THE LISBON AFFAIR

Flying with the Swallows
Volume One

THE LISBON AFFAIR
FLYING WITH THE SWALLOWS, VOLUME ONE
Copyright © 2024 by Cat T. Gardiner
Publisher: Unionport Hill Books
ISBN: 979-8-9897833-0-4

Editor: Kristi Rawley
Cover: Hannah Linder Designs
Pinterest Inspiration Board: tinyurl.com/y5ftkm4h
YouTube Playlist: tinyurl.com/y3kompuk

Unionport Hill
Books

In Memory of
Gert Block,
Dear friend
A loving woman of grace
and radiant beauty.
Your light remains
on every life you touched.
(1925-2022)

CONTENTS

PART I
Liberation in Estado Novo

AMAR
by Florbela Espanca

I want to love, love with abandon!
To love for love's sake: here, there,
this one, that one, another, and everyone.
To make love, to be in love, and to love no one.
To remember? To forget? Makes no difference.
To hold on or let go? Neither bad nor good.
But to say you can love one your entire life,
is a lie.
There is one Spring in each life:
You must sing it like Spring, floridly,
For if God gave us voice, it was to sing!
And if one day I must be dust, ashes, and nothing
let my night be a dawn,
let me know how to lose myself…to find myself.

CHARACTERS

Family / Household / Friends

Evelyn Rousseau Somerset, Pseudonym Amelia Snow
Lieutenant Richard Somerset - Husband
Louise Rousseau (Queen Louise) - Mother
Senator Albert Rousseau - Brother
Ann Rousseau – Sister-in-law
Marjorie Rousseau Newbold - Sister
Brewster Newbold – Brother-in-law
Lord Charles Somerset, Baron of Sallingham - Father-in-law
Alice & Vincent - The Dakota staff
Franny - College roommate
Olivia (Livvy) Russell – Nemesis, debutante

New York Daily Spectator

Hank Drucker - Newspaper editor
O'Shea - Foreign desk correspondent

SS Serpa Pinto

Carl Wilson - American clarinetist/Intelligence Agent
Irena & Stephan Olszak - Polish travelers/Intelligence Agents
John da Silva Purvis - Portuguese traveler/Nazi collaborator*
Mrs. Honeywell & Hyacinth Bartlett - British travelers

British Secret Intelligence Service (MI6/SIS)

Preston Musgrove (Berkshire) - Iberian section handler

Lisbon, Portugal

Madam Elena (Magda) Lupescu - Royal Mistress*
Carol II - Hohenzollern - exiled ex-king of Romania*
Drucker Family - Samuel, Rebecca, Ezra, Suzannah, Tovah
Otto Wegener - General in Wehrmacht Sicherung
Baron Oswald von Hoyingen-Huene - German Ambassador*
Rodrigo Esteves - Portuguese banker
Antonio Salazar - Prime Minister of Portugal (Estado Novo)*
Comandante Pedro Ganzaga - Warden Tarrafal Prison

* Denotes real-life historical personage

PROLOGUE

I Let a Song Go Out of My Heart

May 1939

With each step taking her farther away from the hallowed grounds of Vassar College, Evelyn "Evie" Rousseau's heart sank to her stomach. From afar, she watched the family chauffeur Chandler slide her luggage into the Cadillac Fleetwood's trunk. Memories and mementos of the last three years had been packed away—items most likely never to be seen again once she returned home to Lenox Hill in the Upper East Side of New York. Even the clothing in those travel cases would be replaced with more suitable attire for a woman of her upbringing and a special trousseau for her honeymoon. She always knew this day would come, just not this soon.

Exiting Taylor Hall tunnel, she thought of her freshman entrance into the revered institution responsible for her life-changing experience. Liberation, academia, and social ideals had married meaningful traditions—thereby changing her view of life and the world from the ingénue who had entered. Here she had excelled and found a place among like-minded friends of Polite Society, sharing languages, journalism, and poetry. Here, there was no censure, or ideology or expectation to be anything other than a reformer of self and the world. Here, she had been just "Evie." No one cared that her brother was a member of congress or that she was of prominent blue-blooded lineage.

Her sadness and disconcerting upheaval turned into despair when she caught a glimpse of her mother, Louise Beaumont Rousseau's smug profile in the back seat. That haughty lift to "Queen Louise's" chin and that sanctimonious scowl brought back a rush of unpleasant thoughts. Even the tilt of Mother's dark hat sent chills down her spine.

She slowed her gait to barely a snail's pace, fully aware that she should be dancing, running toward her future: marriage to Richard Somerset—hasty as it was. Still, each step she made spoke more of ambivalence than elation and that awareness gnawed inside her. Their initial plan to marry *after* Vassar wasn't for another eighteen months!

Stopping below the arch, she turned back for one last somber, reflective glimpse of the main building. "Good-bye. Thank you, sisters. Onward, right?"

She fingered the flower-motif gold brooch at her shoulder, a matching pin to that of her roommate, exchanged during their sophomore year when they were both honored as two "daisies" carrying the 1938 commencement Daisy Chain.

"Do *not* keep me waiting, Evelyn," her mother's stern voice carried in the air at her back.

She stiffened, then sighed, fighting the tear prick in her eyes. Saying good-bye was painful, but she set her shoulders back optimistically facing her future. Vassar and the friends she had made gave her wings on which to fly but, in her heart, she knew she was a different girl than the one who had accepted Richard Somerset's proposal. Would marriage change the woman she had become? Surely not! Nor would her college experience change the type of wife her fiancé hoped her to become.

This time, her feet moved swiftly, anticipating the wrath sure to come. Oh, where were Margie her sister or Albert her brother when she needed them the most? Alone with Mother was never wise, particularly today when her feelings were raw and forcing composure. If pushed, she might actually say what was on her mind—liberated Vassar girl she'd become! It wasn't that she felt *nothing* for her mother. Hate was something, but she did respect her as the matriarch of the family. She knew the queen's incapacity to love her. The woman's abuse and fault-finding derision toward her youngest "surprise" child had caused deeply buried scars and life-long discord between them.

Chandler opened the car door and immediately Queen Louise took full measure of the fashionable ensemble she wore. Evie swallowed hard and withstood the critical assessment from top to bottom: wide-brimmed straw hat, to green dress and jacket, to stylish shoes. Finally, her mother's pursed lips twitched, whether in satisfaction or disapproval remained to be seen. She hoped the former because even after these formative college years, she still felt a child under the scrutiny.

Of course, Mother was dressed in onyx. Why wouldn't she be? Evil creatures always wore furnace black. The raven color of her hair made her look even more menacing.

"Good afternoon, Mother."

"Evelyn. You're looking…suitable. Quite grown up, in fact."

Whew. "Thank you."

Inside the Fleetwood, the temperature had to be at least one-hundred degrees, and she resisted the passive-aggressive urge to fan herself with her hand when she sat. As expected, Chandler rolled the window half-way down for her before closing the door. He knew. He'd always known: Mother liked the oppressive heat; creatures from hell regenerated in airtight coffins. Sort of like Bela Lugosi in *Dracula*. Yes, Mother was a life-sucker, too.

Careful the queen did not see, dear Chandler gave her a much-welcomed wink and a smile.

"Evie! Wait! Evie!" someone called to her from under the arch.

"Drive," Mother commanded, rapping her fingernail against the half-open partition between driver and passengers.

"No! Wait. It's my roommate."

Franny reached the limousine, out of breath and panting. In her hands, she held a memory never to be revisited again in this lifetime.

"I'm so glad I caught you," she panted. "You forgot your saddle shoes!"

Mother's silent censure was deafening, her glower burning on Evie's profile.

"Thank you. I left them for you since we're the same shoe size." Turning her head, she looked at the stoic, slender figure beside her and that critical furrowed brow. "I won't have need for oxfords any longer, Franny. They're yours now."

"I'll miss you, Evie," her friend said grasping the window. All Evie could muster was a pat to her hand as her emotions once again rose to the surface.

"And I, you. Like I said earlier, I'll never forget this time we shared here. Never forget the fun we had. Founder's Day, the Daisy Chain, late-night study sessions, the newspaper…all of it. It was the best time of my life."

"Will you at least join me and the girls for the Millay Monthly Musings over the summer?"

"I…I'm not sure. You know, I'll be planning my wedding when I get back. Time is of the essence since Richard will be leaving for Chicago for naval training at the end of August. Maybe in October, we can get together for tea and recite some of Vinnie's verses. I promise you, Franny, we won't lose touch." Yet in her heart she knew her promise was hollow. It would be difficult.

"I was hoping—"

Mother's rude, guttural throat clearing interrupted them. Chandler started the limousine. He knew better than to defy Mother twice.

"Write me? Please?" she begged Franny.

"I will!"

The car pulled away and her friend's hand slid from the glass. She called out their private maxim, "Soar, eat ether, see what has never been seen…"

Franny shouted back, finishing Edna St. Vincent Millay's poem. "…Depart, be lost, but climb!"

Keeping her friend in sight as long as possible, she tried to hold onto that last bit of freedom before Best Society dictated her future—and her manner.

"It's best you put young ladies like that Frances behind you. As I indicated to you previously, her family is not the sort a Rousseau should be associating with. You well know that they are not listed in the *Social Register*."

"Maybe not, but Franny is my best friend, Mother."

"*Marjorie* is your best friend."

Resisting a sharp retort, her rising temper quelled. "No, she is my married sister. Dear that she is, we will never share the camaraderie that I have known at Vassar."

Mother narrowed her eyes. "Nevertheless, this college experiment is behind you, now. A prominent future is ahead of you and you should consider yourself lucky, indeed, to be betrothed to a young man such as Richard Somerset."

"You are right; I am lucky. We love each other and I have no doubt Richard will make a good husband."

"Poppycock. Love is irrelevant in making a suitable match. He's from a highly respected and influential family of British peerage—the finest breeding to elevate the Rousseau name to its proper place within Best Society."

Inwardly, she rolled her eyes. Mother always had a way of making men of "their sort" sound like thoroughbred stallions. In fact, in Queen Louise's day a young woman's sole focus was to marry an English Lord. When one didn't offer for her, she had to settle for a wealthy American banker—whom she did not love. Thereby, she was quite pleased her daughter caught the son of a baron, not for Evie, of course, but more for the Rousseau name.

"Now that your nuptials are in sight, Evelyn, you would do well to make sure you keep your impertinence and defiance under control. Lord Somerset shan't be as tolerant as I have been since your father's passing. Your new position demands it, and neither the society pages, nor your husband will be forgiving if you step out of line in your class duties, and you know I shan't."

Step out of line. "It won't be like that, Mother. Richard and I are *new* society now, definitely not *old* society. The ancient days of Caroline Astor's Four Hundred are long over." *We will be modern trendsetters! Rebels against the old guard! Paris and the exciting Montparnasse await us on our honeymoon!*

Mother had always aspired to that useless, self-aggrandizing, fractured list. No, she and Richard will not live by those strictures; she was sure of it.

"You shall see. Your first order of business will be to produce an heir," Mother added. "And I'm sure Lord Somerset will agree."

Evie gazed out the window at the passing, serene Upstate New York landscape, imagining the happiness ahead of her in Manhattan. Although her fiancé was at times quite a serious fellow, he made her feel safe—insulated from the queen's barbs. He was quite dashing and brilliant and boy could he cut a rug. Every deb—particularly her arch nemesis, the snooty Olivia "Livvy" Russell—had eyes for him, yet he'd chosen her and she was smart to have accepted. In this, her mother was right: they would be the talk of the city and their wedding written up in all the society pages from New York to Rhode Island and Philadelphia to Palm Beach, "Son of Baron of Sallingham marries Senator Rousseau's sister!" Their every move would be followed by working class girls and she'd be the envy of everyone in Polite Society. Isn't that what every young woman dreams? Sure. However, she would have liked to have waited just *one* more year before any of it. That had always been the agreed-upon plan. Odd how her mind drifted to her bicycle—another remnant of life at Vassar. She sighed in acceptance that her college days were over, but buoyed in her dream of freedom as Mrs. Richard Somerset. She would embrace the silly obligations and expectations that came with marriage into such noble aristocracy. It was time to grow up now. Marriage to the catch of New York County, a naval officer, was going to be the thrill of a lifetime! They would raise a family and take society by storm by not adhering to its confining restrictions! Millay's poem *On Thought in Harness*, again called to her. "Soar, eat ether," she said under her breath.

"Did you say something?"

"No, Mother," she said continuing to look out at the passing wooded fields, her thoughts drifting in optimistic silence. *Why, August is just around the corner, and as Mrs. Richard Somerset, I'll not have to adhere to her rules or censure. I will no longer be victimized by you! Richard will sweep me away, be my shelter, show me the world. Yes...I will soar! I will see what never has been seen—beside my dear husband!"*

———◈———

# ONE

Don't Cry, Baby

February 20, 1943

At twenty-four, Evelyn Rousseau Somerset was a war widow hating her trite existence in The Dakota Apartments on the Upper West Side of Manhattan. Famed for its opulence and its rumors of ghostly apparitions by a handful of former residents, the building held only haunting memories for her. She resided in this ivory tower with her ghosts and demons.

Neither the opulent lifestyle nor the inhabitants of Best Society could make her enjoy life at the residence. And although she had been nurtured alongside these same denizens mentioned in New York's society pages and *Variety*, she found herself oddly out of place since moving here as a newlywed in August of '39.

There had once been, however, two redeeming traits in Evie's opinion: planning her future there with Richard and the view of Central Park. Neither mattered now. Richard was dead and she could not even find joy in the bird's-eye view of the changing seasons beyond the window. She was lonely. Every day she felt the chill of death's grip upon her heart since receiving the dreaded War Department telegram at the end of September.

She paced before the floor-to-ceiling window, stopping to glance down at the frenetic pace of bundled-up pedestrians. Her heart felt as cold as they looked. The body she inhabited—like The Dakota—felt empty and void of spirit. She was bored, lacking the desire to do anything at all.

Despite the frigid weather, the stalwart Victory War Bond kiosk at the entrance of the park welcomed determined home front patriots for their share in the war effort. Not her! No thank you. She had already given her husband to the cause, and he in turn, had given his life.

It was best to replace these maudlin thoughts with memories of the freshness of springtime and long walks in the park, of the sweetness of her and Richard's budding romance and their bold kisses under Trefoil Arch Bridge. Just shy of eighteen, they'd tenderly kissed beside the boathouse that first time.

Time...they hadn't had enough time together.

She banished the bittersweet reminiscence, that, too, proving painful and she redirected her focus to the checker cabs lined at The Dakota's curb. She searched for the Packard sedan bearing the esteemed United States Senator Albert Rousseau—her brother. One of the men responsible for this blasted war! Despite Albert's insistence, neither Richard nor she had believed America would be at war following Richard's commission as ensign aboard the destroyer U.S.S *Jarvis* in Pearl Harbor. But within a month, the Japanese bombing had sobered them both.

She felt soured by it all—the war *and* Albert's inopportune visit—but attempted to will away her sad-sack attitude. While she could not side-step the issue that her whole life stretched out before her, she did not have the will or wit to plan beyond today. What would she do without her husband? There was no going back to those lofty, idealistic dreams she had as a college girl. She was a different woman now, having matured over their three and half years of marriage.

Not that she sought their guidance, but neither her siblings nor their overbearing mother had offered any sage advice—or comfort—when the horrific news came. The latter was incapable of compassion or any semblance of human emotion. Her brother was a typical male offering only telephone condolences. Dear, sweet Margie had tried, but she never knew what to say to console her grief. What could she really say? Let's go shopping at Saks Fifth Avenue?

Preparing for her brother's visit, she set her shoulders straight, smoothed her skirt, and pretended to smile from the heart. Albert was finally coming home to Manhattan. And, although he'd been most likely sent on a mission by Mother or his wife, she would attempt to find delight in his call. It must be utterly important for him to come home to New York from Washington, D.C. prior to any congressional recess.

Her turn of the radio knob filled the room with an upbeat swing. Benny Goodman was just what the doctor ordered; the weight of her grief and uncertainty lifted. She'd not let Albert see a miserable widow; his masculine stoicism couldn't handle such a display of emotion.

"Mrs. Somerset, Senator Rousseau has arrived," the butler Victor announced from the primary doorway.

Her heart rate sped a little at Albert's arrival. Fourteen years her senior, her brother felt more like a parent at times.

"Shall I put him in the parlor, ma'am?"

"Yes, thank you. Have Alice bring him some tea and a piece of the crumb cake she made this morning. My brother enjoys the occasional sweet."

He nodded as he backed from the room.

She turned off the music, patted the hair at her nape, then forced another smile. She had no idea why he had come for a visit, but she'd be damned sure not to ruffle his feathers. He was most likely stressed by the business of war, and his agitation on any topic they would discuss was inevitable. The dear man just didn't understand women—let alone the emotions associated with love, grief, or loneliness. Indeed, he was a fine example of control and reserve. Mother always noted how she should be more like her brother.

<hr />

From the threshold of the open double doorway between the parlor and the library, Evie smiled tenderly at the image presented to her, which suddenly dispelled all apprehension for this unprecedented visit. Albert's presence filled the soft yellow, fifty-foot parlor. He stood tall, back straight with a slight lean onto his right leg as he gazed up at the oil portrait of her above the fireplace. One hand dragged across the carved mantle and the other stayed tucked in his trouser pocket as was his habit. From behind, she imagined the firm set to his lips. That expression hardly altered, but his blue eyes usually gave a hint to what he was thinking or feeling. Very few could read them, and she wondered if her sister-in-law ever did. Like her parents' marriage, theirs had been a society match, born out of political ambition and gold-digging social climbing. In that instant, she felt both warm and sad for Albert at seeing him after an eight-month long absence from New York. She loved him as only a baby sister could, and she cherished the memories of when he, too, was a different young man—before Father's death, their mother's demands, politics, and a strained marriage had hardened him.

Evie closed the doors upon entering and he turned to face her, his expression softening slightly, but the worry lines on his forehead gave him away. His eyes were filled with something akin to tenderness.

"Evie," he greeted, his smile finally forming as he walked to her, arms outstretched.

"Al! When did you get back in town?"

"This morning. I haven't even been to Mother's yet."

"Does she know you've come home?"

"She does."

His embrace was similar to their father's, something she had missed since their patriarch had passed away twelve years ago. Albert had given her away on her wedding day, and her heart swelled with affection.

His cheek was still chilled from the brisk weather when she deposited a small kiss. "And how are Ann and the children?"

"I don't know." He dropped his arms from her and walked to the gold cigarette box on the coffee table. "I'm only passing through before leaving for Michigan with the Senate Special Committee."

"Sounds important." His disregard of her mention of his family was telling. War wasn't his only stress.

"It is and not to be taken lightly. This war is hardly over, and Ford's plant needs greater scrutiny. It's bad enough we have Truman at the helm of the committee; he's not the man to get war production levels where they need to be. I'll say this though, the President won't tolerate anything but a well-run facility in the National Defense Program."

"Of course, he wouldn't." She resisted rolling her eyes.

He turned to the wing chair then settled himself in as he lit a cigarette. As usual, he scrutinized her like a defense budget when she sat on the settee opposite him while trying not to fidget. His brow furrowed again. "You have lost weight, Evelyn."

He called her "Evelyn." That was never good.

"Perhaps a little." She'd been picking at her meals since that terrible day and dropped two dress sizes in her grief, but she'd not tell him.

"You also let your hair grow," he added.

"My, you are observant today," she teased, refusing to admit she hadn't seen her beautician in months. She didn't like his tone but tried not to take offense. The man was naturally insensitive.

"Margie mentioned she hasn't seen you at the club and you canceled on her at least a dozen times for tea."

"I have been quite busy…preoccupied. I assure you, our sister is not offended." She raised an eyebrow. "Have you been spying on me, Al?"

He leaned forward, took a drag of his cigarette then snuffed it out in the crystal ashtray. Clasping his hands between his knees, he regarded her straight-on before speaking.

Evident by his knit brow, her strong, powerful brother struggled to find his words. She offered a pensive smile, so sure that whatever he was going to say would make her angry. He was like their mother in almost every manner.

"You're not going to like what I have to say."

"Probably not, but I'll love you any way...even when you irritate me," she teased, hoping to soften such seriousness.

"Everyone is worried about you, and we agreed, mutually, that it is best you move back home with Mother. I am told your suite in The Lancashire is as you left it. You need someone to care for you now that Richard is gone."

Her chin dropped. It felt like a sucker-punch to her stomach. Of all the things she'd expect him to say, *this* was not one of them.

"I know you'll buck me on—"

Alice thankfully entered the room, carrying a sterling tea service, her demure smile breaking the tension. The warm beverage and crumb cake were a welcome diversion for Evie before she set loose her red-haired temper.

She slid to the edge of the settee, crossed her ankles to the side and promptly poured, stiffening her trembling fingers. Her blood simmered to a low boil. Her ire always came to the surface when treated like a helpless child by either him or Queen Louise.

"Thank you for your concern, but I am quite happy here," she fibbed, stirring a bit of sugar into his cup. "I'm sorry it can't be two teaspoons, but sugar is rationed, you know," she apologized then held out the cup. A quirk to the corner of his lips told her that he seemed to like that simple nod she made to the government's efforts to deal with shortages during wartime.

"Make sure you remember to pick up Ration Book Number Two next week," he directed right on cue. "You'll have fewer points to shop with and more restrictions. Make sure you instruct your household staff."

"Yes, Al…I'll be sure to remember," she said with a hint—just a hint—of sarcasm.

"Now, about The Lancashire—"

"Al, before you go any further, Richard and I shared many beautiful memories in this apartment prior to his departure for Hawaii. The Dakota is…is home now and no one needs to care for me, I assure you."

"This haunted mausoleum is home? The Lancashire is your home. You are a Rousseau and belong in Lenox Hill."

"No, *that* is *Mother's* home and there is no point in my returning. In case you have forgotten, I've been a *Somerset* for some time, heiress to my husband's fortune, and don't forget the entirety of my trust. Need I remind you that it wasn't too long ago that I was The *Honourable* Evelyn Josephine Somerset?" She looked away from his penetrating gaze, conceding to herself…*well…so what if Richard's father forfeited his barony holdings and title the year after we had married?*

"Don't be so impertinent. This is not about your wealth, or your father-in-law's British peerage, so don't make either an issue. Mother is proof that wealth does not guarantee happiness. I understand you are still grieving and wanting to cling to your memories, but you should be surrounded by those you love. You've built a wall around yourself, grieving in isolation."

"It's what *feeling* people do, Al! Is it not expected that a woman of my station mourns for a period of twelve months?"

"Idiocy! Six months are more than sufficient."

"It has been *five* of mourning—*six* since Richard's passing."

"How ever long it has been, it's gone on too long. It's time to get back to doing the things you once enjoyed. Go to the club, resume your weekly tea with Margie, go shopping with Ann."

"I'm simply not ready."

"Nonsense. Returning home will help to ease you back into society as the socialite you were groomed to be. There are plenty of opportunities to assist in war efforts within our circle. Join Under-secretary Forrestal's wife in the Navy Relief for young widows. You have experience in that now."

Groomed to be? She hadn't felt this way—this sting of harsh reality—since that fateful day when she departed Vassar.

"There's not a thing I can say to any grieving young woman!" She huffed and turned her back to him. "Groomed to be, Albert? Is that what you think of me? In my place? In need of coddling, being taken care of?" She tried to laugh off the insult, reminding herself for the third time that this was Albert, her persuasive politician brother. After a silent few seconds she whipped around to face him, again, snapping, "What's next? You will all conspire to marry me off to some do-nothing loafer who needs my money, or worse yet a politician? Those days of marital indentured servitude are long over!"

The statesman's expression darkened. "Stop being so melodramatic." In a huff, he walked to the fireplace then proceeded to check the hour and minutes of the Ansonia clock against his pocket watch.

Solemnly he said, "It is expected of you, Evelyn. Until you marry again, mother needs a companion in her advancing age."

"Definitely not! That is *not* going to happen! She has Aggie to assist her and my soul is not for sale!"

"You know darned well Agatha is not accepted in society."

"Did Queen Louise summon you from Washington?"

"Yes. *Mother* did." He cleared his throat. "And she was rightly justified in doing so. You need someone to look after you."

"Do you honestly believe I cannot take care of myself? Forget for a moment her unrealistic justifications—or expectations. *You* make decisions and assessments on behalf of a nation—try to make a rational one as it applies to your sister. I was once quite independent, you know."

He reached out and carefully opened the glass bezel to adjust the clock's second hand—perish the thought *his watch* was the inaccurate timepiece, and not the clock given to her by Eleanor Roosevelt's family as a wedding gift.

"The minute hand is off," he said.

"Ignore the blasted clock, and look at me, Al."

A snap to his pocket watch preceded his turn to her. And there it was—that softening in his eyes, his expression considerate, even sympathetic, and reminiscent of when they were naïve and uncorrupted by life and the influence of others.

"Do *you* really think me so incapable of independence now that Richard is gone?"

"I believe you a capable young woman—who is maybe lost right now. Your future is uncertain—no longer wife and homemaker as Mrs. Richard Somerset, not even a mother. It's expected that you reestablish your place as a widow and member of society and, yes, act as companion for Mother. You can't deny that you've become a recluse. Of course, I'm worried about you."

She walked to him then took his hands in hers. "Darling, please don't fret so about me. This grieving process is normal. I miss my husband, that is all, and yes, my life has been forevermore changed by his death. But, I assure you, I intend on doing *something*. Why, only this morning, I considered a great many things I would care to accomplish in his memory." Okay, that was a fib.

"Such as?"

She dropped his hands, leaving him for the console table nearest the Baby Grand. Her heart thundered in her ears as she did the unthinkable. She picked up a newspaper then held it out to him. Honestly, it was the only thing that came to mind in her defiance to committing to any *real* war effort, given her solemn vow to not give anything more than her husband!

"If you must know, for almost three years, I have been writing a weekly women's column in the *New York Daily Spectator* under a pseudonym. Although I've been in hiatus since Richard's death, I plan on resuming my coverage of the importance of the four *F*'s during wartime." She held her chin high, undeterred, and feeling brave, now faced with the miserable future he and Mother had conspired for her.

"What? Are you out of your cotton-picking mind?"

"Of course not. I enjoy journalism."

"Society reporting on the women's pages for some rag is not journalism, Evelyn. You are from a prominent family listed in the *Social Register* for God's sake! Did Richard know?"

"Yes, but not specifically. So...no."

"You lied to your husband? How could you?"

"It wasn't quite the mendacity your censure assumes. He encouraged me to get involved and find something productive to do for the cause after he departed for Midshipman school—and I did. Now that he's gone, I've been doing some thinking and I consider my freelance column as...oh, I don't know, a stepping stone to something bigger—for the war effort." She smoothed the fallen tendril from her brow. "Maybe I'll become a news correspondent or a front-page reporter."

"Now you're talking illogical nonsense."

"Why? Because it's me making the statement or because I am a cultivated, married woman?"

"You know—the latter, of course! I have no doubt your column is acceptable, but it's not proper. It was fine when you were at that college, but you're out in the world now."

"Am I? I beg to differ. I chose Vassar for academia and its cultural curriculum, but you seem to think it was a finishing school, a proper pre-cursor to marriage! Your 'out in the world' does not equate equally to my ideal of 'out in the world.' "

He laughed mockingly, "I *never* thought it a finishing school. Against my better judgment Mother allowed your whim by paying for that socialist incubator. Be that as it may, did you not marry well?"

"Stop it, Al. I married well, not because of Richard's blood line or military aspirations. I married him because I was in *love*. However, I did have *other* dreams, too. I'm not so singular a person. At one point, even Richard knew that about me."

"Your husband understood quite clearly his—and your—role in society. Perhaps, *you* didn't quite understand *him*. I assure you, writing for a paper like *this* would not have garnered his support." He laughed, ridiculing her with a shake to his head. "Respectable wife of prominent upbringing writing a rag gossip column, fantasizing about becoming an inexperienced war correspondent. Have you lost your mind?"

"That is quite enough! I don't hear your disapproval of the First Lady's all-female press corps—some of whom are no doubt, Vassar alumni and married women."

"That's different. You're wanting to play *Brenda Starr*, Evelyn!"

"Well, what about Clare Boothe Luce? She was an editor at *Vanity Fair* and a correspondent for *Life* magazine—both a man's world—and now she is a congresswoman. *She* wasn't born on the funny pages!"

"You, touting the achievements of a Republican? Why, this is quite novel, Sister."

"You know how I abhor politics, but I am trying to appeal to your antiquated ideas. Luce has been successful in a man's world, which gains my respect, even if I don't see eye-to-eye with her policies," she quipped.

"Luce was protected, sheltered by her husband the publisher! Yours is dead," he declared without thinking.

Her back went rigid and she stepped back from him; he had officially crossed the line. She'd always make excuses for his frankness but this went beyond the pale. "This is the last time I will say this: I do not need a husband's protection. This conversation is over, Brother—or should I say Father? Perhaps *Mein Führer* is more appropriate."

"Come now. Evie, don't be like this. We're only trying to help. Let's sit and finish our tea before I have to leave."

As predictable as ever, he now called her Evie. Truly, never backing down was the only way to handle the senator. For Pete's sake, why had it taken her so long to challenge him on anything?

Bolstered and determined—not to mention affronted—she looked down at the watch brooch Richard had given her on their first anniversary then walked to the archway leading out to the hallway, holding her head high and her shoulders back. "I don't think so, Albert. Please forgive me for not being a more generous hostess, but I have a great many things to attend, and calling on me—without an invitation—so late in the afternoon is keeping me from them."

After tugging the velvet chord at the entrance to the room, the butler magically appeared. "Victor, please collect the senator's hat and coat and see him to the door. He has vital government business and his *own* beleaguered familial affairs to attend to."

"Yes, ma'am."

Today, that hint of red highlight in her hair served her well. Although she didn't quite hold her temper at bay, she was proud of herself. For the first time in a number of years, she stood her ground against the formidable Senator Albert Rousseau. Her heart may be slamming against her chest wall, but it was a much-needed confirmation she was still alive.

Albert grunted then stormed past her, quitting the room.

"I do believe, Evie, you may have turned a corner today," she said to herself in proud rebelliousness but there was no mistaking that the hole in her heart just grew to twice its size.

She pushed her fear down and when she heard the foyer door close, let go of her breath. "Next week, I'm going back to the paper. I may have forgotten so, but I am still a Vassar girl, dammit!"

Two

Your Socks Don't Match

February 20—late

*T*he tick-tock of the Ansonia filled the eerie silence within the cold Dakota apartment. Lost in her thoughts, Evie sat in her dressing robe staring blankly at the dusty typewriter on her side of the partner desk in the library. Since the telegram's arrival five months ago, she hadn't given a damn about writing an article or even looking at her typewriter for that matter. In fact, she'd technically quit the paper all together! She ran her hand over the edge of the strong oak and smiled wryly in recollection of the desk's delivery two weeks after her wedding. Richard saw no purpose for her half of the desk, but freely admitted that *he* needed one. As soon as he left for naval training the Corona Zephyr had found its home smack dab in the middle of her side of the desk. Back then she truly believed he'd support her whims and when he returned home one cold winter weekend, his only acknowledge-ment of the typewriter had been a shrug and a "As much as I'll miss your delicate handwriting, type is much more practical. Good decision." He was speaking of her letter writing, not pursuing her interest in becoming a columnist.

She sighed. "Oh, what dreams you had, Evie."

In those first few months of getting acclimated to both life at The Dakota and marriage, there was no time—or place—for her girlish dreams to become a journalist pursuing meaningful stories, and she embraced her wifely role in an even higher society than the one she grew up in, slowly pushing down her alternate ego: Vassar's Evie.

She had learned almost immediately that her new husband had strict expectations, and to make him happy, her tedious days were occupied with planning soirees for when he returned home, lunch at the club with Margie and such prominent women that Queen Louise had not even socialized with. At the personal request of her father-in-law, she became involved in charity fundraisers dear to the Somerset family but in her opinion, they seemed to only benefit Best Society's interests. And of course, she did everything she could to placate Albert's wife's boundless discontent with the absentee statesman. Why, she even took the children to Carnegie Hall and lunch every Saturday just to give Ann some solitude—in her solitude! All these tiresome efforts began in September of '39 and continued until the telegram. Gone were the days of Millay's influence; they had been replaced by Somerset and Rousseau demands the moment she said "I do."

But Richard's assumption that she was fulfilled in his absence provided the perfect cover to her so-called whim in July 1940 when the *New York Daily Spectator* introduced their new gossip columnist "Amelia Snow"—her!—to the women of New York City. In truth, when she finally succumbed to the lure of writing for a newspaper, she was still trying hard to make a good home—even if Richard had been away in Chicago for months at a time. She had planned on telling him of her "moonlighting" when the right time presented itself, but that time never came.

She wrote her column at night. What else was there to do in his absence? Even though those banal articles were meaningless, she was thankful for the opportunity to write what she knew about society and fashion, while her housekeeper fed her information about the other three "Four *Fs*": family, furniture, and food. It had been her secret hope to one day—after the children came and a governess installed—to write on more serious topics, provided Richard approved, of course.

Each topic she'd written, especially the Four *Fs*, held little appeal to her in the scheme of things but she was proving herself with each article! Were the women of the hoi-polloi, truly concerned about those things or were they too busy holding together their households when their men left to fight? Was the society tittle-tattle an escape from the business of war as her editor had stated? Surely, the gossip was the only appeal for those of her social circle, none of whom read the rag tabloid she wrote for any way, and all of whom lived for every word out of Hedda Hopper's mouth, not Amelia Snow's.

In the low lamplight, she shuffled through her desk drawer until she found a pack of Chesterfields, lit a cigarette, then settled back into her chair ignoring the goose flesh on her arms. Finally, the steam radiator clanked.

Hopefully, her editor at the *Spectator* would hire her back at the very least to continue writing *Women's World*. Back then, she hadn't been given a choice of column, but maybe by now he'd hired a hen house of female reporters. Maybe he was offering more substantive positions to women due to the war. Journalist Martha Gelhorn wrote real news articles for *Collier's* news magazine; she could, too.

What would her husband think if he knew? He loved her but would he be displeased? Oh dear…the sudden emergence of guilt at her liberation having come with Richard's death stabbed her heart. Her abject sadness coupled with Albert's pronouncement of attending to their mother had created a surge of confidence and, yet, a maelstrom of uncertainty making her loss feel so much greater. But she'd stay strong and find purpose again, if for no other reason than to prove to her family that she could be something on her own.

A survey to her surroundings brought on the recollection of so many things, and like most days since Richard's passing, she tormented herself with bleak memories and their unfulfilled dreams as husband and wife.

"Organized chaos" he'd once joked of the state of the library— his most favorite place on land. She scanned the bookcase-lined walls, the reading ladder, the stained-glass chandelier and finally, the partially read volumes stacked on both sides of the desk, flanking piles of his papers and Old World navigation maps. This was the only part of Richard's life that wasn't precisely shipshape and arranged.

Even Martha their housekeeper knew not to upset the volumes or to clean the disorder. Although he'd barely lived here, he was particular about his clutter and, well, everyone had expected him to return to it. The room was as he had left it except for tonight: she'd rolled a sheet of paper into the Corona as a sign of things to come. Her intuition told her that good things were on the horizon now that she stood up to Albert.

"Don't be a chicken, Evie. Richard loved you and you adored him. He would want you to do what makes you happy now, not what Mother demands. Do it in his memory."

Her gaze settled on the blank sheet of paper and, like every night since that telegram, a memory rushed to the surface. They'd only been married seven months when on another late night, she sat before the Corona. Odd, how she'd forgotten that terrible night, having suppressed the memory and how it had made her feel. Life went on and so had their marriage: him there and her here.

"What are you doing? Richard asked coming behind her at the typewriter. It was late and she was sure he was asleep—and she had a deadline to meet! Thankfully, she hadn't begun and the paper before her was still blank.

"Oh! Richard! You frightened me. Don't sneak up on me like that, silly!"

"I'm sorry. Come back to bed."

"I can't...I um...forgot to make up the menu for the Cunard dinner party and it is keeping me tossing and turning. I must type it up for Alice."

Tenderly, he brushed the hair from her nape and burrowed his face into her neck depositing a kiss, then another, and she smiled thinking—wishing—he'd make love to her. He'd come home this afternoon for a four-day break and what with getting settled in and dining with her father-in-law, they had yet to be intimate.

"Forget the menu. I can't sleep without you."

She swiveled the chair around and looked up into his blue eyes. *"What do you do without me in Chicago?"* she joked.

He didn't answer her, just placed his finger under her chin, prompting her to rise from the seat into his embrace.

His kiss to her mouth was warm and gentle, sweet but not as hungry as it should be for a man who hadn't slept with his wife in three months. She had fantasized many times that when he returned home they would never leave the bedroom, but he seemed preoccupied. When asked by both her and his father if he was troubled, he reassured them otherwise.

Dragging her hand down his back, she hoped to entice him but he held his ardor at bay. She deepened her kiss, slipping her tongue between his lips and pressed against him.

"Can we...you know...I miss you, darling," she murmured.

"Here?"

"How about on the divan?"

Richard furrowed his brow, pulling back from her slightly as if presented with an untenable option or that he was shocked that she would make the suggestion. Her sexual inhibitions had yet to truly fall away, but she was trying.

"What is it, Richard? There must be something troubling you...either that or you just don't want me anymore?" She tried levity. *"Our honeymoon isn't over yet."*

He smiled softly then entwined his fingers with hers. "Of course, I want you. You're my wife. But not...not here."

Once in their suite, he sat her on the bed. His eyes never left hers as he stood above her undressing. Richard had a magnificent physique, commanding and taut with blond patches accentuating his chest muscles. She nearly swooned at the sight of him after so long, and she brazenly reached out to touch his growing arousal but he snatched her hand up in his, placing it in her lap. His index finger smoothed down her cheek and he tenderly smiled.

Rising, she stood before him, allowing him to lift her nightgown then pressed against him, reveling in the feel of their nude bodies against each other. Inside, she sighed in both satisfaction and relief at his full arousal pressed against her when he took her into his arms.

They made love, but something was missing. That spark, that fire of newlywed fervor. It felt devoid of the passion they'd previously shared in those early months. His touches were brief and, yes, he was fulfilling his husbandly duty, and maybe they'd conceive a child— an heir—but something wasn't right between them. Something was drastically different in him. Maybe he was tired from the long train ride. Was it her? The navy? Training...or was someone else keeping his bed warm in Chicago the many months apart?

She cried in their intimacy but they weren't born from passion. When it was over, he plopped down beside her and dragged her bottom against his naked body and snuggled into her. He no doubt believed he'd loved her just like she wanted and needed and she chastised herself for not being more assertive in bed. She should have enticed him further, prolonged their pleasure—explored. For all her education, she just thought sex would come naturally. The how-to's shouldn't come from a book; they should come from the heart. Apparently, she was wrong.

Five months ago, she'd vowed to herself to never think of their marital troubles, which was only brought on by their separation. Training at Northwestern University in the various midshipman programs and then his commission aboard the *Jarvis* surely had changed him. Those first few months were marital bliss and she'd even traveled sixteen hours to Chicago aboard the 20th Century Limited train on several occasions, but come summer 1940, he insisted that he didn't have the time with all his studies and training, adding "You have better things to involve yourself in back in Manhattan." It was then that Amelia Snow was born, filling the void his absence and studies left.

"It was the war. Things could have been so different if we only had the time."

She gazed up from the typewriter and stared at the short barrister bookcase of alphabetized and meticulously cared for volumes along the right wall. This one small section of novels and poetry books, her husband had set aside for her pleasure when his grandfather shipped a collection of books from the family library in Sallingham. Very few of those old books were from her favorite Romantics Keats and Byron, but a few Victorians graced the shelves alongside Millay and others she had collected. Richard had been particularly pleased that someone in the household could enjoy them for he was not a lover of prose or verse. She, however, was especially thankful for all their company over the long, lonely years of marriage.

In that rare moment of introspection of her duties and disappointments, she thought of Millay's poem "The Spring and the Fall." Her quiet recitation of the stanza barely breached the chilled silence of Richard's space.

"Year be springing or year be falling, the bark will drip and the birds be calling. There's much that's fine to see and hear. In the spring of a year, in the fall of a year. Tis not love's going hurt my days. But that it went in little ways."

———◈———

THREE
Boom Shot

February 22

That'll be a buck, lady," the checker taxicab driver said after raising the "For Hire" flag on the fare meter. He turned to glance back at Evie as she held out three coins. "Say, are you one of dem working gurlz?"

"I beg your pardon?"

"Ya know, one of dem dolls doin' man's work. I figure no one comes to the paper unless they work here or are placin' a death notice and ya don't look none too sad to me."

She chuckled inside, reminded of Albert's incredulity two days before, not to mention she felt pleased with herself that she wasn't wearing her grief on her sleeve. "I suppose I am doing a man's work. I'm a writer for the paper."

"Good fa' ya! We even gotz lady cabbies now since Uncle Sammy is callin' up a lotta the boyz."

From her purse, she removed another coin and handed it to him. "Exciting times," was all she said with a smile.

She exited the cab and stood at the curb, adjusting her leather gloves. The frenzy of Broadway's traffic filled her ears like welcome ambient noise. Afternoon in Midtown, no matter the season, was always exciting to her. There was a frenetic energy down here that Uptown failed to produce. Taking a deep breath of the winter air, her head tilted up at the three floors all occupied by the *Spectator*.

Dressed in her finest suit—an emerald green fall ensemble and a darling feathered homburg hat she'd been saving for Richard's eventual return, she smiled. He'd delight knowing she wore both to signify it was time to go back to living—if not the women's pages, then another desk. Surely this was a sign of healing.

"No time like the present," she whispered to herself, taking her first step toward independence.

In the lobby, the elderly reception clerk recognized her right away, gifting her with a wink as a visitor held most of his attention at the desk. He'd always been a dear whenever she arrived at the newspaper's headquarters—then subsequently making it out alive with a smile and a kind word to spare. Not many could withstand the editor Hank Drucker's irascible personality, and she supposed the clerk admired her for that. She was, at the time of her employment, one of only two women at the *Spectator*, the other being Mr. Drucker's Girl Friday and both of them knew how to play him like a fiddle.

"Mrs. Somerset! Evelyn!" shouted one of the fellows who worked closely with the Office of Censorship to ensure the newspaper adhered to the new Code of Wartime Practices. The man, not a real newsman, wasn't someone she had missed these five months. Poor fellow meant well, but he was a drip of the first order. He ran from the entrance, through the crowd, to where she stood at the elevator bank. Near out of breath, he caught up to her, grinning like a fool.

"Oh hello, Joe," she said.

"Gee, it's grand to see you. Are you coming back to the paper?"

"I am considering it."

An awkward silence fell between them and her skin prickled from his stare upon her profile.

"Um…I'm sorry to hear about Lieutenant Somerset's death," he stammered. "We all were. I didn't know him but I bet he was a swell fella."

"He was. Thank you."

She wanted to die inside but kept the smile plastered to her face as she glanced up at the brass floor dial, the arrow stilled on the third floor taunting her.

"How ya makin' out?" Joe pressed, his beady eyes remaining locked onto her profile. She'd forgotten his fascination with her.

"As good as can be expected, I guess. I think it's quite important to keep myself busy. At least that's what I'm told."

"That's good. It was in the paper, ya know. Did you see it? Old Waddles made sure Jones gave the lieutenant a swell obituary, a real send-off. Of course, we couldn't go into detail because of the censorship, but it was done proper. I oversaw it myself."

"That was thoughtful of you, Joe. Say, don't let Mr. Drucker hear you calling him Waddles if you know what's good for you. He's chewed out men for less."

"Aw, he can't touch me. I'm a protected government man. Uncle Sam is my boss!"

A lady wouldn't roll her eyes, but gosh she wanted to. Saved by the elevator, the doors opened and the attendant squished to the wall as people exited and entered. Thankful for gentlemanly etiquette, she was the first to enter and Joe was the last.

The doors slid open on the third floor and the elevator emptied into a vibrant press room where the tapping sound of typewriter keys hard at work filled the pungent air. The room felt electrified with a boogie woogie rhythm—a sort of Gene Krupa drumming—and she hoped she'd be adding her own beat. At three in the afternoon on Washington's Birthday, the press hadn't stopped from news gathering, evidenced by the half-eaten sand-wiches on scattered papers at every partner desk. No doubt, the latest news and the next big scoop had reporters focused before print deadlines.

"Well, if it ain't Mrs. Somerset," her editor greeted from the middle of the room in his usual brusque Brooklyn accent. Short, round, and almost bald, Drucker waddled to her with a knowing smile, as if he had expected her, which he hadn't. Heck, she hadn't even planned on coming today, but she was ready. Despite the editor's abrasiveness, she liked him. He never treated her like high society; never spoke to her differently than he had the men. The man was a sour puss to everyone, even the fairer sex.

"Hi, boss."

"Boss? Why I thought you quit the paper."

She removed her gloves and spoke with a saucy smile. "Quit? Wherever did you get that idea? You must have misunderstood me."

"I'm sure I heard ya right through all those tears, kid."

"Well they're packed away now, and you'll have to find another desk for me, or reinstate me as Amelia Snow."

He let out a big belly laugh he only did when being a sarcastic hard nose. "Oh, I see! Something has stirred your stumps, so you've come back to the *Spectator*? We'll see. Ya won't get any sympathy or special assignments from me."

"I don't expect any, but I'm sure any of these fellows attempting to write the Amelia Snow column haven't had the inside scoop on the various charity fundraisers and debutante wedding gossip. All those New Year's Eve balls must have been a terrible bore. I wonder what advice they gave the ladies about the shortages of stockings and elastic in their undergarments?"

"I'm impressed, Somerset. You came with your moxie. Step into my office and we'll tawk."

Following behind his rotund form, she unhooked her mink collar and unbuttoned her coat, suddenly flushed under the heated stares as she walked through the pressroom. Some men waved, others simply smiled. Do other war widows feel the same as she?— like she wore a patriotic badge of stalwart courage that garnered sympathy—or was it thanks? Maybe it was a common thing. How many of these older gentlemen lost sons? Maybe she could write about that in a fine editorial.

Surprised to see Evelyn, Drucker led the way into his glass-enclosed office and shut the door to the drum of typewriters, but carriage bells breached the room.

"What's on your mind, kid?" he asked, trying hard not to stare at her shapely figure when she hung her coat on the rack. Evelyn Somerset was one of the most beautiful dames he'd ever seen. Although all class with that perfect enunciation and tight jaw, she never acted hoity-toity when she came to the *Spectator*. Further, the girl had guts, never backing down for anyone. Polite, yet tenacious with personality—she was his favorite reporter.

"As you guessed, something has stirred my stumps. I'd like to come back to the paper."

He sat opposite her. She was right: Crenshaw made a terrible Amelia Snow. Why, it was so boring that the fella couldn't color the copy even with a box of crayons. But he didn't want to admit that to her, so he only nodded.

"But I'm not sure I want the women's desk anymore. I'm bored with writing the four Fs."

"So wattaya thinking? A lonely-hearts advice?"

"Don't be silly! Of course not."

He scratched his head. "I don't know…the paper needs Amelia Snow's weekly column. The government has us pushing the 3 Rs now and the city needs to start encouraging little women about that scrap metal drive coming up in the spring. I wanna see everywhere that new slogan 'Use it up, wear it out, make it do, or do without'—something like that, and you're the one to do it. The women who read the *Spectator* listen to you."

Evelyn sighed, clearly unhappy. "Thanks for the vote of confidence, but I don't think I am the one to write "Woman's World" anymore. Mr. Drucker, I know this is going to sound positively crazy to you, but I want to be a reporter *first* and a woman *second*."

She straightened her shoulders and those expressive eyes of hers locked onto his. A woman second? That was impossible. In his opinion, she was a Grade-A chick all the way—first and foremost. Evelyn made him feel like a young buck and not a grouchy old geezer.

"Now that Richard is...well...you know, I want to be a front-page girl reporting on real stories. No more soft news for me. What you need is a woman's angle on today's headlines. After all, that is who reads your paper."

He laughed, unable to bark at her as was his usual form. "Front page? And what do I tell those boys out there who eat and sleep hard news fighting each other for a byline?"

"Tell them Mrs. Somerset is going to scoop them as the *Spectator's* best investigative reporter. I'm going to go after the stories no one else can get. I did it for the *Vassar Miscellany News* and I can do it here. And if you won't let me, well then, I'll have to go to *The New York Times*."

He'd not admit this to her, but she was a G-d-send in that moment—a gorgeous, heaven-sent doll who could save this paper from going under just by her gumption alone. No more two-bit rag articles or sensationalized slanted stories. He tapped his pen on the desk considering her gumption and the one hot assignment perfectly suited for her. Evelyn could deliver the headline that would catapult the *Spectator* into the big league, right beside the *Herald Tribune* and *Life* magazine. But there were other reasons he needed her for this particular assignment. First off, she had nothing to lose and the moxie to do it. And secondly, maybe she needed to see the face of war and what her husband died fighting. And, well, the last reason was personal to him.

He dropped the pen then leaned forward to his desk, spreading his fingers on the papers before him. "What languages do ya speak?"

"French, Italian, Spanish, and three dialects of German, and some Latin." She furrowed her brow.

"That many? Hmm...good...good. Have you ever seen one of those flying boats?"

"Yesss."

"You might be in luck, kid. I think I have an assignment with ya name written awl over it."

She raised a sculpted eyebrow, those expressive green peepers nearly undoing him.

"It's just the kind of story that'll change the future of our little tabloid here. If you can get this exclusive before the AP Lisbon Bureau does…then I'll give ya a raise and…and an office."

"I'm all ears."

He picked up the four-week-old letter from his cousin, tapping it against the palm of his hand. "There's a catch."

"There always is with you, boss."

"You'll need your passport."

"Whatever for?"

"Because I need you to fly to Lisbon on the *Yankee Clipper*. The *Spectator* has the chance at a real big scoop. We're gonna be the first American newspaper to get an exclusive with Romania's King Carol II and his Jewish mistress on their return to Lisbon for a little holiday."

Evelyn laughed at what she thought was a joke. "He's no longer king."

"Well, he ain't the subject of the article anyway."

"You can't be serious? You want me to go to Portugal—while there is a war on?"

"Portugal ain't in this war."

"But why would our readers care about Lupescu? Her story has been run through the mill. Besides, she's Romanian and, need I remind you?—we declared war on Romania in June of last year."

"You know your news."

"I may write the women's column but that does not mean we're all so clueless to what's going on in the world."

"You got me there. I always knew you were a smart cookie. Look…war with Romania is…a minor detail. It would make a great follow-up story to the one we published in '40 about the unveiling of the king's bust at the World's Fair. But as you know, our readership is mostly women—"

"And no woman likes a homewrecker. Lupescu's story is dead on arrival."

"Now, hold your horses. I thought you said you were willin' to do anything," Drucker said.

"I did, but—"

"And didn't you say you'd go after any story?"

"Yes, but I—"

"And that yaw one of those sophisticated dames from upper-crust society? Didn't you once tell me your father-in-law was some English Baron?"

She chuckled again. "You know I did—it's the reason you hired me to write the woman's pages."

"Well, kid, yaw the only one I know who could infiltrate that international Lisbon crowd and get the ex-king's mistress flappin' her lips about life on the run from the Nazis. It'll be a real sob-sister story. That's what our readers want and why they'd care about Lupescu."

"I can't go to Lisbon! Why, I don't even speak Portuguese." Her fingers toyed with the stunning watch fob she wore on her lapel.

"Like I said, you got the smarts, Evelyn. You'll get the hang of it."

"In time, naturally, but not as quickly as I apparently need to. You said you wouldn't give me any special assignments."

"I lied. What can I say…I'm a pushover for a pretty face."

She laughed.

"I'll tell you what, if you go to Lisbon for me, when ya get back I'll…I'll send ya down to Washington with a recommendation letter to the National Press Club. Maybe you'll get to meet Mrs. R. Think about it, Evelyn. This assignment could change your future." *And others.*

"I already know the first lady and, as I am sure you are well aware, women are *not* allowed into the National Press Club. You can't pull the wool over my eyes, Mr. Drucker."

"All right, all right. You got me on that one."

"Besides, I hate to draw your attention to the obvious, but I don't have press credentials or security clearance as a foreign correspondent. And, since I'm a woman, you know that will take months to get approved. That alone comes from the War Department along with immunizations and rules I have to follow for accreditation as a U.S War Correspondent. The process is a daunting one and most likely a fruitless endeavor for a cub reporter like me."

He chuckled inside at her level of stalling, knowing full-well she itched to take the assignment. "When did a few obstacles keep you from going after something? Look, don't tell that government kid Joe out there, but I don't want you to follow any military rules. As a stringer, you'll travel as a hoity-toity socialite on a little adventure holiday to those fancy beaches in Portugal. Unless of course, you want to give the senator a call and get yourself one of dem field manuals and armbands, take advantage of his preferential treatment." He smirked, making his point.

"Absolutely not!"

"Surely, the baron himself can give you a leg up in Lisbon. Those Portuguese have a tidy relationship with the Brits."

She gasped. "Not on your life!"

"C'mon. Would ya rather me give the scoop to those fellas out there? Each one would jump at the chance with a hi-di-ho and have no problem gettin' their credentials."

"And muck it up, too. Can…can I think about it for a few days?"

"I'm tellin' ya, kid, don't let this opportunity pass you by. Word on the wire is that the playboy king is gonna be high-tailing it out of Lisbon to go back to Mexico soon.

"Ex-king. Why don't I wait for their return and fly to Mexico for the interview?"

No, that wouldn't help him in the least. "Look, if you're worried about what's going on in the war, Jones'll bring you up to speed and you can sit with O'Shea for details on Nazi shenanigans. It's a mess over in Europe, but you can handle it. You got moxie, more than you realize."

"Gee, I don't know, Mr. Drucker. I appreciate your confidence in me but I wasn't thinking *that* big, *that* soon."

"Malarkey. What else do you have to do in The Big Apple—tea at the Colony Club? Attend some high falutin' ball?"

His heart sank, and he vacillated on what more he should tell her until he finally handed her the letter. "There's also this—it could be your second story when you get home." He didn't mean for his hand to shake when he handed her the envelope across his desk. Damn, she just might figure out he had a heart and no self-respecting news editor in New York City would admit to that!

"What's in it?"

"Just read it and try not to turn on the waterworks. I'm not equipped to deal with a leaky dame."

Evie examined the penmanship and the Portuguese postal stamps. She turned the envelope over, searching for a return address but there was none. After removing the small letter, she translated it from German, reading aloud the cramped slanted print.

Dear Cousin Henry and family,

We have left France after many months stay, and arrived in Lisbon where we patiently await the next part of our journey. Each day more refugees arrive, and our situation grows bleak. Although we are out of harm's way for the immediate future, our financial situation keeps us from acquiring the necessary permission document to make sea passage to America or Palestine. We must spend all our funds on lodging and food.

I have heard royalty and the wealthy are securing letters of transit with no difficulty as they pass through this Jewish safe haven, and there is talk Hitler or Spain may invade Portugal. We understand the duplicity of the local secret police requires our vigilance. We have come far yet the Gestapo, and its influence, is never far behind. The British consulate and several charitable organizations assist many, helping them in their journey, and we will remain hopeful our turn will come before our German passport's thirty-day "visit" expires. Outspoken as ever, my father waits in line for days at the Portuguese consul and I will go tomorrow to the Americans. My mother's health is failing, but she is happy to be alive, hoping to see another grandchild come into the world! Yes, my Suzannah is with child.

Give our love to Edith and the children. We will write again soon, hopefully with good news of our expected arrival to America.

Sincerely,

Ezra

She put the letter down, her expression filled with confusion. "Your family escaped Nazi Germany, Mr. Drucker?"

"Yeah, yet another family on the run from those thugs. My young cousin and his parents left Germany about a year ago, making it safely to the south of France for a short time. This letter came about two weeks ago. I'd be grateful to ya if you can find them…use your influence to get them exit visas then bring them back with you after you get your scoop on Elena Lupescu."

"Can't you wire them the money?"

"Personally, the missus and me ain't got that kind a dough or power…but you do."

"I see."

"Besides, they need someone on the inside to sort things out for them—translate, be a go-between, not to mention a sponsor to bring them into America. My uncle Samuel is a bit of a firebrand, but he's a good fella. He once wrote for a small newspaper before the German government shut it down for subversive opinions. Anyway, call it a reporter's hunch, but I think he could be the problem in securing their papers. No one wants a rabble-rouser."

"Surely, with your reputation and press credentials as editor of the *Spectator*, someone in the Lisbon Bureau could help you."

"I tried, but no one wants to touch it with a barge pole. You and your feminine ways might have more luck in person than me and my hard-nose ways over the wire."

"Perhaps. I'd like to—"

A knock on the door interrupted their conversation followed by the entrance of one of the office boys waving a teletype printout. "Boss! This just came in over the UPI wire: 'Pan Am's *Yankee Clipper* crashes outside Lisbon.' "

"Holy smokes! Any casualties?"

"Twenty-four and that war correspondent Richardson. The singer Jane Froman was on board but she survived."

The fella handed Drucker the teletype then left the office, shutting the door behind him.

He glanced down at the print out then up at Evelyn still holding the letter. Dagnabbit, the *Yankee Clipper* was the only plane to Portugal. He hated to ask her the alternative given how her husband died, but he had no choice. "Well, kid, if you're in, then it looks like you're gonna have to sail transatlantic. I won't lie to ya—it's dangerous."

"An ocean liner? Oh dear… I can't do that. I'm …"

"You're what?"

"I'm afraid of the water."

"Hold your horses. You just said you'd been on one of them there flyin' boats."

"You misunderstood me. I said I've *seen* the Clippers, which was your question."

"Front page, Evelyn. Can't you just see the screamer headline by Mrs. Richard Somerset? While all those fellas will be clamoring for a byline about this airplane crash, you'll sail in dripping in diamonds and have a little heart-to-heart with Lupescu."

Looking back down at the letter, she furrowed her brow for a long moment, until she finally spoke quietly, "Well it is important...Richard would want me to go. And your family does need help ..." Another pause before her frown turned into a thoughtful smile. "Oh dear." She sighed. "I guess there's a first time for everything, right?"

"That's my girl."

"Can you provide me with a snapshot of your family?"

"I'll see what I can dig up and messenger it Uptown to ya. Oh, and Evelyn, keep it on the quiet, all right? I don't want to announce to the pressroom that I'm Jewish. You understand. Some people got funny ideas about that."

"Of course. Mums the word."

"And above all, be cautious in Lisbon. It's run amok with Nazi Jew hunters."

FOUR

Always in My Heart

February 23

*E*vie's elder sister Marjorie Rousseau Newbold wasn't an exceptional beauty by society's high standards nor was she born into one of the most aristocratic families, but she did possess three things, which had made her a popular debutante back in '32: her charm, her ease in the ballroom, and her large dowry. It was because of her charm and kind disposition that her husband Brewster loved her as much as he did, because he didn't give a whit about what she would bring into their marriage. Unlike the Rousseau family, the Newbolds had been listed on Astor's First Four Hundred of New York's most important Knickerbocker families. Brewster was a carefree Nob who had millions of his own, even greater than the Somerset family's fortune, after her father-in-law's abdication, of course.

A privately not-so prim but outwardly proper socialite, Margie sat opposite Evie with a glorious smile but a mischievous sparkle in her eyes. She wore Wedgwood blue, a perfect complement to her chestnut tresses and azure eyes. Concealed behind a large potted palm tree at the Divan Parisien restaurant on Forty-fifth Street, the two sisters spoke quietly against the backdrop of clinking china and the din of dining patrons.

"Darling, I'm so delighted you telephoned," her sister's sing-song voice effused as she reached out to take her hand. "I've been so worried about you, but I simply didn't know what to say. How does one console the inconsolable?"

"It's duly impossible I dare say, and in truth, I haven't been talkative lately. As I told Albert on Friday, every widow has their own way of grieving especially during wartime. As usual he just didn't understand that life doesn't smooth itself out or go on as though nothing has happened in a matter of months—whether in Real or Best Society."

"Oh dear, I knew his visit wouldn't go well. The poor man just lacks any empathy at all. The big oaf has become such a stuffy politician. Was he harsh?"

Evie smiled tenderly for both her sister's assessment of their brother and the fact that Margie was doing her best to suppress her normally flighty demeanor. "He was…just being Albert."

"I'm sorry. I wish I could blame the war business he attends, but we both know Mummy's influence over a tad controlling."

"A tad? It's her own form of Nazism."

"Evie! I wouldn't say *that*."

"Of course you wouldn't, darling. You're too sweet," she said before placing a forkful of endive into her mouth.

Margie giggled. "You think too highly of me. I'm not oblivious to Mummy's machinations or that she acts like that Mussolini fellow at times. Why, just last week I gave her a piece of my mind as it pertained to you. So don't declare me so saintly. I'll have you know, I have a fairly devious mind when need be."

"Let me guess, contrary to what Albert said, you told Queen Louise I should remain living in The Dakota."

"How did you ever guess? But I did suggest you should go on an extended holiday to the villa down in Palm Beach. You do know that Washington's Birthday Ball is on the twenty-seventh. It's the event of the season. You simply must attend!"

"No. Not Palm Beach and certainly not a society fête. I'm still in mourning contrary to what Albert believes."

"Oh poo! Don't pay him any mind. Mourning is twelve months—even if you aren't wearing black. Yes, you're right…a ball is out. Well then, how about a trip to Rio? That would be marvelous this time of year. I hear Latin lovers can do wonders for a woman's constitution whether in mourning or not."

"Lover? Oh Margie, what have you been reading?"

Another giggle brought her sister's hand to her cherry lips and she leaned forward whispering beside her fingers, "Not *reading*, dear. I overheard someone at the club. She's having *una aventura amorosa*."

" 'Marjorie, whispering and giggling have no place in Polite Society,' " Evie joked mimicking what their mother would say. "You know you shouldn't have been eavesdropping either."

"Darling, it was positively worth my attention. Her lover, a Spanish artist, snapped the lady in question right out of her doldrums on Monday afternoon. An hour after riding him like one of her Arabians, she was right as rain and arranged another private showing—and vigorous ride—at his gallery on the following afternoon." She whispered, "She claims when seated upon him he could have won the Preakness in both stamina and duration. Oh dear!" She fanned her neck with her hand. "The well-known heiress explained it was priapic prowess that moved her to a finer appreciation of Abstract Expressionism…and Equestrianism. Why, just thinking of it gives me the vapors."

Shocked, she tried not react to such vulgar imagery. "Control yourself, dear. I have no intention of taking a lover, not now, nor in the future. I couldn't…no. My heart was captured the month before coming out and, alive or not, Richard will always own it."

She tried not to glance down at the wedding ring she still wore, but instead toyed with it. Obviously, the object of Margie's gossip didn't think too fondly of the commitment her own wedding ring represented, but that was not her concern. Even if Amelia Snow loved the details of a socialite's tawdry affair, she was no longer writing the column. Evelyn Somerset would never even consider inviting another man into her bed. *An artist! Seated intercourse! Priapic prowess! Really!*

"One day soon, I am sure you will take a lover. How could you not with that face and darling figure, as slender as it's become? A woman has just as many needs as a man does." Margie primped her hair. "Brewster understands. He's quite considerate in that department."

"Then you're a lucky girl." She couldn't help the slight stab of jealousy. The memory from the other night flashed before her eyes, and the mystery of Richard's detachment remained unanswered. Perhaps he'd felt as insecure in his prowess as she had. He'd never been an exceptional lover. Goodness, she never got the vapors! And what specific needs were there to be "considerate" about? The whole act was rather...perfunctory. But she'd not ask her elder, more experienced sister. Theirs was a good relationship, but not one of depth or indelicate sharing.

"Yes, I am lucky. Well then, in the meantime, please consider a small getaway. You have been cooped up for almost a half year now. It's simply not healthy, Evie. All the girls at the club have been asking for you. Why, when last I saw Livvy Russell, she even asked whether—"

"And I hope you told her it was none of her concern."

"Honestly, darling, the girl is a sweetheart. Mind you, as much as she tries to hide it, she's lost her once adorable figure, blew up like a dirigible. Anyway, I just don't understand your dislike of her."

She grew fat! Good! She smiled refusing to acknowledge there was no proper explanation beyond rivalry over everything since they attended Dalton School together.

"Thank you, Margie. Truly, I appreciate your genuine concern for me. It's quite refreshing after my visit with Albert. It's funny you should suggest a trip. Apart from missing you, it's one of the reasons why I've asked you to lunch. You see, I *am* going on a journey, but I'd appreciate it if you kept it our little secret."

"Oh darling! I'm so happy! Where are you going? Somewhere exotic in this dreary weather, I hope! A little sun will help your peaked complexion."

"I leave next week for Philadelphia and—"

In unremitting, breathless interruption Margie opined, "Wonderful! You'll be visiting with Mummy's friend Ellen Frazer and her clan then? Why, I haven't seen her since my wedding. I understand she's working with the Red Cross now. Whatever will you do for relaxation? You know, her son Perky...you remember Perky from those winters in Palm Beach, he's in the Army Air Corps now—"

"And he's engaged. Take a breath, dear. I'm not going to visit with the Frazers. I'm going to Philadelphia to board the ocean liner *Serpa Pinto* bound for Lisbon on the twenty-sixth."

"Oh, I just adore Portugal. It is just simply divine and so romantic. You know Brewster and I honeymooned in..." the fork she held stilled above her salad plate when her mind caught up with her lips. She suddenly stopped chattering and looked up with a confused expression. "What did you say?"

"I said I'm sailing to Lisbon for a holiday. I'm told the beaches in Estoril are stunning and the casinos are a wonderful diversion. But—and this is why I need your assistance—having never been before and recalling you've visited Southern Europe, I need you to accompany me to Bonwit Teller so I can select appropriate travel clothes and new evening wear."

Suddenly, Margie's expression turned dour. "But you're afraid of the water, Evie."

"That is true, but I am determined to get away."

"Does Albert know?"

"Of course not."

"I hope you know what you're doing by not telling him." And just like that her sister took a mouthful, speaking as she ate! "It's always the best course to come clean with him at the onset. He has a way of finding things out—just like Mummy does."

"They'll only find out, and stick their nose in my affairs if someone blabs I am headed to Portugal." She raised an accusing eyebrow.

"Who me? I'll never tell! Unless, of course, Albert raises his voice. You know how I dislike that."

"Seriously, dear. For the life of me, I cannot understand why *you*, of all people, are still afraid of him."

"And I might ask the same question of you about Mummy. You're a married…I mean, you're too old to let her get under your skin the way she does."

"That's different and you know it. From my infancy, our relationship has been…a challenge. However, as much as I may dislike the queen, she's still the matriarch of our family and as such, I tolerate her. Albert is your brother—not your father, and surely your husband has something to say about his influence over you."

"Ha! Brewster is a pussycat. He's a lover not a fighter."

She couldn't help chuckling. "So, you said. You'll keep your promise, right? You won't gossip to Albert or Mother?"

There was that twinkle in her sister's eyes again and a sly smirk to her lips before she said. "I won't say a word."

"Please take heed, Margie. I know how you adore spreading information, but if my travels were to suddenly 'show up' in the society section of the *Times* there would be repercussions."

Margie twisted her pinched fingers before her lips, then pretended to throw the imaginary key over her shoulder. "You have my word, and I'll have you know I keep a great many secrets that I don't even share with dear Brewster."

"Oh?"

"Yes. Even a few about you!" She laughed.

"Do tell."

"Oh, silly girl, then they wouldn't be secrets and telling you would only give your belief of my being a gossip credence." Margie playfully grinned.

Always a kidder. Of all the people in Margie's vast acquaintance, Evie prided herself on having the fewest skeletons. Well, apart from her horrific childhood and alter-ego Amelia Snow.

"You will write, won't you? I simply must hear every detail about your Lisboeta lover."

"Darling, you know it would be fruitless to write you. I'll be returning before my first letter would even reach New York. Besides, the details would hardly be of interest to you...or Brewster. Quite tame, I imagine. I don't have a salacious bone in my body."

"Very well, then you must tell me more of your plans. I'm simply agog. Estoril, you say!"

"Naturally I'm traveling first class—unescorted—for eight days."

"Romance on the high seas! Simply marvelous!"

"Oh, for heaven's sake. Stop being so silly, Margie."

"I'm not silly at all. I saw that Humphrey Bogart film, *Casablanca*. Oh, darling...the intrigue, the spies. Why, everyone, simply everyone is trying to get to Lisbon!"

Having been self-sequestered for so many months, Evie was exhausted following lunch and shopping with her sister for the afternoon. As soon as she walked through the door of the apartment, it felt like a welcome cocoon. Now infused with purpose, she didn't have the same abhorrence for The Dakota as she did only four days ago. Committing to helping a family on behalf of Mr. Drucker and in Richard's honor had made everything feel brighter, her burden and sadness lighter. Her editor was right, what else did she have to do? It's not as if her Engagement Book was filled, and what else should she use her money for? Rescuing her boss's family was an opportunity to do something for the war effort, which actually meant something. For the last few days, she hadn't felt guilty about moving on with her life. She was ready to take the first step.

A hat box dangled from its cord at her wrist as she struggled to place two shopping bags on the entry table in the foyer.

"May I assist you, Mrs. Somerset?" Victor asked.

"Oh hello, Victor. Thank you," she said handing him the hat box, her gloves, and then finally her coat. "Prescott will be up with the rest of my packages. Please place them in my dressing room."

"Yes, ma'am."

"Were there any telephone calls today?"

"No, but you did receive a special delivery, which I placed in your chamber."

She stilled at the mirror, removing her hat, gaze locking on his cautious expression in the reflection. "What is it?"

"I would rather not say...It's personal...sensitive, ma'am."

"Oh. I see." Her heart squeezed. "Thank you, Victor."

He left her standing in the foyer as the fear bubbled up inside her. Nothing good ever came by special delivery. She had a feeling she was going to need something strong to drink—or a cigarette. Not one to hold her liquor, she decided on the latter, promptly turning on her heel toward the library where she occasionally enjoyed a poetry book and a smoke.

The apartment was so quiet that the hourly chime of the Ansonia startled her in her pensive consideration of "sensitive." That distinct hammer strike reverberated against the mahogany walls, sending an ominous chill down her spine. Thankfully the feeling of coming home infused her being when surrounded by Richard's volumes and papers. She admired the framed photograph taken on their wedding day. He had such arresting good looks; he was such a good man.

From her desk drawer, she removed a pack of Chesterfields, trying hard not to glance down at the papers—particularly his unused bookplates. He loved those little pieces of artwork designed in a naval motif. They lay just where his long fingers had last placed them.

"No more sadness, Evie," she breathed to herself picking up the ashtray. Without dillydallying, she turned, quitting the room through the connecting door to the parlor, and then finally entered the chamber she once shared with Richard.

Her trembling heart froze. Her hand clenched the half-full package of cigarettes. There, in the center of her vanity sat a single envelope, bent and having looked to be put through hell.

She put one foot in front of the other with her gaze riveted upon the letter. She knew it contained Richard's strong hand and pragmatic assurances. Six months. For six long months, a piece of him had lingered out there waiting to be delivered home. Her hand shook as she set the ashtray on the glass vanity top. *No!* He'd sketched Trefoil Arch Bridge on the left side of the envelope but it was marred by the crude red words "Opened by Censor" stamped atop his artwork. She'd always appreciated his attempt at sentimentality following his arrival at Northwestern University for the Naval Reserve Midshipman training. Upon every envelope, he had drawn a Big Apple landmark, letting her know—in his way—he was home in spirit.

Gone was the confidence she demonstrated at the newspaper. She wasn't sure if she could do this—if her heart could withstand much more. She lowered onto the stool then blinked several times to focus through the pooling tears on the postage stamp and postmark: Tulagi British Solomon Islands.

Unable to touch the letter, she just stared at it, transfixed by Richard's handwriting. She mindlessly lit a cigarette, her fingers trembling as flame touched paper tip. One at a time, tears rolled down her cheeks, dangling then dropping from her chin. It wasn't supposed to happen like this. Their marriage was supposed to last until old age. He was not yet twenty-five when the U.S.S *Jarvis* went down, and she didn't even know the details. Damn Albert for not investigating! Damn the Navy! Damn the war! Damn it all!

She sat there, her heart beating wildly, tears unabated as she blew long streams of smoke into the air in her chain smoking. Her fear of what lay inside the letter propelled her procrastination, and she allowed her thoughts to wander, her stare still locked on the envelope. Other wives had also gone through this. She considered, yet again, how things might have gone differently for Richard had she done more than shop at Henri Bendel and throw dinner parties during his service.

The deep ache fueled her guilt, recrimination...self-pity. This war ruined their future and now she was alone! The Catholics had their novenas, the Jews had their Sabbath, and the pacifists had their rallies, but without Richard she had nothing beyond this last remaining missive and his personal belongings in this apartment. Neither of them had been believers in divinity despite his Anglican and her Presbyterian upbringings. Was that the reason for his doomed fate? When his ship went down, had he found that mysterious god everyone assumed existed?

"No. There is no God," she whispered, half doubting her own proclamation.

She had considered the *Jarvis* a lucky break, having escaped the bombing by the skin of its teeth, musing that its fate, at the time, had been because she'd done her bit by participating in her sister-in-law's "Bundles for Britain" drive.

Life had a funny way of doling out good fortune. She had once believed "for every good deed done, luck was sure to follow."

Not any longer. How wrong she had been!

Staring at the letter, she sobbed and was forced to snuff the Chesterfield out. Evidenced by this last correspondence and the crater in her heart, there was no turning the clock back, hoping to "do more patriotic activities" with the expectation that fate—or what was probably revenge for lack of religiosity—could be reversed. Richard was dead.

She bent over the letter without touching it to examine the postmark. August 8, 1942. The day before his death.

"I can't do this Richard," she blubbered.

"You can, Evie," she imagined what his reply would be, or rather, what she wanted it to be. "You're stronger than you think. Go on, darling, open the letter."

"But I'm *not* strong. Who am I kidding? I'm nothing without you."

"That's not true. You're talented and brave and you don't need me to have an incredible life. Before me, you were daring and uninhibited!"

"But I miss you so much."

"I know. Now, pick up the letter. It's time to say good-bye and hello to the future ahead."

"I ca...n't," she blubbered.

"It is just a letter. It cannot hurt you."

Finally, she bit her lip to keep it from quivering when she reached for the envelope. She ran her index finger over his name in the upper left corner, and then carefully opened the top flap.

As she slid out the stained letter, she smiled softly at the tiny hearts he had uncharacteristically drawn around the edges. His fine penmanship written in pencil soothed her somewhat. This correspondence from the grave was different from all the others— he had not penned it on officer's U.S Navy letterhead nor was it in a War Department V-mail—it was stained scrap paper and written in haste with a few words cut out by the military censors.

Dearest Evie,

It is late, and we will be headed out to sea back into battle ▓▓▓▓▓▓▓▓ *but I could not let this moment pass without writing you. Our ship has been towed to a small island for emergency repair after being torpedoed by a Japanese bomber. We lost 14 brave souls today and will leave behind seven wounded for care. I am as well as can be expected, not wounded physically, but more so emotionally and mentally exhausted. I am shaken, yet proud of our men who seamlessly worked together against the enemy, just as we did at Pearl*

Harbor. I have no doubt that we earned another battle star today. But rest assured, our tin can will see another day, another fight, as will I.

I cannot lie to you, the one who knows me best. I prayed today, and I ask for *your* prayers and forgiveness. I was wrong. Having seen how evil war is, I believe now God is real and come what may, He will give us both strength. Lately, I've been dreaming of simpler, happier times before things got so complicated with me in Chicago and then Hawaii, and I close my eyes and think of you and me dancing at the Drake Hotel on New Year's Eve bringing in '40 with such newlywed optimism. We were happiest then. I've made more mistakes and demonstrated the poorest of judgment more times than I care to count, but I've always loved you. I may not have shown it but I have. You've been the best wife a fella could have and never once complained about any and all of my family's demands or my failures and sins as a husband. Know that although we are apart, you are always in my heart and I am always with you.

Yours,

Richard

P.S. Never Forget Pearl Harbor!

She wept. Her heart torn from her chest. This cannot be happening! Did he know he wouldn't make it home? This unusually heart-felt letter, reading as though a confession, was so unlike Richard.

"Come back to me, Richard! I don't care about the bad times, just the good," she cried, sliding from the stool into a heap on the floor. She curled into a ball and clutched the letter to her chest. Sobs uncontrollably wracked her body as every emotion collided with each other, crushing her like an anvil.

Some time later, Alice found her fast asleep beside the vanity and she awoke feeling as empty as when the telegram announcing Richard's death arrived.

"Come, Mrs. Somerset, let me help you into bed. It'll be all right, my dear. Tomorrow is a new day," the older woman comforted. "There, there. In time, you'll heal. You'll see. One day at a time."

FIVE

I Walk Alone

February 26

*W*orking the night shift at the Philadelphia Naval Yard had turned out to be *boa fortuna* for John Da Silva Purvis. While he went about his lowly tasks of sweeping and maintenance on the docks, his real work went unnoticed—just like he did. Since no one at the yard was a slouch, the other workers kept focused on their duties through the night, never noticing his note taking and swift photographing, particularly around the assembly of those merchant Liberty Ships headed for England. Yes, it had been a productive three months here in the "Cradle of Liberty," following a nine-month employment at the New York Naval Shipyard.

From the stacks, thick billows of smoke filled the morning sky as the night shift ended. At the end of the twelve-hour workday, the whistle blew, and the workers left their tools for those "Wendy the Welders" to resume the unfinished construction of the U.S.S. *Wisconsin*, now that the U.S.S *New Jersey* had been launched. Dubbed "The Black Dragon," the U.S. Navy considered the *New Jersey* the fastest battleship in the fleet. It sat waiting for its commission while they assembled the crew, installed the guns, and carpenters went to work on the inside. The *Abwehr* would pay handsomely for those blueprints and the projected date of the New Jersey's commission. He and his broom had had access to it all.

He'd come close to getting exposed once, but his discoverer, a Ship Fitter, had an unfortunate mishap with a crowbar one night followed by a toss into the Delaware River. Such a shame—the fella had some of the best Cuban cigars.

He stood beside pallets of steel plates at his right near the yard's entrance, his intent hidden out in the open. He cupped his hands to his mouth and warmed them as he surveyed the one-armed giant cranes and towering shipway. The massive structures backdropped the army of laborers headed toward busses and ferry to carry them home; it was quite the patriotic image of America's Arsenal of Democracy. Chuckling under his breath, he imagined the battleships' destruction one day, as well as the bombing of this shipyard—the birthplace of the United States Navy—but that wouldn't happen for some time.

Although Portuguese by birth, Purvis was clandestinely German by temporary allegiance to the Reich. It was a profitable fidelity and one he'd thrown his commitment behind for the last year, disliking American men as much as he did. Their arrogant patriotic idealism and isolated perception of the world got under his skin. This young country had the nerve to think themselves superior to Germany or even Portugal—the *Estado Novo*. But he couldn't deny—as a lover of all women—American women and their independent know-how impressed him. He'd been surprised by their diligent acumen on the docks by day and their eagerness for the company of a real man by night. Easily wooed by his European charm, accent, and dashing good looks, they were not as uncompromising as American men and not as piously uncooperative as Portuguese women. Never flaunted and always behind closed doors, dancing with Americana women usually led to other things.

After three years living in America and securing his position as a yard laborer, everything had gone as planned. And this afternoon, he'd be departing in style for Lisbon where contacts, payment, and new investors for his next subversive endeavor awaited. Hopefully, he'd still have a job upon his return to the States, and hopefully he could arrange security clearance to work in the naval yard's atomic bomb testing facility. His German—or any other nation—contacts would find *that* intelligence worth the price tag of an investment.

Turning from the surrounding activity, he faced the waterfront. *Only a few more snapshots and I am home free.* Sure his hand was quicker than the eye, he snapped several photos of the shipbuilding docks around League Island with the subminiature camera provided to him on his last trip home to Portugal. To his left, down the Delaware, one of the Liberty Ships was being loaded with supplies for their departure across the Atlantic.

Snap. Snap. Snap.

From the second floor of the building closest to the Philadelphia Navy Yard's main gate, an Englishman laughed as he gazed down out the window at Purvis standing beside the river. "The poor chap has no bloody idea he's been under surveillance," he said to his Canadian partner filming the mole using a motion picture camera. "Look at him down there…'Ello, govna," he called down jokingly in an exaggerated cockney, unheard beyond the glass.

The two men in the cordoned-off drafting room were agents for the British Security Co-ordination (BSC,) a highly covert organization within the Secret Intelligence Service (SIS.)

"He's done for when he gets back from Lisbon, eh?" the Canadian stated.

"Quite sure of it. The Americans now employ the electric chair for spies. You remember those Jerries that came ashore last year. Frankly, I prefer the old-fashioned way—firing squad in the Tower of London."

"Purvis is such a dolt; he doesn't even have the intelligence to work both sides against each other. If only we can tie the murder of the dock worker to him."

"It's a bit dodgy and 'Intrepid' wants a weapon, but buggers like Purvis always strike again. He'll pay for his high crimes."

The subject of their conversation turned to face the building, tilting his head upward to look at the sky. The Canadian grinned. "That's it...up here. Giv'r a smile for the camera, buddy."

Evie had lied, and she didn't feel bad about it in the least bit. Still in pain from last week's surprise letter from Richard and smarting over Albert's insensitive telephone call following his visit, there was no stopping her determination. Further, she'd get over her fear of the water. Lisbon awaited and today was the day the Portuguese liner S.S. *Serpa Pinto* would leave for its journey. That was why she had lied. With a sob story about needing to get away and visit a Vassar friend, her sister-in-law Ann was only too eager to loan her the Packard and driver for the two-hour trip south to Philadelphia. How else could she obtain an unlimited amount of fuel on the ration? Members of Congress were exempt from such restrictions, even though they enforced them on every other citizen. She had considered the hypocrisy, but reminded herself that her brother was vital in winning the war. Maybe he could oversee the production of a ship impervious to Japanese dive bombers and save another woman's husband!

In the near distance, League Island's enormous cranes towered over Philadelphia's Naval shipyard. Albert had once commented that thousands of men and women had come from all over to work together and, again, her thoughts traveled to Richard and how proud he would be of her. She had never traveled by sea before, choosing instead to remain in the States for their brief honeymoon. This sailing was significant in so many ways. There would be much time to think on them as the *Serpa* crossed the Atlantic and she smiled slightly with her own sense of pride at doing her bit for Mr. Drucker's family. She couldn't help reflecting on how, standing here wearing mink while waiting to embark the luxury ocean liner, she didn't *feel* the war at all. Well...apart from Richard's death and the newsboy pushing through the crowded pier, selling *The Philadelphia Inquirer*.

The newsie waved a paper aloft. "Rommel retreats in Tunisia!" he called out trying to entice readers with the newspaper headlines. "Our fighters are hot on those Nazi heels! Americans take Kasserine Pass! Read all about it."

The fellas in the newsroom had brought her up to speed on the geo-political atmosphere and the number the Germans were doing in Europe, and the Japanese in the Pacific. She was a reporter now, and would get her own scoop!

The stark comparison of her first-class accommodations and her position in society versus the hard work of the average Joe building destroyers and carriers just beyond this shipway was dispro-portionately evident. Still, in her way, she was joining the ranks of those in Real Society, doing something for the war effort just as Albert had encouraged.

Painted upon the steamship's hull at her back, the Portuguese flag and the name of the ship backdropped her half-frozen form. She clasped the fur around her neck when the wind blew across the Delaware River, whipping up through the ship's slip. For a Sunday morning, the gangplank was packed with tear-filled travelers ascending two-by-two onto the main deck. No doubt, they were excited and apprehensive for the potentially dangerous passage, just as she was. Flanked by steamer trunks stacked on the pier, well-wishers waved good-bye to passengers. No one was there to send her off with a bon voyage, but she realized she didn't feel alone. She carried with her Mr. Drucker's confidence, her re-discovered independent streak, and the last line in Richard's letter that he'd be with her in spirit.

One white chimney and four flapping small flags bid travelers welcome onto the older ship as many people gazed over the deck balconies at their families and friends below. Ready to embark, Evie took a deep breath and recalled the Millay verse: See what never has been seen! She tightly grasped the handle of her alligator purse and took her first step toward the gangplank. Trailing directly behind a group of men, she could not help but to overhear their conversation.

"Third class. Ya think Dutch could've gotten us better sleepin' digs," a fresh-faced young man complained to his traveling companion when they stepped onto the gangway.

"Do you wanna swim to Portugal, Billy-boy? If you axs me, we were a bunch of lucky fellas to get this gig, and I'm sure as heck not going to look a gift horse in the mouth. Free is free," the older said with an indiscernible American dialect.

"Yeah. I guess you're right. It's not as crummy as getting called up—that's for sure."

The man laughed. "You can't outrun Uncle Sam. He'll find you."

"I ain't chicken if that's what you mean. I'm a trumpeter."

He slapped his young friend on the back with another hearty laugh. "Kid, you can play the bugle in the Army just the same as ya do with Dutch. Haven't you ever heard 'Boogie Woogie Bugle Boy?' "

"So what's your excuse for not signing up?"

"Because there's a reason it's called a *bugle* call, not a clarinet call."

"That's cock-eyed!"

"You hoo, Carl. Oh Carl! Wait for me, darling!" Evie heard from behind her before a strong whiff of cheap perfume assaulted her. The wearer pushed forward through the crowd making her rude way up the gangplank, bumping her from behind.

"Sorry, doll. I'm with him," she said pointing to the clarinetist before shoving past.

"Oof!" Evie exclaimed, losing her footing as she fell half on the man in question and half onto the metal railing. Within a second, he dropped his instrument case then turned, catching her in his arms before she went over the guardrail.

"Jeez! Are you okay, Miss?"

"I…I think so."

He examined her face, most likely assessing her mortified blush. She looked away, righting her posture and her hat.

"Are ya sure? I could carry you up the gangplank if you're hurt." Both of his hands remained on her waist as his gaze searched hers even though the line of passengers ahead of them had moved and they blocked embarkation.

"No. Really, I'm quite fine," she brusquely said, hoping he would turn around and go back to his girlfriend.

"Carl! She said she's okay," the woman said, attempting to remove the man's hand from her. "We have to go, darrrling."

"I'm sorry, Miss," he said giving her a contrite smile before dropping his arms.

The woman tucked her arm into his after he picked up his instrument case.

<hr />

Six

I Hear a Rhapsody

March 1

*W*earing golden silk, *she* entered the small ballroom to the Canadian Dutch Ellerton Orchestra performance of "Frenesi." With each poised step the elegant woman took, her evening gown moved in luxurious waves as though melted ore flowing around her sensuous shape, and Carl Wilson couldn't help staring. Even from the stage, with a clarinet reed pinched between his lips, his attention diverted from the sheet music laid out before him. This high-class dame stole all his attention from making music and everything else in the room. Oblivious to the choppy seas and the rock of the ship, she seemingly moved to the rhythm of the music, gracefully sashaying across the dance floor toward her destination at the edge of the wood. It was as if she'd been taught how to make an entrance, how to cross the polished floor while inflicting the maximum amount of damage to every male in the room.

Her strawberry locks were elegantly pinned up, but not so hidden beneath the sheer veil loosely draped over her head. Adorned with tiny, sparkling rhinestones the diaphanous fabric swept across the jewels hugging her neck. She sparkled like stars under the ballroom's chandelier. Although kissed with coppery red, no smile graced her perfect lips, but those lips were made for all kinds of smiling—and kissing. The thought of doing just that had occupied his mind since the band's female vocalist Kay Shaw had rudely pushed the mysterious woman on the gangway during embarkation three days ago. He could still recall the feeling of soft mink and her waist in his arms and that beguiling embarrassed flush to her cheeks when she fell into him.

As he played from his stage position in the second row, he admired how the beauty settled at a table for two but sat alone. Of course she did—she had boarded the ship unaccompanied. That too brief exchange between them had caused all sorts of wondering about her. Why would she travel to Lisbon alone? Was she meeting someone? An *affaire d'amour* perhaps? Was she oblivious to the danger? She didn't seem to be one of those adventure tourists, nor was she a British refugee returning to Europe. Maybe she, like others on this ship, was not as she appeared. Pretty as a picture, she crossed her legs and his gaze traveled their length imagining what hid below the cascading fabric.

The steward arrived beside her, filling her coupe glass with champagne, reserved only for this swanky European set. He and the boys were just third class fellas aboard the *Serpa*—it was more like beer and peanuts for them down below, but he sure liked playing for aristocrats. Dutch's orchestra wasn't Glenn Miller, and Dutch himself wasn't the "King of Swing," but they did all right and the gig awaiting them in Lisbon was a lucky break for these boys. As for him, getting the job with Dutch's orchestra was all in the cards.

The soft illumination from the table lamp commingled with the dancing bubbles within the glass. Again, "Red's" lips spellbound him when they touched the rim. Seductive flame and golden effervescence met in a delicious drink, and he freely admitted to himself he was gawking, stirred…affected by her. That feeling was something new. Not a playboy, unless absolutely necessary, and always level headed, he wasn't prone to manipulation by the fairer sex, even if it was unintended.

Thankful the song ended, he lowered his clarinet, turned then wiped his moistened brow with his pocket square trying to refocus.

He readied for the next song and faced the dance floor. Sure enough, like a bad penny that kept turning up, Kay entered stage left for the swinging vocal "I Have Eyes." Her quick glance over a shoulder in his direction followed by a sly wink annoyed him. In fact, everything about the wacky woman annoyed him, particularly her designs on him.

The more he stared at the classy vixen at the table for two, the more Kay's rendition of the lyrics felt like something *he* should be singing to the woman. Yeah…just like the song said…she has lips that fill his soul with flame. He played his solo with desire, hoping even just one note would cause her to look up, search for the clarinetist performing for her alone and maybe recognize him as the man who had briefly held her in his arms.

The song ended and to his knowledge, she hadn't looked up, but Kay thankfully moved from the spotlight and he continued to drink in the only other person in the room. The socialite was alone and looked bored. No, she looked distracted, maybe lost and he wanted to go to her, put on some genuine charm he'd been holding in reserve for just the right woman. Maybe offer an uncomplicated gesture of his hand with an invitation to dance, but it wasn't gonna happen. Make no mistake, although young, she was all woman—not some jukebox bobbysoxer he'd grown accustomed to seeing at each music gig he played in either London or New York. Despite his many personas, he was, at his core, just a simple music man from Pittsburgh who knew his place in a world that he was trying to make better, and she was a socialite who would never venture from her aristocratic place in it.

Dutch signaled him and the band and with clarinet in hand, Carl stepped down three steps to the microphone on the dance floor then smiled when the bandleader gave him the spotlight. Oddly, he felt nervous even though he'd played this song hundreds of times for hundreds of people, but to his recollection none had garnered his attention like Red.

"Ladies and Gentlemen," he said. "I hope ya enjoy our version of the American Billboard hit, 'Moonglow.' "

Within seconds of his introduction, she glanced up.

Their eyes met over the length of the clarinet when he began his performance.

No siree, he wasn't mistaken when those stunning, long-lashed emerald peepers stayed locked on his during each solo of liquid tone his clarinet made and each breath he took—just for her.

Yuh-huh, he was a goner and admittedly grandstanding as he played. When it was over, he gave her a small salute and a grin, but what he didn't expect was her gift of a tiny, barely perceptible smile to send him back to his place on the stage—mind reeling, heart pounding, and now determined to meet her no matter her station or his.

———⬦———

What are you doing?

Evie chastised, fully aware of the fact that she'd just spent the last four minutes enraptured by the clarinetist—and not just the music he played. Before those first notes, she'd been lost in memories of hers and Richard's wedding reception at the Waldorf Astoria when suddenly pulled from them by the sound of the clarinet and "Moonglow." She recognized the musician's face from the gangplank but, at that time, she hadn't *noticed* him. How could she? First and foremost, her mortification had consumed her attention, and secondly, he had been ostensibly hidden below a fedora and overcoat. But now, decked out in a double-breasted tuxedo over a trim, yet substantial frame, the clarinetist *made* her take notice. She had to admit, the man was dreamy looking—a real sender—with brown bedroom eyes and dark chestnut waves. His honeyed voice conveyed confidence. How had she missed that on the gangway? And then he began to play one of her favorite songs. Oh, how she must have looked, sitting there captivated by the way he had made love to his instrument, seducing the melody from it with strong fingers gently caressing and tapping, creating a velvety sound, which enveloped her. It resonated like a romantic sonnet recital or better yet, a bansuri flute, charming her as though she were a serpentine. At his solo breaks, he'd snap his fingers to the rhythm, turning to the other musicians to lead them. The clarinetist was not only a talented instrumentalist, but also a natural showman.

At the song's finale with the clarinet's mellow exit, she released the breath she strangely had been holding. Handsome grinned to the crowd, then to her and, unnerved by the whole experience, all she could manage was a small smile in response. She could not deny his music—rather *he*—awakened something long dead in her. But he'd done something personal—which he couldn't have known: he saluted her, just as Richard had always done as a tease, calling her his captain whenever she asked a favor.

She glanced down to her gloved left hand, and her heart filled with absolute guilt for even just *looking* at the musician with anything other than indifference. Was she not still in mourning as she had insisted only days before to Albert?

Yes, she should have stayed in her cabin for dinner, just as she had done for the last three nights. This trip wasn't for pleasure and she would just as soon deal with her seasickness in privacy. The further the ship traveled into the deep Atlantic, the angrier the sea had become. She had been prepared to be stopped and boarded by the Germans. Perhaps even torpedoed in error by one of those U-boat wolfpacks Mr. Drucker warned her about. But this seasickness? She was not prepared for the tumultuous waves and ship's rocking. *"When in public, refined ladies must maintain all appearance that her constitution is perfect,"* she recalled her mother lecturing. The warm gold tone of her gown and the coppery rouge on her cheeks hid it well.

"Excuse me, *Senhora*, may I introduce myself? I am John Da Silva Purvis and I would like very much to dance with you," a swarthy gentleman asked, his nasally accent clearly native to the

Iberian Peninsula. His groomed mustache further evidenced his European style.

Regretting the constraints of Polite Society to be friendly not disrespectful, she glanced up with a smile replying, "That would be lovely."

Oh, how she wished she could ignore her upbringing with a resounding, "No, I do not care to dance, but thank you." Her false smile concealed all thoughts of Richard, the clarinetist, her betrayal of her husband, and the fact that she was sorry for taking a sip of champagne.

"And whom do I have the pleasure of dancing with?" he asked.

"*Mrs.* Evelyn Somerset. It is a pleasure to make your acquaintance." She accepted his open hand, and he led her to the empty floor for an awkward fox trot. His dance frame, specifically his touch on her back, felt like a trespass to her person. The dulcet tone of the clarinet carried above all the other instruments, as if it was calling to her. It comforted her uneasiness. Oddly, she'd never had such an affinity for the instrument before even though she enjoyed the music of Woody Herman and Benny Goodman, but now she felt some sort of whacky connection to the instrument.

Her partner was a proficient dancer, keeping her in time to the flow of music despite the sway of the ship. The first minute of silence between them was welcome until he spoke, making polite conversation.

"Are you traveling to see family?" he asked.

"No. I am not. I've heard wonderful things about Estoril."

"Ah, the beaches this time of year are not as frequented as in the summer months, but enjoyable nonetheless."

"And the casinos?"

"Very popular." He smiled, joking, "They are anxious to part visitors from their money. Since the war, my beautiful country has been overrun with Americans, Italians, French, and of course, as always, the British. It is quite cosmopolitan. You will fit right in and enjoy yourself."

"I have no doubt." She indulged the inquisitive, aspiring reporter in her when she inquired, "I hear England's Duke and Duchess of Windsor have vacationed in Lisbon, and that the former king of Romania is currently on holiday in Estoril. Is this true?"

"Since I have been away for some months, I do not know of the Romanian king's visit, but yes, the noble *German*...visited Cascais in '40. The Estado Novo is friendly to every nation and their leaders, particularly those in the British monarchy, through our longstanding alliance."

"Ah, yes, the house of Saxe-Coburg and Gotha. I am aware the royal House of Windsor renamed during The Great War. They are originally from Bavaria, I believe."

"You are well-informed," he grinned.

"Are we not all from *somewhere*?"

"I mean to compliment the British Monarchy's respectable bloodline."

"Indeed. Does Portugal have the same type of amicable friendship with the Reich as it does with Great Britain? Do they welcome members of the Nazi Party?"

"Ah, you are an inquisitive beauty. Perhaps you are an international spy, Senhora?" he asked, turning her under his arm.

What an odd question to ask, but she mused real foreign war correspondents most likely would be asked the same question had they'd been wearing diamonds and a Charles James evening gown while inquiring about a controversial statesman.

"A spy? Of course not! I am just a tourist, but I'm eager for any chance to practice my German," she lied. "*Sprechen Sie Deutsch?*"

He responded as though his native tongue were German. "*Du bist ein wunderbarer Tänzer!*"

"Well done!" she beamed, complimenting him for being such a proficient linguist, adding "*Danke Schoen*," for his compliment to her dancing. "Do you frequently travel via ocean liner?"

"I have lived in New York and Philadelphia for some years, but my profession requires I make this trip frequently—and alone. As such, I have grown accustomed to the violent seas and the danger."

"Personally, I have yet to adjust to what they call 'sea legs' due to the terrible squalls. Was it your profession that brought you to America?"

"*Sim,*" was all Purvis said before looking out at the tables of passengers, giving the impression he hid something. His cordial veneer slipped slightly.

He swept her close to the stage and her eyes met with the narrowing ones of the clarinetist. Was it her imagination that he shook his head—in warning?—before placing the instrument to his lips?

"I do not see your *marido* dining with you. Are *you* traveling alone?" he asked with a sickening smile she didn't quite trust. His inquisitive tone was more than just pleasantries and his observation about the missing Mr. Somerset was a bit unsettling. She sensed the treachery behind his words., and a chill traveled her spine.

"Alone? No, *Senhor* Purvis, I am on my honeymoon, but unfortunately my husband doesn't travel well on sea voyages. He's convalescing in our stateroom until our arrival into Lisbon."

"Oh, I am so sorry to hear of his affliction. It makes for an unfortunate beginning to your future. But perhaps, if he recovers, you would both join me for a small after-dinner party I am hosting tomorrow night. I assure you, you will have much opportunity to practice the German language as many of the guests are native."

Thankfully, the song ended, and he dipped her slightly before she gave her answer. "I appreciate your kindness, but he is rather ill. As it is, I have stayed away from him for far too long. Thank you for the dance, though."

"That is a pity."

Her neck prickled, intuitively feeling his stare upon her back as she exited across the dance floor toward the safety of her cabin.

"Senhora, where may I call on you and your husband in Estoril?" he called after her.

Turning to him she lied, "The Hotel Inglaterra," having been informed it was the hotel where the Allies stayed and where she would *not*.

SEVEN
Strictly Instrumental

March 2

March 2, 1943—Philadelphia to Lisbon, Day 5

After almost five days of queasiness with bouts of illness, Poseidon has calmed the sea today and the sun shines brilliantly. I have taken this short respite for fresh air on the main deck to jot notes of the journey for better recollection when compiling my article for the Spectator.

The captain informed me this morning that the fierceness of the ocean during a transatlantic journey is normal this time of year, assuring me the winter squalls and breeze had been made even more violent because the Serpa Pinto was steaming full speed ahead for the Azores. He explained that in this perilous time, as stalwart as Portugal's neutrality is, Germany's assurances not to sink a Portuguese ship are not as certain as the continually changing political atmosphere with the Iberian Peninsula. While this is unsettling to me, I have resolved that if my fate should be the same as Richard's, so be it.

I met the most mysterious man in the ballroom last evening. Proper in both manner and social graces (and quite dapper), John Da Silva Purvis, a Portuguese, spoke Low Prussian with true proficiency: perfect enunciation and not an iota of variant by mixing dialects. The gentleman's German dialect was as pure as Vassar's Professor Stein's. Although polite and a steady conversationalist, I could not discern his intent. Senhor Purvis has been living in America and indicated his business brings him to travel to and from Lisbon. Yet...my woman's intuition did not comprehend what his "business" is. Frequent trans-Atlantic travel during wartime? It was odd that he should invite me (and Richard) to a private gathering of other German-speaking voyagers. Am I being paranoid? Perhaps. Perhaps I am just unaccustomed to being out in society" or looking at everything and everyone through the eyes of a reporter on the scoop of a lifetime. Or perhaps...there is some skullduggery afoot on the Serpa Pinto.

Traveling alone has caused me to be a bit apprehensive when making other acquaintances on board. Richard's missing companionship and protection on this trip has allowed me to consider Albert's position during these many days of isolation in my cabin. However, I am determined to chart my own course—even on stressful seas of uncertainty.

My first-class accommodations are suitably appointed, but having never traveled by steamship before, I am assuming they are comparable to the reputed lavishness of the Queen Mary as conveyed by Margie. The music...ah...well I can attest is top billing. Dutch Ellerton & His Orchestra hit some lovely high notes last evening and I have found one positive about this journey: the clarinet is an exquisite instrument.

Evie lounged on the main deck where first- and third-class passengers comingled. She glanced up from writing in the leather-bound journal on her lap and surveyed the sea. Fighting the bubbling fear of the dark abyss beyond the railing, she focused on the beauty of the rolling waves and white caps spanning as far as the eye could see, turning fear to poetry in her mind. Clear, crisp blue skies were only marred by the steam from the single white stack at the center of the ship. She snuggled down into her mink collar, enjoying the softness at her chin and smiled at the tranquil feeling it brought. Her imagination was now sparked by the thought of "Moonglow" the evening before. The musician was talented and handsome…and her notice of the latter made her uncomfortable.

She thought she'd put these thoughts to bed last night after assessing her curious fascination with him. After tossing and turning for hours with the Artie Shaw song repeatedly playing in her head, she finally—successfully—convinced herself it was only the *song* that had affected her at a time when she was missing Richard the most. Had she believed otherwise, she would be hiding in her stateroom, avoiding the musician like the plague.

Yet…her thoughts insisted on traveling to how his lips hugged the reed, the way his chest rose and fell, the black wave of hair above his eye, and the way he filled out a tuxedo. Would he stop tormenting her thoughts?

Stop it, Evie! She sat upright refusing to allow him to enter her mind. The smile he had given her at the close of the song appeared sincere, and frankly she had missed a man's attention— appreciation—for far too long. *No. I'm only interested in his instrumental talent.*

"Whataya reading?" that recognizable voice broke through her musings, causing her to snap her head in his direction.

It's him!

Defeated, her heart sank yet rejoiced much to her shame.

Please go away!

She promptly closed the journal on her fountain pen and looked up at the man's unnerving grin she had just recalled. "Just a silly novel. Nothing too absorbing."

Wearing the overcoat he wore on the gangplank, the clarinetist looked dashing in new light, on a new day, with a new perspective. The sun kissed the pomade shine in his hair as it blew in the soft breeze. His cheeks were rosy from the brisk sea air, but his speech was warm with a hint of humor in it when he said, "You left early last evening. I hope my playing didn't run you off."

"Not at all. You play exceedingly well." Her heart pounded.

"Then you enjoyed the orchestra…my clarinet?"

"Yes, very much so. 'Moonglow' is a favorite of mine."

"I'm glad." He craned his neck to look at the book cover. The grooved embossing of a ship's anchor seemed to amuse him when he smirked. "Apart from luxury sailing, I wouldn't have taken such a high-class dame as yourself to be interested in nautical novels."

"You are right. This is my first time on a steamship and this book isn't really mine. It was…my late-husband's. He is—was—a lieutenant in the Navy."

"Gee, I'm awfully sorry to hear that. Was it Pearl Harbor?"

"His destroyer narrowly escaped the attack, only to later be sunk in the Solomon Islands in August of last year."

"My condolences—and thanks. Those navy boys sure are taking a lickin'. I guess this trans-Atlantic trip must be difficult for ya, huh?"

Yes. It is. "In some ways. How is it you're not in the armed services, sir?"

"I'm not as young as the kids being called up now, but I did serve in battle for a short time," was all he said, not elaborating on his service.

America had only been at war for fourteen months. Where had he served if not in the navy? Africa perhaps? How old was he? She promptly changed the topic from war, holding out her hand to him.

"My name is Evelyn Somerset," she greeted.

He took her hand in his—Zap!—and she pulled it away as quickly as their flesh had met.

"I'm sorry! Did I do that—that spark?" he joked.

She rubbed her palm on the mink, panicked, yet trying to keep her composure as he continued to look down at her with a knowing smile, like he read her mind. Maybe he was thinking the same thing.

"Nice to meet ya. I'm Carl Wilson." He presumptuously sat on the edge of the empty lounge chair beside her before she could invite him to join her. "I hope ya don't mind if I take a seat. We third class fellows playing with Dutch don't have much opportunity to get up on C deck to converse with a beautiful first-class woman."

He called me beautiful. She'd never felt particularly lovely. "Are you sure your wife won't mind?"

"Wife? I'm not married."

"Well, then your sweetheart."

"I don't have a girl, but if I did, I'd be true blue. My attention doesn't roam from the object of my affection."

Her palm tingled with perspiration at the intonation in his voice. *What is he implying?*

"Well, what about Miss Shaw?"

Mr. Wilson laughed, and what a nice laugh he had, as he leaned back onto the wooden chair. "Kay's a dish and has a set of pipes, I'll give her that, but she's not my girl. Not even close."

He turned his head to look at her straight on while it still rested on the back of the chair. A smirk played upon his lips as he assessed her. Heck, she didn't even understand *her* intent on asking the question. This stranger's love life was none of her affair. Oddly, he was exempt from her previous apprehension about making new acquaintances. It felt good to talk to someone other than herself in her boredom and miserable anxiety of sea travel.

"What gave ya the idea that Kay and I are an item?" he asked furrowing his brow.

"By the territorial way she hung onto you on the gangway, of course. Women are astute about those things, and I have a keen intuition about almost everything."

"Nah. She might be interested, but I'm not, especially after the way she treated you. I don't like discourteous people."

"I survived—and thank you for your quick assistance."

"Glad to have been of service. Catching you was the highlight of my afternoon."

He turned his face away from her then closed his eyes, lifting his chin to the sun. In their silence, she truly tried not to stare at him from the corner of her vision, but she couldn't help it. There was something comfortable about this man. The frank informality of their discussion and the way they had easily slipped into acquaintance was as if they'd known each other for some time or had been conversing much longer than one minute, and as though their social standing hadn't been an impediment. He wasn't refined like Senhor Purvis; in fact, his manner was quite plebeian. But he wasn't a smooth talker, not really. Yet, in his way, he was flirting with her.

"Sure is a pretty day," he said dreamily, eyes still closed.

She admired his profile, enjoying how his lips rested in a tiny quirk, which fascinated her.

"Yes, it is."

"A man can spend all day like this, so long as the company is good."

"A woman might say the same. A good novel is good company."

He laughed softly.

Silence fell again and he folded his arms across his chest. Perhaps he was chilly. It couldn't be more than forty degrees outside.

She wanted to ask him about his music career and why he was headed to Lisbon, but the quiet between them was nice, too. She closed her own eyes, resting her head back on the chair, enjoying the sun and companionship just as he appeared to be.

"Say listen, if I were you, I'd stay clear of that fella you were dancing with last night," he said breaking the silence.

"Oh? And why is that?" She turned her head to face him and he did the same, their eyes holding fast to the others. He had such expressive eyes; his soul burned evident in them.

Mr. Wilson's expression changed, no longer humored as before. Dead serious and clearly concerned he said, "For starters, because he and his friends are up to no good aboard this ship. And secondly, his hand was a little too low on your waist. I don't like disrespectful people, either."

"I confess, I thought the same—on both accounts and that was why I left following our dance."

"Smart girl. Look, I don't know why you're headed to Lisbon, and it's nunna my beeswax, but ya should be careful whose acquaintance you make. Both the city and the *Serpa Pinto* are crummy with spies and manipulators. A nice girl, with a lot of moolah, could find herself in a tight spot when traveling alone."

"I have considered that, Mr. Wilson. I fibbed to him, indicating my husband was ill in our stateroom where he would remain for the duration of the journey."

"That was quick thinking."

"Besides, do tell how you know the state of his affairs in Lisbon? How can you be so certain *I'm* not a *crummy* spy, just as Senhor Purvis also implied?"

He chuckled a low rumble from his chest. "Because any spy would have known that Purvis would check with the porter about your story of a sick husband."

"I didn't consider that."

"And given that Lieutenant Somerset died for the cause, I'm pretty sure ya aren't a fascist or socialist secret agent."

"Yes, he did. We are both patriotic Americans, and my brother...Senator Albert Rousseau is on The Truman Committee. He would have a fit if anyone he knew was a fascist, let alone a spy!"

"A senator, huh?"

She sighed, regretting the slip of tongue. "Yes. Forgive my name-dropping. I'm not prone to grandstanding, I assure you."

"No offense taken. But there is also the *obvious* fact that no spy I've ever heard of would openly write in a journal then try to pass it off as a maritime novel. Spies are people of action who operate either in the shadow or behind a carefully contrived persona, a cover profile. They don't take notes as they go about their espionage acts, Mrs. Somerset. It could cost them their life."

He raised an eyebrow and she slid the journal under her coat. "I'll have to remember that if I consider the spy business," she joked. "Do...do you know very many spies then?"

"In my line of work, I meet a lot of people."

"Really? Then how do I know I can trust *you*? Maybe you are a German agent. Perhaps your clarinet is the perfect subterfuge."

He paused, and she thought she saw his lips twitch and something flicker in his eyes before he said, "I suppose it could be—but it's not. Like I said, I'm true blue and all-American. Not to mention if I was a bad hat, the spark between our fingers, followed by the beguiling blush to your cheeks, wouldn't have happened. Like *you* said, women are astute about those kinds of things."

"Boy, you are sure of yourself, aren't you?"

"No, just a believer that there is a reason for everything. I try not to waste time when fate points the way."

"Fate and time...horse feathers." *Did it always have to come down to those two things?* She shook her head. "The *spark* between our fingers, Mr. Wilson, was nothing more than a net electric charge caused by the salt air and the fur I am wearing. Charged particles ignited into static electricity when we came into contact."

There was that chuckle again before he stood towering over her. "Exactly what I said."

Backlit by the sun, he gaped down at her, his expression filled with mirth. "Don't kid yourself with some fancy science explanation. We both know you and I felt that *same* spark the first time we made contact—at the end of my clarinet over 'Moonglow'—and we hadn't even touched. Fate, I tell ya."

She laughed trying to make it sound convincing. "Poppycock. I don't believe in destiny. Besides, I've only just met you! *And*, I am a married woman."

"I beg your pardon, Evelyn, but you *were* a married woman up until the Solomon Islands."

He'd informally called her by her first name then stuck a knife in a still open wound. Speechless and struggling for a retort, her chin dropped, and the man turned from her.

"Will I see you in the ballroom tonight?" he cheekily asked over his shoulder, taking his first step in departure.

"Not in your wildest dreams! You, sir, are impolite and for a man who has little tolerance for disrespectful people you should look in the mirror!" she declared in a huff.

He stopped and turned to face her full-on with a beaming, smug smile. The wind blew the wave of hair at his forehead revealing a thick scar above his eye.

"I didn't mean any disrespect, but I *am* confident I'll see ya in the ballroom later. Men are astute about *those* things."

"Then prepare to be disappointed." *The gall!*

"Just out of curiosity…what does your keen intuition say?"

"About you?" she twisted her lips. "My common sense tells me you are trouble with a capital *T*."

"I didn't ask about your common sense. I asked about your gut."

"My *gut*…is queasy from sea travel," she prevaricated.

He laughed, "And how do you feel about Cole Porter?"

"That depends."

"On?"

"Whether or not there is a clarinet solo, Mr. Wilson."

"Oh yeah? Well then, ya better start calling me Carl 'cause— trouble or no—I'm gonna sweep you off your feet—for a second time."

"I wouldn't count on it, sir. I only admit to enjoying your performance, not your manner, nor your presumption to know me."

"We'll see about that, Red."

He turned, leaving her alone on the deck. His whistle carried on the sea air, trailing behind him straight to her. It was "Moonglow."

Red? Did he call me Red? The nerve!

EIGHT

And the Band Played On

March 2—evening

*E*vie had tried to stay away from the ballroom. Truly she had wanted to prove Mr. Wilson wrong, but in direct defiance of his caution, she gave into the lure of examining Purvis's actions. As an aspiring journalist, it was unacceptable to go soft when faced with a potentially great story—no matter how dangerous. This trip was an opportunity for prodigious things, namely the chance to prove to both Albert and their mother that she didn't need to be taken care of by anyone. She would wait all evening for a chance to ask Purvis a few more questions.

There was also the matter of Mr. Wilson himself. She glanced over to the orchestra, her expression softening when they landed on him at his stage position, but when he glanced in her direction, she looked away. Nervously, she rubbed one hand over the other, feeling the gold band on her finger. It pained her that she had wanted to see him tonight.

On the deck this afternoon, he had made his intentions clear. But she wasn't sure if she approved of his directness or if she even wanted *that* kind of attention. And by "intentions, directness, and attention," she assumed it was his desire for a shipboard seduction—just as Margie had suggested she pursue. Yet…she was flattered and captivated. What girl wouldn't respond to the music he made or his appealing smile? He also possessed a positive, light spirit about him. He was intelligent and protective. And observant about people and her. She had to admit, she enjoyed their banter. The man seemed unbothered by the war, maintaining a sense of joie de vivre in contrast to Richard's pensive seriousness. Perhaps whatever "battle" he had experienced had something to do with it. Although, that conclusion defied logic, even to her.

Alone at a table for four on the edge of the dance floor, she expected to be joined by other travelers since seating in the first-class ballroom was limited on the small ship. The music was exceptional, and she absentmindedly tapped her fingers on the linen tablecloth to the snappy tune "Let's Dance," which showcased the clarinet in full swing tempo.

Gay laughter rose from the round table of revelers beside her. Since her arrival into the ballroom, the international group had been a source of intrigue for her, unlike the night before when seasickness, loneliness, and the music consumed her thoughts. But tonight, she was acutely aware of her surroundings and the people in it, particularly the many nationalities of those living it up at the table. Both young and old, they conversed in Slavic, Italian, and German accents as they laughed and drank. Were these the friends of Purvis? It didn't escape her notice that the accents were from Nazi sympathetic nations.

"Mrs. Somerset, may I present Mrs. Honeywell and Miss Bartlett?" the steward stated. "They will be joining you this evening."

A woman in her late forties and a young girl, no more than thirteen years of age, stood before her wearing evening wear, which clearly identified them as from aristocracy.

"How do you do?" she greeted, holding out her hand to Mrs. Honeywell.

"Very good, indeed. I hope you do not mind our supping with you this evening," the woman said with an English accent.

"By all means, please do."

The young girl seemed timid and kept glancing over her shoulder at the loud table, even as the maître d' slid the chair out for her.

"Are you traveling alone, Mrs. Somerset?" Mrs. Honeywell asked, referring to the empty seat across from her. She settled into her chair then promptly placed the napkin across her lap.

"I am, and in dire need of some companionship, I dare say." *So that I don't look at the clarinetist.* "It has been a lonely five days."

"Indeed, we have been spending much of our time in our suite. However, today's reprieve from the rough seas encouraged us to venture out into the fresh air."

"Yes, the seas have been dreadful, not to my liking at all for my first time aboard an ocean liner. Like you, I ventured out this afternoon. The sun felt magnificent."

Mrs. Honeywell frowned. "The captain informed us of a change in the weather later tonight. Rough seas are expected until our arrival in Lisbon."

"Oh dear." She had not heard that, and for once was glad for small talk so as to prepare herself. Thank goodness she'd found a diversion in the library: learning the Portuguese language using outdated newspapers. "Are we expecting rain, too?"

"Yes." The woman looked to the young girl with a wry smile, "But Hyacinth is a great reader, so she does not mind staying in our suite of rooms for the duration. Isn't that right, my dear?"

The girl nodded.

"Books are a wonderful diversion. What are you reading, Hyacinth?" Evie asked.

"*Anne of Green Gables*," she said looking up with a sweet smile on her face.

"Wonderful little tale. I recall being quite fond of it myself."

"Hyacinth is on a grand adventure herself. She is returning home to England after over two years in New York City."

"How exciting! I bet you can't wait to see your family after so long away."

"Yes, ma'am."

"Are you her chaperone, then?"

"She is my sister's youngest child and was sent to me in August of '40 when the Jerries bombed London. At the time, Samantha had every intention to later join us in New York, but unfortunately, even for someone of our position, it has been a frightful challenge to obtain an exit visa to come to America. Now dear Samantha has summoned the poor child home, and here we are, making this terrible journey on a…a Portuguese *barge*." She sighed, glancing around the ballroom. "It is *not* the *Queen Elizabeth*."

Hyacinth ignored her aunt's repugnance and fidgeted in her seat, eyes switching from her folded hands at her lap to the merry makers at the table beside them.

"Don't mind them, darling," the aunt comforted before lowering her voice. "I think it is the German accent frightening her. Her father was lost in that ghastly business at Dunkirk and well, my sister filled her head with fear of invasion."

"Understandably so. Is your sister not afraid of it still? I mean, I have it on good authority the Allied victory is far away, contrary to what many may believe."

"Yes, she still foolishly worries, but has moved away from Westminster and now resides in a marvelous country manor in Wiltshire. It is true Hyacinth will not only be safe but much happier than in my flat where she has few friends. As a young lady, it is expected she return to her mother. Mind you, she must start preparing for her role in society."

"I remember those days well. You are correct, there is much to learn."

"Of course, since Britain declared war on Germany, Hyacinth's finishing will now have to take place in England. Such a shame she won't have the advantage of Germany's fine art and music, to lead her into her season. They are such a cultured people."

Yes, Evie was all too aware of the expectations and "training" for a young woman of Best Society's coming of age, but as for Germany's culture in preparation for coming out, she couldn't agree, having prepared in the States, not abroad like most of her peers. And, well, the statement showed the woman's sympathetic bent toward the Jerries.

She tilted her head to Hyacinth. "We are in exciting times and, just like Anne Shirley and her new adventures in Avonlea, one never knows what lies ahead or the people we will meet. I bet Wiltshire will be a glorious place to explore once you return to your mother. Think of the new friends you will make."

"There are ancient stones, too" the girl said.

"Tell me about them. Are they similar to the mysterious Stonehenge?"

"Yes, ma'am. Mummy said they are prehistoric."

"Simply a marvelous archeological adventure! You know, I'm on an adventure, too."

"You are?" the girl asked.

"Yes, I'll tell you a big secret…I'm a newspaper reporter on my way to interview with—"

Mrs. Honeywell gasped.

"But you're…you're a lady," Hyacinth stated in awe.

"Born and bred—just as you are, but that does not mean you cannot pursue your dreams. I'm doing just that."

"Mannered women are not newspaper reporters," Mrs. Honeywell huffed.

"Some are, several even from Best Society. In fact, our First Lady is a syndicated newspaper columnist." Evie mischievously grinned and delighted to see Hyacinth smile back. This slip of a girl was tomorrow's future and Evie's heart clenched slightly at the thought that she'd never have a daughter of her own to say this to.

A glance up to the older woman's disapproving expression set her shoulders back for she saw her mother's censure in its likeness.

An abrupt change of topic was necessary before her blood boiled at the officious woman's further condemnation of her career pursuit. "Tell me, Mrs. Honeywell, what will happen when you arrive into Lisbon? How will you ladies travel to England?"

"Through the British Consul in Portugal, we have arranged for air transport on a civilian plane, which departs once a week for Bristol. From there, we will endure, as best we can, day coach train travel to Avebury. All this travel is not good for my constitution."

Perhaps you should take a Latin lover. My sister suggests it could do wonders for your constitution. "You are quite fortunate to have such connections to assist you. As I understand, it is not only difficult to acquire exit papers in England, but also in Lisbon for those who are escaping Germany and France. Passage either by sea or air is both crowded and limited."

"I have heard of the so-called Jewish predicament, but it is none of our concern. Our papers and passage home are assured."

Truly, with only having read a letter from the Drucker family, Evie could not assess the situation in Lisbon, and continued in polite conversation, but she had learned one thing in the last few months: the war was everyone's concern. However, the little she knew of the Jewish flight from Europe, conveyed by Mr. Drucker and the boys on the foreign news desk, Mrs. Honeywell's indifference angered her. The woman's blatant arrogance startled her and she, again, saw her mother—and yes, even herself during her pre-college years—through the narrow view of aristocratic isolation—not born from pacifism, but entrenched in elitism and possibly bigotry.

Thankfully, supper arrived and for the duration, the conversation turned back to books, travel, and her honeymoon at the Greenbrier Resort in the Allegheny Mountains before it had been overrun with Axis diplomats. Hyacinth was genuinely interested in its notable American history, and her aunt put on a good front interjecting the occasional jab at the inferiority of

American society in comparison to Great Britain's refined gentry and nobility.

She wanted to blurt out: "My father-in-law, The Right Honorable Lord Charles Somerset, Baron of Sallingham is a naturalized American citizen!" to silence the woman, but then the statement alone would bring further censure. She pursed her lips to keep them from moving. If it hadn't been for the rapt attention of the girl, and propriety, she would have even feigned a headache and foregone the opportunity to speak further with Purvis.

As the older woman chatted on, Evie noticed the man's arrival to the table beside them. Their eyes briefly met and then he sat, engaging the stunning woman to his left in conversation.

During tea and dessert of the traditional Portuguese *pastel de nata* tart, the break from Mrs. Honeywell came when Mr. Purvis asked her to dance.

He smiled a gentlemanly invitation as he extended his hand, which she gladly accepted. Clearly humoring her previously expressed desire to become more proficient, he spoke in fluent German. A moot endeavor, since she had already mastered three dialects of German as well as Austrian-Bavarian *Bairisch*. "Mrs. Somerset, you look lovely this evening, like a Hollywood starlet."

"Thank you," she said in kind.

"May I inquire as to Mr. Somerset's health? I hope he has greatly improved with the calming seas."

"He is feeling much better, but is taking supper in our cabin this evening. Unfortunately, our initial travel plans were upended when the Pan American Clipper crashed. The poor man just cannot tolerate seasickness."

"That is unfortunate for him as well as the seaplane. Yet, I cannot deny both are to my great fortune, as you are dancing with me this evening. We have a word for that where I come from. *Fado*, it means fate." Purvis whisked her around the dance floor in a fast fox trot, thus far his left hand remaining firmly in its proper place on her back. "Have you given thought to my invitation to the intimate gathering for friends?"

"Some consideration…tell me more about your friends." She chuckled, glancing out at the raucous voyagers. "They are quite lively!"

"Some I have traveled with before, but others I have just made the acquaintance of on this journey. My business interests bring together like-minded people."

"Oh? And what business are you in, *Herr* Purvis?"

"Shipping."

"How fascinating. Your friends are quite international."

"Yes. They are from all over the world. In fact, Irena Olszak and her husband Stephan are natives of what is now the General Government of the Third Reich in Poland."

He turned her under his arm, smiling as if he considered her of like mind. This was exactly as Mr. Wilson had suggested. Spies among us? The couple in question was returning to the Nazi zone of occupation.

"Yet she lived in America? How on earth did they escape the occupation of Poland?"

"It is not like that. Herr Olszak is a diplomat, an envoy, and they are now returning home to their country. I have only just met them on this voyage, but he is interested in…investing in shipping and exports, and knowledgeable in State and legal affairs."

"How fascinating. Did they reside in America long?"

"It is my understanding they lived in New York City for four years, but now…the American government has *invited* them to return to Poland."

"She is quite a beautiful woman."

His hand slid downward, resting on her lower back. "I am told Irena Olszak is an heiress, but she is not more beautiful than you."

"Oh, what a charmer you are, Herr Purvis!" she laughed then reached behind to slide the sycophant's hand upward.

Four years in Manhattan? She had not heard the name "Olszak" in her circle, and her circle was *the* circle, filled with blue-blooded families and political heavy-hitters, including dignitaries and even some royalty from other countries. The *New York Social Register's* members were deeply entrenched in "State affairs." If that woman was an heiress, she'd know and Margie—of the oldest, smartest set—would have indeed spoken of her. If only she could get closer to examine the tiara she wore.

Evie glanced over her shoulder as the song ended, and it was just as she had felt: Mr. Wilson's penetrating gaze fixed upon her. Again, he shook his head, and defiantly she added to Purvis, "I would love to meet her. May I join your darling little soirée at the table?"

"But of course!"

What am I thinking? The song ended and Carl bent for the crystal glass at his feet. He took a deep drink, his glare riveted on her retreating back—and bottom—as it subtly swayed. Tonight, she was draped in luxurious silver covered with twinkling diamonds in a Grecian style, which hugged her shape in all the right places. Each movement she made under the ballroom lights spellbound him like shooting stars, but he still fumed at her carelessness.

Had he not made his point strong enough up on C deck this afternoon? Was she deliberately acting carelessly, or was he too concerned where it was none of his business? That was what truly annoyed him. Why her? Why was he so concerned about a highbrow dame, *this* dame? That wasn't his job, but then again, an innocent woman shouldn't become embroiled in what was afoot on the *Serpa Pinto*. She could find herself thrown overboard with this crowd. He considered that maybe there was more to her than what met the eye. Maybe she held secrets; maybe his judgment had been clouded by her captivating presence. *Maybe her brother is using her as a courier? Or maybe her brother is a crooked politician. The book she was writing in might shed some light on her intent.*

She stood at the table as introductions went around, and it was clear someone had made a joke. Evelyn's smile lit the room; her ruby lips framed her pearly whites, her mouth opening into a full grin when she laughed. Carrying above the din, it sounded like a mischievous angel song. Her laughter caused her chin to lift and a shoulder to rotate forward then back presenting a glorious image. Her strawberry locks brushed over one shoulder from the movement, and he answered his own question of "why her?" having said it best on the deck: the spark between them was real. Despite her haughty arrogance and high-class upbringing, he was the thunderclap answer to her lightning bolt siren call.

The steward brought an additional chair to the table, and Carl watched her take a seat next to Purvis. The conversation coming from the saboteurs seated around her bordered on the raucous but Evelyn, with the same demure composure as he witnessed on deck, played along wonderfully. In his line of work, he could tell when people were acting. She was good...very good. *What game is she playing? Who is she? Is she an American spy?*

Perplexed, yet intrigued, by her decision to join the rowdy group, he decided to get her attention, to distract her from further entanglement in Purvis's game of espionage. Discombobulation and confusion were his only options. The aristocrat Mrs. Somerset would embattle, block out her attraction to him but once Cole Porter began taunting her, "Red" would fight to dismantle the veneer—and safety net—Evelyn hid behind.

Carl signaled Dutch that he'd like to end the set list with "Begin the Beguine," then came down the steps just as he had the night before. "Ladies and gentlemen, I'd like to dedicate this next Cole Porter song to one of the most fascinating women aboard ship tonight."

Evie stilled at the sound of his voice, then turned her head in his direction. Again, their eyes locked over the length of his clarinet when he raised it to his mouth. A tiny smile formed on her lips, and he knew then he was speaking to her through the penetrating vocals of his clarinet and she was listening.

He enjoyed playing this piece, and at the moment, the "beguine" was an alluring dance between them having begun over "Moonglow."

Purvis tried to speak to her, yet she only offered the thug a smile as she continued to absorb the music. The German at the table appeared to ask her to dance, yet she shook her head; her attention never wavered from the stage. Eventually, the Italian tried to gain favor, but to no avail; she disregarded his slick manner almost immediately. For three minutes, he alone, the tuneful Pennsylvanian, held her under his spell.

The song finished and this time, he didn't salute her. Instead, he left the stage with his instrument of charm in his hand and a grin on his face.

NINE

Pennsylvania Polka

As cold as it would undoubtedly be outside, Evie needed air. She struggled with the strange and alluring pull Mr. Wilson had on her. It both pleased and disconcerted her that he'd come through with his Cole Porter promise. And what a breathtaking performance it was, having completely overridden all her desire to dissect Purvis and the fraud Mrs. Olszak's machinations. In preparation for a possible scoop, she still had three full days at sea should she decide to uncover the Lisboan's "shipping business" and the woman's reasons for deceit. Right now, the only thing occupying Evie's mind was how she'd responded to the clarinetist's dedication and performance.

The door swung open onto the covered promenade deck and the biting wind hit her face with a blast. The Mid-Atlantic waves pounded against the hull, like her heart against her chest wall, and she took a deep breath trying to clear her mind and override her fear of the dark abyss below. *Just for a minute.* She needed to regroup before heading back to her cabin, and leaned against the wall beside the hatchway, one hand over her chest the other grasped the railing, in fear of losing her footing.

Out of habit, one instilled by her husband, she peered upward into the moonless night and looked to the stars. Though the ship's floodlight spoiled their true brilliance, she located the big dipper and followed it to the North Star. She smiled at the recollection of her husband's appreciation of astronomy, as only a seafarer would.

She'd never before considered their differing tastes in things. His love of maritime, her dislike of it; his love of the cosmos, her ambivalence to it; her love of poetry, his choice of academic journals; her love of music, his preference for silence. In retrospect, they'd only lived together for a month before he left for naval training and then on and off for a year before his commission. That was hardly enough time for their interests to meld or to create shared ones. So peculiar, she'd think of that now, in the ice cold, while gazing up at Polaris. Perhaps Mr. Wilson's music had brought the reflection to the surface, but it was Richard's stargazing custom calming her.

This man, a clarinetist...she'd have to sleep on the puzzling emotions he made her feel. It was too confusing. Would she be wrong to imagine dancing with him? His music did things—stirred things—in her, and if his instrument could do that what could his person do? How much of a betrayal to her marriage vows was it to consider what his hands would feel like upon her skin? She took another cleansing breath, filling her lungs with the crisp air.

A movement in the shadow some twenty feet from her toward the aft of the ship alerted her that she was not alone. Two figures huddled in the darkness below the staircase leading up to the first-class deck. A sudden flicker of flame preceded the hot orange embers of a cigarette's lighting between them. Crystals, like those of Olszak's tiara caught the deck light when the figure moved in the arms of the smoker.

In the shadow, Evie held tightly to the wooden handrail and took a cautious step closer, then two. Murmurings between a man and a woman breached the waves against the hull, and she felt like a voyeur to an obvious shipboard romance, but she was a curious creature. Perhaps her alter ego, Amelia Snow was surfacing. If this woman was indeed Irena Olszak, well, then she left her husband seated at the table!

Still, Evie could not make out their conversation and bravely moved to the fire hose box nearest to them.

The couple whispered in the darkness, but she heard them from her hiding place.

"I have to go back. He'll be suspicious." The accent of the woman was clear: Polish.

"Wait. I need you to do something for me," the man said, his voice also clear: Mr. Wilson.

She stifled a gasp, her hand flying to her mouth as she listened for what that "something" was. As if their "close quarters" wasn't proof enough of their assignation, but she could not hear the words that followed.

Determined, she draped the shawl over her head, not only for concealment but also because of the ocean spray, and crept closer toward the lovers, ears and eyes alert, footing precarious.

"Are you sure?" Olszak asked. "She may be one of them."

Evie stopped, pressing her back flush against the wall, fingers gripping the rail behind her, the waves roiling like her stomach. To her left, the cigarette burned brighter when the clarinetist took a drag.

"I don't think so, but she's cozying and noseying up where she doesn't belong."

"If she is no one, then why are you so concerned?"

"Her brother's an American senator."

"Then I take care of it for you, but I notice this gleam in your eyes, darling."

"There's no gl—"

"Ssh, someone's com—"

Mr. Wilson's lips cut off Olszak's words when he pulled her into him, kissing her passionately.

Panicked by what she'd just witnessed, *heard,* and the possibility of having been seen, Evie ran down the deck toward the nearest door, struggling not to slip and fall in her shock and haste.

———❖———

Perspiring and heated in terror, Evie's fingers trembled as she slid her stateroom porthole open a crack. Her heart raced and mind spun by what she had just witnessed. The man was a wolf, playing her—and Olszak—like an instrument, attempting to woo her with his music and soulful eyes. What had the woman meant by "I take care of it?"

"This isn't happening," she cried, struggling to divest herself from her evening gown. Finally, it gave way and fell to the floor in a puddle of silk. She dropped onto the edge of the bed in despair and burst into tears, her hands covering her face as the sobs released all the confusion and fears building over these many days. What did Mr. Wilson want the Polish woman to do? And what did it matter if Albert was a senator?

"Now you've done it! If Richard were with you, then this never would have happened! You wouldn't be on this ship, in this position!" she bawled feeling like a foolish naïve child duped by the first man to show an interest in her. For the first time in years, she wished for the safety of The Lancashire. "What a fool you are, Evelyn!"

A rushing whistle of wind pierced the crack of the window sending a chill up her bare back, and she rose for her robe and a cigarette. If ever there were a need for one, it was now. The ship pitched, and she nearly toppled over, promptly holding onto the side of the table; her stomach lurched.

A fast rap to her stateroom door felt like a boon, so sure she was that her attentive and intuitive steward was at the ready with tea to quell her seasickness.

"Donato, oh thank goodness!" she said through the door.

"Donato? Aw, you break my heart, Red. It's me, Carl."

She stiffened, and her hand stilled over the doorknob. *Oh no!* Unsure of what to do or even say, her body reacted on impulse by clutching together the lapels of her bathrobe even though the closed door stood between them.

"This is highly improper! Go away!"

"I don't think ya mean what you say."

"You don't know what I'm thinking! What do you want?" she balked.

"I think we need to talk," he said.

"I have nothing to say to you." Yet she found herself wanting to talk to him; her abject fear lessened the more he spoke. Never before had she experienced such overwhelming emotional conflict and confusion. The man exasperated and attracted her at the same time.

"Look, you have my word as a gentleman, I don't have indecent intentions. At least...not tonight."

"A gentleman you say!" She laughed, mocking him, but opened the door anyway. Despite what her eyes had seen and her ears had heard on the promenade deck, she was relying—hoping—her first impression of him had been the correct one. If she was wrong, she'd scream bloody murder for the whole ship to hear.

He looked so debonair standing at the threshold wearing a tuxedo and a contrite smile, and yes, his eyes did rake over her, the admiration evident and it was shamefully gratifying.

"Mr. Wilson, that wolfish expression in your eyes exposes your intentions."

"I can hardly be blamed for your allure, Evelyn. I wouldn't be a man if I didn't admire your near perfection. As for intent, it isn't what you think, as tempting as the thought is." He braced a hand against the door frame when the ship pitched.

"And what of Mrs. Olszak's allure? I'm sure her husband might blame you for her disgrace despite her obvious invitation for romance."

"Ah, so it was you on the deck. Tsk, tsk, tsk...you shouldn't spy on people."

"You, sir, are a cad."

"A cad? Again, you wound me." He placed his hand over his heart and grinned.

"Good, and I don't care to hear an explanation regarding your affair either."

"Well, that's just fine and dandy because I'm not gonna give ya one. It's nunya beeswax." He looked down the hall to his left, then right. "Nor is it anyone else's. Please, let's have a private word in your cabin. You can trust me." He held up three fingers. "Boy Scouts Promise."

"Boy Scout, my eye. We'll see about that," she huffed, stepping aside to allow him entry, but she made sure to keep her distance from him. "Did I hear you say, *near* perfection?"

"Yuh-huh, sure did." He silently observed her from across the room, his searching expression softened. "Were you crying, Evelyn?"

"No, of course not. Why would I cry?"

"I don't know, but the black cosmetic under your eyes is a dead giveaway."

Oh damn! She swiped the wet Maybelline away attempting to appear unfazed, and awaited his next jesting remark. But it did not come.

Instead, he glanced down at her disregarded gown on the floor then furrowed his brow. "I'll get right to it since you got the wrong idea about me. Why are ya going to Lisbon?" he asked point blank. "Unaccompanied and clearly not used to sea travel, a woman of your position wouldn't subject herself to such susceptibility, let alone inconvenience."

"I'm sorry, Mr. Wilson, but one conversation on deck and a clarinet solo does not entitle you to my personal details."

"I guess I just need to be sure you're not involved in all the shenanigans on this ship."

"Honestly, I think you're paranoid believing there is a spy or a saboteur at every corner." She refused to engage in this questioning of his and turned her back to him, walking toward the vanity to the gold cigarette case atop her leather journal.

He crossed the room in two determined steps.

She gasped when he grabbed both her biceps and turned her to face him. His eyes were filled with anger—or passion—she couldn't be sure.

"Damn it, Evelyn! I'm not paranoid. I'm serious! This is not a game you are playing with Purvis. He *is* a God-damn spy for Nazi Germany, and he most likely thinks you're sympathetic to their cause! Are you? Is that why you're headed to Lisbon? Are ya in cahoots with him and his unsavory friends?"

"Let go of me! You're hurting me!"

Immediately, his grip loosened and she wiggled from him. *Now,* she really needed a smoke!

She picked up the cigarette case and lighter then crossed the room away from his penetrating stare.

Rooted beside the vanity, he watched her futile effort to open the stuck case, until he softened his brow and walked to her. Stopping mere inches from her struggle, with only her trembling hands and the cigarettes bridging the gap between them, he gently removed the lighter from her grasp. She almost swooned from his intoxicating cologne and continued to look down at the gold compact when he then slowly withdrew it from her fingers, his own lingering. She looked up into his eyes, their faces so close, his lips so inviting, the air between them charged like electrons on a wire in their silence. His head dipped to hers ever so slightly and her breath caught in anticipation of his kiss.

But nothing happened.

His effortless lift of the latch snapped open the case and he withdrew two smokes, lighting one then the other.

Carl's gentle voice soothed her when he held out a burning cigarette to her. "I'm sorry. Frightening you was not my intention. I'd never hurt you, Evelyn. Just answer me this: this afternoon…on the deck…did I judge your character correctly?"

She sighed filling the silence between them and then took a deep drag, calming her anxiety. She knew she shouldn't trust him after what she saw and heard, but he sounded so sincere in that moment. Another pitch rocked the ship but he quickly responded, steadying her with a bracing cup of his hand under her forearm.

"You did judge me correctly," she whispered. Gazing into his eyes, she ignored the image of his shipboard romance with Olszak, a woman who, for whatever reason, had also been enticed into Purvis's net. With reservation, she told him what he wanted to hear: the truth, incomplete as it was. "I am who I say I am, as is my brother, but you may find my reason for travel…quite implausible, contrary to my normal lifestyle."

"Try me."

She raised her chin high. "I'm a reporter for the *New York Daily Spectator*, and, since I am of a certain society, if you will, and multilingual, my editor sent me to Estoril to interview the Jewish Romanian Elena Lupescu. I have reports she and the exiled former king are staying at the Hotel Palácio where I've secured a suite."

"Ah …"

"But my interview isn't technically official, you see. The newspaper could be in hot water because I'm *not* an accredited war correspondent."

Carl's lips twitched in a half smile. "In other words, you're not bound by military rules and ya don't have to ask for permission for every cock-eyed thing and, because of that, it puts your brother, the senator, in a bad position."

"Exactly."

"Does he know you're headed into the spy capital of the world?"

"Albert? No, he would most assuredly not approve, but as frightening as this assignment is, I just had to take it. I needed to get out of New York."

She sat on the bed, crossing her legs, but when he ogled their length, she quickly covered them with the silk bathrobe. He stood over her as she continued her explanation. "I was curious about Purvis, as only a good journalist would be, and I admit, even more so after your warning on deck this afternoon."

"Of course you were...with that strong-minded defiant streak you possess, I figured that's why ya gave my advice the brush off." He raised the scarred eyebrow.

"You seem to know me well in such a short time, sir. How is that?"

"Not much escapes my observation. Besides, you're a red-headed dame. Some things go without sayin'. So you're telling me there is no other reason you're headed to Portugal?"

Her stomach turned over at her lie, and she smoothed the hair at her brow. "That is what I'm saying."

Finally, Carl placed the vanity chair to face her, then handed her the ashtray. She promptly tapped the lengthening ashes of her smoke.

Surveying the room he sidetracked to more prosaic conversation, "Nice digs. A lot bigger and swankier than the set-up me and the boys have. They got us packed in like cattle down below. Why you could sleep the whole orchestra in here!"

"It's sufficient, I suppose. Too much damask for my liking and pink is my least favorite color. The bed is quite uncomfortable."

They sat smoking for long minutes until she blurted, "What are your intentions toward me, Mr. Wilson?"

"Intentions? Well, I had intended on you at least calling me Carl by the end of the night after I played Cole Porter for ya."

"That's not what I meant, and you know it." She took a deep drag of the Chesterfield, her eyes searching his for a glimmer of sincerity—honesty.

"The only intentions I have aboard the *Serpa* are to entertain the passengers and, now, make sure ya safely get off the ship so you can go about your bizness."

"No...no shipboard romance?"

He chuckled and shook his head. "Not unless you want one since, as you insisted this afternoon, we only just met. I'm not the wolf you take me for, Evelyn."

"Oh. I...um...I guess I misconstrued, which—please don't misunderstand me—is fine by me! I mean...I have no intentions of engaging in *that* with *any* man."

"I can respect how you believe that, but it'll change."

"Still so sure of yourself."

"It has nuthin' to do with me. I just think that time heals everything and you'll make up for the loss of it when you're ready. Trust me...I know about these things."

"Are you making up for lost time with Irena Olszak? You seem to have wolfish intentions toward *her* on this journey."

"She's nothing to concern yourself over, but if it makes you feel better, I'm partial to *American* socialites."

Evie chortled in an unladylike manner. Her fear of him and her embarrassment at the silly assumption about his intentions toward her had now completely evaporated. Darn Margie for putting such thoughts in her head! "That woman is no more European nobility than I am Mickey Mouse. I'll have you know, those aren't real diamonds in her tiara and her pearls are dipped! She is not who she says she is."

"Doll, in this war, none of us really are—are we? Heck, I used to be a music teacher and now I'm playing with Dutch for possible spies and collaborators. And, by day, you're a hoity-toity debutante masquerading at night as an intrepid newspaper reporter."

"True, but I'm *not* masquerading."

"I believe you...for now."

"I'll make sure I look you up and send you my article as proof."

"And I'll look forward to it."

"Since you know about Mrs. Olszak's deception, why are *you* 'involved' with one of Purvis's cohorts in crime? And what did you ask her to take care of?"

"Aw, you were spying *and* listening? I'm shocked, Evelyn." He looked away, took a drag then blew it out. "Like I said, I'm not here to answer questions about things, which are nunya bizness."

"It is my business...It was about my brother."

"No it isn't and no it wasn't."

"I know what I heard, Mr. Wilson."

He said nothing in reply, but his eyes locked with hers in pig-headed challenge told her she wasn't going to get anywhere with him. "Well then what do you consider appropriate questions?"

"Off the record or to be jotted down in that journal for the *Spectator*?"

"Neither, just simply to satisfy my *strong-minded* curiosity."

"Ask whatever you want—*if* I answer, I'll answer truthfully."

She smiled at his frankness and the way his lips puckered around his cigarette after he spoke. "Very well. First, where are you from?" she asked, stamping out the cigarette.

He paused, dragging on his smoke as he examined her curiously as though debating whether to answer this first question.

"I grew up in Aliquippa on the Ohio River. It's a mill town outside The Smokey City, Pixburgh."

"Ah, so that's where your accent hails from. It's not exactly proper English."

"And here I'd been thinkin' I hid my Pixburgese well."

She tilted her head and examined him with a soft smile. "It comes out...axs, Pixburgh, and my favorite nunya. What exactly is a nunya?"

"You're a real corker, aren't ya?"

"No. I'm a New *Yorker*—the Upper West Side. The Dakota Apartments, in fact." Not that someone from his side of the tracks would know The Dakota. There she went again: name dropping.

"So, what you're sayin' is only New Yorkers speak proper English? Cawfee and tawk and all that Brooklynese. Nuh-uh, those aren't in any *American Dictionary of the English Language* I ever read."

"I have *never* spoken in such an unrefined manner!"

"Naturally, not. A high-society dame such as yourself wouldn't dream of it. You, instead, lift your chin and drop your *R*'s. You people aren't Brits ya know."

"What*ever* are you talking about?"

He raised his chin and put on a show, clipping his *T*s and sounding very much like her brother-in-law. "The cultchaad Dakotaa Apaatments are puufectly daaling in the wintaa."

She should be affronted, but she wasn't and tried not to giggle. "Point noted. Next question. How long have you been playing the clarinet, *daaling*?"

"Oh, for about twenty-one years now."

"Really? How old *are* you?"

"A bit older than you. I'm twenty-nine."

"Just five years older than I am. You do play divinely."

"Thanks. I get by. And you sure know how to cut a rug."

"Thanks. I get by, too" she joked. "Do you play any other instruments?"

"I tickle the ivories some, but not enough to dazzle an audience."

"I'm a proficient pianist. Why, I can play Chopin's 'Opus Twenty-Eight' in precisely sixty seconds."

"Sure you can, but the *Minute* Waltz is commonly performed between one and half to two and half minutes." He quirked his eyebrow, again.

Admittedly, she was provoking him, not expecting him to know the classical piece so she ignored the arrogant tease in his voice. There was one question she was curious to know and gave into impulse as impolite as it was. She lifted her hand to his brow, startling him, but she smiled softly to reassure him that it was not going to be a slap. "How did you get this scar above your eye? It must have been a terrible accident."

He didn't answer, just looked away and took another puff on his cigarette followed by its crush in the ashtray.

"Was it in battle? You mentioned you once served in the armed forces. Where? In North Africa?" she persisted, hungry for more information about the puzzling man.

Carl abruptly stood, then slid the chair back to its rightful place, clearly unwilling to answer. His attention fell to her journal before he said, "Well, Red, I'm tuckered out after the night I had, and you need some shut-eye, too."

"Wait! I'm sorry...I shouldn't have been so rude...I'm sure it's personal and—"

"Look, we're heading into a storm, so Dutch's band may not be playin' for the rest of the trip," he interrupted, turning his back to her. He walked to the door and added, "I suggest ya take my advice this time and stay in your cabin far away from Purvis and his pals if you hope to make it back to The Big Apple. It might be a darned tempting scoop, but it could cost ya your life."

She believed him. She'd take his advice to heart—this time—but still couldn't help wondering how he knew what Purvis's intentions were.

"And do yourself a favor when you get to Lisbon. If ya meet any nosey Germans don't go tellin' 'em who your brother is. Not only is name-dropping a bad habit, but with an American senator as a brother, you'll be headed for trouble. Mark my words, them nasty fellows know every bigwig in Washington and would use you to make a statement, so keep the Rousseau name outta it."

"I understand," she acquiesced resisting the urge to prod him further on how he knew these things. It was clear she would get nothing further from him when he turned away from her.

"Mr. Wilson!...I mean, *Carl*. Won't I see you again?"

He appeared to struggle with his answer when he furrowed his brow, then stammered, "I...I don't think so. Just be careful, Evelyn. Lisbon isn't what you think it is, and—"

"Evie. Please call me Evie," she nervously blurted.

"All right...Evie. Anyway, good luck with your interview. It's been nice knowin' ya."

"But I thought you said meeting me was destiny?" His abrupt good-bye affected her more than she imagined and, instead of feeling pleased over the prospect of not seeing him again, she felt disappointment.

He smiled wistfully, his fingers grasping the door handle as he glanced up and back over his shoulder at her. "We'll just leave it betwixt the stars and the unaccomplished fate," he said, then left.

Her heart flipped at his poetic recitation from *Sonnets from the Portuguese*. He liked poetry. Was he a romantic, like her?

March 4, 1943

Fear. I'm trying not to respond to it in my inept and uninformed view of what is truly going on in this war—and aboard the Serpa Pinto, but I cannot deny the encounter I just had with Carl Wilson has left me shaken. Whatever his purpose, he has cautioned me twice now against pursuing a possible lead on John Da Silva Purvis's onboard activities, which confirms my instinct—there is a big story there.

Those at Purvis's table in the dining room were: Italian, Polish, German, and Czech (possibly Bohemian-Moravia.) Most from Best Society. Stephan and Irena Olszak the obvious exception. Immediately, I knew by the very manner in which she held her dinner fork, and I tried not to laugh when she mistakenly used the ice cream fork instead of the pastry fork. There is no mistaking those two! Well-bred, my eye! They are parvenus in society at the very least.

I would have liked to stay longer at the table, particularly when conversation turned to the development of something called "atomic," but Mr. Wilson's promise of Cole Porter left me speechless and unable to focus.

Trust. Can I trust Mr. Wilson? Is he a man of integrity? He is a stranger—perhaps an orchestra playboy—yet there is something about him, which feels genuine. He keeps abreast of world events, unlike many I know who do not even understand why we are at war, but there is something more there. Perhaps, playing for an international orchestra requires his astuteness, maybe he is well-read. For now, at his insistence I shall relegate Purvis to the back of my mind, as difficult as that may be because I feel in my bones there is a scoop here. But I will keep my distance, trusting that Mr. Wilson has observed—or heard—of misdeeds perpetrated by the Lisboeta. I will also ignore Mr. Wilson's shipboard romance with Olszak (none of my affair—but perhaps he was cautioning her as well.) No matter; I will take his word that he was <u>not</u> discussing Albert during their tête-à-tête on deck. I am sure my own guilt (as it pertains to Brother) clouds and misdirects my perception of events.

Reality. I must remain focused on the intent of this trip: Madam Elena Lupescu and the Drucker family. Unrelated to any of the above, my intrigue of and physical attraction to Mr. Wilson is not only shameful, but must be tempered at all costs. He represents everything that both Mother and Albert (and society) would disdain, everything I do not dislike but should, particularly as a married woman! Despite the seasickness that will no doubt afflict me, I am thankful for the rough seas and ill weather so that I will remain in my cabin until our arrival in Lisbon.

TEN

Oh Look at Me Now

March 6—morning

From the top deck, Carl gazed down at the passengers as they walked down the *Serpa Pinto*'s gangplank and overcame their sea legs. He tipped his fedora back in appreciation of only one person's graceful disembarkation, recalling how his arms had circled her waist only eight days before. He knew he should be paying closer attention to the barricaded crowd of refugees on the pier, but he only watched one brilliant beacon: Mrs. Evelyn Somerset.

Like a beacon against the watercolor sunrise sky of shades of pink, she wore a light blue dress and a complementing tilted hat. Her strawberry-kissed locks cascaded down her nape. A gentle Portuguese breeze billowed the skirt lightly and his breath caught at the sight. *Style and grace*, he reflected; Evie was all class, right down to the seams rising up the back of her shapely gams. He sighed. It was just as well she was having a hard time letting go of her late-husband, and for that he felt truly sorry for her loss. Death in battle was a tough pill to swallow; closure was harder to accept. He was wrong to have pointed out to her that she was no longer a married woman.

Be that as it may, it was in *both* their best interest to avoid forming a deeper attachment. In his line of work, romantic entanglements were *verboten*, even if she *had* been ready for it. Aw, who was he kidding…he was a goner and had come close to kissing her in her stateroom. The innate gentleman in him kept him from seeking her lips against his—not to mention the expectation of her slap across his face. Yeah, he'd have done the unthinkable: allowed himself to be manipulated by her unintentional charm. Her smile and her laugh were enough to pull him in, but the pretentious, decisive veneer she put on was the ultimate honey trap. Deep down, though, he knew Evie was a vulnerable woman and, because of that, he wanted to watch over her.

Just because he put an end to anything before it had begun didn't mean he couldn't keep a protective eye on her until her return to New York. Lisbon was a small city and Estoril even smaller. He smiled at the thought of seeing her again, having lied to her two days earlier when he had said good-bye to her in her stateroom. It really wasn't a *true* good-bye, just a bunch of malarkey to end her questions about his past—and present. In fact, he hadn't planned on going to her cabin that night, but seeing her in Purvis's arms had caused concern, made him consider he had uncharacteristically misjudged someone, suspecting her to be a bad hat after all. Leaving with her journal tucked under his tuxedo jacket had been his plan from the onset, but thankfully, she came clean to her own "operation."

Naturally, his protectiveness for her kicked in and he needed to scare the dickens out of her so she'd stay in her stateroom for the rest of the passage. Purvis and another in his circle, someone with suspected connections to the fascist Mussolini, were dangerous men, but he couldn't tell Evie everything. He shook his head in amazement. *A reporter…go figure. I didn't see that one coming, and it's a danger alone.*

Unbeknownst to Evie, her ritzy hotel selection was the belly of the beast in the coastal town of Cascais where every slick spy and businessman made their shady deals. It was a well-known fact among those in-the-know that German riff-raff ventured to the rooftop of the Palácio for a smoke as they awaited signal lights out in the Atlantic. Many in the Gestapo had suites beside members of

Soviet and/or British Intelligence, not to mention the plethora of smugglers and diamond dealers who took advantage of Portugal's uninvited Jewish guests.

Evie would end up at the Hotel Metrópole for dinner and dancing to the Dutch Ellerton Orchestra. At least he could watch her—along with everyone else—from his band position.

Lisbon would change the young socialite's life, but he'd be right there should that strawberry red hair, fire in her eyes, and blind willfulness lead her down a dark alley. Lucky for her, she had unintentionally wormed her way into his heart with the first blush to her cheeks on the gangway.

Kay came up beside him, jolting him from his thoughts and he smiled, not from his heart, but because it was the polite thing to do, even toward a wacky hanger-on.

"Are you ready, darling?" she cooed. "There's supposed to be a car waiting to take us to the hotel. Can I hitch a ride with you?"

"Sorry, Kay. I'll have to meet up with the band later. There's a few things in town I need to take care of first."

"Oh? What could you possibly need to do? You don't know anyone in Lisbon—do you?"

He tapped her nose, giving her just what she wanted: attention. "Don't you worry your pretty little head. I'll be back in time for practice."

"Well, alright then. Will you at least be a gem and escort me down the gangplank? It looks so unsafe and I need a strong man to assist me."

"Sure."

She tucked her arm into the crook of his and he lifted his clarinet case; his observation never left Evie's person until she safely drove away in a local taxicab.

———— ✥ ————

After ditching Kay and the boys in the band, Carl walked to the edge of the port and scanned the cars lined up along the street until he found the black sedan left for him. The German-made 1939

BMW convertible was a car he particularly enjoyed two months ago on his first trip to Lisbon.

Thankfully, the *Serpa* had arrived earlier than expected because it was going to be a long day of driving and rushing to get back to practice at four this afternoon. Not that they needed the practice, but with the set list changing to accommodate the Germans at the hotel, they needed to fine tune their performance. It wasn't just his mouth the song selections left a bad taste in. Some of the older fellas, particularly the Canadians in the orchestra, had put up quite a fuss demanding to play only American dance music, but it was Dutch's band and catering to his audience's preferences was his decision.

He glanced around the shipyard, then bent pretending to check the tire. The single key to the car and an envelope of escudo notes were hidden just where he expected them: inside the wheel well. Once he secured his travel bag and instrument case in the cargo, he was ready for the three-hour trip north. Again, he carefully perused his surroundings before settling in the driver's seat. From the corner of his eye, he located the Olszaks, one on each side of Purvis, walking toward a waiting sedan used for diplomatic visitors.

He turned the engine key and the BMW purred to life; the scent of stagnant petrol filled his lungs. No doubt, the vehicle had been sitting for some time waiting for his return.

Before the mass arrival of exiles, the once tranquil city looked like what he assumed was its sleepy old self as he drove down bumpy cobblestone streets away from the docks. Apart from the occasional vagrant and the empty trolley cars, the pot-holed byways were desolate.

He was back in the thick of it, back where all the mystery and espionage took place—hidden, yet out in the open. He felt a heady rush, loving the thrill, which came when his cunning mind could be put to good use, which was more than the role of clarinetist. From his orchestra station as his fingers automatically worked, he'd piece together who was up to what at any given moment as they collaborated under the guise of social entertainment.

Apart from speaking three languages, Carl was skilled at unpacking lies. The only one to have flummoxed him was Red. She'd sent him in a tailspin, and if he knew one thing about her, for a fantastic scoop, she would be like a tenacious Spitfire engaging in a dogfight pursuing Purvis for an all-out assault until one or the other crashed. He'd have to consider the benefit *and* detriment of Evie's allure and put his personal feelings aside when next they met. Hopefully, he scared her away and Irena kept the Lisboeta busy enough to keep arm's length from the socialite.

The fresh sea air hit his face through the open window. He breathed deeply enjoying the scenic two-lane road heading toward central Portugal traveling along the Tagus River, through the heart of the country. As he drove northeast, the geography changed from featureless, dry pastures dotted with cork oak trees in the lower basin to increasing elevations of craggy, limestone mountains and narrow valleys. At times, the river became a deep ravine and the roadway a series of sharp twists and dangerous curves. He gassed the car, getting a kick at cheating death with each turn.

In the silence of the countryside Carl's mind traveled, as it often did whenever he was alone for long periods of time. As usual, he reflected on what life would have been had he stayed in Pittsburgh with Doris—the girl he had left back home in '39, along with the belching smoke stacks and filthy stairway streets. He could still hear her words as clear as a bell, "If you go, I won't wait. This is not what we had planned."

She was right. It wasn't what "we" had planned. He left, and she didn't wait. Teaching music had never been his plan—it was hers. Along with the girlhood dream of happily ever after in domestic mediocrity and a gray picket fence surrounding a soot covered house. He just happened to be the boy next door and the only schmoe who aspired to do something other than steelwork like his brother, father, and grandfather. There had never been any sort of great love between him and Doris, anyway; it was something they had just fallen into.

Recalling every detail of the fateful afternoon when he had passed the U.S. Army Air Corps recruiting office, he relaxed his grip on the wheel. On that day, his life had changed, and he smiled, innately feeling his life had changed, yet again, when Evie Somerset fell onto him.

"I'm going to England," he'd written Doris in the summer of 1940 and by the time she'd written back, he was gone, having volunteered for the Number Seventy-One Eagle Squadron of the Royal Air Force. America hadn't been at war yet, and the Battle of Britain was in full force. The Limeys needed fresh meat in the pilot seat to fly those Hurricanes in defensive patrols. Doris's letter didn't say much other than the announcement of her engagement to a former schoolmate who'd promised to purchase her a cottage in Terrace Village overlooking town. Now Pittsburgh must be humming as the epicenter of war production and the sky likely even more polluted and yellow than before. He dodged a metaphoric bullet on that one, and as dangerous as his career choices had been since he joined up, he thrived on the excitement. At first it was just the thrill of being out of western Pennsylvania, but now the intrigue and a chance to lick those Nazis kept him in. Besides, what else did he have? He'd never settle down, marry, and raise a big family. The Game was his future.

The car climbed the mountain range until arriving at a secret destination: an abandoned eighteenth-century farmhouse in the middle of nowhere outside of Castelo Branco. He turned the BMW onto a hacked-out pathway between bramble and slowly drove through the overgrown bushes, making his way to the back of the two-story stone building. As expected, his was the only car visible on the homestead and he made sure that he rolled it quietly into the wood barn some one hundred feet beyond the tree line. He glanced down at his wristwatch, hoping he didn't have to wait long before getting down to the business at hand.

Nothing had changed since the last time he was here; it was a perfect location for a dead drop with his handler, Preston Musgrove, code name Berkshire, from Britain's intelligence gathering organization: the Secret Intelligence Service or MI6, as they referred to it. In fact, in another circumstance, he'd like to spend time here. Once restored, the house and the land could be a swell place to hang his hat one day.

He exited the vehicle, removed his suit jacket, then laid it on the back seat, then rolled up his shirt sleeves. Where he was headed was dirty business— as filthy as a mill town. Once outside, he took several deep-cleansing breaths before closing the barn doors. It was indeed a beautiful day; the azure sky was clear and the crisp temperature in the mountains felt refreshing after the long ride. Memories of life before the SIS had been quickly banished when recalling Evie's tear-stained cheeks.

If only a woman would cry over him like she had over her dead husband the night he visited her cabin—if in fact, it was the cause of her waterworks.

The stream running behind the barn led him through the forest until he came upon a wildflower-scattered clearing surrounded by the mountainscape. Birdsong filled the air mixing with each crunching footstep through the overgrown grass and weeds toward his destination.

Up ahead, he could make out the specific hill he sought on the opposite side of the meadow, and if not for the mossy boulder as a distinguishing landmark, he might otherwise miss it.

Abruptly he stopped, closed his eyes and took another deep breath, pushing all thoughts of the beauty Mrs. Somerset aside before continuing on his mission.

He reached the stone and hill and pushed the vines aside, revealing the slat wooden door tucked into the stone face. Immediately upon opening it, he felt the cold, drafty breeze whistling through the long cavernous tungsten (wolfram) mine set out before him. At his feet lay abandoned wooden tracks and various-sized picks and hammers. A discarded miner's hat lay partially buried under core samples scattered in the dirt. Was there anything left in this mine?—probably not, since the place had been left to rot.

The eerie blackness before him didn't frighten him. There were only a handful of things that did. Not even the threat of being ambushed by the enemy or the prospect of a German Lugar pressed against his temple, which might very well happen in his line of work, made him chicken. A man's time had to run out sooner or later. He wasn't afraid of death, just the demons that followed him after having faced the grim reaper once before.

He removed his lighter and flipped the cover; the pop and whoosh of the fuel illuminated his immediate surroundings and he pulled the door closed behind him. Some sixty feet in, another's pop echoed back, and he followed the tiny light and the tracks at his feet, careful to keep his footing on all the mining debris.

"Phoenix, Jolly good to see you," Musgrove said, his finger running over one side of his blond mustache. It was an annoying habit, but Carl ignored it.

His handler lit the old carbide miner's lantern on the rock ledge beside him.

"And a hi-di-ho to you, Berkshire. How long have you been sitting here in the dark, sir?"

"I only just arrived. How was your trip across the pond? Did the Jerries give the *Serpa* any trouble?"

"Rough seas. I'm better in the air than on the water, but at least the Germans were less damaging."

"And how is that good fellow Dutch?"

"Just as London described. He didn't ask any questions and has been mighty accommodating. There were a few new fellas in the band, so no one was the wiser. It's the perfect cover."

The big cheese stood to his full short stature of five-foot-seven. As Carl suspected, the Brit had hiked the mountain. The avid outdoorsman wore rolled pants and a plaid shirt; his walking stick and fur-covered rucksack lay on the floor.

"Capital news!"

"It was good to go back to the States for a short spell. I missed American food."

"Indeed. I know how you feel. Dreams of dear Old Blighty and bangers and mash keep me focused. I suppose we will just have to hope this bloody war ends soon, but then we will both be out of work—aye?"

"I might not be able to fly again, but at least I have my clarinet to fall back on. Maybe I'll stay on with Dutch's band and see Europe when it's all over."

"At least we are better off than those unfortunate blokes with the SOE. They won't live long enough to dance in Piccadilly after the Jerries get their comeuppance."

Carl nodded. Sure, he was steeped in danger, but the men and women within the Security Operations Executive were the covert boots-on-the-ground, parachuting in behind enemy lines, bombing railways and vital German supply lines, and organizing networks of resistance. Among other things, he was just military intelligence gathering.

"Let's get down to business. Have we got our man, yet? What is the status of Operation Night Shift?" Musgrove asked.

"Purvis, our two-bit dock worker, is right where we want him, going so far as acting courier for his own gathered intelligence and pretending to be a wealthy playboy onboard. Irena and Stephan infiltrated his core of well-heeled sympathizers, and he's surprisingly recruited some new ones, mostly scattering cock-roaches kicked out of the States, but a few worth the SIS's surveillance."

Carl handed him the list of names. "We found his cut-out aboard ship. One of the crew members is also working for the Germans. I've underlined his name."

"Capital. I'll pass these along to the Iberian Station Chief so he can direct the Ship Observer for the *Serpa*. As suspected, no one is neutral especially in neutral countries. Have the Americans been notified of Purvis's espionage?"

"Nuh-uh. BSC assured me that although there's a boat load of evidence involving his shipyard shenanigans in New York and Philadelphia, the hand-off of his intelligence to Germany's naval *Abwher* or to a courier from their espionage service in Lisbon will be the clincher. Until there is indisputable proof of spying for the Germans to sabotage those Liberty ship convoys headed to England, Stephenson in New York wants to wait before tipping off Hoover in the FBI."

"Quite. Has Irena made the switch?"

"Yuh-huh. While Purvis was otherwise occupied with her in her stateroom, Stephan switched the microfilm, which he found inside a shoe heel. After Irena gets photographic evidence of Purvis's hand-off with the Germans, we and the boys in New York will have a nice case of espionage to package up for the Feds and they'll have a set of handcuffs waiting for him when he docks back in the States."

"A shoe heel? Quite the amateur, isn't he?"

"He sure is out of his league."

"You have all done very well!" Musgrove ran his pinky over his mustache again. "And the FBI will be in our debt—once again. Ah, where would American Intelligence be without us tipping them off through the BSC in New York? The Yanks—"

"Hey, watchaht, bub."

"So sorry. I forget sometimes how lucky we are you work for us and not our American friends in the OSS."

"Or the SOE."

"Right you are! Jolly fortunate."

"Yeah. They couldn't sucker me when they offered the opportunity to make bombs. Not sure I could play the horn with only a few fingers."

Musgrove laughed; its bellow echoed back down the shaft.

"When is Purvis's return trip to America?" Carl asked. He lit a cigarette then blew out the smoke in a smooth stream.

"He leaves in five days aboard the S.S *Mouzinho*, but you'll be staying on in Lisbon with Dutch. We have a new assignment for you since you are playing in German territory at the Metrópole." Musgrove looked around the mining shaft. "Bloody appropriate we chose this location for our dead drop. Going forward, we are teaming up with Beevor's local SOE crew on Germany's smuggling of wolfram ore out of Portugal."

"Teaming up? I'm not happy about that plan. Too many agents spoil the soup."

"I agree, particularly that bloody grandstanding lot, but the SOE's hands are tied in Spain and the directive came from the top: no covert activities in appeasement of Franco. The SOE needs us and we need them."

Musgrove dug into his rucksack, removing a leather document portfolio. "Here's everything you'll need. Once we gather the Intel, the SOE will execute their plan."

Carl opened it, glanced inside, then jokingly turned it upside down. Only two photographs of a German official floated out and down to the debris at his feet.

"All you need to know is written in invisible ink on the inside, under the flaps. We thought the case would be a nifty item for you to keep your sheet music."

"Is this our subject?"

"Yes. Take a good look. He is General Otto Wegener, of the *Wehrmacht's Sicherung*. He flew into Lisbon this morning."

He examined the military photographs—one a portrait, the other a full length—and immediately committed them to memory, which was a good thing because several seconds later, Musgrove's lighter flipped when he held it to the corners. Wegener disappeared into flame.

"There's something ya need to know. There's an American socialite—someone Purvis took a shine to aboard the *Serpa*."

"Take care of her."

"It's a bit more complicated, sir. Her brother is a U.S. senator and she's a curious newspaper reporter. Irena convinced Purvis that the girl isn't worth his attention, but I'm afraid she'll get into a mess if he decides to pursue her. He's bound to discover who she is."

"But *is* she who she says she is?"

"I believe so. My gut says so, but the dame is mysterious and possibly hiding something."

Musgrove groaned. "Then shadow her and do what you must to keep her away from Purvis until we wrap up Operation Night Shift. We can't have any reporters noseying around looking for a story—and the last thing the Crown needs is a cock-up involving an American politician's sister."

"I don't know…any 'hand's on' treatment of the situation could blow my cover at the Metrópole. A clarinetist romancing a high-brow dame isn't a likely combination."

"I don't care how you do it, but do what you have to. Things are politically fragile now. All this negotiating over tungsten and Churchill's proposed economic blockade against Portugal is bound to get England expelled from the country."

"While putting the Germans on Salazar's good side…"

"Right you are. You can't blame Salazar. There is a tidy profit to be made." Musgrove tented his fingers. "Business begets war and war begets business. It doesn't matter the generation. It's all the same bloody buggers running circles around all of us poor blokes who take the bullet."

"All for the almighty dollar, pound, franc, and mark." War was a profitable investment. It had pulled America, particularly The Smokey City, out of its economic woes.

"Stay with the girl, but if you botch your cover, we will disavow."

Carl sighed and looked down the mineshaft. "You put me in a tough position. Well…I had already planned on keeping an eye on the woman just to be sure she is who she says she is."

"Like I said, do *more* than keep an eye on her, Wilson—at least until Purvis is headed back to the States."

"You mean…"

"Old man, you know what I mean. I hope for your sake, she's a real beauty. There's less chance of your being compromised in the field if you compromise her in bed. Now *that's* hands on."

He was unsure how he felt about that. Sure, he was a man and she a gorgeous dame, but he'd not resort to such actions. Other swallows like Irena, a true femme fatale operating without a conscience, may have done so. But he avoided that untoward behavior unless absolutely warranted. Not with Evie.

"In the meantime, what's her name? I'll contact the Section Chief's office and have them vet her, just to be sure."

"Mrs. Evelyn Rousseau Somerset."

"Is there anything else you can tell me?"

"She lives in some place called The Dakota in New York City, and works for the *New York Daily Spectator*. Her husband…went down on the U.S.S. *Jarvis* in the Pacific."

"Bad luck."

———◈———

ELEVEN
A Room with a View

March 6—morning

*E*vie's first impression of the Hotel Palácio was that it wasn't worth the famed reputation. Only the colorful native flowers in the garden and the swaying palm trees surrounding the drive provided the white façade with any character. Once inside though, she admitted it was truly a grand hotel. Of course, she did not admire its splendor too openly. She had frequented hundreds of opulent residences and hotels for society balls and teas, and the Palácio décor and architecture ranked among the finest. But for the assignment she was on—and the purported danger lurking within the town—she would need to truly portray ambivalence to the lodging's uniqueness and hide her appreciation of the classic style. An aristocrat or royalty would expect nothing less and everything would be considered beneath or entitled to them. She imagined Queen Louise and Mrs. Honeywell aboard the *Serpa* would feel that way, too.

After filling out the hotel's detailed registration document, she slid it and her passport across the marble reception desk to the head concierge, then signed the recording book, adding her name below all the foreign ones listed above. *The Honourable Mrs. Evelyn J. Somerset.* From this point forward, she would be borrowing her father-in-law's forsaken peerage. Barons were a dime a dozen and should her title be questioned, no one would be the wiser that he was no longer one.

"I hope you enjoy your stay on the Riviera, Senhora Somerset," the clerk said with a pleasant smile, speaking English. "The porter will bring your luggage up to your suite. Please notify me if you require anything at all to make your visit more comfortable. My name is Arnaldo."

His attention fixed on the diamond-encrusted watch pinned at her shoulder. "We have a safe for your valuables, should you desire," then handed the room key to the young bellman standing to her right. "You are in one of our finest suites, number four ten."

"Very good. I was wondering, Arnaldo...can you tell me, if Madam Lupescu is still in residence at the hotel?"

"Sim. She and her traveling companion are expected to depart in four days' time. Do you know the party?"

"Not officially, but I do hope to make her acquaintance during my stay."

She covertly passed a few escudo notes across the reception counter. "Do you know where I might find her?"

Apparently, he was familiar with this type of inducement for acquiring secret information. As Carl informed her several times, Lisbon was rife with spies and everyone in Portugal hoped to profit from the war. Evie smiled inside, absolutely pleased with herself when the clerk's hand closed over the currency followed by his acquiescing grin. "She frequents the Casino Estoril." He leaned toward her, whispering, "And cocktails and poker in the English Bar in the guesthouse beside the casino."

He tucked the money into his suit breast pocket and grinned. Yes, she was sure the concierge would be a willing ally in securing an interview with the controversial woman who influenced a king.

"The color...her hair is like yours. Flame," he said, tapping the hair at his forehead.

Of course, she already knew that detail. The woman's hair color has been a topic of journalistic slander since the thirties. "Well, then Madam Lupescu is a woman not to be trifled with. Thank you for the warning. To your knowledge, might I find her at the English Bar tonight?"

"Not tonight. But tomorrow, yes." He whispered, "It is known for the gin. Tonight, she will be at Casino Estoril."

"If you'd be so kind, can you make arrangements for me at the English Bar? And please send a lady's maid to my room to attend my luggage and personal needs."

"Of course, Senhora. And would you care for something to refresh you this morning? Room service, perhaps?"

"That would be lovely. Thank you. American coffee, fresh fruit, toast, and a four-minute boiled egg—no more, no less. Oh, and two local newspapers. One in English, the other Portuguese. Do you have the *Diário da Manhã*?"

If she was going to be here for two weeks, she had better continue the language lessons she began in the library aboard ship. Comparing the content in the newspapers to learn the words and familiarizing herself with the local happenings had proven indispensable.

"Yes, madam, right away. Would you also care to read the *Konigsberger Allgemein Zeitung*?"

"A German newspaper? Here? In Lisbon?"

"There is also an information shop in the Chiado district."

"Fascinating. And yet, the British co-exist in the capital city?"

"And the Americans, the French—all without incident. It is demanded by our leader Salazar. He is committed to neutralia, and our visitors require confidentiality of their political allegiance. It is quite entertaining to most Lisboetas, as we can always tell their nationality by their manner of dress."

"Oh?"

"The Germans are sloppy and the French are lazy dressers."

She laughed for the first time today. "I'll have to remember. And what is your opinion of American apparel?"

"Fashionable." He smiled politely.

"That's astutely diplomatic. Please include the *Zeitung*. I'm sure I'll find it quite interesting. Just out of curiosity, of course, do you have Russian newspapers as well?"

He stiffened. "No. No *Comunista* papers allowed."

After the bellman escorted her to the suite, he opened the French doors to the balcony with a wide smile. She tipped him, then turned to examine where she'd be living for the next two weeks, walking from room to room, admiring the furnishings, and surprisingly impressed by each tiny detail. The bedroom, where she would spend little time, was decorated in pale, soothing colors—and not an iota of pink in sight! The morning sun shining through the picture window brought the boudoir to life, infusing her with a sense of tranquility. The parlor looked perfectly suited for tea and she considered it could be a lavish enough room in which to privately talk with Madam Lupescu. The welcoming doors leading out to the balcony revealed a stunning view of the sea beyond towering palm trees. She stepped out onto the spacious terrace and immediately filled her lungs with a refreshing breath of the salty air. Closing her eyes, she breathed again, relishing the reset to her equilibrium from the last two days of terrible seas. Unfortunately, she would have to do it all over again on her return sailing.

When her thoughts traveled to Carl, she opened her eyes, disturbed that her first reflection wasn't how much *Richard* would enjoy the view. She furrowed her brow, troubled that she just may have fallen for the stranger—ever so slightly. Where was he now? Where was the orchestra playing? "Stop it, Evelyn. You are Mrs. Richard Somerset." She bit her lip before voicing her greatest concern, "…but are you still? Is it as Carl said?" Further…when would she fully allow herself to cease being a married woman?

"Never!" She said with a huff and turn from the exotic view before her. "He is an insignificant musician, beneath your notice…and you are still in mourning!"

A knock to the door caused her heart to jolt, and her first thought was that it might be the subject of her musing. Had he come to her room just as he had her cabin, with a smile and joke? Oh, their near-moment of kissing when he took the cigarette case from her hands!—Was she so terrible a person to have wished it so?

She smoothed her coiffure before opening the door, only to see the white-jacketed waiter and a service cart; her heart dropped. The man pushed her breakfast through the parlor, stopping the cart before the open doors to the balcony. As instructed, three newspapers lay fanned beside a single red rose, a bone china coffee pot and cup, and a covered dish. With a flourish of his arm, the waiter lifted the stainless cover revealing an assortment of beautiful fruit and a brown egg perched in a cup. Although having never tried them, she shuddered inside at the obligatory dish of sardines.

"Four minutes?" she confirmed as he placed the desk chair at her place setting.

"Sim, Senhora."

"Do you speak English?"

He nodded, his eyes lighting as she reached for her purse on the coffee table.

"How may I be of further assistance?"

"*Onde Fica*...the Jewish quarter—the location of the poorer transient visitors to the Estado Novo?"

"Senhora? You wish to go there?"

She raised an eyebrow and pursed her lips. "Is there a problem?"

"No, Senhora. It is unexpected. Lisboetas have welcomed these unfortunate strangers, but there are those staying at the hotel and some in government who do not."

"Of course. That is why I am asking *you*."

"Some are near Rossio Square—the center of Lisboa, others stay nearest the docks, but it is most dangerous there. Most are in camp in Ericeira, the other tourist destination, or Caldas da Rainha in the north."

"Hmm. If…if I were looking for someone where would be the first—best—place to start my search?"

"Ah…I understand. Then begin in Rossio at the Café Chave d'Ouro or the synagogue."

"A synagogue…I hadn't thought of that." She handed him a large tip and smiled softly, thanking him. *"Muito Obrigado."* Was she allowed to step foot in a synagogue, let alone talk to a rabbi?

"But it will not be easy. There are hundreds and many hide from the *polícia de vigilância.*"

"I see. Well, all I can do is try."

"I would suggest…if you please…beware secret polícia. They are responsible for ensuring order and guidance of foreign visitors, but some of them work for Germans. The *Polícia de Vigilância e de Defesa do Estado* (PVDE) could be dangerous."

"Thank you. You've been quite helpful."

The young man departed, and Evie sat at the dining cart, her thoughts absorbed with the enormity of the task Mr. Drucker had commissioned. She hadn't truly considered how difficult it might be to find them, let alone arrange for their papers and passage. Pouring herself a cup of coffee, she spoke aloud. "Hide from the secret police? It is just as the letter indicated. Where on earth shall I begin?"

But first things first: she needed to get that scoop on Lupescu and wire it to the *Spectator* before the Associated Press's Lisbon Bureau beat her to it. That was, after all, the reason she was here. This article could be the defining moment of her career and future. She tapped the egg with her spoon then sliced the top off. Quite pleased and famished, she admired with satisfaction the perfectly cooked egg, its yolk steaming and runny for bread dipping. So far, she had a good feeling about Lisbon. She just needed to confidently put her shoulders back and let go to the possibilities.

"Yes, Evie…you, my dear, are on your way. I can feel it in my bones. Take that, Albert!"

March 6—night

Casino Estoril was where everyone who was anyone, so she was told, played on any given night until early morning. Evie had heard about high society gambling halls from Albert's tales following his travels to Europe with a few of his Yale Skull and Bones mates, but she never expected to visit one. Organized card games like Bridge with the Cushing sisters were the extent of her gambling. A Somerset, Richard had once declared, would never stake his fortune at a roulette table or baccarat. But she wasn't here to gamble—not in the traditional sense. Such was Richard, always under honorable regulation to redeem the family name after his grandfather's scandalous affair and Father's appalling abdication. The latter had affected Richard more than she expected. He had grown to be a different man than the one she betrothed back in the summer of '36. Society and his place in it as an esteemed naval officer had become quite important and necessary for his career aspirations, which, if she were to acknowledge the truth of it all were *political* aspirations, no matter her objection. "Admiral Richard Somerset" he once joked, but she knew he was thinking even bigger. Secretary of the Navy? Perhaps. It was no wonder Albert adored him so, and no wonder he led such an honorable life.

There was a thrill of the unknown traveling her nerves as she entered the gaming room. She tried to maintain a state of poise and ambivalence to it all even though inside she was wide-eyed and fascinated by the activity and players around her. The click-click-click of multiple roulettes breached the din above international elite and royalty dressed in black tuxedos and evening gowns. Tonight, she wore the shimmering gold Grecian gown first worn the night Carl played "Moonglow." Perhaps her choice of evening wear was more telling than she wanted to consider. He'd plagued her thoughts since debarkation.

Dimly lit, the wood-paneled gaming room embodied mystery and sensuality, and she took in every detail—and person—

recognizing several from the society pages and the general international news coming off the AP wire. In search of Lupescu, she navigated through the smoke-filled room, stopping at each of the crowded card tables, all silent with onlookers as the players considered their hand.

Her purpose tonight was not to interview or even approach the scandalous woman, but rather to size her up, ascertain her personality, her weakness, perhaps discover an "in" to gaining her confidence. Society was no different in that regard: one must understand one's prey before the kill.

With champagne glass in hand, she stopped at one of the many roulette tables, fascinated by the game and wheel of fortune. As was Amelia Snow's custom at social gatherings, she pretended to drink while scrutinizing those in her company over the rim of her flute. From her position at the edge of the table she delighted in the many accents. Here, in this gaming hall, nations—friends and enemies—were united in affluence and vice.

"I find the roulette wheel particularly stimulating," an Iberian man whispered into her ear from behind.

She turned with a smile. "Quite."

He exuded natural charm and not too dissimilar to Purvis, he had amenable looks and spoke English with educated proficiency.

"Is this your first visit to Estoril Casino?" he asked. "I have not seen you here before."

"Oh, yes. I just arrived into Cascais this morning aboard the *Serpa Pinto*."

"Then you are American?"

"Yes. I'm from New York. The weather was so cold and dreary, I simply had to decamp."

"Then welcome to the Estado Novo. Rodrigo Esteves at your service, madam."

"Thank you very much. Mrs. Richard Somerset," she offered, extending a gloved hand, just as her mother always did. Of course, he complied with proper veneration, bending with a kiss.

He glanced around her, perhaps looking for her husband. "And you are here by yourself?"

"I am. Why, Cascais and the Palácio could not be safer for a widow enjoying a grand adventure of sun and game. Would you not agree?"

"But of course. There is no war here, only the hospitality of our people and great leader. But it is always wise, as a beautiful woman, to be wary of those who might seek your company for political or financial gain. You would do well to take care of your jewels."

Cheers went up around them when the wheel stopped and the little ball settled. "How exciting. It's quite a beguiling game."

"Allow me," he said, holding up a chip. "What is your favorite number?"

"Five." Her wedding anniversary date.

Esteves placed the chip on a black square alongside others playing the next round. The croupier turned the wheel and all those sophisticated airs dissipated in chants for their number.

She held her breath when the ball slowed, seeking its destination, and felt quite dashed when it dropped into number twenty-six.

"Oh, I am sorry," he said. "Perhaps the number is not your fate. Would you like to try another, Mrs. Somerset?"

"There is no other, but thank you. I don't believe in fate, Senhor," she laughed.

"It is the way of us Portuguese."

Behind them, a commotion broke out, and the guests around them silenced. "Ah, the Polícia de Vigilância," Esteves stated matter of factly.

"What is happening?"

"It is nothing to be concerned over. The casino is a magnet for criminal impostors and illicit interaction," he whispered to her. "Our police are quite heedful."

The crowded room parted like the fabled Red Sea as all watched in horror as a dozen or more armed, uniformed men stormed the casino shouting commands in Portuguese, which she did not understand.

Suddenly, a man from the baccarat crowd toppled his chair and pushed aside a number of gamblers in his attempted escape.

In unison, the crowd gasped; several pointed to him.

"I have seen this man before. He claims to be a Russian diplomat, but he is of suspect activity," Esteves noted.

"Is he a spy?"

"I do not know. The Portuguese government will soon decree spying a criminal offense for both the Allies and Axis, but the Bolsheviks are not welcome in the Estado Novo."

"I have heard this."

A nightstick made contact to the man's legs before several police trounced the criminal to the floor, apprehending him at the back of the casino. Kicks to his abdomen took all fight from him.

Evie heard from the other end of the table behind her, a German woman proclaimed, "He is a Jew!" the sneer evident in her *Hochdeutsch*.

Leaning into Esteves, she whispered. "Do tell. *Is* he Jewish?"

"Possibly."

He did not elaborate, nor did she ask, but the whole scene was unnerving—nay horrifying—as she watched the PVDE drag the man through the casino. *Could the man be Jewish? Is this what happens to them?* Shocked, she covered her mouth.

A police officer turned to the crowd, again commanding something in Portuguese, and just like that, the whole disgusting affair—and the poor man—were forgotten when the room filled with the sound of chatter and roulette wheels.

Following the exit of the secret police and the return to gambling, she spotted the subject of her article: Madam Lupescu and the former king standing at the end of a craps table. The Romanian woman was just as the decades-old articles she'd read described. Slender framed, short red hair, and a plain face—not comely at all, but the monarch obviously thought so by the way he admired her. Madam Lupescu had an infectious smile, even if her crooked teeth and overbite made her look like a chipmunk. Apart from his bushy mustache, the former king looked as stately and refined as she imagined. Not handsome in her opinion, but she understood the appeal for someone like Lupescu.

The couple seemed completely unaffected by what had just happened.

Evie turned to her new acquaintance, anxious to change topic from what she'd just witnessed. "Tell me, is that the exiled Romanian?"

"Yes. He has recently arrived for a holiday, such as yourself."

"In America, we have heard interesting tales of the couple."

"Then you have heard of their troubles in Spain, I presume?" he imparted with a gleam in his eye similar to Margie's when she was about to tittle-tattle.

"No!"

"Oh, yes. Last year, under my consultation and advice, our benevolent Prime Minister offered the royal couple refuge after a near assassination in Madrid. In their haste they left their luggage filled with enough money to buy two luxury villas in Estoril!"

"How awful!"

"*Sim*. Our friend, Franco is not as accommodating to those who do not sympathize with Germany."

"I see."

"Were the couple not at one point friendly with the Nazis?"

"Oh yes, but times and alliances change like the wind. Would you like for me to introduce you? They are most grateful to me for my influence to Salazar."

"No, I wouldn't want to impose on their party."

"Then, come meet my dearest friend, a most sociable man who enjoys meeting people. I am sure you will enjoy each other's company famously."

They departed the table and walked side-by-side through the crowd. "Are all Portuguese men as amiable as those I've had the fortunate acquaintance to make?"

"Ah! You are too kind. Although my friend is an expert on Portuguese culture, Baron Oswald von Hoyingen-Huene is the German Ambassador to Portugal. He is a man of superior intellect and worth meeting, and I am his humble servant."

<hr />

March 6, 1943

My investigative visit to the casino proved to be quite illuminating as I mixed and mingled among Lisbon's movers and shakers ranging from the influential banker Rodrigo Esteves to the extremely handsome German Ambassador. Quite the diplomat, he showed no prejudice to my being an American, but I was cautious given Albert's position. Instead, I allowed the gentlemen to regale me with stories of their deep friendship and they both made me feel quite comfortable in my widowhood. Not once—to my very shame— did I consider Richard or how alone I felt being back in society without him. Make no mistake, this was Lisbon's crème de la crème in all its glitter and wealth.

The king and his mistress were present, enjoying their drink and gaming. I also enjoyed the company of a French artist and a Canadian exporter. Several British gentlemen seemed to never leave my side, one of whom knew the Somerset family—but he never hinted at the disgrace. The entire evening was quite exhilarating, and I oddly—among the quite continental aristocracy—felt free of anxiety!

Yet...all was not a pleasurable experience. A man was brutally beaten, kicked, and apprehended before my eyes in the casino. Scooped up by the secret police in the middle of high stakes baccarat for being a Bolshevik and/or possibly

Jewish! Yes. I am far away from my sheltered life in America, and even though our democratic President has decreed war relocation for Japanese-Americans in an effort to combat the Fifth Column, we would never act in such a manner as I've witnessed by the PVDE police!

Ten days ago, I would never have imagined myself in a European casino, let alone witness to such brutality. Although the battlefields of war have not come to Portugal, war is here—bloodless and hidden in its very heartbeat at all levels of society. It is just as Carl Wilson explained. Nothing or no one is as they appear. I am fearful, not for myself for I am untouchable in this country where their relationship with Great Britain will protect a peer (no matter the "baron's" standing or scandal.) But I am terrified for the Drucker family and what I may find at the end of this search for them. In that endeavor, I will take judicious care when introducing myself. Perhaps...Eva von Lamberg, my dear childhood governess' name, may be best served when necessary here in Lisbon. Everyone always seems to be enamored by Austrian women.

TWELVE
From Twilight 'Til Dawn

March 7

*T*ittle-tattle from the Palácio's concierge indicated that the popular establishment was named the English Bar not because of its faux-Tudor façade or its hunting lodge décor, but rather because the proprietor was a British spy. The young Lisboeta explained that for last two years the establishment had been the local meeting spot for all Allied secret agents, but he could neither confirm nor deny if the owner was, in fact, truly an agent for the Security Intelligence Service. But goodness! After last night's incident at the casino, what a story it would make. Already Evie's mind whirled with ideas for her next article, one of intrigue and espionage.

Located across from the Estoril Casino and the gardens of the Palácio, it seemed only natural that the former Romanian king, cousin to the King of England, would frequent the English Bar. The restaurant reminded her of the 21 Club with its dark wood dining room and romantic allure sans the comfort she had always felt when dining at 21. Here, she was a stranger among international raptors seeking her own prey: Elena Lupescu.

You can do this. This is your chance. Think big, Evie! Front page news. Find your moxie!

"Madam, will you be dining alone this evening?" The maître d' asked when she entered the restaurant.

"*Sim.* I am Mrs. Richard Somerset. The Palácio made a reservation for me."

Her heart pounded in her ears, louder than the American dance music playing from a radio somewhere at the bar. Reaching out to the man, she slid her gloved hand into his, along with a carefully concealed a one hundred escudo note. "I prefer to dine near Madam Lupescu, please," she said in Portuguese.

He gladly accepted her bribe, smiled broadly, then indicated for her to follow him into a room off the main dining section. Her skin prickled at the feel of many sets of eyes on her and the not-so-quiet speculation about her above the din, which, of course, made her consider the spies and secret agents Carl had warned her about. Perhaps they believe her to be one of their kind.

As they neared her table, a man's raucous laughter followed by a woman's amused tease spoken in Romanian rang out.

"The Hohenzollern party is dining in this room, Senhora."

The richly appointed anteroom overlooked the sea through the small paned windows spanning the western perimeter. The former king and his mistress sat at a round table in the center with another couple drinking and playing cards. A pungent cloud of smoke wafted up to the light fixture above the table. Evie resisted the urge to crinkle her nose at the combined odor of cigars and sweet pipe tobacco mixed with a woman's heavy-handed perfume.

The maître d' sat her at a table for two against the windows, promptly handing her a menu. "May I offer you a Manhattan cocktail? We have the finest on the Riviera."

"No thank you, just soda water."

"Darling, Jose…this room is reserved for friends and poker. If she is not willing to join our party, then remove her post haste!" a brash Elena called out in butchered Portuguese, eyes of fire and flame flashing.

Although taken aback by the woman's forcefulness, there was something instantly likeable about Lupescu.

"We are missing a player tonight," she passively commanded. "We are quite respectable, and only marginally inebriated I assure you."

The former monarch laughed, his eyes dancing as they held the ostentatiously dressed woman in his gaze. She had yet to remove her mink stole, and the diamond and pearl ear pendants she wore were long enough to touch the fur at her shoulder.

"You look quite familiar, little bird." Lupescu scrutinized but more in friendly admiration, than in Queen Louise's manner of study.

"Perhaps you recognize me from the Casino last evening. I spent most of the evening in the solicitous company of your friend Senhor Esteves."

"A jolly good fellow!" the former king announced.

"It was quite an eventful evening was it not?" she added.

"Ha!" She glanced to Carol. "What a dust up! Why, it reminds me of the old days in Romania. Does it not my love? Traitors and spies in Court and your enemies plotting against you!"

"Let us not forget our narrow escape from Madrid," he laughed, as if life on the run from the Nazis was all a game.

"Come, take this seat beside me. What is your name?" Lupescu persisted with a swipe of her hand.

"Mrs. Richard Somerset of New York. You may call me Evelyn."

Jose looked flustered by the forceful woman with hair the color of a setting sun, and quickly relocated Evie beside Lupescu at the round table. The men stood, greeting her with intro-ductions in each his native tongue: English, German, and Portuguese. Turning to the former ruler of Romania, she respectfully dipped her body in a small curtsey. "Your Majesty," she greeted in English.

"Nonsense! That distinction is reserved for my son. I am simply Carol now."

She smiled. "Shall we converse in German for the benefit of your guests?"

"An American in Portugal wants to converse in German, not French? Excellent!"

Everyone laughed with cheers and Elena effused slipping into German. "An American! Well, aren't you a lovely one? Isn't she, my dear?"

"Indeed, Duduia," he said with a leer, which made Evie uncomfortable. Elena elbowed him when his stare went longer than propriety. He hadn't acquired the nickname "the playboy king" for acting the saint.

"Any woman wearing Chanel during the war is a friend of mine. We lived in Paris for some time, and I simply fell in love with French designs. How ever did you get it?"

Portraying arrogance only Queen Louise could appreciate, and Carl would tease, she tightened her jaw even more so. "It is an older style, but one of my favorites. Unfortunately, she has been unable to visit my apartment in New York for a private showing since Paris fell to the Germans" She sighed. "I'm forced to make do. American designers and their paltry offerings are not nearly sufficient. They're simply abysmal."

"Oh, yes! You should see the inferior quality available to me in Mexico. The fabrics are horrendous. Nothing is coming out of Paris these days."

"We are slaves to fashion," she joked. "As I understand it, Coco's friends were keeping her quite busy in the South of France. We do miss her delicious designs during this blasted war and all the restrictions imposed on us in America!"

"You *know* Gabrielle?"

She touched the turban above her ear. "But of course," she lied, having only met her once a few years ago.

"Then you must have heard she took a lover?" Elena leaned toward her, disturbing the playing cards and poker chips stacked before her. "A *Nazi* lover."

Aghast that the designer would become romantically involved with a Nazi, she continued the deception. "I have heard rumors at the club."

"Somerset...Somerset of New York?—any relationship to the Baron of Sallingham?" Carol inquired.

"Yes, he is my father-in-law."

"Yo ho! You know, Binky is my third cousin once removed."

Binky? Oh, how eccentric!

"Carol's mother was a granddaughter to Queen Victoria," Elena proudly added.

"Is it true he renounced his British holdings and title?"

"It is. He thought it best after war broke out, and particularly since he has vowed never to return to England. Not because of their declaration of war, but for other reasons entirely his own."

"Ah, yes. Perhaps the old man is still in a tizzy over his late-father's affair with a commoner all those years ago. He was always a bit pharisaical for my liking. How is the beastly Binky these days?"

"Sadly, he's in mourning. His only son, my late-husband Richard, was lost in the Pacific six months ago."

Elena gasped, patting her hand. "You poor dear! This unfortunate war." The woman clucked her tongue and solemnly shook her head. "And you're so young. Don't you worry, darling. We'll find a suitable young man to wine and dine you while you are in Cascais." Her cupid-bow-shaped, red lips broke into a wide grin.

"That's not necessary. I'm quite content. I'm..." Quickly examining the table contents of half-consumed digestifs and stacks of colored betting chips, she hoped to redirect the company when she declared. "I'm here to learn to play *pochen*! I have heard through the grapevine you are quite the expert, Madam Lupescu."

And with that the party cheerfully continued with their game, dealing her a hand of cards she didn't know what to do with. All conversation about Lord Somerset, Richard, and her widowhood was forgotten when Elena undertook her poker tutelage.

The cocktail arrived, and Jose gave her a sideways glance. She had a feeling this was going to be a long night.

———————⧈———————

At almost two in the morning, Evie stood at the mirror in the small lavatory of the English Bar. A pinch to her tired, pallid cheeks was interrupted by Elena's entrance.

"Darling girl. I'm so impressed! Why, no-one has stripped my dear heart of so much money in one evening as you."

"I think it is what they call beginner's luck."

"Nonsense. You have quite the poker face. You're a skilled bluffer. Watching you play cards was as glorious as *Hamlet* at the National Theatre in Bucharest. Your joining our little party was ever-so delightful. We must have lunch."

"Oh, Elena, you must be a mind-reader." She turned, taking the older woman's warm hand in hers and bolstered her confidence. "Please come to my suite in the Palácio tomorrow. I have the loveliest view of the sea, and lunch on the veranda would be divine."

"Just us two girls?"

"If you wish."

"As much as I adore dear Carol, I sometimes must have female companionship. For my sanity, you understand. The man can be such an insufferable pig head." She laughed.

How odd that Carl should come to her mind. "Would you agree to an interview?"

"An interview? What kind of interview, dear?"

Her cheeks burned. "For the newspaper I work for in New York. I'm a reporter, and I confess, although an unlikely one given my social circle, I would like to set the record straight about who Madam Elena Lupescu *really* is, not who everyone *speculates* she is. My female readers would just adore learning about your romance with Carol and how you both came to settle in Mexico City."

Elena howled, throwing back her head. "Brava, Evelyn! No one has been so successfully deceptive in trapping me."

"I didn't mean to be so deceptive, honestly, but you *did* insist I join your party. I know…you never give interviews, and I am aware that you are private about your relationship, but my female readers would just adore learning about your romance."

The woman sized her up with burning circumspection. This, she had anticipated, having read how suspicious Lupescu was of the press and most people who entered the couple's circle.

"I should have learned long ago to be more careful, but your charming smile and delightful manner caught me unawares. Like I said: poker face."

"From one peer to another, you have my word, Elena, I'll not misrepresent you and vow to print only what is on the record."

"You are a sly one, my little bird. I agree to your interview, but only on one condition."

"Anything."

"I would like for *you to* share with *me* the story behind your Mona Lisa smile. You hide a sadness of the soul and I would like to know why."

———◈———

THIRTEEN
Tea for Two

March 8

*O*n the calm moment before the hurricane Madam Lupescu's arrival, Evie replayed in her mind "the one condition" to the interview. She never considered her smile to be like Mona Lisa's, but she did hide sadness and stories behind it. Life as one of "Best Society's darlings" had been a series of concealed personal disappointments and her share of grief: a wretch of a mother, the death of the woman she once longed to become, and the dreams she once imagined coupled with the deaths of her father and husband. In her shipboard solitude, it had occurred to her that her only true friend after college was Margie, and the sisterhood of deep friendships formed at Vassar had faded away. She had quietly replaced them with Amelia Snow, an imaginary conspirator in her pursuit of fulfillment in the uninspiring life she'd led since marrying.

In Richard's absence during their three and half years together, they hadn't had time to become best friends. She was sure her smile hid that sorrow along with his death, but she was packing up the sad-sack grief now. Still, she couldn't deny he'd left her long ago. Her existence, much as The Dakota had become, was a depressing one and no amount of mention in the society pages could ever fill the void. Once, she had cared about that...no longer.

She closed her eyes and breathed in the salty sea breeze, just as she had upon her arrival to the Palácio, turning her thoughts to the birdsong and the rustle of palm trees. What a strange course of events life had presented to her. How would it all change her and who was she becoming? Perhaps this fortuitous interview with the controversial and mysterious Madam Lupescu could give insight into her own mysteries. Namely, why had she willingly abandoned herself after marrying? Had she learned nothing at all about herself at Vassar? Did the meaning of Millay's musings also die with her free-spirit? Had Richard and the ever-present Queen Louise been the influences to her change or was it society itself?

Did it matter now? She wistfully smiled. "I'm in control now, free to pursue my dreams. The decisions are mine."

Thirty minutes later, she sat opposite Elena as the waiter placed their lunch before them on the table. Dressed in a navy and white print ensemble, the interviewee looked quite at ease for someone who abhorred reporters and what she surely suspected would be an inquisition. Spurred on by the Romanian populace's unfavorable opinion of her, the press had been ruthless to Elena since the beginning of her affair with then-Crown Prince Carol eighteen years ago. Further, there were so many conflicting stories about her lies and truth became blurred. She hoped Elena would be honest in her interview.

"Quite lovely," Elena remarked on the offerings and then looked out at the sea with a warm smile. "I adore Portugal."

"I have only just arrived, but I can see why it is such a popular holiday destination."

"It is all the rage. Carol and I hope to permanently live here in quiet domesticity, perhaps after the war. Although we are content in Mexico, it is dreadful for my health."

The waiter left them to their peace and conversation, and Evie felt compelled to reiterate her promise made the night before at the English Bar.

"Thank you for lunching with me, Elena, and I apologize for taking you unawares last evening. You have my assurance that my questions will be tame in comparison to what you've experienced previously with other reporters."

"You must know, the only reason I agreed is…well, I see so much of myself in you."

Should she be insulted? "You do?"

"Your subterfuge was simply marvelous. It reminded me of the early days with Carol. There were no bounds to my deception. Of course, not with him, but with curiosity-seekers."

"It wasn't meant to be deception. I was merely gathering the courage and when you so kindly invited me to join your party it allowed me to get to know you—personally. I am intrigued, and I know those who follow my column will be as well."

With her fork, Elena pushed aside the pickled carrots then dug into the potato and cod casserole. "It is all off the record, Evelyn."

"All?"

"Well, I will tell you what to print," she directed before placing the utensil into her mouth.

"Perhaps we can meet in the middle. Shall we collaborate on a *forthright* article for the *New York Daily Spectator*, which paints you in the best light, one to put all those inaccuracies to bed once and for all?"

"I do like that alternative."

"Wonderful! American women are quite weary of war news, but I believe your romance in the thick of it could be a story for the ages."

"Yes, I have many American acquaintances in Mexican society who express the same malady. They don't realize how very good the Americans have it."

"I concede we have not been as traumatized as Europe by having war on our doorstep, but our losses are great. American men have died in the fight to liberate Europe, and don't forget we are fighting in the Pacific, too. Pearl Harbor was a deliberate act of war."

Elena frowned. "I'm sorry. I'm not demeaning your husband's death, not at all. It is, you see, my heart is still wounded by Romania's loss of our crown jewel Transylvania to Hungary. And we mourn the death of many men who followed Hitler into Russia." She clucked her tongue and shook her head. "So sad. Such a waste for all in this war."

"On that we can agree. May I quote you?"

"If you wish."

Taken aback—and delighted—that the woman seemed to be amenable to discussing Romania's fascist alliance with the Axis instead of her romance, Evie grinned at the prospect of a more substantive article from what she set out to achieve. "So, you would be agreeable to discussing Romania's geopolitical situation further, Elena? The relationship between your paramour and the Third Reich followed by his eventual ousting is quite perplexing and provocative. Some have said you are at the heart of every political decision he made and now Carol's young son is king. It must be quite heartbreaking to be exiled from your home—the country you both love so much. I imagine it must have strained your relationship."

Elena pursed her lips, clearly not liking the direction in which Evie wanted to steer the conversation. "I would not like to discuss this, but I would enjoy sharing how exciting it has been to be loved by Carol...*after* you tell me about *your* love affair."

"Love affair? I'm not having a love affair!"

"With your late-husband, darling. Unless...of course...your protestation implies something or *someone* else. Have there been others?"

"Of course not. I just didn't know what you meant. Richard...my husband, of course. He was a good man."

"That is very telling, indeed. Carol is a good man of strong character, but I don't refer to my *amour de vie* in such a droll manner. Why, you didn't even smile when recollecting such an admirable attribute."

Flustered, yet unyielding, her gaze met Elena's challenge. "How do you believe I should refer to the man I married if not to recall the most noble aspect of his character?"

"With ardor. Unless, that is what you're hiding behind your placid deportment." Elena twisted her lips.

"I was quite devoted to my husband. But on the record…what do *you* consider ardor?"

"When you can face the devil *together*—undeterred—and survive as inseparable and in love as when you began. Leaning upon and supporting one another in the trials of life, such as leaving Romania, all the while maintaining a flaming passion. This, I understand is difficult for most, but not us. It was our destiny."

Destiny…fate. Was it Richard's fate to have died so young? Was it Carl's fate to have met me, as he implied. Poppycock! She'd not respond to Elena about her vehement disbelief of fate or anything implying a higher power of influence.

"Richard and I did not have enough time together to face many challenges. We had only one. He left for naval training within the first month of our marriage only to return to a whirlwind of social engagements and familial obligations. And then he left for Hawaii. Pearl Harbor shred any remaining semblance of a cohesive marriage. "

"Pity. Then tell me of your flaming passion when you came together in the quiet of your suite before America entered the war. Surely you made up for lost time over many hours of lovemaking."

Definitely not. Their flaming passion had tempered early on in their short marriage. In the quiet of their suite, any romantic intercourse was over in mere minutes followed by his snoring into her ear. Long ago, she had acceded that their marriage was not meant to be *that kind* of passion—and not by design, but rather faulting her own bedroom timidity.

"Elena, I'm to interview *you*," she joked with a false smile before taking a bite of her lunch.

"Very well, but we will continue with dissecting your veneer over dessert."

"I assure you—I have no veneer. I'm an open book, so there is nothing to dissect or uncover. In fact, I'm quite boring. Now…I am curious of the deception *you* mentioned earlier. Would you care to elaborate?"

Elena laughed. "There was a time, when I was so harassed by the press and members of Romania's Iron Guard, that I elicited the help of nine look-a-likes to act as a diversion while I went about my affair."

"How did you find such women?"

"Really, it wasn't too difficult in my younger years and the red hair was easy to imitate. Oh, what fun I had in sending one to the open market in Bucharest and another to a cafe, while my *l'amour de ma vie* and I escaped the city in his sports car. What fun it was to send the press on a wild goose chase!"

"And no one found out?"

"No!" she laughed.

"The art of disguise in all manner is quite important. In fact, I even dressed as a peasant woman waiting outside the royal palace for the king's generosity."

The conversation over lunch continued in this light manner with Elena laughing at her detractors when asked of her personal trials in Bucharest and Carol's first abdication when Crown Prince in 1925 during their Parisian romantic escapade. Evie attempted several times to discuss Queen Helena and Michael, but, again, Elena always brought the conversation back to their great love affair. Of course, they talked of Elena's dogs, even fashion and books until finally Evie insisted on the topic of the woman's Jewish roots, which was the true intent of the article. Hank Drucker wanted a scoop on the couple's, "life on the run from the Nazis." But Elena carefully circumvented the Jewish topic with excuses and well-rehearsed lies—or not. It was becoming difficult to keep track of the contradictions. Finally, the woman declared: "Carol would never take a Jewess to bed!" thereby ending the topic at hand.

This didn't surprise Evie. O'Shea had prepared her for the denial in light of Romania's purported anti-Semitic history under King Carol I. What did surprise her was the woman's turn of the tables. The interviewee had become the interviewer over Portuguese coffee and cigarettes when the red-haired titan attempted to draw out what hid behind the Somerset "Mona Lisa" manner.

"Tell me, little bird, were you a virgin when you married your naval husband?"

Affronted, her chin and cigarette almost dropped in shock and she stuttered to answer. "Of…of course!"

"Then this would explain the lack of passion. You were too young, too inexperienced."

"I never said we lacked passion…just time."

"Time to learn how to please each other in the bedroom."

"Time for so many things. War is a cruel occurrence in marriage."

"Did you not take a lover when he was gone?"

"Elena…please, of course not. I was faithful to my husband."

"There is nothing wrong with a love affair. I understand completely if you did for I, myself, was married to an Army officer who spent much time away from me. Did your Richard excite you?"

"Yes…no…in what way?"

"Oh dear," Elena remonstrated. Her knowing gaze locked onto Evie's as her red lips pursed around the cigarette and she took a deep pull. After a long exhale, she straightforwardly—and rather crudely—asked, "When he climbed upon you, did he just merely rut like a dog or did he take his time, caress your body, call you the most beautiful woman he ever held in his arms? Did he touch you in places that sent you to heaven and back?"

She blushed, answering to herself: yes, no, no, no…and no. "This is quite indelicate and inappropriate."

"Did you not promise me girl talk, a lunch suited for us girls?"

"For one so secretive about so much, I'm surprised you would ask me to share the intimate relationship between my late-husband and me."

Elena softly smiled. "Perhaps, my aim is to only encourage you to open your heart and mind to something more fulfilling. You are clearly a brave, adventure seeker come all the way from New York on your own to pursue a scoop no one has yet to attain. But I can see in your eyes you masterfully hide a hunger—a thirst for passion: heated, intoxicating madness in the moonlight, a vigorous man to shower you in affection and adoration. Have you not desired that? Do you not deserve that?"

She couldn't answer but, in her heart, admitted: yes, yes, and yes!

"You sound like my sister back in New York. She believes I should take a lover. That it would be good for my constitution, help me to move on from my mourning," she laughed.

"It is true. And it is all right to admit that life with your husband may not have been perfect."

"I never said such a thing."

"You didn't need to. You called him a good man, nothing else. Trust me, I understand what you feel. Richard was the son of a baron." She shrugged. "I pursued a Crown Prince, but I was lucky; he was everything I dreamed. But setting your sights on and marrying well can come with its share of disenchantment. Take for example, Carol's ex-wife, Queen Helena. Everyone adores her, but she was terribly unhappy. How sad for her to have married him due to expectations when she could have married another. Ah, but she was queen and now mother to the young King Michael. Don't misunderstand me. Power and nobility are marvelous aspirations, but the true love of a man is a greater treasure and, when you have it, there is nothing he would not do for you—even abandon his birthright."

She reached for a cigarette, attempting to control the subtle shake to her fingers when she lit the tip. No one ever had the gall to even *insinuate* such things to her! This brash woman read her most intimate and disconcerting thoughts like a book.

"Elena...I appreciate your candor, but you couldn't be more wrong about me. I'm quite happy with my past and present. I did not marry for status or further wealth. Richard and I had a wonderful marriage—a passionate marriage—and no one, absolutely no one can ever take the place of him. Please, let's move on from the topic of *my* love life and focus on the subject of our article—yours. Tell my readers about your ex-husband, the army officer."

———◆———

FOURTEEN
Stormy Weather

March 9

Seated in the trolley, Evie allowed the dull click, click, click noise of the car riding over the metal rails to lull her into a sense of familiarity; even the high-pitched scraping sounded similar to a New York City subway. Not that she'd been on the el—or a trolley for that matter—in recent years, but the steady sound made her feel at home as she considered all the questions she would ask upon arrival to Rossio Square, the center hub of Lisbon's activity. Taking a street car was the most common means of travel in the city. Apart from the close quarters, and the sense of being watched at every turn, she liked the ease of travel in getting on and off in her search for the Druckers, even if unsure where the search would leave her. Traveling on the streetcar had also uncovered Lisbon's poverty-stricken districts stressed by the influx of Jewish immigrants. Although wealthy visitors, whether escaping persecution or exiled, were aplenty, they had mostly traveled to the tourist destinations in the south just as she and Madam Lupescu had.

She had been informed most refugees congregated in the center of Lisbon while passing the time awaiting their exit visas. Armed with only a few languages, her charm, and the photographs, she remained hopeful in finding the family despite the failure of her first stop: the American Embassy. Her heart broke at the sight of the long line wrapping around the building and up the stairs to the crowded office. She noted that some travelers had spent the night queued to hold their spot. Unfortunately, given the sheer number of refugees who sought transit documents, the two clerks could not recall and had no paperwork attesting to the fact that either Samuel or Ezra Drucker had ever sought their assistance. If she were a religious person or had any belief system at all, she would have lifted the Druckers in prayer as she squeezed back down the steps—past the waiting, disconsolate visitors from various nations. Instead, she would keep her fingers crossed that time would be on their side.

Overcast and bleak, there was a chill in the air and she buttoned her sweater then absentmindedly toyed with her gloves resuming her stare of the winding, narrow streets beyond the window. So narrow, it hardly seemed possible that the streetcar could fit!

The trolley bell rang a hollow ding and she craned her head to see if this was her stop. Beyond the spanning cables and wrought iron street lanterns, the monument of Dom Pedro VI towering above the square between the hills, indicated it was.

"Pardon me," she said to the man seated beside her, then nudged her way through the standing passengers toward the front exit.

She stepped out onto the ancient stone pavement and took in the magnificence of the condensed center of Lisbon lined by brightly colored shops and cafes. Nervous excitement coursed through her blood, and she admitted it was part intrigue; definitely fear, but mostly determination, and she was proud of herself for taking that extraordinary, unfathomable step in her life. Now that she had cabled the Lupescu interview to the *Spectator*, she had "unofficially" earned foreign correspondent press credentials in her editor's eyes, paving the way to a reporter's future!

Only someone who had walked in her shoes could understand why she delighted in a future, which strayed from her strictly regulated society. She would not make this investigative experience an article, but what a story to tell. Former lead reporter at the *Vassar Miscellany*, columnist Amelia Snow, and now rogue war widow was here, alone, in Lisbon at the height of a worldwide war, surrounded by spies and collaborators at every turn. That would make more than an article. It could be a novel! Although the task before her felt daunting, she was resolute and held her head high. This was for Richard and he'd be proud of her!

Oh! Pretty! A darling floral dress displayed in a shop window caught her attention and she lingered to admire it. Lisbon was just as Purvis had described: an exotic blend of old-world style and continental sophistication. And just like The Big Apple, it, had its hidden underbelly.

More pronounced than when she left the hotel and again at the Embassy, she felt a burning gaze at her back, and nervously clutched her purse. In the window's reflection she searched for anyone who looked suspicious behind her, but there was no one out of place or lingering. She determined her intuition was only heightened—and paranoid—in the culmination of events over the past few days. What she did see in the mirror image was Café Chave d'Ouro's billboard spanning the rooftop of a five-story building on the opposite side of the square. The dress would have to wait. She walked across the street to the open plaza dotted by pigeons and policemen; the latter's keen focus examined everyone, including her. Nearing the fountain, she regarded the picturesque backdrop of the café lined with umbrella tables where patrons socialized and smoked. The sun disappeared behind a cloud and a visible shadow moved across Don Pedro and the white façade of the café. She shivered. The air suddenly felt menacing, ominous, as though a portentous omen—and not of rain. In a flash, her investigative reporter confidence dissipated in the gloominess and her strong intuition caused her hand to grab the watch bob pin at her shoulder. She recognized that in doing so she was reaching out to Richard for protection—from what exactly, she did not know. But then his last missive's invitation echoed in the back of her mind: to pray. Poppycock.

To calm her sudden cold feet, she stopped to sit at the impressive two-tiered fountain, removing her cigarette compact from her purse. The first inhale relaxed her as she surveyed her surroundings and the people in it. Why was she suddenly apprehensive? Boy, Albert had done a number on her confidence. She assumed it was insecurity getting the better of her and speculated when exactly it was that she stopped flying with glee toward the unknown. That Vassar girl and her gumption—where had they gone? It was marriage to a sagacious, serious man of the finest breeding, a man who loved her in a reserved, sensible manner. She had married a man whom her mother and Albert highly approved of and she idolized with steadfast devotion, but in doing so, she lost herself.

People-watching had always been a favorite pastime, and Evie admired how life in Lisbon continued despite the food shortages within and war just beyond their country's boundaries. Despite the influx of invading foreigners and refugees, Lisbon hummed with life and culture. Smiling faces in the passing crowd of denizens were etched by hard work going about their business. Local women chatted and others scurried by with filled baskets masterfully balanced on their head. Most men congregated, speaking privately beside Don Pedro. And everyone wore a hat: a traditional Portuguese fisherman's hat, a bowler, or a French beret, and in her case, the green homburg. Most visitors to Rossio Square were well-dressed.

In spite of the foul weather, she became lost in the vibrant sights and sounds of everyday Lisbon, and her ears perked to Portuguese folk music played by street performers. The sharp plucking of the bandolim carried across the courtyard, lifting her spirits slightly as the fountain's rivulets of water showered in a throbbing, steady rain. Both songs encouraged her as she attempted to regain her reporter's legs.

It was a shadow, Evie. Nothing more.

She turned her attention to the national theatre on the northeast side of the square. Its neoclassical design and stately pillars reminded her of The White House, which, of course, reminded her that Albert was probably furious over her sudden departure from New York and all its—and his—trappings. Goodness, she hoped he didn't try to contact her in Philadelphia!

A police officer walked toward her in curious assessment; his glare caused her to look away toward the music and she smiled nervously, fearful that he would stop to speak with her. After what she witnessed at the casino two nights ago, the secret police were relentless and rough and looking for trouble. Their tan uniforms, and violent reaction, resembled Hitler's own paramilitary group O'Shea called the Brownshirts—and here she was searching for a Jewish family. She could lead them right to the Druckers!

"Do you loiter waiting for someone?" he asked in halting Portuguese, his manner, voice, and expression void of any friendliness.

"No. I am enjoying your lovely city." She swallowed hard, hoping she had not made any mistakes in her pronunciation.

"You are...American?"

She vacillated considering that he could be a Nazi sympathizer, an American enemy. "I am from Salzburg!" she lied in Portuguese, beaming falsely. She called upon her "poker face" to mask her consternation, but her heart thundered.

"And what is your business in Estado Novo?"

"I am on holiday with friends from Germany."

"It is not the usual season for visitors." His beady study of her fixed on the diamond watch brooch and he raised an eyebrow. "You are staying at which hotel, Senhora?"

"The Hotel Atlântico in Estoril," she played to his believed sympathies, having heard that the Germans stayed there. "I have heard such exceptional things about Rossio Square and just had to explore, even on such an inclement day. The weather is not quite suited for beachcombing or sunbathing, and I do so enjoy window shopping."

"Sim. Then you would do well to visit the Chiado district."

"Thank you, I will do that."

"Enjoy your day," he said followed by a half-smile.

The moment he walked away, she let out her breath.

Carl watched Evie from his seemingly relaxed position on a bench at the edge of the park. Peering over the top of the *Konigsberger Allgemein Zeitung* he held, he observed how she calmly smoked a cigarette while people-watching or spying. She appeared to be waiting for someone. A member of the suspect German-sympathizing PVDE approached her beside the fountain, and they chatted briefly and, as expected, she flashed her pearly whites. Just like that, the official took a powder. More than likely the official's questions were shot down by her particular skill: a mixture of spoiled, high-brow indignation and charming sincerity. The object of his budding affection was good at her game, whatever game she was playing, which was more than "in Lisbon to interview the Romanian mistress." Evie certainly kept him guessing as he awaited the information about her from Berkshire.

He'd been shadowing her from the time she left the Palácio this morning and, frankly, he enjoyed every minute of it. It had surprised him that such a sophisticated woman would take the trolley, but it made his surveillance easier. Though right under her nose, he went unnoticed as a fellow traveler concealed behind a newspaper. Her first stop at the American Embassy could have been for any number of reasons—conceivably a problem with her visa, and maybe now she was planning on shopping for a souvenir or two in Rossio Square, but with each glance over her shoulder, she looked to be hiding something or from someone. Perhaps that feminine intuition she relied so heavily on had tipped her off to his presence only steps behind her. He had been careful not to be seen.

The PVDE officer left her seated on the wall and she continued to smoke her cigarette while staring at the wave-like pattern of mosaic stones circling the fountain. He wondered if she could hear the folk music, which made him chuckle given that the name of said folk music, Fado, translated to "Fate," something she did not believe in.

Pedestrians passed her and then a man, dressed in a black suit, stopped at her feet. Towering over her with his lanky, intimidating form, he leaned on his umbrella. *Damn!* If only he was in earshot of their conversation, but the man's profile, the Romanesque, pointed nose and arrogant posture identified him straight away. The image of *that* particular man conversing with Evie made Carl's heart sink to the pit of his stomach. She was meeting with the very man whose dossier he had read the night before: General Otto Wegener, the highest ranking official responsible for security over the German Army's supply routes. SIS suspected that he alone was directing the smuggling of wolfram and transporting it over ratlines through Spain.

A couple stopped walking directly in front of him, blocking his view of the exchange, and he closed the newspaper just about to rise and walk closer to Evie and her suspected cohort.

"Carl! There you are, darling. I've been looking all over for you this morning," Kay said, coming behind him.

Damn! That bad penny again.

"Oh hello, Kay," he said flatly, preoccupied and unnerved by what he had just witnessed.

She touched his shoulder. "I was wondering if you'd like to help me practice for tonight's performance. You and I have the spotlight in 'Deep Purple,' you know."

He rose and smiled, a light bulb going off in his head. Bending his arm, he offered, "I have a better idea. How about we mosey around the square and take a look at the fountain?"

"Really? Oh, daddy! That would be just swell!"

———⬥———

The folk music in the square entertained the patrons seated alfresco in front of Café Chave d'Ouro. Even in overcast weather, men leisurely conversed in hushed tones and smoked, unaffected by the chill in the air. A few sat alone reading, and it appeared to Evie that they were the most aware of their surroundings, eyes shifting as though keenly taking note of her when she strolled past the flower stand to the coffee house entrance. A gentleman wearing a black beret glanced up and his gaze met hers. She smiled, but his lips only twitched slightly as he examined her suspiciously.

A few casually dressed women in the brightly decorated two-story establishment examined her curiously when she sat at a table beside the window looking out at the square and Don Pedro. What could be so peculiar about her patronage? It was mid-morning after all. In the short time she'd been in Lisbon, she'd learned that Lisboetas enjoyed their coffee breaks at this hour.

The photographs of Mr. Drucker's family burned in her purse and she hoped that someone here would recognize them, but at that moment it was not opportune to inquire.

"Senhora, welcome to Café Chave d'Ouro. What may I serve you?" the elderly waiter asked, his hunched, short stature was barely taller than her seated form, but his delighted expression filled the café. Perhaps she was the only paying customer in the relatively empty restaurant.

She spoke in butchered Portuguese, making mistakes, but confident her effort would be appreciated. No doubt, many of these patrons did not speak the language. "*Bom dia*. Please excuse my poor Portuguese. I would like coffee," she said with a smile. "And rice pudding, thank you."

"You speak very well," the waiter answered before glancing over his shoulder to the two men seated closest to the bar. Sneaking a peek around his thin frame, she noted that they were dressed in black suits and still wore their fedoras. The dark-haired one sported a graying mustache, the fairer had narrow eyes of ice blue—both watched the exchange. One brought a demitasse cup to his thin lips. His stare burned the waiter's back.

"German Secret Police," the waiter said in barely a whisper as though cautioning her, sympathetic to the refugee plight.

When he turned toward the bar, she removed her gloves, unnerved at how clammy her palms felt even though she had nothing to fear. But the indication that these two men were the dreaded Gestapo made her uneasy. Back at the *Spectator*, O'Shea explained their purported "Jew-hunting" in occupied countries and there were some other unsubstantiated stories he had picked up across the AP wire: horrific happenings such as mass deportations and ghettos throughout Poland. To her knowledge Old Waddles had never printed these events in the *Spectator* but still, she wouldn't question the journalistic source.

The thick air in the café hung with a palpable dark energy as though it emanated from those two men. Their presence might explain the lack of patronage and her earlier presentiment. Her curiosity about them grew and she glanced up and around, pretending to admire the architectural details of the popular establishment: the massive clock overseeing the activities on the ground floor, the art deco balustrades and columns, and then finally the two Germans, sitting stoically as if Baroque statuary quietly surveying with intimidation.

The fairer of the two touched his hat in greeting and leered; his cold scrutiny unnerved her. She crossed her ankles and gave him a pleasing look, batting her lashes to disarm any negative scrutiny. It worked! He placed his cup down, spoke quietly to his accomplice and they both mechanically rose. He walked to her table as they made their way to the door.

"*Guten Morgen, Fräulein,*" he greeted, towering over her like a black shadow.

"Guten Morgen."

"You are from *Deutchland*?"

"Yes. Quite near to the Führer's home, but today, I'm enjoying this lovely city."

"Are you from Vienna?" He raised a suspecting eyebrow. She knew Vienna had a significant Jewish population.

"Goodness, no. I am from Aigen Mitte in Salzburg."

"I know this place."

"Then you know the von Lamberg villa, Herr…?"

He did not offer his last name, but his gaze bore into her. "I do not. And what is your business in Lisboa?"

"I'm visiting a family friend…Baron Oswald von Hoyingen-Huene." She smiled, quickly recalling the German Ambassador she'd spent the evening with at the casino.

He smiled and tipped his hat to her with an *"Auf Wiedersehen"* and departed the restaurant.

Below the table she clenched her fists in fear and relief then let out a ragged breath.

Bearing gifts of *arroz doce* and *um bica*, the waiter bustled to her table; his manner almost gleeful. "I thought they would not leave. They have been here since opening this morning. What did you say to them to make them go?"

"Nothing more than polite conversation."

"You ran the wolf off with your charm." The waiter placed the items on the table, complaining, "Ach! The newspapers said that Salazar had shut down the Germans spying in Lisboa, but they are still here making mischief. Our patrons do not come, and when they do, they worry. Some we never see again."

"I had been cautioned to be careful of the PVDE, but I didn't realize it is this bad in Rossio Square."

"It is mostly safe…but for the few who look for trouble. They all can go to the place where Judas lost his boots. Before the war, it was peaceful in Lisboa."

"I imagine so. Are the Jews safe?"

"From the Portuguese people? Certainly!"

This was her opportunity. "If you please, Senhor…I'm looking for someone. Perhaps they are patrons of the café." Reaching into her purse she removed the photograph. "They are German."

The waiter took the photograph into his hands and examined the family.

"Have they come here?"

"No. I do not recognize them, but I only work three days."

She handed him the other photographs for examination.

Shaking his head as he shuffled through them, he stated. "I am sorry. They are not familiar. Perhaps the men come to the café at night for the billiards. You should ask at the docks, too. The women frequent the taverns there to make money for passage."

She gasped. *Prostitution?*

"I do not know this family. But there is a Frenchman at the table closest to the door. I am told he is here every day—all day—waiting for travel papers." He shook his head. "It has been one year," he whispered. "I think he is Comunista."

She'd never seen a Bolshevik, at least not one she knew of. Perhaps that was why the Frenchman remained, perhaps the reason for not being granted an exit visa. America certainly would not allow his entrance, even if we were allied to Russia to defeat Germany, but according to O'Shea, that was only a convenience for victory. The ancient proverb: The enemy of my enemy and all that.

"Would it be okay if I asked your patrons if they recognize the family?"

"Of course. I cannot assure they will help you. The Jewish community is always cautious. The stories I hear would break your heart."

"I understand. I will be delicate in my questions. Thank you."

Now alone, she sat there enjoying the strong coffee and pudding, waiting for the precise moment for her moxie to arrive as her thoughts traveled to her interview at the Palácio with Elena Lupescu.

"Elena, over the years in America, we have read much about your love affair with the king. Since as early as a 1930 <u>New York Times</u> article, and again in 1934 with a <u>Washington Post</u> exposé titled 'Attacks Are Renewed on Red-Haired Magda.' And lastly in 1938, the esteemed <u>Time</u> magazine declared you 'His Majesty's titan-haired Jewish Pompadour.' In light of the negative press, what would you say are some of the lessons you've learned since meeting Carol? What helped you to overcome the criticism for your influence over the king and, of all things, the color of your hair?"

The king's mistress smirked, clearly humored by the press's fascination with her.

"The American press is so very cruel and harsh. There is only one lesson of importance that I learned early on and it has been my champion. In my experience, nothing should stand between you and your goal. Darling, you only live once, make it an adventure! It is when you realize this—you understand that the press's opinion is merely either a form of sport or political posturing, but always means to sell newspapers with one headline more salacious than the next whether true or not. But, of course, you are aware of this."

"That is true. We call them 'screamer' headlines. It would appear the press is your greatest foe, perhaps even using their words as a weapon. I assure you, Elena, that won't happen with me."

"I have no doubt, darling girl. Anyway…no matter how great your goal, whatever it is—independence, love, sex, money, power, or the mere frivolity of causing a scandal is all part of living. I don't let a few newspaper articles or public opinion ruin your mission! In my case, all these things came with pursuing the Crown Prince. Destined to meet, he was my heart's desire—and I was his since 1925. I learned quickly that sex is the most effective way for a woman—and a man— to achieve one's goal. I don't regret for a moment using my feminine wiles as his mistress because it led to great love. In the end, I was the victor over the lying, slanderous detractors who attempted to stand in

our way to an eternal Romania and our passionate love affair. It's been quite a fabulous whirlwind."

"What you're saying is that your husband at the time was a hindrance, as well as the then-Prince's wife, the beloved Crown Princess Helen?"

She laughed. "Beloved? I will give her that. The people are enamored by the Greek, yes, but dear girl, that frigid woman was never a threat. Well, maybe in the beginning when she would lock her husband in his chamber, but that was just merely an inconvenience, nothing an open window couldn't resolve! They divorced in 1928. As Carol explained she was frightened by the size of his manhood. She did not have the sexual appetite he craved. I alone could satisfy him. No, Helen was never a problem in keeping us apart, and we did not hide our affair d'amour from her! She was fully aware—I believe relieved!"

"Were there others who stood in your way?"

"Apart from the press? Of course. The list of our enemies is long, but to make a worthy statement, Carol proved his love for me by leaving Romania: me over our beloved country. Of course, he took my counsel and in a brilliant plan returned to Bucharest and his rightful place at the throne as king—I joined him several months later."

"Yet not as Queen. Surely, the Romanian monarchy could have approved a morganatic marriage for the King."

She shrugged. "We are married in our hearts. My lesson to you is one of great importance. I offer an example of how nothing should stand between you and your goal. Together, our great love, as partners in the future of Romania, could have accomplished many things, but in the end, Romania could not divide us, nor would it conform to his brilliant plan."

"This brings me to a question that Americans are eager to have answered. Was it your Jewish faith that caused you to go into exile?

Were you forced to run from the Nazis? Was that the real reason behind the king's second abdication in '40?"

"Darling, I'm a baptized Roman Catholic, and any claim my detractors have made about my being the daughter of a Jewish apothecary is merely to slander my reputation in a poorly conceived attempt to strip me of my Romanian citizenship! Lies for political gain. Do I look Jewish? In Bucharest, I was educated by Bavarian nuns!"

Again, she cackled.

"So you're telling me that your mother was not born an Austrian Jew who converted to Catholicism, and your father did not change his name from Wolff?

"Details. Lies, just lies."

In some measure, reflection on the odd conversation with the bold, self-centered woman had brought forth Evie's moxie. Not even fear should stand in her way of success, no matter the endeavor or the insecurity lying below the surface. Undaunted, she dabbed her lips with the napkin, refreshed her lipstick, and pulled back her shoulders before leaving more than enough money on the table for her bill. A happy wave of thanks caused the waiter to grin and wish for her return. On her way to the door, she stopped at a table where two women sat conversing in susurration. With an open, friendly demeanor, she interrupted them hoping not to scare them away. "Pardon me, ladies, perhaps you can help me?"

Neither spoke, they just looked to each other, then back up at her, waiting.

"Parlez-vous français? Sprechen Sie Deutsch? Você fala português?"

"Wir sind Deutsch," the older of the two warily said.

"Our friend—the waiter—thought you might be of assistance. Can either of you tell me if you have seen anyone in this photograph? This family is from Frankfurt am Main and I'm their sponsor to America. Unfortunately, I'm having a difficult time finding them and getting anxious that something may have happened."

Of the two women, the more senior lifted the photograph from the table but the younger nodded in caution, although ignored when her companion spoke in German. "At the Hebrew Hospital for free food, but I have not seen them for many weeks. This one—here—big mouth," she indicated with a point to Mr. Drucker's uncle Samuel, shook her head, then handed the photograph back to her. "He was not welcome there."

Her heart leapt...then sunk. *Not welcome?* "Where can I find the hospital?"

Shaking her head, the woman said, "It is in the Santó Antonio section, but the family is long gone."

"Thank you so much." She hesitated. "Is there anything else you can tell me? Even the smallest detail could be helpful."

"No."

"Do you recall, the little girl, perhaps?"

Again, the woman vehemently shook her head. The conversation was over and she would not hound them. Would giving them money be an insult or welcome? They were proud Germans, so she decided against it, leaving the café as soon as the women continued their conversation in a Germanic dialect she did not recognize.

The suspected communist sat in the same posture from when she had last seen him: nose in book, surrounded by newspapers; a lit cigarette rested in an ashtray to his left—looping ribbons of smoke rose from the embers.

"*Bonjour.* May I join you?" she greeted in French.

He glanced up then lowered his round eyeglasses to his nose, raising an eyebrow before warily opening his hand in invitation.

"*Merci beaucoup.* My name is Mrs. Richard Somerset," she said, taking the empty chair opposite him.

"What do you want, *Madam*?"

"I'm sorry to bother you, but I'm searching for someone. As a representative for their family in New York, I'm trying to arrange for their passage to the United States but, unfortunately, they seemed to have vanished from Lisbon and the American Embassy has no information. The waiter inside suggested you might recognize the family since you are here most days."

"It is a large community," he said curtly. "What is the name?"

"Drucker from Frankfurt am Main. The family of Samuel and his son Ezra. They arrived in Lisbon two months ago after living in the South of France. I have a photograph," she anxiously offered, nervously opening her purse.

"There is no need. I know the family." He raised the cigarette to his lips, dark eyes locked onto hers, his bushy brow furrowing. After blowing out a long stream of smoke he spoke. "I have not seen them since they went to live in Caldas da Rainha at the mandatory migrant camp. The old woman was ill and they were out of money to continue to stay in Lisbon. The PVDE and Jewish Distribution Committee moved them to housing." He shrugged. "Maybe for the best for Samuel's wife. There are therapeutic baths at the hospital there."

"Oh dear. Did you know the family well?"

"*Oui*. Both father and son..." He nodded. "It was good that Samuel left Lisbon. It was good he left my acquaintance."

"Because..."

"He draws too much attention, and I prefer solitude. His kind is different from my kind, but we are both not welcome in Portugal."

"Your kind? You mean Jewish?"

He chuckled wryly, shaking his head but did not answer.

"What is your name?" she asked.

"It is not important. I hope you can help Ezra. His wife is with child and he is a good man. Educated, unassuming. He is a peacemaker in these troubled times."

"I'll stay in Lisbon for as long as I need to find them, especially given what you have shared. Thank you. You've given me hope."

"There is little of that, but for what we have we are grateful. I am sorry, *Madam*, but I cannot tell you anything more. I think you will find answers in the north."

Hoping it would help this man's efforts to secure passage from Portugal, Evie removed a five-hundred escudo note from her purse and placed it under the ashtray. "I am very grateful."

"Be careful, Mrs. Somerset."

She smiled pensively, her mind already made up on visiting the Jewish Hospital and the docks before going back to the Palácio to arrange for a hired car to take her to this Caldas da Rainha. When she walked from the table, she thought she heard him say, "I hope you are not disappointed in what you find," but did not turn back.

FIFTEEN

Spring is Here Again

*S*ituated on the corner of a quiet intersection where the sidewalks and façade were tiled with cobalt blue, Moor-inspired mosaic, Livraria Lagos held the largest selection of books in the country, but by appearances, passersby would never know that. Evie had been apprised of its reputation by Lupescu, a great lover of not only Carol but also one of the written word. Will wonders never cease?

Evie couldn't resist stopping at the display windows before she hailed a taxi back to the Palácio. Rain was imminent, and her spectators pinched her feet given the amount of fruitless walking this morning. In her heart, she held onto the small fragment of promise both the old German woman and the French communist had offered. She tried not to feel disheartened, ignoring that intuitive sense of foreboding she'd had earlier when crossing the square, and vowed again not to return to New York without Mr. Drucker's family. It was just as she feared, the PVDE, in possible collaboration with the Germans, had transferred them to a "camp." What kind of camp? The kind that O'Shea had told her about? The kind that required the reported cattle cars? Oh goodness! She hated the thought and despised that her humanitarian effort was what made front-page screamers, not the Jewish plight. Tomorrow she would venture north to the refugee camp and continue the search.

Pushing the last warning from the Frenchman to the back of her mind, she focused on the positive: At least the interview with the Romanian had gone off without a hitch. Impossible as it was to get Lupescu to own to her Jewish heritage or remark on the widespread anti-Semitism in Romania she had read about, she still had a strong article. For that, she could hold her head high, having achieved her primary goal to independence.

The chilled wind blew, and she clutched the brim of her hat to keep it in place, then promptly entered the old bookshop. The door slammed behind her from the gale force. The dimly lit shop smelled like Richard's library, which had come by its scent from his grandfather's antiquities shipped from England. She delighted in the shop's rich wood paneling and the old world feel of the floor to ceiling ebony and dark rosewood book cases, some with glass doors to protect special editions. The arched entryways, accented by Florentine gilt carvings, led to each of the reading rooms reminding her of those within The Dakota. Small details showed the age—and care—that the bookshop had been cherished. She unbuttoned her sweater then removed her gloves as she noted the few browsing bibliophiles, mostly men, their manner of dress different than native Lisboetas; baggy trousers and well-worn shoes were indications that they were transient visitors from France or Germany. The one thing she had learned today was the Portuguese, when in town, were dapper dressers, and their fashion style more tailored than other European countries.

She cleared her throat and the shop girl looked up from her task. The girl's face alighted in joy when she greeted, *"Boa tarde."*

"Hello. *Você fala inglês?*"

"Yes."

"I was wondering if you have any poetry books? Perhaps Portuguese romanticism?"

"Of course!" she said, her voice rising in punctuated enthusiasm as though she had waited all day to be asked that question.

"Portugal has many poets, but unfortunately we do not have any books in English, Senhora."

"That's fine."

"Splendid! I normally recommend the father of Portuguese romanticism Almeida Garrett, but, for you, I suggest the modernist Florbela Espanca, a favorite poetess of mine—tortured words, yet beautiful; sonnets filled with yearning."

Suddenly the young woman broke out in recitation in her native tongue, her enunciation of a poem so impassioned upon each word spoken Evie didn't even attempt to translate—just allowed herself to get lost in the evocative romance language. The verse sounded daringly erotic, enrapturing; the recitation almost took Evie's breath away.

The shop girl pinched her fingers together, enunciating, surprisingly well, the translation with the same intensity. "In English, it means: 'There is one Spring in each life: You *must* sing it like Spring, floridly. For if God gave us voice, it was to sing!' This is from volume *Charneca em Flor*, Senhora Espanca's greatest works published after her death. These are the sonnets for you. Come. I show you."

Trailing behind the girl, Evie glanced into each book-filled room they passed until they stopped at the threshold of a tiny alcove at the back of the quiet shop. It could barely fit two people at the same time. A window looked out onto the cobblestone street where a trolley passed by the café at the street corner. No doubt, on a sunny day, this space with its arched stained glass above the window was breathtaking—a tribute to the books within.

"This is our poetry section," the girl said before entering. "It is small, but we do not get many patrons in search of Senhora Espanca or Almeida Garrett." She removed a book from the wooden stack then handed it to her. "*Charneca em Flor*. I hope you will enjoy—it invites the reader to let go of all inhibition. That is a must to understand her work. One must have an open heart and mind, and when you do…well, you will see."

And just like that the girl bowed her head with a shy smile, all enthusiasm gone when she went about her business leaving Evie with her thoughts and consolation and a book written in a language she was just beginning to understand.

After placing her purse and gloves on the step stool, she opened the volume to a random page, allowing the book its providence to direct her. The poem was titled *Amar* or *To Love* and Evie stilled, her mind taking the time to process and translate, as she read in a whisper the second verse: "To remember? To forget? Makes no difference, To hold on or let go? Neither bad nor good, But to say you can love one your entire life, is a lie."

"That's a lovely hat you're wearing, Red."

She jumped at the unmistakable voice and slammed the book shut as if caught in forbidden salacious reading.

"Oh! Carl. Thank you."

His smile lit his eyes. Gosh, he looked so debonair in the brown double-breasted suit he wore, his fedora tipped just right. He stood only a foot from her within the tight alcove.

"How are ya?" he asked with a slight nervous tremble to his voice. She, too, felt a bit discombobulated by his appearance as if on command of the stanza she had just read aloud.

"I'm fine. And you?"

"Couldn't be better. You called me Carl. That's a good start."

"You...you asked me to."

"Axsin' doesn't necessarily mean you'll do me the honor." Examining her face, he smiled endearingly, nodding. "It sure is good to see you, Evie. What brings ya to this part of town?"

She lied, touching the hair at the nape of her neck. "Books!"

"Yeah. I'm a sucker for a good mystery. Have you been up here from the beaches all day—just for a few books—in the rain?"

"Um...no. I just arrived. I've been told of the book shop's reputation." His inquiry into her daily routine made her uneasy. Her visit to the café and its surroundings were none of his affair so she didn't expound on the details of her visit.

"You didn't say, but where in Lisbon is the orchestra playing?" she asked, redirecting the polite, but too inquisitive, small talk.

"Dutch got us a real good gig at the Metrópole. Funny how, when away from the Reich's watchful eye, those Jerries don't mind listening to some verboten boogie woogie."

"The *Jerries*? Have you turned British since your arrival?" she teased, familiar with the British slang for the Germans, thanks to her father-in-law's distaste for them.

"Nah. It's just a nickname. Lisbon's crummy with Brits."

"Crummy with Poles, too," she said, still unable to dismiss the image of him and his lover under the deck stairs, she couldn't help being peevish. "Tell me, how is your friend Mrs. Olszak?"

"I haven't seen her since we docked. Why? Are ya jealous?"

"Not in the least. That would imply a romantic interest, which, as you know, there is none."

"Hmm. So you keep insistin'…How was your interview with the *infamous* Elena Lupescu? Were you at least interested in her secrets on how to steal a fella's heart?" he teased with a grin.

She playfully smiled because—in truth—his smile was infectious even if his transparent question showed his renewed intentions, and yes, Lupescu did share—a bit too much—about her love affair. "Some. She's a master at deflection and quite the narcissist, but I have enough information for a substantial article. I had been misinformed about several things, so I will be setting the record straight."

"Good for you. I'm looking forward to reading it on the front page of the *Spectator*!"

"Me, too. I dare say, much of what she shared isn't fit to print—unless it's in a tawdry dime store novel."

"Did you at least write them down for future reference?"

"No! Of course not!"

He tilted his head, examining the book spines. "Pity. What does the royal mistress recommend to encourage affection?"

As he continued to read the shelved books, she looked down at the top of his hat, honestly replying, "Like you, she believes that fate requires little work, but when one's romantic aspirations meet obstacles then you should do all you can. *I*, on the other hand, suggest that *patience*—and perhaps a few lovely sonnets—encourage affection." Darn, now she was the one unable to hide her responsiveness to his presence.

The deep chuckle she enjoyed—and had missed—rumbled from his chest. "The food of love," he remarked.

Had he read Austen as well? The man was turning out to be full of surprises. An awkward silence and heavy tension settled between them, feeling odd—strained—unlike their previous conversations, which had been spoken with candor and ease aboard the *Serpa*. Her heart hadn't stopped its steady, rapid cadence from minutes before. In fact, his intimate proximity made it beat faster. The warmth of a rosy flush on her cheeks increased, particularly when he glanced up, his sight holding hers fast as they searched for something. Evie felt her veneer slipping; she was regrettably succumbing to his undeniable charm and handsome looks, ignoring that little voice in her demanding answers to his evasiveness on so many issues.

"What are you reading? Another nautical novel?"

"Ha. Ha. You're quite the comedian, Carl. I'll have you know it's a poetry book."

He removed the small volume from her grasp, then examined the cover. "Do you understand Portuguese?"

"I've been teaching myself since departing Philadelphia."

"I'm impressed. Will you read something to me?"

"I...um...no, I don't think so."

Carl's eyes pled; his lips quirked. "Please." Opening the book, he pointed to a page, then handed it out to her. "Translate *this* verse for me."

She looked down at his neatly manicured index finger and the stanza in question, her mind translating the words with ease. *Oh no. No.* She swallowed hard—the heat on her cheeks no doubt burned brightly in mortification. "I can't."

Again, he removed the book from her hand; he was so close to her she thought she'd faint from his nearness, but she was a true goner when he recited the poem in perfect Portuguese. Spellbound by his mouth, she imagined the rolling of his tongue as it spoke the words with masterful pronunciation in a paced rhythm meant only for seduction.

He glanced up to her seeking a response, and then he read the stanza again, this time in English: "My body trembles seeking yours, my hands are hot on your skin smelling of amber, vanilla, and honey, my crazed arms long to embrace you."

His honeyed tone washed over her. Like his clarinet song, he delivered the verse with unbridled ardor, making love to her.

Carl closed the book, unwavering in his fixed gaze. The silence and air between them pulsed with electricity. She bit her lip at how his pupils dilated and his lips parted. He felt it, too.

"Have dinner with me tomorrow night, Evie," he said, inching closer to her as he handed the book back to her. Their hands touched under the volume during the exchange.

"I cannot. I have a previous engagement and even if I didn't, I just don't think—"

His impetuous kiss silenced her objection. A delectable soft pucker caressed her, shattering any remaining defiance she had into a million tiny fragments. He captured her upper lip, drawing it into his mouth, consuming it as the heat between them grew. Her flushed body betrayed her when her hand, of its own volition, slid up his firm bicep. *Oh goodness!* This kiss…made her fly. The intensity of their mouths increased and he swept her up into a tight hold around her waist, pulling her against him.

Again, her body betrayed her, unable to hold back an audible purr. Her womanhood fluttered like a cocooned butterfly awoken for its first flight. She didn't want this kiss to end.

Regretfully, he withdrew from her, breathlessly whispering, "I'll pick you up at seven."

She nodded, the craving she had for him and that erotic interlude overwhelmed all sense and sensibility.

Carl turned, tipped his hat, then quit the room.

The book slid to the floor from her left hand as the right went to her lips in wonderment. What had she done? What had she agreed to? She could no longer deny the attraction. Carl Wilson's kiss was like *none* she had ever received. And she wanted more.

Twenty minutes later, completely shaken, she approached the sales clerk at the cash register and tried to smile when she nudged *Charneca em Flor* across the counter. "Thank you ever so much for the suggestion. I would like to purchase the book."

"It has already been paid for, Senhora. A gift from the handsome gentleman." The shop girl wrapped the book in brown paper then tied it with cord. "And he left this for you," she added, handing Evie an envelope.

"*Muito obrigada.*"

"It is no problem. Come back to see us again. Perhaps you will read from Luis de Camoens on your next visit."

Evie exited the shop in the rain and stood at the threshold of the door, quickly raising her arm to the passing taxicab. Once on her way back to the hotel, she settled against the hard seat, watching the rain stream against the windows. The morning of searching for the family—and the small glimmer of hope she'd had in that endeavor—had been surreptitiously replaced. All she could think about was the tingle on her lips and the way her body responded. She wasn't a married woman any longer.

She opened Carl's note:

Some lovely sonnets to help you learn the sweet, mysterious language of love. -Carl.

SIXTEEN
Moonlight Cocktail

March 10

*C*arl paced the lobby of the swanky Palácio as the concierge watched his attempt at wearing out the marble flooring. The hoped-for dinner with Evie was about to happen. Comingled with his apprehension at being duped by her true reasons for being in Lisbon, he also couldn't fight his attraction to her, feeling as if he had a schoolboy crush, because truly, that kiss they had shared yesterday afternoon felt like the first one he'd ever had. And she hadn't slapped him for being such a worm. Further, reading *Amar* to her was the most erotic moment he'd experienced—and he'd had several "experiences" in his day after leaving Pittsburgh.

But romance wasn't his game tonight. What he needed from her were answers—specifically why she was meeting with Wegener. She had been up to no good. Both he and the secret police were certain of that—and her lie in the book shop proved she was covering something up. Was she on another scoop for the *Spectator*, or was she truly involved in espionage? The woman had a talent for obfuscation. Hell, from the start of their acquaintance, she had kept him guessing and still tied in knots. *Perhaps this is all orchestrated. Perhaps she's a honey trap and I'm not on my game— caught off guard and hoodwinked. What is your gut telling you?*

"Senhor would you like for me to have the bartender bring a cocktail while you wait? We have the best martinis in Estoril," the clerk stated in English, his mouth twisting in a knowing grin. Carl didn't mean to be so transparent.

"No, thanks. She shouldn't be long, right?"

The man glanced down at the oversized, colorful basket in the center of the floor. "You may miss the sunset, but the stars are not going home for many hours."

Carl chuckled then finally took a seat. "When you're right, you're right. I have all the time in the world, and Mrs. Somerset is worth the wait."

"Sim, Senhor."

He heard the elevator gate slide open and he promptly stood at attention, righting his suit jacket.

Her sandals tapped the marble, growing louder as she neared him.

Then she turned the corner.

His heart stopped.

Evie's radiant elegance filled the lobby when she sashayed toward him with a timid smile. Long, tan gloves encased her arms and nothing encased her long legs. The black and beige halter dress she wore and her swept-up tresses bared her shoulders, causing a physical reaction in him. In that unchecked instant, he reminded himself that his objective was not to seduce her, contrary to Musgrove's suggestion. His purpose was to spend a lovely evening with the mysterious enchantress whom he hadn't stopped speculating about—and, of course, he planned on getting her to confess what she had been doing in Rossio Square the day before.

"Hello, Carl," she greeted, the timbre of her voice sounded so seductive that he wondered if *she* had romantic intentions, but then she blushed—a sure sign of her romantic reticence.

"You look lovely, Red."

"I hope I'm dressed appropriately. You didn't say where we would be dining."

Grinning, he walked to her. "It's a surprise, and you look *perfect*. Are you hungry?"

"Famished."

Yeah. He was hungry, too. Wolfishly hungry. Unfortunately, she had that power over him and he kept falling for her ambush.

He grasped the picnic basket's handle with one hand, then guided her toward the exit with the other, his palm lightly touching the center of her back.

"Well, now you have me curious. What a darling hamper," she effused.

But he did not reply; for the second time in several minutes his heart stopped when a familiar face came through the door.

"Senhora Somerset!" The spy Purvis greeted in English, his thin mustache lifting in the devilish sneer Carl had come to know these last two and a half months of surveillance.

He felt Evie's back stiffen as his.

"Mr. Purvis, what a surprise," she said with a polite smile, the tone in her voice stiff, so unlike when she greeted Carl.

Purvis looked to him, examining him curiously, and Carl knew then that his cover in Dutch's band both aboard the *Serpa* and now playing at the Metrópole could be blown. For the moment, he would count on the fact that being out from behind the clarinet would afford him anonymity. Most amateurs, like this low-class Lisboeta, foolishly dabbling in espionage had difficulty in connecting faces with names and locations. A lowly clarinetist in a swing band wouldn't be stepping out with such a ritzy woman as Evie.

"Senhor, we have met before, no?" he asked, tilting his head. "You look familiar."

Just as he was about to answer, Evie blurted, "I'm sure you have not met my husband, Mr. Purvis. If you recall he did not leave our stateroom aboard the *Serpa Pinto*. Perhaps you recognize him at boarding in Philadelphia."

Although shocked, Carl did not react, but quickly remembered his deck-side discussion with Evie about her "seasick" husband. Clearly, his earlier warning and her woman's intuition felt it necessary to introduce him as Mr. Somerset. He couldn't help himself; he smiled at the delectable thought of being her husband and played along with whatever game she had in mind. She was inadvertently giving him concealment and proving to him more and more that she was not involved in Purvis's machinations.

"Darling, this is the kind gentleman aboard the ship whom I told you about. Mr. John Da Silva Purvis."

Not that he should be surprised, given Evie's artful charm, which possibly was another performance aboard the *Serpa Pinto* the night she joined Purvis's party in the ballroom. But she was exceptional tonight, just sliding right into the role of his lover without even a change of expression. In fact, she even tucked her arm into the crook of his and leaned into him, cooing. Well-bred dames weren't likely to perform *any* public displays of affection, yet her body language was in complete harmony with her words. She was entirely believable.

With a tightened aristocratic jaw, like the one he had teased Evie with, Carl addressed the spy, "Ah, yes, a pleasure to meet you. Thank you for your kindness to my new bride in my unfortunate absence."

The Lisboeta's smile grew, his eyes widening in delight and he brazenly spoke in German, further sinking himself in the British Intelligence officer's opinion. "Herr Somerset! It is an honor to finally meet you. *Gnädige Frau* Somerset is a skilled dancer, and her company delightful, but I am most pleased to see you feeling better."

Purvis held out his hand for a shake, and Carl cringed inwardly when their flesh met, but made polite conversation also in German, putting on his best airs. "Evelyn informs me you make the transatlantic trip to Lisbon frequently. How ever do you do it?"

"Herr Purvis is in shipping," Evie interjected in perfect German. The realization she understood and conversed in the language set warning bells off in Carl.

"One grows accustomed to the sea," Purvis flippantly said before examining them both with a head tilt and a slight furrow to his brow. "It is truly fortuitous that I should find you staying here at the Palácio before my dinner meeting with a friend. I had inquired after you at The Hotel Inglaterra, but it is curious, they did not have a reservation for Somerset."

"Yes, we changed accommodations upon our arrival. The Palácio is more to our expectations, so much more…romantic for a honeymoon. You understand," Carl stated.

"But of course. It is the finest in Cascais. There is none more suited for a new bride, a palace for your queen."

"You said you are meeting someone? Here? Tonight?" Evie inquired, which further piqued Carl's curiosity and renewed suspicion of her.

"Yes! The lovely Irena Olszak and her husband."

"How delightful. Will you—"

"Please, excuse us, but we are late for an important appointment." Carl interrupted. This time, he intimately placed his hand on the small of Evie's back, trying to guide her past Purvis and her questions regarding Irena, but the man obstructed their departure with a step to his left.

"An appointment with a reed basket?"

Carl smiled. "The setting sun—like time—waits for no man, and there is romance in the air, my good friend," he said with a wink. "You would not keep me from impressing my wife, would you?"

"No. No. The sunsets at Tamariz Beach are the finest in Portugal." Purvis stared him down, narrowing his eyes. "There is…something about your eyes…very familiar."

"I guess I just have one of those common faces." He looked to Evie. "Well, shall we my dear?"

She nodded.

"Please excuse us, Herr Purvis. It was quite nice to make your acquaintance."

"Tell me, Herr Somerset do you speculate on foreign affairs?"

Carl laughed. "Not if I can help it."

"But perhaps, you will indulge me later at the English Bar for drinks. I have a lucrative business opportunity that I would like to discuss with you before I return to America."

He slid his hand protectively into his "new wife's." Irena and Stephan Olszak had Operation Night Shift now and he had wolfram—and Evie—to concentrate on. Unfortunately, after witnessing her meeting yesterday, he considered that wolfram and Mrs. Evelyn Somerset may be *one* mission not two. "We must decline. I promised that I would not discuss finance while on honeymoon, but we are much obliged."

"You are a lucky man, Herr Somerset."

He looked to Evie and the delightful, teasing smile playing on her lips. "I am the luckiest of men. There is no other woman like Frau Somerset." And with that he gently led her to the door.

"Good evening, Herr Purvis," she giggled, a sound Carl had yet to hear from her.

"Don't look back," he said.

"Why ever not?"

"Because he's smarter than you think. It'll come to him where he saw me. I'm afraid my scar will give me away. I shouldn't have been so foolish. Dagnabbit."

"He won't. You were quite convincing as a Metropolitan Club member. Why, every word you spoke was right out of the *American Dictionary of the English Language*, not a 'nunya' in sight!"

Even in her levity he could still feel the disconcerting burn of Purvis's eyes on them and abruptly stopped in front of the hotel windows. Turning to face Evie, he set the hamper down. "You might not like this out in the open, but I have to do it."

"Do what?"

"This."

He kissed her full-on despite propriety, but Purvis was just the sort of man who would expect it from newlyweds and relish it like a voyeur.

What surprised him most was Evie's willing response when she kissed him back. Her lips moved slowly below his in the sweetest torment. Tender, moist and eager, her mouth made his temperature rise and he wrapped his arm around her bare shoulders, pulling her closer. Her soft skin below his palm set him aflame, but he reluctantly ended the kiss, lest he embarrass her further.

"Red is perfect for you," she cooed breathlessly, their faces so close to each other.

"I agree. You are."

"I meant my lipstick. You wear it well."

"Like a badge of honor."

"Do you think he's still watching us?" she asked.

"I don't know, but I sure wanna kiss you again, Evie." His heart hammered.

"This embrace is only an act, Carl. Nothing more than my determination to keep Purvis far from me."

"Then what was yesterday's kiss? Ya did respond, and I didn't see him in the book shop."

She took a deep breath, her eyes locked onto his. "It was ...confusing."

He let go of her and shook his head, sobering. "Gee, I'm sorry. Yesterday was ungentlemanly of me, and confusing you wasn't my intent. Like a jerk, I acted on impulse." He sniggered. "But ya have to admit the spark between us is more electrified than ever."

"I know no such thing, nevertheless your apology is not necessary. I would be lying if I said that I didn't enjoy your kiss, both then and now. I *want* to be here with you tonight despite my confusion. So, let's go and have a good time."

"I'd like that." He wiped his mouth on his handkerchief and glanced over his shoulder, making sure that Purvis had left the hotel lobby. "I hope that's the last we see of him before he goes back to the States in a couple of days."

"How do you know when he is returning?"

"I don't…I'm just assuming given his eagerness and that's when the next ship leaves for the United States." With a bit of luck, she wouldn't press him on that slip of the tongue. "Let's hope for both our sakes, he doesn't show up at the Metrópole to visit with some of his friends." He glanced at her sideways, questioning to himself who she really was. "The place is infiltrated by the worst German riff-raff, and he's too eager to rope people into his nefarious game."

Once again, he slid his hand into her gloved one and led her along the path, which trailed to the back of the hotel. "Anyway, enough about him. I'm just glad ya took my advice to keep away from the thug."

"I did. Thank you for the warning. Now, did I understand you correctly? You're taking me on a picnic to watch the sunset?"

"I sure am."

"Well, Carl, you certainly surprise a girl."

"I try."

"I think it comes naturally to you. Thank you for the book."

"Sure. Maybe one day *you'll* read to *me* a few sonnets." He couldn't help the intonation in his voice and she did not answer, only laughed.

The salty scent of the sea mixed with sweet jasmine in a heavenly aroma as they walked through the garden. In the distance, the secluded place below two palm trees he'd chosen for their picnic was thankfully vacant and quite picturesque backdropped by the vibrant orange of the setting sun. Painted in wisps of watercolored shades of ginger and charcoal, the sky gave the water a mysterious charm as it ebbed and flowed, breaking on the shoreline.

Evie suddenly stopped when they reached the beach and rested her hand on his bicep to support her. It took him aback when she slipped her sandals from her feet and dug her toes in the sand.

"Oh, that feels simply marvelous. I haven't been to the seashore in ages. Richard and I never…I'm sorry."

"Don't be…It's good that you remember your husband so fondly." *Although, I wish I could make you forget him.*

She dangled the shoes from her clasped fingers as they walked silently toward the palm trees.

"You should take off your shoes, Carl. You won't be disappointed," she announced, her voice filled with mirth. It fascinated him how her demeanor had changed on a dime, her whole countenance light, Purvis—and her sophisticated airs— seemed a distant memory. Perhaps he'd be lucky enough if the ghost of Richard Somerset was forgotten, too. No matter her suspect game of un-American activities, it was clear that her dead husband's invisible death grip remained on the dormant blithe spirit hidden below her sophisticated control.

"When was the last time you went to the beach, Evie?"

"We have a villa in Palm Beach and another on Martha's Vineyard. But I haven't felt the sand between my toes in I don't know how long—probably Vassar, on a weekend trip to Orchard Beach, but I didn't swim."

"Why not?"

"I'm afraid of the water, have been since I was a child."

"You don't know *how* to swim?"

"I do, but I haven't in many years. How about you? I suppose you didn't have opportunity for the beach in Pittsburgh."

"You're right. We did have a few lakes in Butler County, though. I looked for any opportunity I could to get out of the big city, but I didn't see a real beach until about…'41." *When I was recuperating in Brighton.*

Stopping below the trees, he removed a tightly rolled blanket from the hamper and with a snap to his wrists it floated in the air, finally settling down between the two palms.

"Here?" she asked with a hint of haughtiness.

"Whatya think, I'd have a couple of beach chairs hiding for us somewhere?"

"No....um, of course not. There are no cabana boys at this hour." She sat on the blanket, bending her legs beside her.

Spellbound by the image she presented, he stood over her admiring the seductive action of peeling the long gloves down her arms. Slow...measured...and when finally removed, she wiggled her elegant fingers; her wedding band mocked him as she smoothed her hands over the blanket. That little action ...wowza!

Evie leaned back on one hand and glanced over a bare shoulder at him. A knowing—and maybe even self-satisfied—smile played on her lips. "Aren't you joining me, Carl?"

"Of course. Am I not your husband for the night?" Gladly obeying her gentle command, he unbuttoned his jacket then sat beside her. If she kept up these subtle overtures, he wasn't so sure he could remain a gentleman.

Digging into the hamper, he removed a bottle of Muscatel de Setubal and a cork puller. "I hope you like red wine."

"I try not to imbibe, but thank you."

Dagnabbit! A little intoxicant would woo a confession out of her.

She looked out to the ocean and then up to the still dusky evening sky, sighing. A few stars twinkled. "Not a cloud in the sky. It truly is an exquisite night for a picnic."

"Sure is; the company is lovelier though," he said unwrapping the cheese and rustic bread, laying them out on the blanket with several small dishes of *acepipes*.

"Escargot, octopus...and what's this made of?" she asked.

"Looks like what you high-society types call pâté...it's sardine, a staple around here."

"I'm impressed!"

"Don't be. The maître'd at the Metrópole chose the menu," he said handing her a two-pronged fork for the snails. "I picked the wine, and you can see where that got me."

"Oh! I'm sorry but, unfortunately, alcohol goes to my head too quickly—and I have a feeling I'll need all my faculties around you this evening."

Smart girl.

"Evie, I promise you, there will be no passes made tonight. Scouts honor." *Damn!*

"There you go again with that Boy Scout mumbo jumbo. Hmm, we'll see just what a good scout you really are."

"I didn't say I was impervious to your charisma, just under good regulation is all."

As they enjoyed the assortment of food, they sat in silence gazing out at the sea and back at each other several times. She seemed to mull over his promise to not get fresh. Could it be that the kiss in front of the hotel had sparked something in her?

As she dug into a snail she asked, "Carl, tell me—where did you learn to speak such fluent Portuguese and German? I must admit, you took me off guard. Are you a polyglot or merely trilingual?"

"A what?"

"A multi-linguistic, proficient in speaking at least five languages. I am awed because I assumed Pittsburgh wouldn't be particularly—"

"In other words, you wouldn't expect the son of a steel-working family to speak a few languages?"

"No! Please, don't misunderstand me. I'm giving you a compliment."

"Well good, because my *Portuguese* mother—living in The Smokey City—would be surprised to hear that her son is a dope. I was a teacher at one time, you know."

"You are no dope, I am sure. Your *Plattdeutsch* is quite expert."

"I credit private secondary school for that. Music and language always came easily to me, but I only speak three."

"It is the same for me. They are quite simple to master when you factor in the similarity of each, such as Spanish and Italian. I assume Russian will be a taxing endeavor when I decide to explore the language. One day, Cantonese."

"Yeah, I'm working on learning Russian. It isn't easy, but ya never know where Dutch's orchestra will take us after the war now that we're all chummy with those Bolshies."

"Exactly my thinking. I would love to visit Moscow one day."

"And where did *you* learn to speak German so fluently?"

"Ah, well, my Austrian governess taught me Bairisch. She was quite strict on my tutelage from the time I could speak and immensely proud of her Bavarian ancestral roots having emigrated from Salzburg. It is, by far, my favorite language. Later, I learned Plattdeutsch and Hochdeutsch in college."

He disregarded her refusal of the wine and filled two short glasses anyway, hoping she'd change her mind as she grew more comfortable. Although he felt bad about the ruse, he needed to loosen those hoity-toity inhibitions keeping her secrets in check.

Pointing out with her fork to two ships on the horizon, Evie attempted to converse in Portuguese, which took him aback.

He smiled through her minor mistakes, but did not correct her or tease her. She was remarkably good considering she'd only begun her lessons ten days ago. "Yuh-huh. Those pesky German ships are communicating with each other as they survey the coast," he said in English. "If you ask me, Salazar should just blow them to smithereens."

"What are they saying?"

"Well as best as my eagle-eye can see…using its signal lamp, the one on the right has just said, 'Get a load of the gorgeous, red-headed Fräulein seated between the palm trees on Tamariz Beach.' "

Evie laughed. "And what is the other replying?"

He squinted. "I think the blinker just flashed: *Jawohl*! She's…with the…best licorice stick player…in Portugal. Go to Metrópole for a swell show.' "

"Gee, those Jerries sure know music. I agree! You are the best I have ever heard."

"That's swell of you to say. You should hear the applause the band gets, especially when we play 'Minnie the Moocher.' They sing along with all their Nazi propaganda lyrics, getting a real big kick out of it. You'd think those Gestapo thugs were a bunch of *Swing heinis*."

"Hmm, I not familiar with that term."

"No?" *Until recently some were the best informants the SIS had, but I won't tell you that.* "Let's just say they're a group of smart—defiant—German kids obsessed with the Brits, the silver screen, and swing music. In their way, they're a clandestine resistance to the Third Reich and anyone else for that matter. As such, Hitler branded the *Swingjugend* dangerous."

"Fascinating. How do you know so much about Nazism?"

"I listen, and like I said, I meet a lot of people in my work. Doesn't the senator tell you about what's going on over in Europe?"

"No, he doesn't. After Richard departed for the Pacific, I tried to stay abreast of all the war news. I read everything I could get my hands on. When he died…everything changed but I did learn quite a bit from the boys on the foreign desk at the paper to prepare for my trip."

"I understand. There was a time when I wanted nothing to do with the war, too. Things happen that change our perspective."

"Hmm…my perspective. Both Albert *and* my mother's perspective is that I should pass my days at the Colony Club, uninformed and sheltered now that Richard is gone." Her gaze drifted to the sea and she added, "Oh, the control she has wielded for far too long."

"Your mother?"

"Yes. But this…here…in Portugal is far from her power and influence. It's the most *exciting* time I have ever experienced even with the war on. Maybe it's so exciting *because* there is a war on."

She shook her head in wonderment. "I learned to play poker from Elena Lupescu! If Mother had any idea…it's so unrefined for Polite Society!"

Evie drank from her goblet redirecting her conflicted conscience and defiance. Evidently, she was torn between duty and obligation versus self-reliance and thrill seeking. Perhaps her husband's death brought about this self-awareness.

"And was their shared opinion the reason you 'needed to get out of New York?' "

"Yes. If I am to be truthful with myself, it was also to prove that I am something more than what I was raised to be. And now that Richard is gone, I want to be a bona fide reporter, and my editor gave me an opportunity to pursue my ambitions. Ambitions that my society wouldn't wholly approve. In fact, I met a woman aboard the ship who dished out a heavy dose of snobbish condemnation when I shared the purpose for my journey. Her reply was that 'Ladies are not newspaper reporters.' "

"Hogwash. You can be anything, Evie, no matter the obstruction. Heck, you've already interviewed Lupescu. That's quite an accomplishment."

"True and as shocking as parts of her interview were, I did find inspiration and rediscovered my fearless nature. She spoke of maintaining confidence to achieve one's goals, no matter the obstacles."

"She's right. Look at me. I'm living proof of overcoming the odds—a multilingual boy from Pixsburgh, sitting under the stars with the most exciting woman I have ever met. Who'd-a thought it? Certainly, not those Yinzers back home who expected me to teach music surrounded by soot and steel."

Snorting in an unladylike manner she laughed, "Most exciting? Hardly that!" She drank again from the wine goblet.

"Look at you—here all alone at this dangerous time with scoundrels all around you. I'd say that you're a remarkable woman."

Under the palm tree canopy, their conversation felt natural, and it was good to see Evie relax, put away that Park Avenue veneer, and come off her lofty perch. Every minute they spent together convinced him she was true blue, but he needed confirmation. He needed to search her eyes and see for himself that she wasn't wrapped up in cahoots with the Germans like everyone else in Lisbon.

He, too, drank more wine then leaned back on an elbow, stretching his legs out on the blanket.

She gazed down at him then touched his eyebrow, brushing her fingers over the jagged mark. "Tell me about your scar."

"I thought you said it was improper to ask such things."

"You're right, I did. But tonight...I don't know...I feel a bit rebellious and you did say I'm strong-minded. I must admit, you have me curious. Was it a boyhood accident or a scorned lover?"

Evie's lips quirked into a saucy smile and he searched her expression. What harm could there be about telling the truth about that part of his life? He'd lied to her about other things already, but foolishly told her where he'd grown up.

"I wish I could lay claim to either, but—if you *must* know— before America entered the war, I was a pilot for several months with the RAF in one of their Eagle Squadrons."

"What is an Eagle Squadron?"

"Well, a couple hundred of us fellas back home were recruited outta the Air Corps by an Army Colonel to help the Brits fight off the Germans. England was getting bombed to kingdom come, and we volunteered for an outfit to fly escort sorties in fighter sweeps."

"I had no idea America helped the British beyond sending care bundles and military supplies."

He laughed wryly. "Not something you would read in the papers, but 'America'...didn't want us to help. Ask your brother. He'll tell ya. In '39 we declared neutrality. So, enlisting to help any belligerent in the war was illegal. But we didn't care...we went anyway. A whole squadron of fellas snuck into Canada to do so. Heck, the FBI are probably still lookin' for us."

"But…then we were in the war."

"Yeah, most of us wanted to come home to fight for revenge for Pearl Harbor, but the Brits wouldn't let us."

"How dreadful and how noble of you!"

"Oh, I don't know about noble for going in the first place. I wanted to fly, to see the world, and be an ace. I suppose I got what was coming to me for being such a cowboy up there, but those Jerries sure did deserve it, and I tell ya those fellas with the RAF sure needed us."

"What happened?"

"On a mission, my Hurricane got shot up during a dogfight. Both the plane and I were barely hanging on as we headed back, but I made it to Martlesham Heath in one piece—crash landed in flames—recuperated, and here I am a little worse for the wear with a few ugly scars that make beautiful women cringe."

"Irena Olszak wasn't cringing and *I'm* certainly not either. I find it…mysterious and…."

She took another gulp of wine.

"And?"

"Attractive."

"Be careful, Evie. That sounded like a second compliment. I might get in too deep from all this unexpected flattery." *Yes, damn if it hasn't already happened. In fact, I'm in over my head now even if she's toying with me.*

"Point noted. I'll have to try harder to dissuade you of any romantic notions you may be courting."

"If there's one thing you'll learn about me, Evie, it's that I'm a romantic fella—no getting around it, most musicians are, but you have my word—I won't get fresh again."

She stared at the piece of bread in her hand as if contemplating the sardine pâté, then crinkled her nose before stating, "I'm sorry about your injuries."

"It's nothing compared to what others have sacrificed." As much as he didn't want to bring her husband back into the conversation that remark was about him.

She must have been tipsy because not only did she call him attractive, but she also did not comment on Richard, instead she bit into the manna then spoke with a full mouth. "Mmm...sardines aren't half bad. Do you still fly planes?"

It gutted him to reply with a carefree, "Nope. Enough about me. It's my turn to ask a question."

"To coin your words, I may choose not to answer."

"But, I'd be grateful if you did."

She grinned. "How can I deny your request after this lovely moonlit picnic, not to mention saving me from Purvis? You have earned my complete honesty. I'm an open book, Carl. Ask away."

"Open book, you say? All right then. I saw you yesterday morning in Rossio Square, yet when I asked you about it in the livraria, you lied, said you only just arrived in town. And that got me thinkin' that something smells a little fishy with your story. You'd already wrapped up your interview with Lupescu."

Her face drained of all color and she shivered, which elicited an immediate response from him. He removed his jacket then draped it over her shoulders before continuing his questioning.

"After your cigarette beside the fountain, you walked on over to Café Chave d'Ouro and had a coffee. Afterwards, you were asking strangers a lot of questions. What are you up to? Is there another reason you're in Lisbon?"

"Carl Wilson! How long were you spying on me?"

"Not spying, just watching, and it was only for a minute or two," he lied. "I stepped out my hotel and there you were across the street waiting to meet with someone. Besides, as I recall, *you* once spied on *me*."

She shrugged. "Meet with someone? I talked to no one other than the police officer."

"That's not entirely truthful. You were having a smoke—the secret police stopped, talked with you then went his way with a puss on his face. For a few minutes, you stared out at the plaza and then another fella approached you."

"I am being truthful. I honestly don't recall speaking to another." She folded her arms across her chest attempting to block out his questions.

"Evie, I saw you conversing with another man—an officer in the *Wehrmacht's Sicherung*—a German."

Her chin dropped, and then something flashed in her eyes. "You're right! I am so sorry. Now I recall, someone asked me for a light to his cigarette. Goodness! He did have a heavy German accent. We spoke about the weather and how it felt like rain, which prompted his offer of his umbrella, but I politely declined. Then he invited me for a cup of coffee at the café. His name, I think was Otto, Hmm…his surname…Wegener! I didn't know him, believe me, please!"

The tone of her panicked voice and the clarity of her green eyes led him to believe she had not known the man previously. "That's the fellow. Did you introduce yourself?"

She pulled her shoulders back and unfolded her arms. "I did, but you'll be pleased to know that I took your advice. From the start of my day, I had a strong premonition, a sense of foreboding. My instinct directed me to fib."

"And?"

"I told him, and the policeman, that my name was Eva von Lamberg from Salzburg. After I turned down his invitation for coffee, he left me alone to finish my cigarette."

"That was before you walked over to the café. Did he put you up to that so you could meet with the two Gestapo brutes who exited shortly after your arrival?"

"What? No! Carl, I take offense at this line of questioning. Who I have spoken to is *none* of your affair."

"In Lisbon, you *are* my affair. I've cautioned you several times. Lisbon isn't what you think it is. No one here is on holiday. No one. Not you, not me, not Purvis, and certainly not Wegener, and in case ya haven't noticed—I care. Whether I should or not is another issue, but when ya start mingling with dangerous Krauts and poor shmoes loitering at a café, I can't help but to question yours—and other's—motives."

"They're not shmoes! Those men and women at the café are *refugees*."

Shocked, his chin dropped. "Jewish refugees?"

She glanced away.

"Evie?"

"If it makes you feel better...I'll repeat what I told you on the ship. I'm not a spy, Carl! I'm...I'm looking for someone."

"I didn't say you were a spy."

"You didn't have to. I'm not a *dope*. I thought we had ended your suspicions of me aboard the *Serpa*."

He sighed, found wrong again in his assumptions, but he wouldn't apologize. Everyone was suspect, especially a beautiful woman whose path crossed with more Germans than he was comfortable with. "All right. Then...will you let me help you?"

"No. I'm on my own for this assignment."

"So, it's for the newspaper?"

"It's personal and frankly, I'd rather not discuss it."

"Is it *your* family?" *Could she be Jewish?*

"No! Please don't ask. I gave my word to someone back home to keep the details hush. Their family may be in trouble and I have the finances to be of assistance."

"But I might be able to help ya."

She turned to him with challenge in her voice. "You play a clarinet for an orchestra at a Nazi-infiltrated hotel—the very people who are the reason for the refugee plight and the cause of fear I read in everyone that I spoke with yesterday. I, too, was terrified sitting in the café. I know what is going on in Germany!"

Looking out at the moonlit ocean, he frowned and nodded. She understood what was going on, but this war wasn't confined to Germany alone.

"Carl, I just don't see how you could possibly assist me."

"At least gimme a chance to try. I might surprise you. I may be an insignificant clarinet player, but I just might know some people who could help. Besides, who else do ya have?"

"Right now, the only thing you can help with is in telling me how to get to Caldas da Rainha."

"It's a rough drive north of here, or you could take the train."

She crinkled her pert nose.

"If you like, I could drive you there tomorrow. I'd gladly play chauffeur for you, madam."

"You'd do that for me?"

"Yuh-huh. I'd do that and more for you, if you'd axs me." And that was the God's honest truth and it wasn't because Berkshire commanded him to or because there was more information hiding behind her limpid pools.

"Don't you have to play at the Metrópole tomorrow night?"

"There's a back-up clarinetist. I'm sure Dutch could give me the night off."

She knit her brow. "Where did you get a car here in Lisbon?"

He opened his mouth to deliver a well-rehearsed lie, but she cut him off, holding up her hand. "Wait. Don't tell me again…you know people."

"How did ya guess?"

After a few minutes of silence, a soft—humbled—and maybe even relieved smile lit her face. "Carl…will you please take me?"

"I can't think of anything that I'd rather do tomorrow."

He removed his shoes, unhooked his sock garters, and then tugged his argyles off, absolutely reveling in the horrified expression on her face. "Let's focus on tonight…it's still young and I'd like to go for a stroll along the beach. Don't you recall encouraging me to feel the sand between my toes?"

Standing before her, he held out his hand breaking the tension, hoping to see that light heart of hers exposed just a little more. He had a *new* mission as it pertained to Red: release Evelyn Somerset from the prison of Best Society. "C'mon, Evie. Let's have some fun and try to forget that I axst what you were up to. I was an oaf not to trust ya. It won't happen again."

Chuckling, Evie shook her head, acquiescing when she took his hand. His suit jacket dropped from her shoulders when he tugged her up from the blanket.

"Let's run!" he encouraged breaking out into a dash for the shoreline—and she followed right behind him, hand clasped in his, her laughter carrying in the moonlight.

Even at one in the morning, Carl heard the Dutch Ellerton Orchestra playing from the ballroom on the floor below his hotel room. After the evening he'd just enjoyed with Evie, his head spun and, because of that, he was thankful he didn't have to share a room with any of the fellas from the band. He'd made that arrangement with Dutch when he signed on. The Canadian band leader, an on-again, off-again collaborator with MI6, had gladly brought him on as an additional clarinetist—for a price, of course. Of course, Dutch was getting the better part of the deal because, if he did say so himself, he was one of the more talented clarinetists in the business.

He quietly strolled toward his room at the end of the hallway, preoccupied with thoughts of the three or four times he almost kissed Evie: on the blanket, in the sand, walking along the beach. The way the moonlight illuminated her strawberry waves spellbound him, her lips invited him, that laugh! He could go all night naming and analyzing every little nuance of Evelyn Somerset that triggered the romantic fella in him. Whether it was intentional or not, it had worked; she had him wound so tight his spring was ready to burst. In the end, he didn't possess the absence of character to invite himself up to her room and for that he was grateful. It would remain in his dreams. He'd done as his handler wanted: kept her occupied, romanced her, and got the truth out of her. She was no more a spy than he was a choir boy, and he wouldn't take advantage of her to keep her from pursuing a story.

Arriving at his room, he slipped the key in the door and removed his hat, tossing it onto the bed in the dark. From the bathroom, a sliver of light breached the door into the darkness. He stilled, listening, aware that he had not left the light on when he departed for the evening.

Silence.

Slowly, he walked to the bed then slid his hand below the mattress, removing a hidden Beretta from the bed springs. Careful not to cast his shadow onto the light, he stood off to the right of the threshold, vigilant not to knock the radio off its stand. His gun was poised at the ready.

He heard a splash.

Casually he turned the doorknob, releasing it so that the door crept open.

Within the bathtub, bubbles surrounded a nude Irena Olszak. Her golden tresses were piled high on her head and a smirk played upon her thin ruby lips. She raised a slender leg and dragged the sponge down her shin without even looking in his direction.

"You're not going to shoot me, are you?" she asked.

"The thought had occurred to me."

"I thought you would not arrive. Was your little debutante worth the time?"

He turned the radio on so that the music would swallow their conversation. Stepping into the bathroom, he unknotted his necktie with one hand, sliding the pistol into his jacket pocket with the other. Any humor left in him had disappeared; an eager and stunningly naked Irena in his hotel room was serious business. "As I understand it, you were busy tonight, too. How was your evening with Purvis at the Palácio?"

"How did you know?"

"Because we ran smack into him on our way to the beach, and he indicated that he was meeting a friend."

"Yes. I enjoy myself before he goes back to New York. It is best way to keep him under surveillance. He sparked flame." She chuckled. "Now you will ignite. Spies—and friendly agents—make exciting lovers."

"I wouldn't know."

"Do I hear censure in voice or is it jealousy?"

"Neither. Like your husband, it's nunna my beeswax how you conduct your mission," he said, removing his suit jacket. He tried not to look at her in the reflection of the mirror as he pulled his necktie from his collar, unbuttoned then took off his shirt, followed by a turn to the water faucet.

"Then why do you ask of Purvis?"

"I was being polite."

"Always gallant. And how do you conduct mission tonight? Was it same as always or did you finally give in to those animal instincts you hide?" she purred, prodding him, mocking him to be a man of action—the type of action she had been hoping to elicit since Operation Night Shift began. Only tonight there was no beating around the bush.

He stood in his undershirt at the sink, cupping his hands full of water, then splashing and rubbing his face. "I followed my orders as usual." His eyes met her ice blue ones in the mirror. She clearly liked that answer and leered, assuming he'd taken Evie to bed. Being an Intelligence agent didn't warrant that he'd sleep with every dame who fell into his net—or bathtub.

The bubbles moved when Irena's body shifted toward his stare, exposing her full breasts to him, and he did what any man would do: grabbed the towel and dried his face. He turned, facing her with his hands on his hips. Gazing down at her, he leered, acknowledging the seductive image she presented to him. Against her porcelain white skin, a faux-diamond necklace glittered, her pert pink nipples kissed the water, the blonde patch of womanhood evident below the dissipating bubbles bid him to reach down and touch her. She looked like a sexy pin-up calendar—but was real and wanting him, inviting him when she opened her legs to him.

He sniggered in apathy, declining her offer. Irena did nothing for him. Unmoved by her attempted seduction he spoke as dispassionately as he felt, "Get dressed. I'm not interested."

"Do you remember…Stephan does not mind if you practice body-searching technique."

"I don't need any practice. Why are you *really* here, Irena?"

"It is as I said, Jack, as I have always said. I want to be lovers."

His mouth set into a thin line; his eyes narrowed to slits. This was the side of him few witnessed. He'd not been called his real name for nine months. "Well, as I have always stated, I *don't* wanna take you to bed, Irena, and I prefer keeping to our covers. The name is Carl."

"Fine." She slid the sponge down her arm. "Berkshire asked me to deliver dossier on your little diversion. It is on desk."

"And?"

"He said she checks out. Of course, it is sealed, so I could not read report but I am told she comes with pedigree and is worth millions. Is she an American?"

He quit the room.

"Carl, surely you cannot walk away from me like this?"

"I just did."

"I know you want to…I saw gleam in your eyes."

"If the gleam is there…it's not for you, doll. Enjoy your bath and let yourself out. I'm going down to the bar for a nightcap."

He grabbed a freshly laundered shirt from the dresser, leaving the file on the desk. He already knew Red was true blue and her money didn't mean anything to him.

"Secure the dossier before you close the door behind you." Hopefully, Irena would be gone when he got back.

———✦———

SEVENTEEN
You Made Me Care

March 11

"Are you feeling apprehensive about visiting the camp?" Carl asked Evie, looking over at her with a soft smile.

"No. I have a really good feeling. I just hope that I can get all their paperwork processed in time before I leave for New York."

"You know…you *will* have to tell me all about the family when we arrive."

"Perhaps," she grinned, having already decided last night before retiring to do just that. In his own words, he was "true blue," and she trusted him. "And one day, you're going to have to confess how you know so much about Purvis's game."

"Aw, Evie, you had to go and bring him up? Here I thought we were havin' a swell morning with neither a thuggish spy nor a Nazi in sight."

"You're right. I'll let you off the hook for now—only because you're such a gem to drive me to Caldas da Rainha."

The windswept coolness felt invigorating, but the morning sun warmed her cheeks as Carl's BMW hugged the Portuguese coast driving northbound. The glorious day infused her whole being with optimism about finding the Druckers. Despite a headache from the wine the night before, she was simply giddy. It wasn't because the car's convertible top was down and the view was sublime—it was because of Carl. What had begun as a delightful evening the night before ended magically and *that* wasn't attributed to said wine and her tipsiness.

In many ways, her new friend was an enigma. His knowledge of people, places, and things fascinated her. As far as she could tell he was honest in his frankness. Well, apart from his reticence about Purvis.

She smiled at the recollection of his proper kiss to her hand when they parted ways in the lobby at midnight. He had kept his promise to remain a gentleman all evening, yet, in his way he managed to woo her just the same, simply by holding her hand in the moonlight as they strolled along the seashore.

Now, seated beside Carl in the sleek four-seat, she banished the creeping, guilt-ridden feelings of her late husband. It wasn't fair to either his memory or to Carl to dwell over and again on the things she missed—or regretted—about her marriage to Richard. However, for the second time of this journey, it hadn't escaped her notice that the list of interests they had enjoyed *together* was relatively small. Not much of a romantic, a moonlit picnic would never have crossed Richard's mind; and he never would have rolled up his trousers to run through the breaking shore. And Carl knew just as much about the constellations as Richard, only when Carl pointed them out, he regaled her with mythological stories. As they walked and talked he had amused her with scintillating wit, sharing Portuguese folk lore about sea travel and their native sons: Ferdinand Magellan and his wooden leg and another explorer, the Viscount of Serpa Pinto! And what's more, for at least an hour straight he had *listened* to her, allowing her to talk about her columns in the *Miscellany* and her long-held private dreams of traveling the world reporting on substantive issues for a newspaper. She even told him about her stint as Amelia Snow. Carl's attention and encouragement had never wavered. She didn't mean to compare the two men, but she had never had a night like last night—not with Richard.

She stopped herself from allowing guilt to resurface for being captivated by this arresting, complex—yet uncomplicated—musician. Guilt was the byproduct of wrongdoing, and it wasn't wrong to enjoy herself in the chaste company of a gentleman, no matter that his presence stirred desirous yearnings in her or that he was riddled with mystery. But she couldn't help his magnetism any more than she could deny that something beyond their physical attraction had happened last night.

"What are you thinking?" Carl asked with a beaming smile when he glanced over at her.

"Just, what a beautiful day it is. We don't even need music."

"I could sing."

She laughed. *He can sing, too?* "Do you?"

"Better than I can play the piano, which isn't saying much."

His grin made her heart flip.

"Say, would you like to get behind the wheel?"

Embarrassed by the question, she debated for a minute before answering; the prospect of driving was tempting, but she wasn't sure if it was a good idea. There was probably a certain excitement that came when seated behind the wheel, but she was enjoying being a passenger in the front seat soaking up Carl's profile and rural Portugal. Since their departure from Lisbon an hour ago, she'd watched him acutely. Her admiration switched from the changing countryside and seashore back to his one hand whenever it reached for the gear shift and his other hand clutching the steering wheel. Not to mention, from her position she could best appreciate his fine profile and the way his dark hair blew in the breeze.

"I don't know how to drive," she finally admitted.

"That's cock-eyed!"

"I am a city girl. Either Prescott drives me or I take a checker cab." She shrugged, ashamed about such a small thing but it was, yet again, another indication of their difference in upbringing.

Suddenly Carl turned the wheel, driving it to the side of the dusty roadway then cut the engine followed by a pull of the handbrake.

"What are you doing?"

Turning to face her he said, "We're switching seats, and you're gonna get your first lesson."

"Oh no! I can't."

"Why not? Are you incapable of learning?"

"I…" She searched her mind for an excuse, but there was none. Why couldn't she learn? Where was it written that for the rest of her life all she needed was a chauffeur or a taxicab?

Recalling the last verse from the Portuguese poem, *Let me know how to lose myself, to find myself,* she smiled and spoke with alacrity, "I can't think of a reason. You'll really teach me?"

Carl opened the driver's door then stood looking down at her. There was a twinkle in his eyes. "Slide on over, Red."

She did as commanded and he walked around the front of the car to the passenger side whistling an unfamiliar tune. Suddenly nervous, her heart sped.

"Carl…What if I accidentally drive off the cliff and we plunge into the sea?" she asked when he settled beside her.

"Then we die."

Aghast, her head snapped to look at him. His cheeky humored expression made her heart skip a beat. "That would be terribly inconvenient since I haven't had my first headline printed yet," she said.

"Yeah, and I'm still waitin' for my big break to headline at Roseland or Carnegie Hall, so don't drive off the cliff."

She put both hands on the steering wheel and poised her wedge shoes upward to do something with the peddles on the floor. A quick glance to the tranquil water to her left, followed by a last-minute tightening of the scarf around her head prepared for the unknown. "I'm ready now."

Inside, her heart did tiny anticipatory leaps. She was a far cry away from her life in The Dakota.

Carl moved closer to her so that their bodies touched. Taking her gloved hand in his, he dragged hers down the gear stick. The action was…oh!…her eyes widened on the image it presented—and her imagined one!—and then glanced over at him in embarrassment, intrigue, and shock. His face was so close to hers…the act so familiar. She was a widow—not dead—and she recalled that intimate act.

A smile played on his lips as her hand, covered by his, surrounded the knob at the tip…reminding her of…

She gasped, pulling her hand from his, covering her mouth.

"What is it?"

"Noth…nothing," she stammered, feeling the heated flush to her cheeks.

Oh dear, she was too affected by his nearness and that repeated tickle of desire at the thought of what her hand…His sly smile mortified her further. It was as though he knew what she was feeling, as if he was teasing her, deliberately provoking her.

"As I was saying." He took her hand again, repeating the action, even more slowly. "As the car's speed increases, you'll need to shift. Like this. First here…" He went through the movements. "Then here, and finally up here."

Goodness, is he wearing cologne? She almost swooned.

"Each time you shift press that far peddle down with your left foot, then slowly let it up as you increase your speed pressing the fuel peddle down."

"It sounds easy," she struggled to reply—undone. Undone by a driving lesson!

"It takes a bit of coordination but once you get the hang of it it's duck soup. But the first thing you need to do is start the engine by pulling that knob." Unaided, her fingers surrounded the tip and she drew it toward her.

The car sputtered to life, shaking slightly from the chugging vibration. Just like her. All of it was highly titillating and a metaphor for something her sister would state Brewster highly approved of.

"Are you ready? I'm gonna keep my hand on yours and together we'll change gears until you can do it yourself. Press the left peddle to the floor, shift with me, and slowly depress the right peddle while raising your left foot. You have to do this all at the same time."

They shifted gears and she did as he instructed; the car jerked—then stopped.

"It's okay. We'll do it again, more slowly. There's no need to rush. You have all the time we need."

"You're a patient man."

"Nah. I'm enjoying the excuse to hold your hand."

After several tries, they finally were on the road, stopping and stalling—waving cars to pass them into the oncoming lane—and laughing the entire time. Once she even slapped his hand away from the gear stick wanting to do it on her own. Goodness, she felt liberated! And although not driving very fast, the whole experience was thrilling.

Regrettably, Carl slid back to the passenger side, which was only a few inches away from her, but she missed the slight pressure of his broad shoulder against hers.

"Well, look at that…you're a real natural," he said, leaning back in the seat, clearly giving her the legs to take control, and then he started to whistle that tune again.

"What is that you're whistling?"

He softly smiled. "That Jimmy Dorsey song: 'The Things I Love.' "

"And what are some things, Carl?"

"One day I'll tell ya, but not today. You might drive off the cliff," he quipped, resuming his whistling and cheerful attitude.

"Do you make everything a joke?"

He sighed and looked over to her. "I try to. Life's too short not to. Sure, it takes a lot to ignore my demons, but I remind myself that life's a whole heck of a lot easier when I look at the bright side of things."

Although more curious than ever, she decided not to ask what demons, apart from his plane crash, he fought. What makes Carl Wilson tick? Why was he always so evasive?

She enjoyed controlling the BMW, navigating the two-lane road; she daringly pressed the fuel peddle increasing their speed.

To her left, the coastline passed in a blur but she tried to remain focused on the roadway, attempting to keep her imagination away from speculating on the things he loved and the demons he battled.

"How much further until we arrive at Caldas da Rainha?"

"Oh, about another hour. You don't mind if I take a snooze, do ya?"

"I beg your pardon? Yes, I mind!" Her fingers gripped the steering wheel in fear of driving without being under his watchful eye.

"Aw, Red, you're doing fine without me holdin' your hand. You're a capable girl. Just make sure you obey the traffic signs now that you added Portuguese to your polyglot list."

"I...um...can't speak fluently yet," she made a desperate excuse, lying because the few signs on the road she had mastered.

"Sure you can." He folded his arms across his chest and tilted his face to the sun, closing his eyes. "You just need to exercise your mouth and tongue."

"Excuse me?"

He chuckled, "For better control to trill your *R*s."

She spoke something in Bairisch, proving she was skilled in working her tongue and throat with exaggerated rolling *R*s.

"Okay, you convinced me." Particularly affected by what she could do with her mouth, he turned his head to face the door to hide his grin.

"Please don't sleep. I enjoy your company."

Carl bolted upright from his relaxed position as though that was the best news he'd heard all morning. "Like I said—all you have to do is axs."

Bustling with activity, the República Square of Caldas da Rainha was different from Rossio Square in the Capital. The ancient spa town was filled with shoppers and vendors at its open-air market beside a Sixteenth-Century chapel. Verdant green landscape and colorful buildings added to the charming ambiance of the vibrant native dress and Portuguese traditional music floating in the crisp air. In blatant black marketeering, under fabric canopies, merchants peddled fish, fruit, vegetables, and ceramics to a public stressed by new ration restrictions, food shortages and increasing poverty. Yet the people seemed unaffected in their conviviality.

Evie parked the BMW behind a truck filled with crates and pulled the brake, just as Carl had taught her. Excitement coursed through her veins from both the prospect of having driven the second leg of the trip and at having arrived safely!

"You did good, Red, a real queen of the road. Except for that cat you ran over back there."

"Ha. Ha. *That* is a bold-faced lie. I thoroughly enjoyed myself and avoided plunging into the sea!"

He said something in Portuguese, which she could not understand and then he laughed.

"What did you call me?"

"One day I'll tell ya."

"Of course you will. The list of things you'll tell me about one day is growing. Be careful, darling, I may stick around and hold you to your promises." *Where did that come from? Darling?*

"Be careful, Evie. I may hold you to that claim."

They both smiled at the other, then scanned the crowd a hundred feet from the car; it was time for her confession.

She turned to face him. Digging into her purse, she withdrew one of the three photographs Mr. Drucker had given her. "Now that we've arrived, I suppose you're in too deep to get out and deserve an explanation as I promised."

"Well, you did say you were an open book."

"This is the Drucker family," she stated, handing him a cabinet card and he examined the image as she pointed to each person. "This gentleman is Samuel, and this is his wife Rebecca, son Ezra and *his* wife, Suzannah. The little girl is Tovah. She's about five-years-old in this photograph."

She continued her explanation after he tucked the photograph into his jacket's inside pocket.

"They are my editor's relatives from Frankfurt...his *Jewish* relatives." Pausing, she waited for Carl's reply, but he continued to do what he did best: listen. "In the hope of finding them to arrange for their passage, I visited the American Embassy, Rossio Square, and the Jewish Hospital on the day you saw me in Lisbon. At the suggestion of a Frenchman I spoke with outside the café, my search led me here. Apparently, the refugee camp is their last known destination."

"This family—are they having trouble getting transit papers or just securing passage?"

"Both. They came via France and, as expected, their funds have dried up. If I find them, I have a letter from their cousin explaining what I hope to accomplish while here—money, sponsorship, papers, whatever they need."

She didn't mean to cry, but finally admitting to herself the truth and giving it voice broke her heart. "The commitment to helping them represents...my final *good-bye* to Richard. I'm doing this in his memory...for his and his crew's sacrifice—and, of course, the family needs help."

"That's a swell memorial. He'd be pleased, I'm sure."

"You see, although my late-husband was a serious man, he was a man of principled conviction and believed in doing what he could for humanity. His family has always been quite philanthropic, more than mine could ever be. While he didn't think war would come to fruition after his naval commission, he did embrace the fight believing it the right thing to do following Japan's attack at Pearl Harbor. He hated dirty sneaks, and the Japanese had pulled one over on America, killing many friends."

Carl's attention never wavered, and he reached over, taking her hand into his with a gentle smile.

"Before his death, in his last letter, he wanted me to understand that this war is necessary, that we're fighting evil on two fronts. Not that I believe in heaven or hell, god or satan, but that's irrelevant—in his final hours *he* did."

She paused again, expecting him to comment on her admission of atheism, but he said nothing, just remained in that same attentive, open posture.

"When my editor confided in me, sharing the correspondence from his cousin, I knew in my heart that even traveling by ship would be my continuation of Richard's service. It took me some time to consider, to fully committing, but the contents of that letter made me realize I have the power and resources to do good for another by venturing out of my sheltered life. I didn't before but I want to do my bit now."

"Your efforts are extraordinary, much more than doing your bit for the war effort, Evie."

"I know, but my intuition said it was the right thing to do, and what the boys at the paper filled me in on confirmed it. This country is the Drucker family's last hope, but if Portugal is invaded then they'll have no hope. They need to be safe with their family in America. I vowed to bring them to a new home in honor of Richard who never made it back to his." She looked away, holding back an unladylike blubber. "Now he rests somewhere at the bottom of the Pacific Ocean."

Carl squeezed her hand and she wiped an embarrassing tear with her other one, turning to him. "Anyway…there is something else, and that's more to do with the selfish creature in me. We touched on it last night, but I need to say it again to clear my conscience. I'm doing this for *me*, too. What good am I if I'm nothing more than a wealthy widowed socialite who can play the Minute Waltz?" She smiled wistfully.

"I'm not your confessor, so don't feel the need to come clean on your private reasons, but I respect your altruism. Sometimes it's hard to look in the mirror. As for ya being not any good—I think you're a lotta good. Heck, ya got me twisted up like a knot. No one's ever done that before. In my book, you're one special girl with many gifts and a boat load of guts."

"That's kind of you. Mr. Drucker says I have moxie, too."

"Yeah, moxie. The Portuguese would call that *corajoso*. I'd expect nothing less from a redhead of *any* nationality."

He winked then smiled reassuringly. "Now c'mon, let's go fulfill your vow to Richard together."

Carl's simple offer of "together" left her speechless, and for several seconds she sat silently, a gentle smile touching her lips as they held each other's gaze. Those brown bedroom eyes conveyed the goodness in his soul. She swallowed down her mawkishness. "Thank you, Carl."

"Don't mention it."

Again, this man had magically lifted her spirits.

"Well! I better not look like a sad sack on this search. There is too much to feel optimistic about," she declared turning the rearview mirror to face her. She felt Carl watching her as she removed her scarf, combed her hair, then applied a fresh layer of lipstick followed by a blot of powder to her tear-streaked cheek.

"Are you ready now, gorgeous?" he teased.

They exited the car, and he joined her at the rear. After lifting the trunk, he removed his Fedora from the floor then settled it on his head. "I think the best place to start is the market. It's part of their daily life in this town."

"How do you know that?"

"Because my mother grew up thirty minutes from here. She'd tell me stories about the fishermen and the hot springs."

"You didn't say."

"There was no need to."

Chuckling, Evie shook her head. "You're full of surprises and secrets. Were you really a Boy Scout?"

He held up his three fingers again. "Duty to God and country, duty to other people, and duty to self."

She could clearly see that he lived by that credo.

Side by side they walked to the busy marketplace, vendors calling out their specials for the day. Here there was an odd mix of international denizens made up of mostly older folk, many of whom spoke British English and French, others—peasants and merchants— spoke Portuguese.

"We should separate," Carl offered as they navigated through the throng of people. "I'll start at the east end of the market, by the church. You start here with those fishmongers."

The inquiries began: "Have you seen..." "I'm looking for..." and "Hello, my name is..." All were answered with smiles, an offer of something to eat or buy, and the repeated, "I'm sorry."

By the minute, Evie's spirits were sinking like the U.S.S. *Jarvis*. She learned that many of the visitors to the market were newly arrived Britons evacuated from Italy where they had resided for many years. Now displaced, they were "exiled" in Portugal for the duration of the war. She even conversed with several men her age. Americans!—downed airmen sitting tight until they could be rescued after having hiked over the Pyrenees Mountains from France into Spain. Boy, those fellas sure were glad to see her, and she kissed them all on the cheek in thanks and encouragement to figuratively keep 'em flying.

All hope seemed lost at finding the Druckers in the market, and her heart sank.

She looked in the direction of the church and Carl's fedora, above the crowd, caught her attention as he approached her from the opposite side of the square. The throng moved and then her focus fell to his beaming smile.

A little girl clasped his hand: Tovah.

EIGHTEEN
Over the Hill

*T*ovah Drucker proved to be a little German chatterbox, animated and rambling with stories, her thoughts taking her mouth wherever it went as the BMW carried them over the hill just outside of town. At seven years of age, she was quite a little lady but had a keen imagination, and it was no wonder considering what her family had been through over the last year. In the short span of fifteen minutes, Carl and Evie had learned about the stray three-legged dog that comes to visit with them, her love of music and something called hamentasche, an invisible friend named Zuzu who dances on the piano, and the most astonishing of all—a fairy frog that came in the night and had stolen her grandfather from bed ten days ago, which was the reason for her visit to the marketplace. None of it made any sense at all. Why would it? She was seven.

Carl glanced over Tovah's looped chestnut braids to Evie as the little girl talked a mile a minute, sitting on Evie's lap. Red appeared unfazed by that pronouncement of Samuel's strange disappearance, but maybe she believed the girl was telling whole tales and not half-truths. Nevertheless, they'd find out what was real and what was fancy when they got to "the black bird house."

Other than the few he taught, he'd not had experience with children and did not know if Evie had either, but she conversed with the child beautifully, encouraging her to regale them with her fairytales. He smiled thoughtfully imagining Red as a mother one day. If she'd come down to earth more often, let go of her hoity-toity long enough to completely escape its prison, she could be magnificent. Inside, his heart tugged slightly, the truth staring him in the face: He was in love with her.

"And what is your puppy's name?" Evie asked.

"*Bello!*"

"I guess it's got a gift for gab, too," he said to Evie in English and she chuckled.

The neighborhood they entered resembled the summer bungalow community where his family had vacationed near the lake in '32. Each house looked the same: white clapboard, three rooms at the most, a clothesline, and the beginnings of a vegetable garden. Today must be wash day at every residence; bedclothes and underclothes billowed in the sea breeze after having been spread. Several cars belonging either to refugees or state officials were parked along the street line.

"There it is," Tovah announced, pointing to a cottage displaying a singular distinction from the others: five decorative, black swallows in flight hung in a row beside the front door, a good omen in Portugal. "See...there is Mother. I told you—I am going to be a big sister!" Beside the house, a very pregnant woman stretched her back after pinning a shirtwaist frock onto the line.

Carl stopped the BMW then pulled the handbrake and without a second's delay Tovah opened the door, dashing to her mother, excitedly shouting in German.

They sat in the car watching the happy girl tug on her mother's skirt, but his attention shifted to Evie and the relieved smile on her lips and the softening to her apprehensive brow.

"You did it," Evie tenderly said.

"No, *you* did it. I'm just along for the ride. Now *we* have to get them to America." And he meant that. He'd pull whatever strings he needed to with the Brits to get this family out of Portugal. And in that blinding moment, he realized that Evie would be leaving, too. They had joked about it in the car, but as usual he made light of it, not really acknowledging that it was a bona-fide fact. Now that she got her interview and found the Druckers, she had a life and a world separate from the business of war to resume. She was a true-blue reporter now. Damn it. He should be saying "good riddance" because he had Nazis to spy on and Irena to fend off. Yet…his heart sank, and the smile he wore slowly receded from his face.

"Is something wrong, Carl?"

"Nuh-uh. Everything is fine. C'mon, let's go say a hi-di-ho."

They exited the car, and he took her hand, helping her up the incline leading to the house. There was no walkway or grass, just a mound of sandy soil and weeds that led up to the front stoop. Evident by the rake and shovels, it was clear they were attempting to make the cottage look like a home.

Samuel's daughter-in-law trailed behind Tovah, struggling in her waddle to keep up as the girl excitedly pulled her mother's arm. With a furrowed brow, she greeted them with a wary, "Guten Tag."

Evie smiled warmly, hoping to dispel the woman's understandable wariness. She spoke in German, confirming her identity. "Frau Drucker?"

"*Ja.*"

"Suzannah Drucker, wife of Ezra from Frankfurt am Main?"

"Ja." The woman's frown turned darker and Evie quickly opened her purse, removing the letter the editor had written for this anticipated meeting.

"*Mein Name ist Evelyn Somerset und dies ist Carl Wilson,*" she softly introduced them, holding out the letter. "*Dies ist von ihrem Cousin in New York City.*"

"Cousin Heinrich?"

"Ja."

As Suzannah silently read the note, she bit her lip, her hand smoothing over her belly, and then her eyes filled with tears.

"*Mutter!*" she cried out, folding the letter. "*Mutter! Kommen Sie!*" And then she sobbed. Wracking emotions mixed with prayers of thanksgiving flowed out of her. Her knees buckled, and Carl grabbed both her upper arms to keep her heavy form from dropping to the ground.

Never one to handle a woman's waterworks with any type of aplomb, he felt completely inept bracing Suzannah when her head fell forward onto his shoulder. His eyes met Evie's own tear-filled ones. Deeply moved, it occurred to him that Evie was their savior, the bearer of good news and light, and his heart swelled with pride and honor to be a part of this experience and part of her own liberation. He regretted ever suspecting her involvement in espionage, but it was his job to distrust and suspect everyone. He'd seen a lot of things—and performed some unsavory acts—during his time with the SIS, but the delicate human plight wasn't something he witnessed often. His world was lies and trickery, cloak and dagger, death and war all hidden behind an orchestra, sheet music, and a clarinet.

Still clinging to him, Suzannah reached her hand out to grasp Evie's. *"Herzlichen Dank."*

The front door opened and a full-figured elderly woman wearing a brown dress and a floral headscarf watched the exchange with a furrowed brow. The little girl spoke to her rapidly in a dialect he had not heard, but was able to glean a few words from. The woman clasped her hands together and raised them into the air in prayer...then she scolded Tovah for running too far from home by going to the market...yet again.

The little girl pouted. "I went to find Grandpapa."

"I know, *Engelchen*," Rebecca kissed her granddaughter's cheek then whispered something into her ear.

Carefully supporting Suzannah, Carl made his way up the small hill to the house where she held the letter out to the old woman. "It is from Cousin Heinrich," she said sniffling.

"Maybe now the fairies will return Grandpapa, so we can all go to America!" Tovah persisted.

Evie blanched and rightfully so. She'd heard of refugees gone in the night.

"Return? Is Samuel missing?" she inquired.

"Come, come inside. Little pitchers have big ears," Rebecca said, clasping the letter to her chest. "I will make tea. We will talk." She took Evie's hand in her free one, leading her into the house. "Thank you. Thank you. You are a G-dsend."

What did Evie think of the woman's proclamation? Yes, it had surprised him earlier to hear she was devoid of any faith or belief system. To him, having grown up in a devout Catholic family, that notion seemed wacky.

Though scant in personal belongings or mementos, the tiny cottage was surprisingly well-appointed. He'd been expecting something significantly less for the refugees, particularly since he knew, but had not told Evie, that residence in Caldas da Rainha was mandatory and could be prolonged for the duration of the war—unless, of course, they decided to send you back from whence you came. He didn't have the heart to tell her that Jewish visitors were essentially interned and needed permission to leave to pursue their visas and travel arrangements. Even with these restrictions in place, Carl was pleased to see that, here in Caldas, "Neutralia" also meant humanitarian treatment of refugees. Despite Salazar's totalitarianism, he saw the refugees as Germans, French, Italian, etc. first, and Jewish second. Jewish aid organizations were allowed to help; unless they were communists, they were no real threat to Portugal.

He felt like a third wheel when the women congregated in the kitchen area speaking German faster than he could keep up. So, as they discussed New York and Hank Drucker, he wandered the cozy main room facing the street, removed his hat and examined the details of the living quarters. A few newspapers were stacked on a footstool, an embroidery project on the sofa, a hairless doll, and a prayer book all indicated that as best they could—they'd made the cottage a home. He picked up a *Zeitung* and an outdated bulletin of anti-Nazi sentiment by the Central Federation of German Citizens of the Jewish Faith dropped out. *Interesting,* he thought, sliding it back where it came from before placing the newspaper back on the hassock.

An upright piano covered half a wall, and he smiled thinking of Tovah's proclamation of her love of music and her imaginary friend dancing on top. Funny how his mind conjured up a red-haired nymph wearing a light blue dress, similar to the one Evie wore disembarking the *Serpa*.

He was lost in his thoughts when Tovah came to stand beside him. Her index finger touched his gold cufflink and she giggled at the music symbol engraving.

"Sit. Let's play music for Zuzu," she said, pulling him toward the piano obviously feeling left out from the women, too. Having an imaginary playmate could only mean that there were few children in this community for her to befriend. She was hungry for a real playmate and most likely scared by all the changes.

She sat beside him, making up her own song by banging the keys until her grandmother scolded her again. The little girl frowned, removing her hands and clasping them on her lap.

Fondly, he recalled how music had changed his difficult childhood when his father was too tired to give him any real attention, and his younger brother was determined on competing with him for the little attention that did come. He smiled to himself remembering the actual joys he had when teaching music as a younger man before joining up.

"Let's go outside, Tovah," he said, rising from the stool.

Without question, she obediently followed behind him out the door toward the car. Upon lifting the boot, he removed the clarinet case. "Would you like for me to play a song on my horn?"

"Yes! Yes!" She jumped up and down before dashing toward the house, her skinny legs climbing the small hill to the stoop.

Carl met her at the steps; he sat and opened the black instrument case. Wide-eyed she watched him suck on the wooden reed, wetting it so he could play for her. "This is called a reed; it's made from a type of grass," he explained removing it from his lips then attached it to the mouthpiece. "And these are called keys," he said assembling the pieces of the clarinet. "Now, I'm gonna show you what they can do together when I blow into the black stick."

"Can you blow 'Hatikvah?' "

"Hmmm... I don't know that one, but I know a swell song that children your age love where I come from."

Unmoved, she watched him play "Hi-Ho-Hi-Ho" from *Snow White and the Seven Dwarves* but her eyes were fixed on his fingers. This would not do. He decided on an old Benny Goodman song, "That's a Plenty," and was rewarded with her laughter and hand clapping to the tune. Her animated reaction to the boogie woogie filled his heart as she danced.

Hearing voices at his back, he glanced over his shoulder at the three women peering through the open windows of the house.

Other residents came out from their homes, curious as the lively rhythm floated down the street. His heart felt gayer with each note he played; his head felt lighter, yet his spirit was more grounded than ever seeing Evie's smile grow. Tovah's mother exited the house, standing with both hands clasped over her baby; she, too, grinned.

More songs by the King of Swing flowed in a medley from his clarinet to entertain his growing audience: "Sing, Sing, Sing," "Boy Meets Goy," and "Swingtime in the Rockies."

After a fifteen-minute performance, he finally took a decent breath and even though the music had ended, Tovah continued to dance across the front yard and Suzannah's earlier tears of joy had now turned to laughter. The neighbors assembled in front of the black bird house clapped and cheered along with Evie, Rebecca, and her.

"We have not heard such music! Ezra plays the piano, but it is not the same. Thank you! You made Tovah so happy."

"She sure seems to be. Music is good for the soul of every age." They looked to the little girl lost in her dance with Zuzu, pretending to hold hands.

"You are very kind to my daughter."

"She's a good kid."

"Do you have children in America?"

"Nope. Not me," he said regretfully, his heart slightly sinking to his stomach at voicing one of those demons he mentioned earlier. There would never be joking about that: not in the past, the present, or in the future.

"Then one day you will."

He softly smiled. That wasn't gonna happen, not for him. Family wasn't in the cards for this music man, this Intelligence agent. He'd most likely be dead by the end of the war.

"Please come join us. The tea is ready. We will tell you about Samuel. Tovah, you stay here and play with Zuzu. I have marzipan if you are a good girl."

Once inside, he placed his instrument case atop the piano then sat beside Evie at the table. Tea, served in glasses, with biscuits, cheese, and fruit offered as an early lunch on unmatched dishes. The ecru lace tablecloth had not been there when they'd arrived, and looked to be an heirloom of special importance. As strangers to this family—and this private world—he couldn't help but to feel flattered and honored by the attention and fuss.

Rebecca dropped heavily into her chair at the head of the table. Placing her palms down before her, she spoke with commendable bravado. "I will just come out with it. It has been many days that we have not seen my husband since the secret police took him away."

Evie gasped. "Did you see them take him?"

"Yes. They came to the house where we had let a room near the hospital in Lisbon and they arrested him late in the night. Thank G-d, our Tovah was asleep."

Carl cleared his throat as he leaned toward the table. "What were the charges?"

"They say for speaking out against the conditions on the docks and the slow pace in which the embassies process the exit visas," Rebecca said.

"I'm sorry...I don't mean to be discourteous, but there must have been something else. The Portuguese government is not known to be such thugs. Some of the police, yes, but not for belly aching over red tape. The prisons are lousy, but they're mostly for hardened criminals. Grumbling over bureaucracy isn't a reason for forced labor in Portugal. Not that Salazar is an angel, but that kind of brutality is more Franco's style."

Rebecca's gaze met Suzannah's before sharing more details, her strength now shaky, her eyes brimming. "Samuel made it known that he disapproved of the wealthy visitors' preferential treatment in getting transit visas and passage while we poorer Jews languished in limbo awaiting eviction back to Germany or France. The Quakers and Unitarians did their best for us but without the many documents we need, they cannot help negotiate further." She brought the glass to her lips and looked away.

"I will finish, Mutter. They accuse Samuel of being a communist agitator. When they took him away, they put us here. We do receive a stipend to live, and we are thankful for that. Troubles are easier to take with soup than without, you understand. We have Tovah and the baby to consider, too."

Evie's sigh and Rebecca's tears almost broke him. There was no upside to this—at all. It was just as he had surmised, and he hated the thought of telling Evie that her women's intuition had failed her today. Samuel's conviction without questioning most likely meant that he was imprisoned far from Lisbon, or quite possibly transferred to Spain. Franco had set up such miserable conditions that there was little chance of survival. His fingers rubbed several times across his mouth as he considered what to do, what next to say. He was usually a man of optimism, but this situation...

The intense glare of all three women burned him as they searched his face for any hope he could offer. He couldn't joke his way out of this. He couldn't play them a happy tune.

"Carl?"

"I'm thinking."

"There is nothing we can do," Rebecca hopelessly stated.

"I could pay someone to help us. I have money, and I could wire home for more," Evie offered. "Surely there is someone within the police who could be of assistance."

"I'm afraid you'll find few sympathetic ears," he said.

"But didn't you say that everyone has a price in Lisbon?"

As impolite as it was, he spoke to her in Portuguese not wanting to say this to the women. "Following Spain's civil war, few think kindly of communists on the Iberian Peninsula. I'm not saying that Samuel is one, but if he is a political prisoner then he doesn't stand a Chinaman's chance at getting released."

She knit her eyebrows, biting the corner of her lip.

"Look, Evie, if the Quakers didn't succeed in helping them, then I'm afraid, this could be one situation that a few escudo notes can't buy our way out of."

Despite the gravity of their discussion, he couldn't help but to be impressed at how quickly she was able to converse in Portuguese, making only a few errors when she spoke. "I refuse to believe that. Oh dear, my editor was afraid of this. He said his uncle was a firebrand and possibly the reason the family was stuck here. Just like the Frenchman in the café. No wonder he didn't want to be associated with Samuel. Please, Carl, we must find a way. We must! *I* must! Look at this family. I can't leave Lisbon without having succeeded." Her hand touched his forearm. "For Tovah and the baby."

"Even if we know it's a bum rap and we're able to find someone to help us, Samuel isn't gonna be allowed on any boat headed to any country."

"Not even America?"

"You said it yourself. Your brother would have apoplexy. I'd bet the farm, he'd have a heart attack if he learned that some of Stalin's agents had *already* arrived and are seated in Roosevelt's administration."

She naively laughed. "That would never happen. Impossible."

He twisted his lips before steering the topic away from the dangers of exposing too much of what British Intelligence knew. "Be that as it may, we're not lettin' *anyone* in, not even Jewish asylum seekers."

"I do recall that terrible situation a couple of years ago with the S.S. *St. Louis*. Both Albert and Richard defended the decision vehemently and I suppose, at the time, I agreed with them."

Her red lips set, and she knit her brow. It appeared to him she was now viewing that tragedy through another prism; her once decided opinion, perhaps influenced by the opinions of those in her exclusive world, had altered.

"Look. I don't mean to put a damper on your optimism, but we have to face all the facts. There is also the possibility that the PVDE turned Samuel over to the Gestapo. He's Jewish—he could be dead."

"No! I refuse to consider that. He's alive and we must find him. I will do whatever I need to do to get the family passage to America or Palestine."

"I dunno, Evie."

"I do! Perhaps the British Embassy can help us. My father-in-law is...was...is the Baron of Sallingham. Surely, they would help, maybe bend a few rules for a peer?"

Jeez! What the hell have I gotten into? A baron?

Yes, this was turning out to be the cock-up Musgrove was trying to avoid. And no more than thirty minutes ago he had vowed to himself to help bring this family to America. He reminded himself that this family's plight was, in essence, what they were all fighting against happening in America and Great Britain—and the reason he was shot down, for Christ's sake!

He sighed then smiled as optimistically as he could muster, but knew that any effort on his part would be fruitless. His hand dragged over his scarred brow. "I'll take care of it."

"How?"

"Don't ask me any questions. I'll just take care of it, is all. I'll find out where they took him and see what strings I can pull."

Evie placed her hand on his, her eyes soft and limpid. "You're a dear friend, Carl. The best I've ever had. Thank you."

That wasn't quite what he'd like to hear but it would do—for now. He held her gaze and spoke from his heart. "I'll always be your friend. Like I said, all you have to do is axs, duchess. I'd move mountains for ya if I could, and I'm sure gonna try to move this one."

"I'll be indebted to you."

"Nuh-uh. You don't owe me nuthin.' "

In German, he spoke to Rebecca and Suzannah eagerly awaiting his input. "I'm sorry to ask this, and I mean no offense, but I need you to be honest with me, Mrs. Drucker otherwise I can't help you. *Is* your husband a communist?"

"Oh no. I promise you he is not. Samuel is a good man, just an old fool. His heart is in the right place, but he just does not know when to shut up and mind his business!"

He chuckled lightly at her frankness, which only a wife of her age could deliver with such affection. "Then, I give you my word— by the grace of God, I'll try to find him."

Rebecca clasped her hands again, raising them like she did before, prayer flowing from her lips in pious, grateful recitation as she looked up to heaven. From the corner of his eye, he witnessed Evie's head bow, her lips touching in gentle repose. She closed her eyes and he considered—for a fleeting moment—that she was moved to humility or meekness in sight of such devout faithfulness in the face of darkness. A glimmer of hope lit his heart when he considered that maybe she was trying out prayer for the first time.

With tears in her eyes, Suzannah placed her hand upon her back and rose from the chair. "I want to give you something," she said leaving the kitchen. Mere seconds later, she returned, holding a sixth black swallow.

"We had planned to place this outside the house when the baby came, but Ezra can make another. I would like for you both to have it. It is the bird of freedom and home—a swallow—from the Sefer Tehillim." She held it out to Carl, reciting a prayer in Hebrew, which he did not understand.

"That's very kind of you. I'm much obliged." He turned the bird, admiring the fine woodturning's detailed craftsmanship. The man possessed great skill. "This is mighty fine work. You say your husband made this?"

"Yes. Sometimes, he sells them in the market to help make money for our passage to America. Today, he is fishing though."

Carl held the wooden bird out to Evie, imparting the Portuguese tradition and why this gift was no ordinary gift—and why five in flight hung outside the front door. "Swallows, *andorinha*, are migratory birds and hold a long tradition in Portugal. They represent hope and, because they stay close to the coastline, they also mean home."

"*Ja*, and family, love, loyalty...they are for lovers, too." Suzannah added with a shy smile.

As though petting the wooden bird, Evie stroked its back. Her face burned scarlet. Yeah, she knew deep down what he—and Suzannah—suspected: he was more than a friend, despite all her protestations and the ever-present, deceased Lieutenant Somerset.

"Christians also believe they represent happiness and new beginnings," he said, feeling the gift was apropos of many things.

"I've never seen a swallow before," Evie said. "But, of course, I've heard of them from the song 'When the Swallows Come Back to Capistrano.' "

"That's right!"

"Thank you, Suzannah."

"You'd love to watch them, Red. They're not afraid of anything. The way they go from dive bombing to dancing to flying upside down—they're determined little fighters, squabbling with each other one second then playing catch-me-if-you-can the next. In fact, they sound like someone I know." He raised an eyebrow with a teasing quirk to his lips.

The expression on her face told him he was about to get an ear full, but lucky for him Tovah came through the front door like a whirlwind. The screen door slammed behind her with a loud whack disturbing Evie's expected retort.

"Play more!" The little girl's flushed face beamed; her hazel eyes sparkled as she tugged on his suit sleeve. "Zuzu wants to dance on the piano."

"Shoo! Leave Herr Wilson alone," the old woman said.

"It is all right, Mrs. Drucker. I don't mind. I have a few songs up my sleeve." He scratched his neck. "Hmm...what I really need is a piano accompaniment." He rose from his seat and held his hand out to Evie.

"What are you doing?"

"I need your help. You did say that you were a proficient pianist, right?"

"Although I enjoy listening to swing, I cannot play it."

"Go on, Evelyn! Play for us," Suzannah said.

"It's like learning to drive. The measure is duck soup. Trust me, you'll be a natural at beating eight to the bar."

She placed the bird on the table then warily took his hand, placing her trust in him once again when he led her to the piano. With a charming smile, he invited her to sit. The struggle within her was evident, trying to hold back her own pleased response— that mask of hers was slipping. Tovah snuggled beside her with hands at the ready to join in if asked.

Shuffling through a thin stack of sheet music kept at the bottom of his instrument case, he found a song that only he had ever played. After the crash, he needed something to lift him out of his depression and the endless pain. So, he composed this score while recuperating at the seashore. Today, he hoped its upbeat tempo would challenge her to leave Chopin, maybe for good, and to keep her spirits up about Mr. Drucker's uncertain fate. He debated for a second as everyone watched him grasp the sheet music, his eyes locked on the words "Better Days Ahead." *Yes. This is perfect.*

Placing the score on the music rack before her, he said, "I hope you like this. It's my own composition."

Evie looked up at him with a confused furrow to her brow. "You write music, too?"

"Of course. I told ya, I'm no dope."

"You most certainly are not." To his ears that sounded like more than a compliment. It teetered on admiration. The gift of her beaming grin was confirmation.

"Is Zuzu ready, Tovah?" he asked.

"Yes!"

His first notes were sweet and long, like pulling taffy from his clarinet. He loved this song because its birth had come from his heart. Evie waited, nervously bouncing her fingers in the air above the keys and he tried to ignore the gold wedding band, instead focusing on a strawberry blonde tendril fallen over her right eye as she looked at the music and then the keys. Finally, she glanced up at him standing beside her. Her smile made his fingers dance on his horn, but one day, he'd dance with her in his arms, he vowed.

He cued her up with a wink. The slow and languid melody quickly grew to a rhythmic tempo and her sensuous fingers deftly kept in beat on the slightly out-of-tune piano. Evie was his perfect duet partner and the boogie beat came naturally to her. She was feeling *his* music, reveling in *his* song. Not Carl Wilson's, a pseudonym he was living under, but Jack McGrath's—the real name of the man in his soul.

Notes flew from them both, joining in the air, harmoniously making beautiful, spirited boogie woogie. They played off each other, their parts fitting snugly like a kid leather glove.

Benny Goodman had once called swing "free speech in music." Together, as partners, he and Evie were freely, without censure, speaking the same language: no Fifth Avenue tight jaw, no Yinzer Pittsburghese. They were soaring, dancing, singing—flying—in the house of swallows.

Their eyes met over the length of his clarinet and it was then he knew that their connection would be everlasting. Their language was formed in their hearts and the music in the air.

NINETEEN

Amen

$\mathcal{T}$he high Evie felt when making music with Carl was soon overshadowed by the good-byes she made when leaving Caldas da Rainha. Tovah's tears had taken her by surprise, leaving her with a sense of despair. She could count on one hand the times she had felt such gloom. The last time was with the arrival of Richard's final letter before she had left for Portugal. The time before that was the receipt of the dreaded Western Union telegram. Then there was the occasion of her forced withdrawal from Vassar to marry earlier than she had planned. And, finally, the time that could not be eclipsed by any of them: the death of her beloved father.

Today, in her heart, she knew that Carl's efforts in finding Samuel wouldn't amount to much, but what a dear he was to vow to try. She knew he was doing it for her—impossible endeavor that it was.

The little car navigated dirt roads winding between green pastures cordoned off by stone walls to protect the wandering of shepherds' wards. She stared thoughtfully out the window of the BMW keenly aware that Carl drove north not south, but she was too consumed by her thoughts of the unborn babe to say anything. No child should be born into a camp without a true home, certainly not a temporary one in a strange land—on the run and persecuted for religion. Try as the Druckers might, their cottage hovel was hardly idyllic, lacking few creature comforts and even fewer niceties, yet they had faith. And goodness, the women had confidence in her and Carl, too. Her heart squeezed again. Tomorrow, she would go to the Portuguese *and* the British consuls—she'd use whatever remaining influence her father-in-law still had. She'd wire his cousins in England if necessary, and dammit, if she had to, she'd wire Albert in Washington! She'd beg. Yes, beg—maybe even bargain. If he agreed to help them, she'd consider moving back to The Lancashire and become that miserable, society widow they wanted her to be. She'd hold the queen's hand and lie through her teeth that she was happy in proclaiming that her mother was the most loved and wonderful woman she knew.

But could she? That little voice of intuition in her soul fought that last option.

Carl glanced over at her for the hundredth time in her rumination. He was learning to read her well, just as she was trying to understand him. His handsome face etched in deep contemplation hadn't softened in the last hour, yet his humor lay just below the surface of his furrowed brow when he held out his hand to her, wiggling his fingers playfully. Should she take it?

Gloveless, because frankly, propriety was the last thing on her mind when she departed Caldas da Rainha, she placed her hand in his open palm. His fingers clenched around it.

"What are ya thinking?" he asked softly, clearly concerned for her.

"About Suzannah's baby." She sighed. "I'll never be a mother, but I know how Suzannah must feel, her desire to give the best and protect her children. She's about to bring a child into the world when their futures are all so uncertain. Oh, I…feel so helpless. I couldn't save Richard either!" The tears threatened and she swallowed them down.

"Take solace in that they're safe where they are, for now. We'll help them. Don't worry about it, Red." He squeezed her hand then turned the wheel, taking yet another dirt road, evident by the cloud of dust the sedan kicked up when he pressed the gas pedal.

"Carl, I don't mean to be rude, but we've been driving northeast for some time. Shouldn't we be headed south?"

He laughed, once again redirecting the state of her mind. "Sheesh, one opportunity behind the wheel and you're already an expert navigator."

"I'll have you know that I have an excellent sense of direction. Lisbon is south."

"That's right. It is."

"Then where are we headed?"

"There's someplace special I'd like to show ya. Every time I come back to Portugal, I make a pilgrimage for my mother, light a few candles, and say a few prayers. It'll do you good, might even cheer you up."

Her first instinct was to recoil at the thought of visiting a holy place, but...oddly, because Carl was suggesting it, she didn't balk. Sure, the emptiness inside her heart needed something to fill it with, a temporary bandage, but religion or any god couldn't do it. "I don't think anything could help, but I'll go with an open mind."

"You can stay in the car if ya like, but I made a promise to my mother—I'm sure you understand."

"That's sweet of you. Will you be long?"

"Nuh-uh. I'll have you back to your swanky hotel before the sun sets. Hopefully."

"If you don't mind me asking...are you...Roman Catholic?" she asked tentatively.

"Born and raised. Does that bother you?"

"Not at all." She knew a practicing Catholic in Vassar, but at the time, she had the same negative opinion of Papists as she had of Jews. The latter opinion had decidedly changed, and she was open to changing the former, seeing that it was Carl who was the Catholic. Elena Lupescu claimed to be a Catholic, too, but of that she was skeptical; the woman was adept at deception and lacked a moral compass.

He said nothing further about this mysterious place of pilgrimage as they drove for another twenty minutes through hills and valleys, and stunning wooded grasslands. She passed the time admiring the landscape while lost in her thoughts, reconciling her future with an equal measure of logic and self-convincing. Deep reflection obviously occupied both their minds, yet he hadn't let go of her hand, and she was thankful for that. It comforted her as she mentally prepared for the choices and commitments she'd have to make when she got back to New York. She wished she could demonstrate Carl's sanguinity when facing obstacles, but that wasn't her nature—not anymore.

Finally, they stopped at a narrow lane where a sign pointed to *Capela das Apariçoes* (Chapel of the Apparition) somewhere hidden at the end of a green field dotted by holly oak trees and filled with flowers.

"Where are we?"

"It's called Cova da Iria. The hamlet is Fatima," he said, letting go of her hand.

"It's lovely here. Peaceful."

"Yuh-huh. It's a special place in Catholic history."

He didn't elaborate, and she wondered if he was being deliberately cryptic, respectful of her beliefs, in light of her voiced atheism.

The BMW slowly drove down the lane and she could see a few other visitors strolling through the field, and others kneeling in prayer surrounding a priest dressed in a black cassock.

At the end of the lane, a tiny one-room building made of white stucco and a dark shingled roof marked their arrival. Its gold cross poised at the roof peak bid them welcome.

"Here we are," Carl announced with a smile, cutting the engine. Turning to her he said, "I won't be long, but feel free to walk around the grounds."

THE LISBON AFFAIR

"I'll probably just stay put and listen to the birdsong until you come back. Maybe I'll have a smoke while I wait."

"As you wish. Say, Red, can I axs ya a personal question?"

"Anything."

"Did you ever believe in God?"

"Oh yes! As a child, well…before college."

"And was Richard an unbeliever, too?"

"Quite so, but in the end—in battle—it changed."

Without reply, he opened the car door then exited. Resting hands on the door, he leaned down to face her still seated within. "And if ya had a *wish*…what would it be?"

"I think you know."

"Is that all? Nuthin' else?"

"What could I possibly wish for that I don't already have?"

He simply smiled again, without even attempting to proselytize or explain the history of Cova da Irina or ask further questions about her and Richard's religious views. Admittedly, there were quite a few things she'd wish for, but they were mostly impossible selfish desires. *More time with Richard. A baby.* Other wishes just seemed like lofty platitudes, but she voiced them with a sigh anyway. "I suppose I'd wish for the war to end. For the boys to come home to their families. For an end to fascism. For peace in the world."

"Peace…it's been the message of Fatima since 1917. That's a swell wish."

He removed his hat then placed it on the seat before turning to the chapel. He shut her out when he closed the chapel door behind him. Oddly, she didn't like that feeling of him within and her without. He with his quiet confidence, and she, feeling like a fool sitting there all alone waiting for him to do whatever Catholics did with rosaries and novenas in their prayer life. She opened the cigarette case and looked down at the contents. Carl had hope and prayer. All she had were six Portuguese cigarettes and despair.

Looking up at the closed door, she couldn't help being curious—drawn to the unknown and wanting more. What happened in 1917? Whose message of peace was it? What made this Fatima place so special that for twenty-six years pilgrims gathered in prayer in an empty field of wildflowers and a makeshift chapel?

Outside the one-room house, bouquets of flowers had been left on the stoop.

With a sharp snap, she closed the case then exited the car. She tied the scarf over her head and then climbed the steps to the door, heart thundering as she turned the doorknob.

It hit her like a wave: the peace, the heavy—yet not oppressive—silence of prayerful repose. And there was Carl with his back to her, in all his masculine strength kneeling in prayer before what she assumed was a statue of The Blessed Virgin Mary atop a marble pillar. He'd humbled that powerful self-assurance of his in this hallowed place of entreaty. Here, he found consolation from his demons and sought guidance in whatever struggles life threw at him.

In the dim light, candles flickered all around the perimeter of the chapel and the afternoon sun streamed through the lone stained-glass window, casting a colorful kaleidoscope across the floor and his brown suit jacket. What should she do? Go back to the car? Stay?

Choosing the latter, she sat in the last pew, eyes resting on the man she had come to admire more than almost all in her circle. Steadfast and true, faithful and devout, forthright and good-humored, talented and now, humbled; Carl Wilson was everything she had been missing.

After many minutes of admiring him from behind, her gaze roamed upward to the crucifix overlooking the chapel. The nails and the red stains below them conveyed the struggle of a man persecuted for preaching love and forgiveness, and her heart swelled with compassion. She closed her eyes at the sight, reflecting on what Carl and others believed: this statue represented the Son of God. In a world on fire, it was he they sought to find solace. As she had once reflected, what did she have to comfort her?

In her contemplation, someone sat beside her—a familiar warm hand—took hers. Carl said nothing, just sat there, his shoulder touching hers. She gazed up and her eyes met his infused with understanding, and dare she believe—love?

Even though her heart was full, she could not admit to mirroring that emotion, but she would concede that Carl Wilson moved her beyond words and music. He was more than a good friend, and the guilt in admitting such to herself had disappeared in the comfort of her hand cradled in his.

It was well past dark when Evie switched a lamplight on in her hotel suite's parlor. What a day of emotional upheaval. She was exhausted mentally and physically. Their long drive back to Estoril was spent mostly in silence, exchanging only a few pleasantries after she prodded Carl to tell her more about Cova da Irina. She vowed to herself to give his explanation of Marian apparitions with calls to prayer consideration in deference to him, as implausible as it sounded. Yet, she couldn't deny the peace she'd felt when there.

As she walked to the bedroom, she disrobed, dropping one garment at a time to the floor, glad to be free of the confines of clothing. Having left a trail behind her, she sat on the bed, liberating her body with a relieved sigh from its final restricting undergarment and tossed her uncomfortable garter belt onto the nearby slipper chair.

The cigarettes called to her. After slipping into her robe, she walked across the darkened room to the window. *Such a glorious night.* The high moon over the sea inspired reflection on how the ebb and flow—high and low tides—were like life. Richard…Lisbon…Lupescu…the Druckers…and a clarinetist had changed her life forevermore. The good came with the bad in their constant fluctuation under the stars and the scrutiny of the man in the moon. Or in Carl's opinion, God Almighty. When she stepped aboard the *Serpa Pinto* thirteen days earlier she had no conception of what lay ahead. Admittedly, there was no turning back to her existence at The Dakota. Her entire being was fighting the idea of cabling Albert for assistance. Yes, he could help the Druckers, but would he *agree to* was another matter. Further, could she truly resolve to living at The Lancashire? Could she forget Carl, the man who brought her to life, and helped her move through her grief?

Underneath all her confusion and undeniable feelings for Carl, she wondered if she had been a fraud all these years by playing a role that Mother required her to play and Richard expected her to play. She had cut short her last year of Vassar by marrying, denying herself the opportunity to see Europe, pursue even more education. She loved Richard, but it wasn't a consuming love. What was love?—a comfortable blanket to hide under? Living together or apart in amiable companionship, like Albert and Ann shared for the sake of nation and family? She and Richard seemed to be carving out a similar marriage for the sake of his naval service.

She blew out a long stream of smoke then asked the moon, "Or is love a topsy-turvy rollercoaster ride filled with passion and selflessness? Is it an arousing exploration of self and the world beside a mate who not only encourages but takes on even more demons without expectation of reciprocation? Is true love a feeling that makes your heart stop in the same manner at the thought that you'll never see him again or when you lay eyes on him every time?"

She'd not been standing before the window for more than ten minutes and already she missed Carl's company. Despite the many secrets she knew he hid and his evasiveness on more issues than she could count, he *was* the warm blanket that soothed her. He was also a selfless, frustrating man who drove her nuts like the moon drove the seas to its quiet ebb and stormy flow! He was her Magellan, guiding and challenging her to explore life to its fullest as she struggled to navigate on the surest—safest—fulfilling—course. Was she the swallow, and he the land—home?

Madam Lupescu's words came to mind as she admired the moonglow on the rippling water.

"Please, let's move on from the topic of my love life and focus on the subject of our article—yours. Tell my readers about your ex-husband, the army officer."

"Ah...Ion Tâmpeanu, he was handsome officer in Romanian Royal Army, and I was a foolish twenty-four-year-old girl. What did I know of love? I thought life would be so daring and thrilling as wife of a strong military man, but that was a child's fancy. The truth was not so much exciting. I was quickly bored with life in the garrison, and he was interested in his drink. It lasted only a short while—four years in total, but in truth, darling, I was through with the major after one year. By the time I met Carol in '23, I had already taken several meaningless lovers to pass time. Then I discovered true love—thrilling love in '25 when I met Carol again. He taught me devotion."

"What happened to Ion?"

"I do not know. I have not thought of him in years. You may think my world is so eventful—Romania to Paris back to Romania. Escaping to Spain then Lisbon, Bermuda, and Mexico City. All these places, spouses, lovers, palace intrigue, detractors, war. But there is one world and one adventure of importance: mine and Carol's love affair. Together we enjoy the quiet of cards and books and the excitement of race cars, horses, and the occasional glass of champagne. We live for today and make love in moonlight! My only regret is that time causes us to age. Seize the day, darling. Time goes too fast."

She snuffed the cigarette in the ashtray on her way to the vanity and the bird-shaped brooch Richard had given her. He knew how much she loved that Millay poem. Yet, this bird sat stoically upon a branch. It was time to soar, time to fly.

Reverently, she placed it back down then walked to the parlor and her travel diary.

March 11, 1943

My life has come to an impasse. Either I continue to languish in my grief for Richard and my droll unfulfilling life, or I change course. Today's events have opened the door to greater introspection. The outcome will determine my future. No! I cannot—absolutely cannot—return to New York until my commitment to the Druckers' safety is brought to a happy conclusion. I will remain in Lisbon as a champion for them doing what I can until they can return with me, no matter how long that takes.

And, as for Carl, it's high time that I admit to myself that try as I might to fight the feeling, I have fallen for him. In fact, I have been attracted to him from the first moment I saw him aboard the Serpa Pinto—as insufferable as he is!

Degraded bird, I give you back your eyes forever, ascend now whither you are tossed; Forsake this wrist, forsake this rhyme; Soar, eat ether, see what has never been seen; depart, be lost, But climb!"

———◇———

TWENTY
All for You

March 13

$\mathcal{A}$ smoky haze hung in the intimate ballroom of the Hotel Metrópole where a lone couple swayed to the mellow sound of "Blue Champagne" on the dance floor. They were lost in each other's arms, far away from the evening's crowd of merrymakers and the war destroying Europe beyond Portugal. Here, it was evident that the Germans loved the capitol city and its leader, having come to consider Salazar's regime acceptably fascist in his totalitarian and anti-communist rule.

A dozen arms raised cocktails at the bar as a group of businessmen toasted *der Führer* with vows to annihilate Churchill and Roosevelt, but the fellas in the band kept playing, not understanding the language.

Wearing a black tuxedo, Otto Wegener sat ram-rod straight with crossed long legs, his chair turned to face the orchestra. His steely glare was front and center at the stage end, enjoying Dutch's music and Kay's pitch-perfect voice. Evident by the Nazi's leer, her vocals weren't the only things he appreciated about Kay. Her bare midriff and on-stage performance—as though she sang just for him—were highly provocative. The girl was good like that. Carl watched it all from his window dressing: stage position with clarinet blowing while his eyes and mind dissected it all.

As he'd explained to Evie, these visiting Krauts weren't bothered by the American dance music set. Perhaps, Portugal's neutrality lulled them into letting their hair down, so to speak. Dutch had finally acquiesced to changing the music after the rebellious Canadians in the band threatened to strike. Lord knows he wasn't too happy with pandering to the Jerries, either. Those thugs snuffed out his future, but he'd kept his opinion about the music selection to himself. None of it was any of his beeswax. His heart was not invested in the Dutch Ellerton Orchestra but playing for the Germans was just what he needed to be doing at this time.

Wegener's party included two high ranking officials within Salazar's government. Tomorrow, Carl would place their activities as a top priority and contact one of the SIS's inside men at the Bank of Portugal. It was likely that they were on the Reich's payroll in securing wolfram beyond the German's agreed upon contract amounts.

Wearing a greedy, wide grin, *the* Lisboeta banker, strolled into the ballroom. Known by all Intelligence bureaus for his cozy rapport with the Nazis, particularly his friendship with the German Ambassador, and his relationship as host to the Duke and Duchess of Windsor in '41, Rodrigo Esteves brandished suave charisma and devilishly good looks. The man played with, for, and among, all sides—including the Jewish one—at Salazar's insistence and acted as middle man to anyone who wanted to do business with the Estado Novo. Carl wasn't surprised to see him stride to the table of his dear friend, the German Ambassador. The two men greeted each other with a hearty handshake of genuine appreciation then, together, left the ballroom through the corridor beside the bar.

Although Wegener and Operation Midas were Carl's assignment, he awaited the arrival of one other man to the Metrópole: Berkshire.

Begrudgingly arranged through Irena—now that Purvis had left for America—he'd asked for her to get word to their handler and arrange for a meeting at the hotel since there was no time to travel north to their customary dead-drop at the farmhouse. A plan had formed in his mind that if he could locate Drucker, then he just might accomplish two things at once. The first objective was admittedly purely selfish: keep Evie in Lisbon. The other would fulfill his promise to her: secure passage for the family in four days. But the latter was contingent on the former.

Musgrove walked in wearing a PVDE uniform, cigarette rising to his lips as he examined the players nearest to his entrance. The man was a clandestine genius who could assume any role with any cover and carry it off seamlessly. In fact, he was better than that fella with the SOE, Beevor. The crowd separated making way for the intimidating uniform, even if the man wearing it was shorter than most in the room. The big cheese took a seat at a deuce table against the wall, continuing to smoke. They acknowledged each other with a nod before Musgrove ran his pinky over his thin mustache. It wasn't code for anything, just that annoying habit of his.

"Ladies and Gentlemen, this next Benny Goodman number you'll be sure to love. 'The Wang Wang Blues' featuring the talent-ed Carl Wilson on the licorice stick, and Fingers Hughes tickling the ivories," Dutch said.

Germans loved the clarinet, and for a few seconds all eyes turned to him when he took flight and generally on any night, under any circumstance, he'd revel in the attention, but not tonight. His heart stopped dead because Evie unexpectedly entered the ballroom.

She stole the show right out from under him when she sashayed past the bar then the tables. She wore a siren-red silk gown with slight train that followed behind her. With ruby red lips and hair cascading in rose-gold ripples to her shoulders she was a knockout. A peek-a-boo wave covered one eye in alluring, Veronica Lake seduction. Evie's aura and diamond, ruby necklace cut through the smoke in a million facets of light—and heads turned—including Wegener's and Musgrove's. His girl sure knew how to make an entrance. Controlled and fluid, she moved through the room effortlessly, unaffected by a hundred sets of eyes on her shapely figure, but her peepers were locked with *his* as she drew closer to an empty table nearest the stage. A seductive smirk played upon her kisser. Wowza!

Evie sat. She was there to see him, but her smile receded when her attention fell to the lanky German approaching her.

Wegener's smile grew with recollection of the beauty, and as Carl worked liquid notes from his stick, he prayed she'd remember her impromptu cover in Rossio Square: Eva von Lamberg. He was helpless to help her.

As expected, the thug offered her a seat at his table after introductions were made, making it impossible for her to decline his attention yet again. The situation sent Carl's warning bells into overdrive. His two worlds were now colliding.

The song came to an end and Musgrove signaled him with a scratch to his eyebrow, but he was torn, afraid to leave Evie unattended. Damn! He had no choice but to exit behind a curtain. His commanding officer waited. Down a dimly lit service corridor, he arrived at the kitchen where the delivery entrance at the back of the hotel bid his escape.

Even in this magical City of Light, there was enough shadow in which to hide as he made his way between old buildings and narrow streets to a private garden behind an eighteenth-century townhome. Moments later, Musgrove pushed the rickety gate open and they met under jacaranda tree.

"You are looking quite spiffy, old man."

"Thanx. Where'd you steal the uniform from?"

"One of my moles always comes through. It pays to be a man of my stature on the Iberian Peninsula."

"Right."

"I see you took my advice about the senator's sister. Jolly good job, Phoenix."

"Yes, sir. I've kept my eye on her—nothing else—just my eye."

"What is so urgent that you needed to see me?"

He paced. "It's about the girl. Turns out she was sent to Lisbon by her editor to locate a German Jewish family and bring them back to America."

"Ah, sticky situation."

"But one of them, the patriarch, was taken by the secret police to an undisclosed location. They think he's a communist, an intellectual refugee."

"Bad luck. Those PVDE blokes think everyone is a Bolshy."

"I'd like to locate the German and arrange for his release, and..." He took a breath, "obtain the necessary paperwork to see him and his family to safe passage aboard the *Serpa Pinto* in four days."

Musgrove laughed. "What you ask is bloody impossible. You know as well as I that the Yanks will never let him in."

"I'll vouch that he's not part of any dissident group. When children are involved, I don't believe in impossibilities."

"And you'd take a national security risk on a dame's word that he's not a communist?"

He didn't answer because in his heart he knew that was exactly what he was doing. Faith, charity, and love—for Evie—were steering his actions.

His superior shook his head. "She must be quite a woman. Why, even Wegener couldn't take his eyes off her when she came into the ballroom."

"She is. Sir, look here, I've axst nothing of the SIS since my recruitment at the hospital, but I'm axsin' now, and I'm not just axsin'—I'm demanding my due—calling in that IOU ya owe me before I give up my life for this bizness. What trouble could it be to get MI9 to process their paperwork through the repatriation office? What's five more Jewish refugees to the Embassy? Small potatoes, I tell ya."

"Don't get miffed, old man. I have not said no yet. But if I make enquiries for you, what are you further willing to do for me?"

"That's not the way IOUs work, but if I must…I'll continue my service for *your* king and country until the end of the war. I won't lie to ya. I'm loyal to my oath, but I'm loyal to my country first. This is an American senator's sister sent on a humanitarian mission we're talking about and I'm an all-American fella committed to that life, liberty, and the pursuit of happiness credo we Yanks extol." *And I made a holy vow to God to intervene.*

"Your patriotic loyalty is commendable—and insubordinate—but Mrs. Somerset is also the Baron of Sallingham's daughter-in-law. *British* peerage."

"I won't pretend that I didn't know that."

Musgrove leaned against the tree trunk, propping a foot up behind him as he considered the situation and ultimatum. After a long minute, he stated with a sneer. "If I didn't know any better, I would guess you are in love with the redhead, am I correct?"

"That's nunya beeswax."

"It is all my affair. There might not be room aboard the *Serpa*. Berths are a rare commodity, these days."

"Yeah, well, my plan is to send the family to America using Mrs. Somerset's first-class ticket. Her suite aboard the ship is large enough for four adults and a child."

Chuckling, Musgrove eyed him. "Well, well! You've been to her stateroom."

"It's not like that, *old man.*"

"Have you considered the advantage a woman such as this Mrs. Somerset could be in the service of the SIS? She's already passed Intelligence musters."

"Wuttya getting at?"

"If I locate this chap, and miraculously get him released, then acquire the necessary travel papers…the Crown's payment is *her* service, along with your continued service until *we* deem appropriate to relieve you both of duty. You saw the way every Jerry in that ballroom responded to her. Wegener himself could not peel his eyes away. And, well, not only can MI6 use another leggy swallow, but you inadvertently have acquired an alluring agent who has already set a trap for Herr General."

"She's not that type of girl."

"Neither was Irena, but that changed and now the Polish chippy is having a gay old time. For her, all it takes is a good stiff john thomas, which Stephan seems to be denying her."

His sentiments exactly, but he didn't care about Irena and Stephan or her method of extracting information from her prey. Further, he didn't like Musgrove's price at all. Evie was not chattel to be sold to the Brits in exchange for a mercenary act. "I'm not sure Mrs. Somerset will agree to the Crown's terms...and that would mean I have to blow my cover. Won't that be in violation of Britain's Official Secrets Act?"

Musgrove stood straight, and then lit another cigarette. "A minor detail, easily overlooked. If you don't speak with her then the Jews will remain in Lisbon. Either you both agree to my terms or bugger off. I don't give a toss if she is a Brit by marriage, the sister of a senator, or the object of your affection."

"You play a mean game of stickball, Berkshire. I'll discuss it with her *after* you get me the intelligence. If you don't come through, then I will *bugger off*—back to America or the OSS—and the SIS loses a good agent. Somehow, I don't think the Foreign Office will appreciate that." He dug his fingers below the tuxedo pocket square, withdrawing a slip of paper. "Here are the names and relevant information for their travel papers. You can find them in Caldas da Rainha. The first name is our missing friend."

"You Yanks really are tenacious, rebellious fellows, but I'm sure you will see things my way in the end." He raised an eyebrow making his point clear. "Expect Irena tomorrow with my findings and further instructions."

Carl wanted to groan. Fending off her advances was getting tiresome. There was only one dame that his john thomas was interested in getting stiff for. "Anyone but Irena," he said.

Twenty minutes later, Carl traversed the path from which he came. Walking through the kitchen, he swiped a cluster of red grapes from a tray of fruit as he passed by, promptly popping one into his mouth. He felt oddly self-satisfied at having laid down the law to Musgrove. Nope, he'd not continue to put his life in jeopardy if the SIS was unwilling to help a persecuted family. What the hell was it all for then? It's not as if the Allies didn't know what was going on in Poland and Germany at those work camps. He'd read the intelligence himself, some of it even found its way into the press. Helping the Druckers toward safety was the very least the British could do in a country where they had influence.

He crushed a grape in his teeth, his thoughts turning dark…Evie. What would he say? How would she react? No. He could not put her in the position that Musgrove was asking. Not Evie. Not ever. Yet he had, hadn't he?

He swung the door open into the passageway and plowed smack into Evie. His unoccupied hand immediately responded with a securing clasp behind her shoulders; his other hand dropped the grapes. At the opening back of the gown, her skin felt as smooth as cream, and she smelled like blossoming honeysuckle on a hot summer night. He was caught up in her literally and figuratively. The fruit lay at his feet in a distant memory.

"There you are! I was so worried about you, Carl. You disappeared."

"Gee, I'm sorry, Red. I…um…had to take a break. That last set left me a little winded."

Under the soft sconce lamplight, she glared at him sideways. Yeah, even to his own ears it sounded like malarkey; he never got winded when playing the horn.

"Did you see who was in the ballroom? It was that Wegener man. Goodness, I thought my heart would stop."

"I hope you remembered Eva von Lamberg."

"I did!"

"Did you dance with him?"

"How could I deny him? It would have been considerably rude and he's quite intimidating. I daresay, he wouldn't take no for a second time."

Carl smiled playfully. "Neither would I. You look beautiful tonight. You smell even better."

"Thank you." She blushed, and his hand slid a little lower, unwilling to relinquish their proximity.

"You'll have to go back, placate him with a dance, ya know?"

"Yes. He's expecting me. Hopefully, someone will rescue me from his clutches."

If only he could tonight. Perhaps Musgrove would be the gentleman to do so.

His heart skipped; his groin stirred at the feel of the small of her back, that sexy indentation concealed under luxurious draping. This kind of love that tugged at his heart was an unfamiliar emotion for him, but with Evie as the recipient of it, it was the most powerful sensation he'd ever felt. It was more than physical attraction. Every cell in his being came alive in her nearness. He was tinder to her match.

Their mouths were poised for love making, and his admiration switched from her kissable lips up to her eyes sparkling like emeralds. He fell to her allure, unable to resist her intoxicant. Banishing the gentleman in him, he pulled her closer bringing her body flush against his. There was no objection. In fact, she welcomed this intimate trespass.

"*Com licença*," a passing waiter said on his way to the kitchen, causing them both to fluster apart in embarrassment when he bent to pick up the scattered grapes.

Silently, Carl took her hand, guiding her toward a shadowy corner where he resumed his hold on her inches from his frame. Again, his hand slowly caressed down her back, resting dangerously low.

"You came to see me play tonight."

She breathed heavily, "I did."

"Because you want to know about the Druckers?"

He smoothed the hair at her temple, admiring her stunning countenance. Oh yes, he loved everything about her.

"No. I'm here because..."

"Because you missed me," he said softly finishing her sentence, unable to hide his feelings any longer.

"Yes."

"And you don't want to go back to New York."

"No."

"That's good, 'cause I don't want ya to go either."

"Oh?"

He slowly dragged his thumb pad over her kissable cherry lips and whispered, "In case you didn't notice, I'm in love with ya, Red."

"I know. In case you forgot, women are intuitive about those things," she said with a saucy smile.

His head inched closer to hers. She breathed in anticipation.

Sparks ignited between them and he delighted in how her skin burned with passion below his palm. They both were ready to combust.

Her plump soft lips fit against his perfectly when they met in a deep kiss. Consuming. Heated. And Evie responded with a sensual purr and the gift of her tongue, searching for his. Her fingers smoothed up his arm, rising, raking through the back of his hair. All his gentlemanly restraint ceased at her caress, in the taste of her mouth, from the sweet fragrance of passion. He catapulted like a shooting star when she pressed her hip against his manhood, pushing red silk against straining black cloth.

That too-short but memorable lip-lock branded him, but the proper Mrs. Evelyn Somerset came to her senses and she pulled away—embarrassed, ashamed—and beautifully flushed. Her eyes and rosy-hued cheeks gave her heart away; he had awoken the sleeping provocateur in her, yet she still fought the freedom to soar.

"One day you'll let yourself fly, Evie," he groaned, unable to release his hold on her, unable to end this intimate tryst in the dark. He kissed her neck with lingering suckles and nibbles, reveling in the way her hot flesh felt against his mouth. She dipped her head back, allowing him greater access.

"My wings are no longer clipped," she said dreamily.

"Then let me kiss you again so we can fly together," he murmured, his lips clinging at the hollow of her soft throat.

Her gloved hand raised his chin. Breathy pants from those luscious, open lips of hers tickled his mouth as her full bosom heaved against him. Their connected gaze spoke volumes. She was as enraptured as he.

He could take her to bed tonight. Love her completely, like she needed to be loved. She wanted him—all of him, but he'd wait to prove himself to her and come clean with her, so that when he made her his, it would be honest and pure. He'd love her so perfectly that all their demons would vanish.

Evie deposited a tender brush to his lips filled with so much promise and unadulterated passion that her knees went weak.

But he was right there to catch her.

——◈——

TWENTY-ONE
We'll Meet Again

*E*vie's flesh crawled under Wegener's hand upon her bare back during her promised dance—all under the attentive eye of her hero Carl and his performance of "Perfidia." His examination of them upon the dance floor of the Metrópole was welcomed, unlike when aboard the *Serpa Pinto*. What a gem! He was always looking out for her.

In silence, the lanky German navigated the crowded dance floor as she attempted to focus her thoughts away from the experience by recalling how her skin felt in the erotic moment she'd just spent with the Yinzer who had won her affection. Carl had touched her soul and not just through his kisses and sensual caress, but through his goodness and brilliant essence. She'd never felt so…so desired before.

But it was not to be. Her dance partner awkwardly cleared his throat, bringing her from her musing. The song segued into another and he did not release her. One dance had seamlessly turned into two.

She looked up and softly smiled but did not refuse the man. And even though Carl was at her back, at the bar there were at least a dozen Germans and the intense stare of one PVDE officer. Fear kept her dancing. At least two decades older than she, he was not physically ugly. On the contrary. He was quite distinguished at face value, but she identified sinister lurking behind his gray, hooded eyes. His aura was dark and menacing; she had felt it while near

Café Chave d'auro when searching for the Druckers, but her intuition had nothing to do with her circumspection. Although disguised behind a finely tailored black tuxedo, her dance partner was an important general in the Wehermacht, and this was all she needed to know about him.

She recalled the tale of Madam Lupescu's skillful deceptions and reliance upon the art of disguise, like when she infiltrated the palace, dressed as a chamber maid. Evie prepared herself, getting into character, playing her own part when Wegener took her into his arms for a Fox Trot. Their small talk was cordial and pleasant, even if she was lying through her teeth about almost everything. Eva von Lamberg—not Mrs. Evelyn Somerset—was doing the talking and dancing. Goodness, she was acting the part of a secret agent in the City of Spies, under dissecting eyes and in the embrace of the enemy.

She stored away each experience for that one-day sensational article or novel, just as she had when dancing with Purvis aboard the *Serpa*...but that metaphoric ship had sailed under Carl's protective insistence.

It was all so mysterious and would be highly titillating if she wasn't in this Nazi thug's embrace, following his tight lead.

"You are a lovely dancer," Wegener whispered in clipped German into her ear and she closed her eyes imagining it was her music man's seductive voice doing the wooing and his masterful fingers pressed against her back, not the rigid hand of a man allied to evil.

"Thank you. It is easy for a lady to look proficient when she has such a strong lead," she mollified.

"You did not say what has brought you to Lisbon, Fräulein?"

"Lisbon is enticing with its sun and continental visitors of the finest families. Frankly, I often grow tired of Salzburg society. My mother credits wanderlust. I credit boredom. The summer festival is too far away and I hate idleness. Lisbon has enough diversions to keep me quite happy."

"Unfortunately, I do not have the luxury of boredom. The sea is what I most enjoy about the Iberian Peninsula. I was born in a small fishing village south of Munich. Ah, how I miss the simple life of upper Bavaria."

She gazed up at his face, noting a softening to his features, but he quickly recovered from his fond recollection, his dance frame stiffening.

"But my father felt my duty to country was more important, so I left many years ago. I appreciate the fisherman's life in Diessen am Ammersee and in Lisbon, but I reside in Berlin for important undertakings."

Jeepers, she was a long way from New York City. If her brother could see her now discussing life's pleasantries with a Jerry! If *Richard* could see her now! Evelyn Somerset was slowly slipping from her sight in a frightening, and yet fascinating, turn of events.

Silence returned between them as they danced through the cloud of cigarette smoke over the ballroom.

"Will you remain long in Estoril?" he blurted. "I would like very much to see you again."

"I'm sorry. I'll be leaving Portugal shortly, but thank you."

"Will you consider remaining until my business for the Reich is complete? I would hate to return home to Berlin without having had the pleasure to dine with you or take you to the theatre or a bullfight. Portuguese horsemen are extraordinary."

"You are kind, but regrettably, I cannot."

"Perhaps you will postpone your travel and allow me to escort you to Prime Minister Salazar's reception next week. It is in honor of our ambassador's achievements on behalf of the *Führer*. There will be visitors from the highest-born families in attendance—those who are most supportive of the Reich."

The German Ambassador! No! He would know her as Evelyn Somerset after having spent two hours in his delightful company at the casino when she first arrived.

The song ended and Wegener finally led her from the dance floor. Unfortunately, she could not extricate herself from his gentle hold's subtle insistence as he continued pressing for her attention and promise to see him again.

At her table, he scooped up her purse and kept their advance toward *his* deuce table. This was not what she had planned at all and she wished upon all Carl believed holy to come and save her. Wegener slid out the chair across from his and she accepted, waiting for him to sit before refusing his invitation. Almost immediately the waiter bustled over with a bottle of wine, which Wegener approved, and without asking her, he directed the young man to pour them both a glass.

This was quickly becoming more than just a dance to placate the German's fascination with her.

"You were about to tell me that you would be delighted to accompany me to the Prime Minister's home."

She chuckled. "Was I?"

Leaning toward her, he raised his glass for a toast. Internally, she cringed expecting a declaration to Hitler's good health, or a hearty "*Sieg Heil*," but was surprised when Wegener relaxed his posture and looked her straight in the eye. "Here is to you, Eva."

"*Zum Wohl*," she said. Her heart hammered now that his intentions were as clear as a bell—a warning bell.

Goodness, she could almost feel Carl's penetrating stare at her back when their glasses clinked and a teeny tiny thought crossed her mind at the first notes of Cole Porter's "Night and Day." His timing of the song and its purpose was also as resounding—he was jealous and reminding her that he was right behind her. She smirked at the thought then took a small sip of the sweet wine.

"So, you will stay in Lisbon," the German confidently stated before lighting a cigarette for himself, but not offering one to her.

"Herr Wegener, I am truly flattered but I am sorry, I cannot join you at the reception either. You see, I'm meeting friends in Nice in a few days and I simply must keep my commitment."

"This is noble and unfortunate. Ah well, perhaps another time you will enjoy a bullfight. Perhaps on your travels through Spain you will make a stop to Madrid. I encourage this as it is a display of man's victory over beast. Such will be the Wehrmacht's fate, yes?"

"Of course. Is that your business here? Are you in the military? Given your love of the sea, I assume you joined the *Kreigsmarine*?"

"I wish it was so, but I began my service as a soldier in the *Heer*. I am now a general of the Wehrmacht."

"Well then, victory on land is assured!" she pandered. This made her sick to say, but again, her intuition told her to tread lightly until she could break away from his attempted seduction.

"Apparently not tonight, not in Lisbon."

"Please don't think of my departure as failure. It is just poor timing, I think. In my experience, time is never a favorable accomplice to one's schemes."

"Too true."

"Of course, I will consider your recommendation to view the *Cavaleiros* when in Spain. I'm sure I'll be quite affected by such a demonstration of superiority and prowess. Such determination almost always assures conquest." *But not for you. Ever.*

"Are you affected now?" His question and intonation were clear: he no longer spoke of bullfighting.

"As only a woman of the *Volksgemeinschaft* could and should be," she complimented, hoping it did not sound too much like flirting.

"*I* am affected by *you*. In case you have not noticed, I am very impressed. I admit, I was pleasantly surprised to see you this evening and have considered over these many days since Rossio Square your sparkling green eyes. Your pure and graceful manner personifies what Magda Goebbels considers the best of the German woman, one meant for a husband—and many children. A wife from *Alpenund Donau-Reichsgaue*, our Führer's birthplace, is sought after."

She'd heard about that Goebbels thug and the Reich's expected role for their women. It sure sounded like the life Albert and Queen Louise had sought to carve for her. Repulsed, she struggled to keep her smile in place. Lupescu would be proud at all the secrets she concealed behind it.

"Such a compliment!" She chuckled. "Are you truly impressed or merely attracted?"

"Both, but I think you are playing coy to arouse further interest. You may be a woman who enjoys the pursuit before the conquest, and this I can understand and appreciate. It is a way to separate the wheat from the chaff."

She smiled because what else could she do when her heart thundered in fear. "I am not a woman who toys with men, but I am honored by your interest. Shall we not just enjoy this evening for what it is…"

"A beginning until we meet again?"

With spies at every corner, she was surprised that this playboy Nazi was so eager and trusting of her. How had she evaded the minuscule scrutiny the Germans were known for? Was this simply his libido foolishly guiding him? Perhaps all he was interested in was someone to share his bed while in Lisbon.

She changed the topic to something more prosaic. "And how long will you remain in Lisbon, Herr Wegener?" Not only was it good manners to ask, but she was curious what he might divulge to her allure.

"I will be leaving in one month for Germany but while here it does not exclude my enjoyment of the company of a beautiful woman."

"Portuguese women are quite exotic."

"As are those with Bavarian blood."

Her chuckle lifted in the air. "You are quite tenacious, sir,"

"Yes." He smiled wickedly. "It is my profession."

"As a Münchner, you share my Bavarian heart. For most in Salzburg, it is a delicate subject in society, but most believe the

Anschluss succeeded in reuniting what once was lost. Our victory at the ballot box assured us that we are finally home now, restored to full German rule as it should have always remained. *Heim ins Reich*."

"I am delighted to hear such sentiment. Perhaps my duties will bring me to the *Reichsgau* Salzburg in my travels to Berlin." He took a sip of wine, then asked, "Would you like to see me again? I am not so easily dissuaded and eager to conquer your coyness." The severity of his manner was replaced by a boyish charm in his countenance.

Reichsgau Salzburg? What is that? "Regrettably, I won't be returning to Salzburg until the summer—for the annual festival and familial obligations."

She promptly sipped her wine to hide her growing fear that she would not be able to continue this ruse. There was too much she did not know about the changes to Austria following its annexation by Nazi Germany. The real Eva von Lamberg had returned to her homeland five years before the Anschluss.

Her heart jolted, when over the rim of her glass, her gaze fell to the corridor opening nearest the bar. In animated conversation, Ambassador Oswald von Hoyingen-Huene and his friend the Portuguese Banker, Rodrigo Esteves entered the ballroom.

"Oh dear...oh my," she feigned placing the glass back on the table, then blotted her brow and lips with the linen napkin.

"Are you unwell?"

"Forgive me, Herr Wegener, but I'm afraid I must leave."

"So soon? But we have only just begun to know each other."

"It has been a lovely evening and the wine is superb, as is the company, but I suddenly feel lightheaded," she abruptly stood, as did he, and she turned her back to the two important men before they spotted her.

"Then allow me to escort you back to your hotel."

"That won't be necessary. Please...stay, enjoy the orchestra and the rest of your evening."

He took her trembling hand in his and kissed it, but her gaze sought Carl's helpless narrowing of his eyes as he played.

Wegener's regretful voice broke through her panic. "*Auf Wiedersehen*. Until we meet again, Eva von Lamberg,"

"If the fates allow, Herr Wegener."

"Otto, please."

She simply smiled then left him standing at their table, feeling the burning gaze of two men at her back.

Carl watched as Evie abruptly stood when the ambassador and the banker entered the ballroom. Was it a coincidence? Why would their sudden appearance run her off, if in fact, that was the reason? Perhaps it was something Wegener had said or maybe she'd had enough of his leer. Unfortunately, he was in no position to go to her! He felt trapped by the very instrument used as his method of disguise.

He wanted to kick himself for insisting that she give up a dance to the German, but he had hoped that Musgrove would come to her aid, at least before the second dance. A glance to the big cheese leaning against the bar when the song changed dashed any hope he had. Evident by his snicker and the drag of his finger across his mustache, his superior was enjoying the scene taking place before him, allowing Evie to chart her fate. The man's inaction was a deliberate attempt at her solidification of cover no matter the cost to her for the SIS's benefit. The fool! She'd never agree to recruitment into the spy game. Further, the Foreign Office wouldn't be pleased with the extortion of an American senator's sister in exchange for a favor.

Still…Carl was angry at himself for giving Musgrove the carrot. Six weeks…six blasted weeks was all a new recruit into British Intelligence was expected to live. Sure, he'd defied the odds, but could Evie? Not likely, and his heart broke at the thought. He should have turned a deaf ear to fate when on the *Serpa Pinto*. She should have never met him! No, he'd not put her in the position

Musgrove demanded. He'd not even tell her the proposal if or
when Musgrove came through with the information they sought.
The only part of the discussion that mattered was the one where
he left his superior standing, with demand in hand, below the
Jacaranda.

Bright-eyed and loving the spotlight upon her, Kay sashayed
onto the stage. Tonight, the ditsy vocalist was a lucky penny when
she turned up because her talented pipes seduced Wegener from
his hard stare upon Evie's swaying bottom in her exit from the
ballroom.

Carl glanced over to Musgrove in conversation with the
ambassador, and he silently rejoiced in a temporary reprieve from
spying behind his clarinet. For the next few minutes, he took leave
to think only on one thing: the music he'd made with Evie in the
corridor, indulging in the memory of how she felt in his arms, the
taste of her luscious mouth, his slow caress down her spine to her
shapely bottom. Oh yes…as sinful and shameful as it all was, he'd
recall every touch. He was a man, after all. He imagined how she
would look wearing nothing but her smile in his bed, below his
body, loving him without any inhibition. And with her release,
would come the three words he longed to hear from her: "I am
yours." Not Richard Somerset's.

TWENTY-TWO
All or Nothing at All

March 14

*E*ven though his head pounded, Carl couldn't deny that he was on cloud nine. Evie'd all but admitted her mutual feelings for him the night before when he brazenly kissed her. Those few stolen minutes made him play for her from his soul in the next set, even pulling out Cole Porter for her when the Jerry got a little too close to her. This early morning, he'd revel in this elation, fleeting as it was, reconciling that her admiration of him would disappear the moment he came clean to his operation and deceit. No doubt, she was going to misinterpret his interest as part of some mission.

The elevator stopped on the ground floor of the Metrópole with a sudden jerk before the gate slid open. Stepping into the lobby, he nearly collided with a young newspaper hawker, no more than eight years of age. He wasn't the run-of-the-mill newsboy given that he wore traditional pescador attire, but he did hold a stack of papers in the crook of his arm.

"*Diário De Notícias*, Senhor," the kid said sliding one out from the bottom of the pile. "It is a special one, just for you," he said holding it out, with a cheerful grin.

Ah…he was one of Musgrove's local couriers. He withdrew a coin from his trouser pocket, flipped it into the air, caught it, then handed it to the lad. "Thanx, kid."

Ten minutes later, Carl was seated at a secluded table, enjoying a cup of coffee while listening to Helen Forrest and Harry James's

"I Had a Dream" coming over the radio within the café. After making sure he wasn't being watched, he opened the newspaper where a ciphered note waited for him on page three. He removed a pen from his inside jacket pocket and quickly translated the handwritten numbers against the newspaper page's paragraphs, lines, and letters.

Musgrove hadn't disappointed. As usual, his contacts in the Portuguese Foreign Ministry had bent to either his forceful will or the will of the British ambassador, known to pull strings for special cases.

You win, but on the conditions we discussed.

Campo da Morte Lenta, Tarrafal, on Santiago in Cape Verde

Dakota departs at 1900 hours from Lisbon Portela. Paperwork and proper attire will be waiting for you and your friend aboard. Transportation to Tarrafal be waiting for you at the hangar upon arrival. Officials will not look too closely when extraction is made.

Papers are processing. Contact new swallow to bring family to farmhouse until departure.

We had an agreement and I bloody well expect both you and her to hold to it. Renege and I turn you both over to the PVDE.

A Dakota—dammit! Musgrove was probably laughing up his sleeve when he wrote that bit. *Bad luck, old man*, he probably said to himself while writing the cipher. It's not like he wasn't witness to Carl's first flight after the accident. The two of them shared a flask of scotch to calm his shaking hands en-route to Lisbon on their first leg of Operation Night Shift.

He was furious over Musgrove's presumption that Evie was on board with the scheme. Recalling their conversation last night, he hadn't committed her involvement with MI6. In fact, he was vehemently opposed to it, but apparently Musgrove didn't care and wasn't waiting for her answer. The deal was done, and he was on the hook for both their souls. He shrugged about the looming flight considering the commitment Evie would now have to make. Getting on a plane was the least he could do.

Further, Tarrafal was no ordinary camp or typical prison. What had Drucker done to land in the worst of the worst where they hid away political menaces to society? Could he actually be a rabble-rousing communist? He wasn't sure if he should be pleased or not at having found him.

The strike of a match preceded setting flame to the corner of the letter and its burning message tossed into the ashtray. It was too late to turn back now. Both he and Evie were committed. His heart sank at the realization that telling her would ruin the best thing he had going for him since 1939. He glanced at his watch: seven in the morning; he could be at the Palácio within an hour.

After greasing the concierge's palm, Carl stood at Evie's hotel room door. His fist hovered, stilled before rapping the wood as he considered for the one-hundredth time what exactly he would say to her. Confessions, except the ones made with a priest, weren't something he was prone to do. Neither was falling in love, but he was now a master at it. Maybe it was best if he didn't knock; no one liked getting awoken by someone pounding on the door. He retrieved her room key from his suit pocket then slipped it into the lock.

The suite was basked in sunlight and the balcony doors were wide open. She sat there looking out at the sea far beyond the swaying palms as she placed a spoonful of something into her mouth. Kissed by the morning sun and backlit by the vibrant cornflower blue sky her strawberry waves fell in an alluring mess around her shoulders. His heart tugged at the glorious vision she presented. Yes, he could see himself waking every day beside her.

He cleared his throat and she jumped, clinking the spoon onto a dish.

"I'm sorry to startle you, Red," he said taking off his hat, hanging it on the coat rack.

Funny how her hand didn't clench the opening of her robe gown like it had aboard the *Serpa*. Instead, she said as though his bold intrusion was the most natural thing. "Good morning. I'm assuming your visit is important enough for you to barge in unannounced." She raised a satirical eyebrow. "Might I assume that Arnaldo gave you the key in exchange for a few escado notes?"

"You learn fast. I hope you don't mind, but I thought you might still be asleep, and the thought of surprising ya like *Sleepin' Beauty* was too tempting to pass on."

"Hmm …" she took a drink of coffee, neither confirming nor denying her pleasure or displeasure at such an act.

He promptly changed the subject. "I was concerned last night when you beat a path to the door. What did the German say to you?"

"Nothing of importance. I just realized that Eva von Lamberg was in a little too deep. My knowledge, or lack thereof, of Austria post-Anschluss could get me in a bit of trouble."

"Good thinking. He seemed a little too cozy from where I stood."

"Unnervingly so."

He walked to her, wanting to lift her from the chair and kiss her. That troubled brow on her fresh face and those untainted lips slightly pursing made his heart sink a little at the news he bore.

"But that's not why I'm here. I need to speak with you about our friends in Caldas da Rainha."

"You have news already?"

"Yuh-huh."

"Then please, join me for breakfast. I'll call down for room service and have them bring you something. What would you like? A poached egg, perhaps? Portuguese coffee?"

"No, thanx. What I have to say is gonna require something stronger than coffee and eggs for breakfast."

"Oh dear, that doesn't sound promising at all."

"On the contrary. I have good news. It's more your reaction to what I have to say that has me needing a gin and tonic."

He slid out the wrought iron chair across the table from her, then took a seat, promptly lighting two cigarettes from her gold case lying on the table.

"Now, you have my full attention. Your usual cheerfulness is gone," she said accepting the smoke from his outstretched arm.

"Before I begin, I hope ya don't take offense if I tell ya just how breathtaking you look in the morning and that...that those stolen kisses last night—"

"Of course I don't mind your compliment, and I assure you, I have no regrets at all, but...bear with me, Carl. This is highly emotional. What I feel for you is entirely...unexpected so soon after Richard's passing. I'm technically still in mourning. And, well, we only just met, really."

He took a long drag, holding her gaze and she smiled wistfully, her way of reassuring him of her affection even in her struggles. "Time doesn't matter when destiny plays its hand, Evie, but I understand. Perhaps what I am about to tell you will make whatever struggle you are working out easier to reconcile one way or another."

"I'm not sure if anything that anyone says can make this easier."

"I found Samuel."

She beamed liked he'd never seen before and gushed in a way that made him feel so gallant. "That's wonderful news! Where is he? Is he safe? Can we reunite him with his family?"

"He's in a crummy prison in the Cape Verde islands, about a three-hour flight from here, and well...I'll be leaving later this afternoon to bring him back to Lisbon. I've also made arrangements for the entire family's transit papers and..." He swallowed then took another inhale, struggling to find the right words to break it all to her. Damn. No woman had ever unnerved him like this before.

"You came through, just like you said you would. Oh, thank you, Carl!"

"Not so fast. There's more. They'll be sailing on the *Serpa Pinto* on March seventeenth."

"Perfect, darling! That's when I'm sailing. I can see them to their new home, assist them on arrival into customs."

"You won't be with them. They'll be traveling using *your* first-class ticket back to Philadelphia. It's the only way I could secure them passage."

"But what will I do?"

"You'll have other plans."

"Surely you are joking with me again. Oh, you're such a tease!"

"Unfortunately, this situation is nuthin' to joke about."

"Is this because of what I said last night in the heat of our tryst? As tempting a prospect as staying in Lisbon—with you—is, it's just not feasible. Now that we've found the Druckers, I must get back to New York, back to the paper—my life. I have obligations."

He stood, then faced the balcony railing, gazing out at the calm water unable to look at her searching, confused expression.

"The paper...Answer me this, Evie. Where is that determined reporter in ya, the one lookin' for the greatest front-page story?"

"What do you mean? She's right here. I accomplished exactly what I set out to do—interview Elena Lupescu and find the Drucker family."

"And you did real good making both happen, but aren't you going to ask me how *I* did *this*? What powerful friends I must have to release a prisoner into *my* care and arrange for transit documentation for a possible communist? Like you've said before 'I'm just a clarinetist.' "

"Why should I question you? I...You've repeatedly told me not to inquire how you know people. In fact, your reply was—I quote—'it's nunya beeswax.' I trust you, Carl, despite the specter of your side-stepping secrecy."

"I told you that you shouldn't trust anyone."

"Are you implying that I shouldn't have trusted you?"

He ran his hand through his hair. "My point is...you're not fooling me one bit, Evie. You're like that bird watch fob you wear every day. Pinned to your heart, it sits there on the branch looking pretty watching time and life tick-tock away. You *are* afraid to fly— that's your problem. And you know how I know? Every time you're anxious or stressed, you toy with the bird as though willing it to flight or finding comfort in its inertia."

"That's not true!"

"You've stifled that reporter's instinct and have stopped listening to that touted intuition of yours. Your confidence is an empty suit."

"I'm offended you think so little of me and my efforts here in Lisbon." She looked away from his challenging stare. "What does any of this have to do with the Druckers?"

"After all that ambitious talk of hot scoops, you let go of two of the biggest ones ever. You could have shined a light on that specter if only—"

"Two? The only scoop I let go of was Purvis and that was at your continued avoidance and insistence, which I begrudgingly acquiesced to."

She was correct in that. He turned to her in towering intimidation, his gaze burning down between challenge and compassion. "There's another scoop. Look. I believe you can go for bigger. It's inya, but at my slightest brush off, you never pursued what your gut told you all along. That day, on deck, you were *right* about me, but then you let it go, believed my cockamamie stories. But if I know you like I think I do, it's been nigglin' in the back of your mind for two weeks, trying to break free. You lack absolute confidence in your reporter's instinct."

Evie's mouth gaped, the cigarette stilling in her hand as she struggled to find words until she blurted. "That's...that's fiddlesticks!"

"Then maybe there's something else holding you back."

She blinked again, putting the pieces together as he hoped she would. Snuffing the smoke in the ashtray she attempted to speak, "I don't know what you are talking about."

"Replay our conversations in the back of your mind. Recall every word. How do you think I know the things I know? The people I know? How do I know so much about Purvis, about Wegener? The answer has been there all along and you guessed it in the first ten minutes of conversation with me. My clarinet. I know *why* I showed ya my cards. Do you know why you remained willfully blind to them? What are ya afraid of?"

"I don't..."

Her lip trembled, and she was near to tears when he rushed to her side, kneeling beside her.

"Red, you didn't pursue your gut feeling because you're in love with me as much as you don't want to admit it. It became clear that you stopped asking tough questions because you were guided by your heart over your instinct. You didn't wanna go after what could have been the story of a lifetime 'cause you were afraid of what you'd find out."

"What...what are you telling me? What would have I found out about your clarinet?" She leaned back from him. "Say it!"

He lowered his voice to barely a whisper as his gaze held hers, "The man you fell hook, line, and sinker for is a British Intelligence agent hiding within an orchestra. I'm a spy, Evie, a bona fide agent with the Secret Intelligence Service."

Her eyes widened.

An expected silence fell like a steel door between them.

She said nothing, but her expression said everything. She was blazing mad but the well-deserved slap never came.

"You deceived me!" she exclaimed.

"Don't take it so personally. It's what I do, Evie. Surely you can understand that. But I want you to know that from almost the beginning I *wanted* to bare my soul to you. I just had to be sure who *you* were, and now I know. You're true blue. I wouldn't be doing this if I had any doubts."

He moved to take her hand, but she reviled him as though he was tainted—as if nothing had transpired between them over the last few days.

"That's quite noble of you," she said sarcastically then turned her head from him bemoaning, "Leave. Just go."

"I won't. 'Cause now that you know…I'm gonna wait for that Vassar *Miscellany* girl you told me about—the one you've hidden away beneath The Honorable Evelyn Somerset."

"I didn't hide anything! I grew up! I married—and married well—I might add!"

"For love or status?"

Abruptly, she stood pushing back the chair. Her porcelain skin burned scarlet in fury. "That is quite enough! How dare you speak to me as if you know me so well! You don't, Carl. You don't, at all! Is that even your name? Are you even from Pittsburgh?"

There she was: Red. Hot tempered with a fanned fire in her belly that he knew had always been there, growing…waiting.

He stood with arms akimbo. "It's not my name, but I *am* a Yinzer and everything I told you about me was the God's-honest truth."

"What is your real name? I demand your absolute honesty!"

He left her on the balcony and entered the suite but she and her exasperated huff followed quick on his heels.

"My name is Jack McGrath, but you can keep calling me Carl if it suits. I like the way your tight jaw moves when ya pronounce it," he joked.

Those angry, confused tears rolling down her soft cheeks were almost his undoing, but for the road she had ahead of her, he'd play the heel—he'd put aside his feelings for her and his impulse to take her into his arms to comfort her. Perhaps her society life had done just the same when—if—things had gone topsy-turvy. He'd not coddle her from truth or real life—ever.

"How do I know you haven't used me to get to my brother? You work for the British, not for your own government! Why is that?"

"*There* you are—asking questions just like you did that night in your cabin."

"Well?"

"If I was manipulatin' you, I wouldn't have just blown my cover nor would I be about to risk my life to rescue Samuel Drucker. Let alone get on a dagnabbit airplane to do so!"

Shoving his hands into his trouser pockets, he paced as she waited for further explanation.

"Look, those damn Brits recruited me while I was getting patched up in the hospital after my crash. When they learned that I spoke a couple of languages, they thought they had a real live sucker in me, and they were right! The only thing worth living for was revenge for what the Jerries did to me. It's more than just a *few* scars." He stopped and looked up at her changed expression. "But that doesn't matter now. All that matters is that ya understand that I'm doing this for *you*…this is *all* for you because you're the best damn thing to ever happen in my life. Call me a dope, but I'm in love with you, Evie. As sure as the sun rises and sets, I'm gonna be in love with ya forever. All of ya…including your high society lockjaw, uptight hoity-toity airs, and spoiled-rotten debutante assumptions."

Her chin dropped from his brutal honesty. "I would like for you to leave, Mr. Whatever-Your-Name-Is. Forget I asked for your assistance in the first place. Go. Just go. I'll get to this Cape island myself without any help from the British or you. Me and my spoiled rotten assumptions will do just fine on our own."

"No, you won't. Cape Verde is off West Africa. Besides, the wheels are already in motion and you can't renege on deals made with the British government. What the SIS is doing for ya is an indirect favor to the senator and I gave my word—"

"Your *word* is meaningless!" she shouted.

"You may think so now, but my word is who I am. I'm not entirely the heel you take me for—and ya know it. You've known it since meeting me otherwise you wouldn't have fought it or come to the Metrópole last night. You wouldn't have kissed me like that or let me touch you...where I did."

"Where?"

"Your heart."

He couldn't be sure if she was crying when she covered her face, dropping chin to chest.

"Look, I'm sorry, Evie, but the way I see it is you have two choices. Either you call the whole thing off and let the Druckers go on as before and face the consequences of putting the British in a compromised position. Or two, you let us proceed as planned." He ran his hand through his hair. "Sure, you can go it alone, find some poor schmoe to fly you down there, but then you risk getting' locked up yourself."

Her head snapped up, eyes wide.

"In the process, you'll expose your relationship with an American politician, calling into question your involvement and interference in the Portuguese refugee policy pertaining to communist agitators." He couldn't help exaggerating by adding this last bit, but he didn't have time for guilt when playing upon hers. Without her agreement, he'd sold her soul last night and now he needed her commitment. "The newspapers will call out your brother, implying he's a traitor, accusing him of sending you to Lisbon to return with a member of the Communist Party. Is that what you want? A scandal that'll rock your high society world?"

"But that's not the truth! He doesn't even know I'm here!"

"Those Limeys'll make it the truth and every international paper will run with whatever 'official' story they're told. It's called propaganda and every side dishes it out. I'm sure even your editor will have to print it when it comes across the AP wire at the *Spectator*. My guess is you already have one of them government fellas calling the shots over there. Imagine the headline."

She plopped down onto the settee. "This is such a mess! What am I to do?"

"The thing is, Evie, we're tied in this thing together. You need my help and I need your help and the Druckers need both our help. What's it gonna be? Am I getting on that plane to Cape Verde or not?"

He observed her analytic deliberation in the changing emotions playing across her face, until she looked up at him, silent and clear-eyed. The real Evelyn Somerset emerged from hiding when challenged, and the so-called moxie she prided herself on replaced her confusion.

"If you are doing this for me, what will I have to owe you in return? Like you said, everyone has a price, and your so-called employer would not do this without compensation worthy of the danger and risk," she stated.

"That's a mighty fine reporter's question. Off the record, I called in my one and only IOU, made hospital bedside with my handler, and in return, last night I committed my continued service to the Crown until God knows when. I sold my soul for you and the Druckers, but like I said to ya in Caldas da Rainha, you don't owe *me* anything. As for what you owe the Brits, they expect the same commitment from you. They would like for you to work for them."

Again, her chin dropped. "Pardon me? They want me to work for them? In what manner?"

"As what we call a 'swallow,' sort of like Mata Hari during the last war, only you have infinitely more skill. You can make a real big difference in this war. It's way more than doin' your bit, but I promise it'll be worth it."

"A spy? They want me to be a spy?"

"Sure, and you'd make a darned good one, too. We need a classy woman with real connections to high society. Someone whose diamond tiara is the real McCoy." He raised an eyebrow, alluding to Irena.

"Someone like Irena? She's one of you?"

He took a seat next to her. "Well, she ain't my lover like you thought, and before you get ahead of yourself, that kiss *was* just an act."

"A very convincing one, like all your others."

He'd not dignify that accusation—yet again.

"And that day, in Rossio Square, you were following me, weren't you?"

"You got me there. I was."

"I knew it...I knew it all along. You were there behind me from the moment I left the hotel."

"Yuh-huh."

The wheels were turning in her head; her eyes narrowed as she considered his admission and the options laid out before her. It hadn't escaped his notice that her tone had changed, her demeanor guarded but inquisitive. Was she intrigued by the offer? Did she find merit in his argument?

She repeated, "A spy? They...the British...want me to be a...secret agent?"

"You have a certain femme fatale appeal that could be of assistance to them as it pertains to Otto Wegener and the mission I'm on."

"Wegener? So, that's how you knew who he was. Would I be working with you directly?"

Carl threw his head back in laughter. "Is that what it would take for you to agree?"

"No. Quite the opposite," she said flatly, not giving him an inch. "What else are you offering as enticement?"

"There's—my feelings for you."

She looked at him dubiously with a mocking smirk. Admittedly, he deserved that, too, even if his intentions were honest and heartfelt.

"I want something no one else will have."

"You have my word, no one else has, or ever will have, what I want to give ya. My heart is in my hands, Evie."

"Humph! So you say. There is equal danger in both the espionage business and a romantic entanglement with a man who makes his living by lying to unsuspecting wealthy widows traveling alone," she said.

Fine. He deserved that, too.

"I never lied about my feelings for you. In fact, I think I've proven my intentions time and again." He raised both eyebrows with a—take that!—nod to his head.

"Perhaps but that doesn't negate your subterfuge."

"Yeah, well, there's equal danger in your returning to a dull life in The Dakota, writing fluff pieces for a dead-end woman's rag. You'll never obtain your dreams that way."

"That we can agree on."

"What's it gonna be?"

"It seems you leave me little choice, having masterfully manipulated the situation in regard to Samuel's rescue, and it appears you've already committed my service to the British."

"Believe you-me, *that* was not my intention. I never agreed to that on your behalf, but those fellas see it differently. The last thing they want to do is let go of a woman of your caliber."

Her lips twisted as she considered his words.

From his position on the settee, he examined Evie acutely when she rose, straightened her dressing robe, and then strode to the French doors. She exited out to the balcony, leaving the door open, but her body language shut him out. Facing the seashore, she lit a cigarette then took a long drag, followed by a smooth pet of her hand down her waves. Her silent deliberation with her back to him felt like interminable minutes.

Finally, she turned with her chin held high and entered the parlor, closing the door behind her. She spoke with a confidence he'd not witnessed in her previously. "Very well then...I'll tell you what is going to be...I want—without any romantic complications—an exclusive scoop. I want you, Mr. British Spy, to tell me all about Purvis and his Nazi-sympathizing friends. I want to know every detail about your mission aboard the *Serpa Pinto*. And I expect neither you nor your friends to stand in my way from wiring it to the *Spectator* for a front-page screamer headline worthy of *The New York Times*. Further, I demand absolute secrecy within your Secret Intelligence Service. Both my brother and my father-in-law's history are not to be made known. Under those conditions, I agree to join your merry band of British spies in the deadly gambit of espionage."

Self-satisfied, she grinned. With chin still aloft, she took a final drag from her cigarette then blew out a smooth stream of smoke into the air above her head.

Could she actually be excited about this? Despite her claim of no romantic involvement, which he knew at this point was an impossible endeavor following their late-night tryst at the Metrópole, he didn't waiver despite the fact that he'd be divulging British secrets about Purvis and possibly pay a heavy penalty for doing so. Aw hell. He was a dead man walking anyway. He clapped his hands together and smiled. "You have a deal even if I could hang for telling you."

Her lips twitched from the suppression of a smile. "Do I get an alias, like you?"

"You already have one—the Austrian beauty Fräulein Eva von Lamberg who is a skilled polyglot and has already trapped her prey with her arts and allurement." He walked to her then took her hand, which she begrudgingly allowed. "Red, I'll give you that scoop, and I'll also give you my solemn vow that I won't let anything happen to you. Scout's honor."

Clearly doubting that he had been a Boy Scout, too, she chortled. "That's the only other reason I'll agree to this. Look, I know in my heart that your feelings for me are genuine, Carl. I do, but—"

"Don't say it. You'll regret those words later, 'cause you won't be able to fight against the feeling."

"Still so confident."

"About *you* loving *me*? I sure am. I told ya from the start, right there on the *Serpa*. We're fated."

"Ha! You darned well know that I don't believe in fate." She dropped his hand then sashayed to the balcony. "Let's change the subject, shall we? Join me on the veranda and we'll discuss what we have to do to reunite Samuel with his family."

He grinned. "For starters, are you ready to go solo behind the wheel of the BMW?"

"I think so."

"It's a lot of driving."

"I can handle it."

"You'll have to travel through the mountains in the dark. It'll be dangerous."

She smiled alluringly with a new quirk to her lips he hadn't seen before. "Dangerous? Nuh-uh, it'll be duck soup."

God, she was incredible.

TWENTY-THREE
Solo Flight

As though a portent of things to come, a storm blew harder with each leg of Carl's flight south toward the Portuguese colony: an archipelago called Cape Verde. Frankly, he had been relying on a stunning sunset along the Sahara Desert and the pristine green South Atlantic to take his mind off his demons. No doubt, Cape Verdeans living on the sandier, savannah-like islands welcomed the inclement weather, but he didn't. The unusual rainstorm made for terrible airborne conditions, but Carl had piloted in worse for the RAF and their God-awful weather! Even still, he loved the challenge and dodging the Luftwaffe in sorties over France had once excited him, but that was before…

The plane shuttling him—a two-engine C-47 transport—held it together just fine, but admittedly his nerves were shot. Although not in the cockpit, he couldn't fight off the beads of perspiration forming on his forehead or the memories of that nightmare dogfight over the Channel. As he once indicated to Musgrove, it wasn't that he *couldn't* fly. It was that the shell shock came back ten-fold within minutes after take-off. He *feared* flying.

The further south they flew along the African coastline, the worse the turbulence and his mood became. There was no getting above the clouds and when lightning missed the right wing by a few feet, he nearly lost his remaining humor all together. He kept reminding himself what was at stake and who he really was making this trip for—even if she wanted nothing to do with him romantically. Despite the weather and poor airstrip lighting, the RAF pilot did a bang-up job seeing them to a safe landing on the largest of the ten islands: the mountainous Santiago.

Carl might have kissed the ground when he disembarked if not for the teeming rain, but the heavens opened-up as though monsoon season, blowing sideways from the Sahara winds the islands were known for. Perhaps the weather was fated, for it would help with his cover. Flight activity and the nominal military presence at this late hour was at a minimum and only a diffused glow came from the dilapidated control tower. Other islands had larger military garrisons since Hitler had set his sights on Gibraltar and the Cape Verde islands in '40, and, of course, since Mussolini purchased one of the airports on the small island of Sai. Here, in the most northern part of Santiago where there were the fewest inhabitants, the prison vis–à–vis the Portuguese military operated this small airstrip to shuttle political prisoners from Lisbon.

Barely visible beside the air field's flood lamp, a Portuguese police car waited for him. Through the downpour, he sprinted from the plane to the vehicle some fifty-feet away. The ill-fitting PVDE uniform he wore was soaking fast as he located the key in the wheel well.

Within seconds, the old car sputtered to life and he glanced at the Portuguese wristwatch Musgrove often wore. Nine o'clock. The guards wouldn't be expecting him at this late hour for a prisoner transfer.

The tree-lined road cutting through the winding hill had turned into slick mud in the torrent but the car sped through it, as dangerous as it was. The thumping beat of the short windshield wipers and the heavy rain drumming against the steel roof sounded like a timpani orchestration, and he whistled a few bars of "Chattanooga Choo Choo" to lighten the intensity.

He gripped the wheel and let up on the gas pedal as he took a hair-pin turn and thought of Evie's driving lesson and her fear of plunging off the cliff. "Duck soup," he said aloud and lifted a prayer, not for himself, but for her and her brave road trip from Caldhas da Rainha to Castelo Branco tonight. Hopefully, the weather would hold for her equally mountainous drive from the seashore to Western Portugal. The winding roads and rugged terrain would be difficult for a green driver no matter how much she thought herself capable. He hoped Ezra would take the wheel and she would be happy navigating the map.

After ten minutes of hand-gripping intensity, he parked at the wrought-iron gates connecting a massive perimeter wall. Rolling down the driver's window, he ignored the rain splatters beating on his face as a guard approached the car from the gatehouse. The young man shone his flashlight into the back seat and then the rank insignia pinned on his collar before standing at attention.

Carl spoke in Portuguese when he withdrew the transport papers from inside his uniform pocket.

"I'm here for prisoner transfer back to Lisbon at the direct order of Captain Lourenço."

"At this hour, sir?"

"Do you question me? The weather delayed my arrival, and now I am already three hours behind schedule. Let me in, immediately," he commanded, motioning to the gates, and the hapless guard promptly complied. He had conquered the first obstacle. He was in.

He slowly drove alongside the darkened, quadrangle-laid compound, passing various buildings, and waiting for the guard tower's search light to gradually illuminate each. Through the rapid motion of the wiper blades, he read the cell block numbers until finding the one he sought.

He cut the engine and took another quick glance at his watch with a frown. He'd lost precious time due to the inclement weather and the RAF plane was scheduled to leave in twenty minutes whether he and Drucker were on it or not. If they missed it, they'd be on their own and forced to find a boat. At this hour, in this weather—after making this prison break—there wasn't a

Chinaman's chance either of them would get off the island alive if not on that Dakota.

The rain pummeled him when he dashed through the mud to the barrack door, but he kept his composure while pounding on the wood until a light switched on. A sleepy-eyed, unkempt guard opened the door, meeting Carl's steely-eyed glower. He authoritatively pushed his way in, brandishing the paperwork from his uniform inside pocket. "You are sleeping? Did you not get orders to have this prisoner waiting at the gatehouse for transport to Lisbon?"

"I...I...am sorry, sir." The guard rubbed his eyes then righted his jacket, fastening the top two buttons. "I did not receive those orders."

Another guard, clearly his superior, joined them from the office. This officer was different, not as hapless as the first two and significantly older. He took the papers from the other, his lips set in a stern scowl, his heavy brow frowning as he read the perfectly crafted forgery.

"Drucker? No. We did not receive word for any prisoner transfer, especially one from 32A," he groused. "Under whose orders?"

"It's right there in front of you. See for yourself. Is that not Captain Lourenço's signature? The Comunista Drucker is to be sent to Spain, so Franco can deal with him."

The officer twisted his lips. "I am not familiar with you. What is your name?"

"Lieutenant Frederico Braga."

"Let me see *your* identification, Lieutenant Braga."

He didn't have time for this and made known his displeasure by growling. "My papers? What is *your* name?"

"I am Comandante Pedro Ganzaga, the warden of Tarrafal camp. I have not received any orders from my superior in Lisbon about this transfer. I repeat, let me see your identification."

There were two options before him: just kill them both and be done with this charade, or hope for the best. Ever the optimist, and adverse to knocking someone off, unless absolutely necessary, he procured the necessary papers, confident that Musgrove hadn't disappointed him. "Perhaps you should telephone PVDE headquarters for quick authorization to this transfer." His glare challenged, yet his demeanor remained calm as he twisted the tip of the fake mustache he wore.

Examining the paperwork side-by-side, the warden nodded. "And how is the captain's son? Has he recovered from the accident?"

"Captain Lourenço's *daughter* has recovered from her *illness*. I will inform him of your concern." Yes. Musgrove, and most likely the MI6-friendly Lourenço had come through with the intel.

"Diego, collect the prisoner from section forty-two *A*, cell eleven."

The guard departed, only to reemerge from a room with a jangling ring of keys. In that short time, he'd cleaned up his act by straightening his uniform and donning his tan beret, which seemed like a ridiculous endeavor since the prison conditions were deplorably inhumane. The stench hanging in the stagnant air presumably originated from the prisoner cells. The whole rotting place needed fumigation, and Carl inwardly cringed imagining the fleas and disease.

From the well-lit doorway, the guard descended the hallway into the darkness, taps of his footfall and jingle of keys echoed down the long corridor until he stopped at the end, sliding key into padlock.

Carl and the warden watched from their station at the office entrance, heads turned, and frowns firmly set when Diego roughly pulled an elderly man from the cell, chains clanking in the darkness. His hand tightly clasped around the prisoner's upper arm, holding the frail man up as he shuffled his shackled feet. With each step closer into the light, the man—Samuel Drucker—came into view. Torn clothing, matted grey beard, dark circles on wan skin surrounded blue eyes filled with suffering. The shackles on his wrists had created such bruising his skin appeared black. The expressionless prisoner before him was not a living man of sixty, but had been reduced to a lifeless husk, a shell, appearing eighty-years-old, blank and devoid of will.

This broken man righted any misgivings Carl may have had and—Evie or no Evie—he would do this a thousand times over if he could.

"Do you not feed your prisoners, warden?"

"We cannot spare what little there is, and it is none of your concern what we do at Tarrafel."

"It is my concern when I have to facilitate the passage of a bag of bones barely kept alive, malnourished and, judging from the caked blood on his head, beaten into submission. This man is to stand trial in Madrid!"

"You would do well to hold your opinions of what goes on here, Braga. Tarrafel is under my authority."

Carl stood to his full height, eyes boring into the older, shorter man before him as the younger guard and Drucker watched the standoff, the former in stunned awe and the other suffering from long-term traumatic shock.

"Your authority? I will inform Captain Lourenço and the Prime Minister of that. Remove those ankle manacles at once or you will face consequences by my hand—the Captain's right one," placing his hand upon the night stick hanging from his belt.

Stepping back, the warden nodded to the guard who bent releasing the iron cuffs. Drucker's eyes widened in disbelief.

Carl clasped his hand firmly upon the old man's shoulder and guided him toward the exit. As he opened the door into the torrential rain outside, he glanced back to the warden. "I will be back to check on the conditions in this prison and its prisoners. You'll be wise to heed my warning, Ganzaga."

They exited the building. Any response from the warden was drowned out by the torrent. The precipitation was probably the first cleansing the poor man had in a long time and these were most likely the first unshackled steps he'd taken since his arrival. No words passed between them, but the freed man's head snapped up when Carl opened the car door without delay.

"You can trust me, Mr. Drucker," he said in German. "I'm a friend, and it won't be long until you are reunited with your family. We must hurry."

Painstakingly the man settled into the back seat, promptly resting his head against the cushion. His crusted lips barely moved when he whispered into the air, "*die Meinigen ...*"

"Yes, and you're all on your way to America, but first we need to get the hell out of here before they figure out that I'm no police officer." He started the engine, then drove like a bat out of hell down the mountainside toward the airport. The rain continued coming down in sideway streams and he prayed at each passing mile that the warden wouldn't pick up that telephone before The Dakota took off. If it hadn't already.

The Worm Moon was more than Evie could have asked for on the thrilling drive north to Caldas da Rainha. The little car traversed the same roads as before, and although they were now unlit, a thousand stars above and the brilliant moonglow were sufficient. The wind blew through the open window; the crisp night air felt electrified. A kinetic energy charged with excitement and—dare she say?—madness filled the atmosphere. She was drunk on the danger and the mystery. Unfettered. Liberated. Perhaps it was the moon, or perhaps it was the excitement of the whirlwind events of the day.

Carl's admission to his real mission in Lisbon, which yes—he was right!—was there all along for her to deduce, yet she chose to ignore the signs. He was a spy, an enigmatic, clever, and talented special agent! He trusted her with this information even fully aware that she was a newspaper reporter. Further, he had put himself in harm's way for her. Once again, he was right: she was in love with him. Though she was unreconciled with his deceit, a lingering suspicion remained that she could never be rid of him or her overwhelming feelings for him, no matter her verbal protestation. He was under her skin, burning her with an even more fervent desire than before. Was it the knowledge that there was a dangerous side to him that burst her heart? He had professed his undying love twice now. Could she ever bring herself to admitting to him the same ardent feelings so soon after Richard's death?

*Richard…*She sighed. Would he be proud of her actions tonight? She hoped so. What would he think of her feelings for Carl so soon?

She forced her rumination back to something much more pressing and dangerous than abandoning her late-husband's memory by falling hopelessly in love with a clarinetist from Pittsburgh. Ha! That alone would send her mother into a tizzy.

The prospect of her enlistment—entrapment—to join Carl's covert friends was too delicious a commitment to pass on. This was surely a "take that, Albert" moment, a watershed event for her and one that, if her brother only knew, would change his opinion of her. "Vapid" would no longer be a word associated with Mrs. Evelyn Somerset's life. Evie was living the dream she'd secretly dreamed of before marrying. Was this the fate that Carl so often spoke of?

She'd not had this feeling since the month before leaving Vassar when she wrote that front-page story for the paper following her reporter's excursion to the 1939 New York World's Fair. That magnificent experience, surrounded by ingenuity and invention reached a zenith while viewing President Roosevelt give the first presidential speech on RCA's television. Anything and everything were possible!

The BMW zipped beneath a cluster of trees lining the final stretch of road before reaching the quaint town, evident by the lights ahead. Her blood rushed, the scarf tie around her neck billowed in a trail out the open window. Quite unexpectedly and most assuredly out of character, she threw her head back in laughter. For the moment, all thoughts of Richard and Carl were banished in the thrill of living life on the edge and the prospect of a new life—absolute liberation—in America for the Drucker family.

A narrow lane led to the illuminated town square of Caldas da Rainha, which looked very different from the busy marketplace she had visited only days before. As expected, it was desolate at this late hour. That was the plan because one did not simply "leave" the Jewish camp. While the refugees were not fenced in, per se, the invisible restriction of punishment relied upon the residents' honesty. Permission must be granted. Tonight, it would not be, and she understood the danger to the Druckers and her if discovered sneaking out under the cover of darkness.

Evie followed the same roads they had driven with Tovah. Her hands clenched around the steering wheel, and her mind worked out the details recalling Carl's explicit instructions for what he called "extraction." The family's hiding location was to be a farmhouse in the mountains somewhere in Central Portugal and where Carl, accompanying Samuel, would join them until the Druckers' departure in three days.

She turned down the sleepy street of the black bird house and turned off the headlights, creeping along the crunching gravel. Just as Carl had warned search lights traveled slowly across the houses. As instructed, she kept the car close to what—back in New York— they called a "curb," but here was where roadway met plot of land.

Her heart thundered when she suddenly stopped the car, promptly ducking when the light scanned over her with nary a notice of her trespass. Hers was just another vehicle among the several parked along the dirt road. Once the spot light had passed and darkness returned, she resumed her travel until finally parking beside an empty lot, two houses down from the Druckers' five black birds.

Tonight, she wore dark clothes, slacks, and sensible shoes, which seemed more appropriate for a dangerous covert escape.

She climbed the small hill then hurried to the back door of the house. After several quiet attempts at knocking, Ezra, whom she had not previously met, answered with a confused brow. It was no wonder, the hour was past one in the morning, and he did not know her. "Guten Abend. Mein Name ist Evelyn Somerset," she quickly whispered; time was of the essence. His smile beamed, and he made to speak, but she put her index finger to her lips and was promptly let in. They stood in the darkened kitchen, the moonlight breaching the makeshift curtain, the air charged with danger and excitement. He closed the door, but left the light switched off.

"Guten Abend, Frau Somerset!"

"We...my friend, Carl, found your father."

He placed his hand upon the top of his messed hair, brown hooded eyes widening. "*Danken Got!* Where is he? Is he hurt?"

"I don't know if he is but, but he is in a prison camp several hours from here. Don't worry. He and Carl will join us tonight—somewhere safe—until you sail for America."

"But, we do not—"

She placed her hand upon his forearm, softening her hurried words. "It is all taken care of, Ezra. Your family will be leaving in three days aboard the *Serpa Pinto*."

"America?...But how? Oh, we cannot ever repay you, Frau Somerset. Thank you. Thank you!"

"I am only the messenger sent by your cousin, and my friend Carl has made the arrangements. He was the one who made this all happen. Now, I'll wake Tovah and Rebecca and help them, as you and Suzannah pack your belongings. We don't have much time, nor space in the car, so take what you need." She nodded with a gentle smile, assuring that all will be well. "Take what is most precious."

"Of course! Yes! Then I only take my family."

"And the swallows. Don't forget the swallows for your new home," she added with a tender smile.

Hastily, he left the kitchen for the bedroom and she went to the small living area. In the dark, she saw Tovah lying on a makeshift bed on the floor beside her grandmother on the sofa, curls of chestnut plastered the pillow and her face. The child held the hairless doll in the crook of her arm. What a beautiful sight—in such pitiful conditions, not the worst, but certainly not the best.

Time stood still as she admired the dear one. Her heart squeezed with longing observing how the innocent child slumbered with a peaceful expression as though sugar plums danced in her head. Evie would give anything in this world to be a mother, to know and give a mother's deep abiding love, something she had never received. As all trains of thought went of late, this one traveled to Carl. *Did he desire children, too?*

Kneeling, she gently shook Tovah's arm. "Darling Tovah, wake up little one. Zuzu wants to go to America."

"A…merica?" The girl yawned, swiping the lock of hair from her forehead. "Will the fairies bring grandpapa back, so he can come, too?"

"Yes, sweetheart."

They hugged, and Rebecca woke with a grandmotherly smile brought on from the hushed conversation, their eyes locking over the child's shoulder.

Goodness, any second now, she'd be blubbering like a fool!

Twenty minutes later, with a trunk filled with luggage, Ezra and Evie dropped down beside the BMW as the searchlight crept passed the parked car.

"As soon as it passes. Get your family and I'll start the car," she whispered. Her heart slammed with nervous staccato, as though it would leap through her chest.

He nodded, then bolted up the dirt incline, passed two houses, and helped his pregnant wife with satchel down the steps of the cottage. Not even a minute had passed. Behind them, Rebecca removed the five black swallows from the clapboard beside the door.

Exiting the driver's side of the car, Evie welcomed little Tovah with a smile at her running approach. The girl's curly head of hair was now neatly concealed below a kerchief, her eyes wide with wonder, but not fear. The hairless doll barely hung on from the crook of her arm.

It all happened so swiftly, so silently, under the watchful Worm Moon looking down upon their escape. She breathed in the clear night air infused with the sea's salty aroma as if a portent of a fresh beginning, a passage to the Druckers' future.

With the women squished in the back and Ezra in the passenger seat beside her, the BMW crept lights-out at the curb edge, stopping, along with her heart, each time the searchlight passed. Once clear from the refugee cottages, the only thing attesting to the Drucker family's presence was the lingering tire dust-up before the search light passed.

She tried not to cry with joy when they reached freedom at the edge of Caldas da Rainha. Rebecca shed the tears for her, weeping onto Tovah's head as she held her granddaughter.

If there is a God, please...protect this family, and please ensure the men's safety tonight. Please be with Carl as he flies for the first time in a long time," she thought, not praying of course, because that would mean she believed. She fully doubted, but half-hoped—for Carl and Samuel's sake. What was there to lose in the thought?

TWENTY-FOUR
Bluebirds in the Moonlight

*D*uring the long drive to Castelo Branco in central Portugal, conversation flowed between Ezra and her, and she learned many things about the family and what it had been like living under the Reich. She also learned that although Samuel was not an avowed Bolshevik, he had written a subversive, anti-Hitler newspaper column back in Frankfurt am Main and distributed his share of counter-propaganda as far back as '30. Ezra's father was not afraid to speak out against anti-Semitism and persecution, and that oftentimes branded him a communist like some of his peers. In her opinion that was brave considering the consequences and, as a journalist, she understood his commitment to truth! Samuel was just liberal-minded and a bother to no one other than Hitler's goons.

She gazed into the rear-view mirror at Tovah's sleeping form slacked against her mother's bosom. One day, when the child was old enough to understand it all, she'd have quite a history to pass on to her own children.

There were other things that had taken Evie aback—conditions she had not known about living as a Jewish family under German rule. The Nazi anti-Jewish policies broke her heart: the yellow Star of David they were forced to wear, the pogroms and curfews, arrests for no-apparent reason. She wanted to sob at Ezra's account of that awful night of terror in '38 he referred to as *Reichspogramnacht*. She had been in college back then and recalled reading the front-page column in *The New York Times*. Nazism's burning of Frankfurt am Main's Boerneplatz Synagogue, among others throughout Germany, was a clear example of government denying freedom of religion. After reading about these atrocities, a few of the girls on the *Miscellany* wanted to write an article about the Constitution's First Amendment. In hindsight, most of those girls had been quite blind to their own racial and religious discrimination. To her knowledge, there wasn't a Jew or Catholic on the paper, and several of her schoolmates were not as outraged by that article as they should have been. Only dear sweet Franny had been sick over it for a week. In hindsight, several of the girls had studied in Munich for a semester and refused to believe it was "as bad as all that." All that idealism her schoolmates professed, yet they were so naïve, so sheltered and exclusive in many ways. Only the editor seemed to have any grasp on the reality when she covered the happenings in an article.

In the pitch night, even with Carl's detailed directions, they nearly missed the turnoff to their destination: the farmhouse. With Ezra acting as navigator at first, then later as driver, they had no difficulty on their three-hour journey despite the winding roads and darkness. The full moon hadn't abandoned them, and it led the way upward while the ladies slept. They had climbed and climbed and were so close to the midnight sky that thousands of brilliant stars appeared to be in reach through the windshield.

"There!" She pointed to a bramble-covered dirt path.

"Are you sure this is the road?" Ezra asked, braking in uncertainty.

"Yes, Carl said there would be a fig tree at the entrance. The house should be up ahead in the clearing. He said to drive to the back where there is an old barn to hide the car."

The car squeezed between the overgrown bushes as branches and leaves tore, yielding to the slow trespass until finally breaking into the clearing. It was just as Carl had described: rundown with neglect and age. Surrounded by overgrown thicket, the stone façade was covered with vines. The moonlight created a silhouette of the mountains surrounding and sheltering the secluded homestead.

How did Carl know of this farmhouse? Was it his? Was it his mother's childhood home? She wrung her hands, hoping he and Samuel were safe.

She narrowed her gaze onto the tiny single flicker of light somewhere within the house. It wasn't abandoned. Her breath caught and then her heart sped. Had Samuel and Carl arrived before them? Anxiously, her hand rested on her chest to calm the stirred racing within. She'd only be fooling herself in not acknowledging that the prospect of seeing her music man added to her already heightened emotions.

"There is a candle beyond the broken window," Ezra said. "Look, smoke comes from the chimney."

"Perhaps it's your father. Continue to the barn."

The headlights shined through the tree-lined footpath as the BMW followed Carl's directions to the old barn, and Evie jumped out as soon as it stopped in front of the doors. The ferocity of her heartbeat pounding in her ears broke the midnight silence, and she tugged the barn doors open, revealing a delivery sedan parked within.

"Wake up, Suzannah, Mother. We have arrived." Ezra said before pulling the car into the ramshackle shelter.

Evie chastised herself, feeling guilty that her first and foremost concern was not Samuel's reuniting with his family, but rather running to the house to find Carl. Worrying over his flight and how it had affected him had frayed her nerves.

Behind her, a branch moved in the breezeless night.

She froze, her fingers still grasping the door pull.

A hand slid around her waist and pulled her backward but she didn't have time to scream.

Carl whispered into her ear.

"I'm proud of ya, Red. You did, it."

That tickle of warm breath stopped her heart. Feverishly, she turned in his arms and enfolded her own around him, hugging him to her tightly, her cheek pressing against his. She thought her legs would go weak from relief, from excitement, from his very nearness. "It's you. Oh, thank goodness you're safe," she breathed.

"Were you worried about me?"

In the dark, even with the commotion of the Druckers exiting the car behind them, she gazed into his sparkling eyes and smiled. "You bet the dickens I was," then kissed him—deeply and without any reservation. He grabbed her up into him tighter, his mouth claiming her with an intense newness, a rekindling in their reunion.

No romantic entanglements, indeed! She was a fraud. Beneath the power of his love and silent declaration, she swooned, particularly since her skilled clarinetist's lip control delivered the perfect kiss. Her insides turned to jelly and an overwhelming sensation like none other rose from her belly to her heart, a quivering fire. The act alone hadn't produced sublime rapture—it was the emotion behind it that elicited it.

"Wowza," Carl breathed in stunned amazement when their lips parted. "Does this mean, you forgive me?"

"It means that I'm glad you're safe."

"I should enter danger more often."

She wasn't that much of a fool to tell him, here and now, what was in her heart. Although that playful smirk on his lips told her that her kiss had confirmed what he already knew.

Tovah tugged on his pant leg. "Hello, Herr Wilson. Where's grandpapa?" she asked in German.

Carl squatted before her, affectionately touching the child's cheek. "Why, hello, my friend. I'll take you and Zuzu to him right away, but first who is *this* you're holding?"

"Hannah! Like Grandmother in Frankfurt, but *Oma* has black hair. Hannah left hers in Germany. Did you bring your horn?"

"I did, and there is a piano in the farmhouse. Maybe when your grandfather is feeling better, we can perform for him."

He looked up to Evie with a wicked smile, and she silently delighted at playing with him again. Her heart swelled. He had a way with children and with her.

"Is this the man Carl?" Ezra asked, approaching with a suitcase in each hand.

"Yes. Carl Wilson, this is Samuel's son, Ezra."

Carl stood and offered his hand for a shake, "I'm pleased to meet you, sir. Your father is inside sleeping beside the fire." Quite surprisingly, the thankful man dropped the travel cases and embraced him without words.

She doubted that her strong fella had ever been hugged by another man before, but it was clear that Ezra, like she, had bottled up emotion.

Determined and no doubt, anxious to see her husband, Rebecca could not wait. She was already to the door by the time Carl had removed the valise from Suzannah's hand. Tovah ran after her grandmother.

The old woman's voice carried out into the pitch from inside the stone house, "Samuel? Samuel. *Wo bist Du?*" And then her cries followed. Tovah's own weeps came. "*Opa!*"

Evie's heart clenched, imagining the child running to her beloved grandfather. What condition had she found Samuel? Were his wife's tears those of relief or shock?

As they walked to the back door, Carl solemnly shook his head when her eyes met his. She mentally braced herself when he held the door open for her.

Entering the house, she controlled her repulsion by the layer of soot covering the old kitchen table and chairs. An inch-thick layer of dust covered the sink counter. It was clear it had been unoccupied for many years, attested by cobwebs and the leaves fallen through the broken window over the sink. Yet, in the candlelight, there was an old-world charm of simplicity.

They entered the living space where it smelled like dirt and ash, and a gray haze from the fire hung over the stone hearth. There were two colors to this room's décor: brown and grey.

Beside the fireplace, Samuel sat on a threadbare sofa, a bowl of unfinished soup rested on the coffee table. His slight frame was consumed by his wife's chubby arms as she showered kisses upon him, tears rolling down her cheeks. Tovah watched in silent awe at her grandmother's affection.

Suddenly, Rebecca halted, cupped her hands upon his gaunt cheeks, gazed into his eyes, and reverently spoke, *"Meine Lieber."* Samuel wrapped his arms around her and dropped his head to her shoulder. As if her husband was the most precious thing in her world, she cradled him with such tenderness, such pure agape, that Evie had to look away. Her heart could not withstand—nor should she intrude upon—beholding such unadulterated intimacy without bursting. She had never witnessed this type of love before.

Ezra and Suzannah entered the room and Evie turned toward the door, leaving the farmhouse…and Carl followed.

A tear trickled down her cheek when he slid his hand into hers, leading her through the woods. The still night looked and felt magical, broken only by their footfall with each crush of dried leaves and broken twig. Lest they break the spell between them, they did not speak. They reached a pond and stood side-by-side for some time, gazing at the moonlight's kiss upon the water as though it were diamonds floating on the surface. Carl squeezed her hand, and his thumb brushed back and forth against the pad of hers. In this quiet serenity of profound emotion, the war was so very far away. At this moment only she and Carl mattered.

The words encapsulated within her heart flowed from her without thought, only heart-felt ardor. "Because of you, everything has changed. I have changed, Carl. You've changed my life."

"And you changed mine, Red."

"Did I?"

"More than any person."

"There's something I need to confess. You were right," she softly said, unable to look at him. "I married for both status and love, but our union was…hollow, a convenience for both of us and I'm ashamed to admit that."

"Well, you were young when you married."

"I was immature and too easily persuaded by my mother. I think…somewhere deep inside of me, I looked upon marriage as an escape, and I made excuses for the lack of passion or even shared interests between us."

"But you did care for him. Based on what you've told me, I have no doubt that you loved him."

"I *did* love him, and still do, but…but it was a naïve love. We both changed."

"Did…he…love ya like you should have been loved?"

Oh goodness, this hurt. This admission to something she'd suspected for so long but had refused to face, particularly after his death. It was Madam Lupescu's frankness, which forced deeper contemplation about her marriage to Richard. "I believe, in the beginning he loved me … maybe in some form. Later, there were moments when I was sure he had grown to adore me, but I think it was just to placate me. His last letter said that he loved me and he regretted our marital troubles, but I know now…what we had wasn't what I dreamed we would have or any semblance of true love." She tried not to cry. "Oh goodness, I painted a pretty picture of us to the world so as to avoid derision and censure from my family—and, of course, gossip."

"I'm sorry, Evie." He turned her to face him. "Listen to me…if he didn't love you then that was his failure because you're one hell of a woman and worthy of all the love in the world. It was his shortcoming—not yours."

"Thank you."

"I mean it, and like I said, I'll never stop loving you. It isn't going anywhere and it's real—true blue, true love. You'll never have any doubt about it—ever."

"I…feel the same way. I can no longer deny that what I feel for you is all encompassing. It takes my breath away." She sniffled. "It's unfathomable that I came to find you at the end of a clarinet and gave you my heart in only three weeks."

"It's our destiny." The moonglow and the stars glittered in his expressive chocolate eyes as he searched her soul for a reply. He was so handsome, even the jagged scar. Everything about Carl Wilson was perfect, including his flaws.

"I now believe in destiny, and I can't imagine my tomorrow ever having meaning without you in it. I love you."

His thumb stroked in soft, gentle movements against her cheek, wiping away her tears.

"Say it again, Evie, 'cause I think I must be dreaming."

"I'm in love with you, Carl, more than I ever dreamed I could love someone."

"No. Not Carl."

In the same way Rebecca made her solemn declaration to Samuel, she cupped his chilled cheeks in her hands. "I love you with *all* my heart, *Jack McGrath*. 'I love thee with the breath, smiles, tears, of all my life.' "

His dazzling smile turned the lock imprisoning her heart these many years. He kissed her…and it set her free. She was no longer a caged, gilded bird as the widowed Mrs. Richard Somerset, New York City socialite. She was no longer the would-be Rousseau ward. She was once again Evie—a girl in love—freed and now soaring high among the swallows. Jack McGrath's heart was her home.

———◆❊◆———

TWENTY-FIVE
My Shining Hour

March 17

$\mathcal{S}$ince that fateful day in 1939 when leaving Vassar for the last time, good-byes had never been easy for Evie. Today, two good-byes were more than she could handle, but both gave the promise of reuniting under different circumstances.

Hours before, in the early morning, she'd stood on the dock, hugging the Drucker family before they climbed the gang-plank of the *Serpa Pinto*. Both she and Carl had felt an odd sense of satisfaction and peace, not one born out of their pride in having saved this family, but born out of the knowledge that this Jewish family beat those darned Nazis by escaping. They would survive to tell their story to the unborn babe and future generations would hear how they lived like nomads for a year to find true freedom from religious persecution. She had shed tears at the dock and it appeared that even Carl's eyes watered some when Tovah held him tightly. The man was proving to be quite sensitive under that Yinzer veneer.

His clarinet and cheerfulness stayed silent for the rest of the day, and few words had passed between them for they knew that their good-bye would be the one that broke them both.

England awaited her—without him.

She sat beside Carl in the BMW and stared out the windshield at the nearly full moon, recalling the first farewell of the day and tried not to think of the imminent one.

Despite the inclement weather, the Druckers had been unfazed and looked a picture wearing new clothes and hats purchased by her in Chiado the day before. They were traveling first class and embarking on a new life, after all. And in eight days, her editor would meet them in Philadelphia, most likely taking them to Brooklyn to live with his family until they could get settled in a home of their own. Perhaps a job at the *Spectator* awaited Samuel.

Meeting and getting to know them had changed her life. She had spent the last three days living with a "real" family, caring for them, sharing with them, cooking and cleaning, and entertaining Tovah on long walks through the spectacular meadow and the entire clan with music. She'd never had this experience before, and it seemed that with each passing day, she was no longer Evie the Vassar girl, nor Polite Society's Evelyn, obedient daughter and wife. Not only were her haughty highbrow airs fading but so, too, were the idealistic and naïve beliefs of her debutante college experience. Three weeks of introspection and freedom had renewed her. Yes, she was anxious for what the future held, but alive nonetheless. There is one spring in life, the Florbela Espanca poem stated. Yes, and she was being reborn into it.

Carl's long fingers wrapped around the gear stick and she smiled, her mind recalling her good-bye to the wise, Samuel Drucker.

Surrounded by the crush of sea-faring travelers, the sweet man turned to face her then patted her cheek. "Let me see that pretty smile, that I should remember it always as the woman who came far to save strangers."

She grinned, eyes brimming. "Truly, it was your cousin and Carl."

"Ach! Without you, I would not be traveling like a king, nor wearing such fine clothing. I would not have a bissel in my pocket

and a spring in my broken step. You brought hope and freedom to my family, and now my grandchild will be born in America!"

"I will always cherish this time spent with your family, and I will look forward to seeing you when I get back to New York. Please rest and try to enjoy the passage." She handed him an envelope containing the prescriptive she'd written Donato and spending money—*just in case of anything. "Give this letter to your steward Donato. He'll take exceptional care of you all and the money inside is for you."*

"Ezra and I will repay you when we find work."

"That is not my wish. My wish is that you get healthy again."

"You worry too much, and should not worry for me. Time and prayer are the best healers."

"Time is quite the thorn in my side and, I'm sorry, but I don't pray."

"Of course, you do! Charity is a prayer. Joy is a prayer. Sacrifice is a prayer." He turned his head, eyes taking in his family waiting for him at the top of the ramp. *"Family...children are a prayer. A gift we give to Adonai. Life is a prayer, Evelyn. Love. Love is the greatest prayer."*

"But I don't believe in God."

"Perhaps now is the time. It is through prayer that we connect with Him so we can heal this broken world and defeat evil."

"Perhaps."

"But you are right about time...it is too short. You and Carl should not waste it in the expectation that this war will end soon. Adonai's timeline is not always ours."

"When will I see you again?" she asked, turning to Carl as the car made its final leg to Portela Airport.

"I don't know. Training will take up most of your time, and I need to remain here. This assignment I'm on needs all my attention until you're ready to join me in the field—and well, Dutch has been more than generous with my absence from the orchestra. I'll be burning both ends of the candle for a while."

Her heart sank. What had she been expecting? "Oh. I guess you won't be getting on another plane any time soon, either."

"Not if I can help it."

"Right."

"Hey, don't sound so disappointed. This is a swell opportunity and ya don't need me noseying around in your bizness."

"Maybe I want you around—in my business."

He abruptly pulled the car over then stopped at a corner. Shifting in his seat, he faced her, his expression pensive. "Look, ya don't. This is *your* time, Evie. *Your* shining hour. This is where ya get to do all the things you've always wanted to do. In England, you'll meet all sorts of fellas, learn all sorts of exciting tradecraft and dangerous things. You'll think and rethink what we promised to each other at the farmhouse, and you'll be so wacky with missing me that you'll find yourself *praying* I'll fly to England to see you."

She gave him a dubious look about that last part. She'd come far, but she was still an unbeliever in divinity. "Would you come no matter the manner in which I asked?"

"If you need me, just get word to Berkshire. They'll read ya letters, so don't be sayin' anything that'll make a grown man blush."

"And aren't you the least bit concerned that some other fella will try to steal me away from you?"

"They'll try, but they won't."

"Always so confident."

"Sweetheart, haven't ya learned by now that when it comes to you and me, I *am* confident? I'm confident that you're not gonna fall for any Limey when you get there. I'm confident that I'm the only man you want to make music with."

"Make music?" She swallowed, understanding exactly what he meant and, yes, she'd pondered that several times in many a restless night since meeting him. Was he a "considerate lover" as Margie stated every man should be?

That absolutely adorable twisting smirk played upon his lips. "Make *all* kinds of music."

"Boogie woogie?" she teased.

"Beat it eight to the bar and not in any one-minute waltz. I can play all night long for ya."

"You'll tickle the ivories?"

He laughed lightly. "Yuh-huh, and I'll teach you how to play the horn."

Embarrassed, she bit the corner of her lip and he chuckled, having succeeded in once again redirecting the course of her disposition. She grinned like a love-struck fool. Marjorie—and Brewster—would highly approve of her would-be lover's double entendre.

Getting through this good-bye would be so much easier knowing that he'd wait for her and when they finally did come together it would be a symphony.

"Even in the dark, I can see you blushing, Red."

"Yes I am, darling. You've given me much to dream about in our separation."

"As do I...so much so, that I just might get on another plane so I can hold ya in my arms and show ya how much I love you."

Blacked out at this late hour, Portela Airport was covered in darkness, but the shadow of the British Overseas Airways Corporation (BOAC) Douglas DC-3 parked on the tarmac could not be missed as the BMW neared. The heavy fog clinging to the flight line reminded Carl of a Lon Chaney movie. The thick rolling mist from the river conjured the image of the Wolfman roaming the hillside, hunting its next kill. He tried to shake the bad feeling and looked over at his girl sitting beside him. Her pensive expression didn't help at all. That ominous shadow was to take her and several others—most likely dignitaries or secret agents—from Lisbon to Bristol. No doubt, like he did on that infamous first flight after the crash, they were praying that German Junkers would keep their distance. The Luftwaffe had little respect for flights coming in and out of Portugal of late; anything could happen.

"That's it up ahead," he said.

"It's bigger than a Clipper."

"Yuh-huh."

"Over the ocean or over land?"

"You'll be flying over the Bay of Biscay."

"Hmm. Water is water."

"You'll be fine. These BOAC fellas know what they're doing."

"You're my inspiration. I mean…you flew, right?"

"And over water."

He noted how she twisted her fingers, but did not let on that he was afraid for her, too. She may have suspected that life in London would be less than perfect, but she had no idea what she was getting into. London was a mess; nothing like New York's safe and secluded home front. She'd have the best of what was available when training with the SIS, but could she really adapt to other inconveniences piled upon the British populace after four years of bombing, air raids, and rationing? She was tough, but not tough enough to evade a German bomb. With her sophisticated airs and Parisian fashion sense, she might scoff at the mandatory gas mask satchel and lack of stockings.

For the hundredth time, he silently browbeat himself for putting her in this position. Further, he couldn't be there to catch her if she fell. Evelyn Somerset would be on her own the moment the plane left the ground.

Their playful banter and sexual innuendo had done wonders for his fleeting sanguinity. He loved her with a fierceness and protectiveness that he'd never experienced before, but he had to let her go. Had to let her spread her wings and fly. If they survived this war, she'd come back to him—not Carl—but to Jack McGrath, the man who held her heart. Second to his near-death, sending her away into the dangerous unknown was the scariest thing he'd ever had to face.

He felt Evie's gaze upon him and he tightly smiled, reaching over to grasp her gloved hand in his. She looked stunning today in that green suit and matching hat. But the watch broach was gone, and he couldn't help wondering about the reasons. Nevertheless, he was glad she banished it. Every time she touched it had been a tip-off to her insecurity and anxiety. He glanced over to her and softly smiled. There was a special rosiness to her cheeks, her eyelashes seemed longer, and her hair appeared more strawberry than blonde today. Perhaps everything about her was heightened in his observation. The picture she presented would have to last him a long time and be at the ready when conjured as he skulked in the darkness on some op, or when he played "Begin the Beguine" just for her from his stage position.

"You're a natural."

"I hope you're right. I'm afraid, Carl."

He stopped the car as close to the flight line as he could get and cut the engine.

"You? Afraid? Nah. Just listen to ya intuition and keep believing in yourself. You're the intrepid reporter who got Lupescu to flap her lips. The same girl who—in three weeks, mind ya—conquered sea travel; learned to drive, speak Portuguese, and play poker; *and* rescued the Druckers in a daring escape. Hell, you're the first dame to get me to feel *anything* in a long time and that's sayin' something." The knot in his throat near choked him with guilt for committing her to the danger ahead.

She chuckled. "You make me sound like Brenda Star, but you're wrong…I did those things despite—and for—the men in my life."

Unconsciously, he fixed his necktie. "Doin' this…going to work for the Brits is a fine way for you to continue honoring Richard," he uncomfortably said.

"No, darling. I found Ezra and his family for Richard, Mr. Drucker, and the men who went down on the *Jarvis*. *This*, going to work for the SIS, I do for Uncle Sam and *you*—for what the Germans did to you."

Choked up, his eyes drank her in when she reached and smoothed his scar. "And the rest is for *you*, Red. It's been inya all along, and now you can be yourself and soar."

"Soar…eat ether."

"Yuh-huh. See what has never been seen."

"You know Millay?"

"A little." He grinned.

"And did you say just *inya?*—there's another fine word," she teased.

He laughed at her ability to find levity when her insides must be turned upside down.

"You won't forget to mail the letter to my sister for me? And wire my editor with my article on Purvis?"

"I won't forget. It's the least I can do. Ya know, that'll be your last article, right?"

"I accept that. There is always tomorrow, after the war, to go back to reporting. This is more pressing now."

He dragged his finger down her cheek. After the war. He would pray there was an 'after the war' for them.

They sat there in an awkward stillness for several minutes as he found the nerve to give her something he'd hoped she'd remember him by. He finally withdrew a brown paper wrapped book from his pocket then held it out to her. "I got ya something to remember the time we spent together here in Lisbon."

"Oh, Carl, you shouldn't have."

"I know. Go on…open it. I purchased it at the livraria. You remember the shop, don't ya?"

"How could I forget? I did so enjoy watching your tongue roll at your recitation of Espanca's poetry."

She pulled the green ribbon and the paper dropped open. "*Sonnets from the Portuguese*, translated to German!"

"I thought it was appropriate given your declaration the other night beside the pond. I…um…have a matching book."

"Thank you." Resting the book on her lap, her hand smoothed over the leather binding. "It's perfect. I'll cherish it always, just as I will cherish these last three weeks we spent together."

His heart clenched and he reached up to her cheek, his thumb brushing the pink hue again.

It really was poor form for a fella to be such a sap, but she knew he was a romantic. He regretfully turned away from her gaze and opened the driver-side door, struggling to cut off his feelings, leaving them within the book and its inscription. After removing her travel case from the boot, he walked to the passenger side.

"Ready?" he asked, opening the door.

A small nod and a soft smile attempted to assure him. She was terrified, but she held her head high.

A thick wall of silence and sadness enveloped them as they walked hand-in-hand to the rear of the plane, until finally they stopped at the bottom of the staircase. He set the valise down then faced her taking both her hands in his.

"Yes," she said quietly.

"Yes? To what, Evie?"

"Yes. I want you to come to me in England if you can."

"Because…?"

She glanced up at the plane and shook her head. Swallowing hard, she then looked up into his eyes. "Because I…because everything is so uncertain and I don't want to waste precious time waiting for this blasted war to end until I can *be* with you—like *that*. I don't want to *hear* that stanza from *III* from your lips. I want to *experience* it."

He scooped her lithe figure against him, kissing her until breathless.

With heart soaring high above them and lips hovering above hers he teased, "So it was a sonnet after all and not the prospect of learning to play my horn?"

"That too. You forget, darling, I have seen what you can do with your horn. You make the most divine music with it, and if you can do that on stage, I can only dream of what you'll do in bed."

Wicked girl to leave him with that image.

She winked at him, grabbed the handle of her suitcase, then climbed the steps. Stopping at the door to the fuselage, she turned and blew him a kiss.

Oh, yes, they were going to be good together—if they survived.

Cable to Mr. Hank Drucker, Editor, *New York Daily Spectator*, New York, New York
From: Mrs. Evelyn Somerset
Hotel Palácio, Estoril, Portugal

Dear Mr. Drucker,

I hope you received my cable with the article on Madam Lupescu. Quite by surprise I happened to stumble upon a bigger scoop than even that! Please hold back from running with this front-page story until the arrest has been made on March 23rd after the S.S Mouzinho docks in Newark, NJ. My sources are intimately involved in the investigation and assure me of the subsequent apprehension. The Spectator can thank me upon my return to New York (whenever that may be). I'm off, with my newfound moxie, to London for another "adventure holiday." Boss, I think you can no longer refer to me as a cub reporter, given the magnitude of what I am cabling you!

As for the other "matter," thank you is not necessary <u>at all</u>. The cost of my return ticket, and its accommodation aboard the S.S. Serpa Pinto, has been used for more worthy passengers (five) departing this afternoon for Philadelphia. They will be arriving in eight days, and I trust you will be awaiting them.

By the way, for national security purposes (my brother) please publish this column and the one on Madam Elena Lupescu under pseudonym <u>Amelia Snow</u>. I am sure you are surprised by my change of heart, but, oh, I don't know, having my name big and bold on top billing doesn't seem so important now. This trip abroad has changed so many things I once thought paramount. Perhaps it's the war. Thank you for all your support and encouragement, Mr. Drucker. Thank you for believing in me! You are a gem among men!

Sincerely,

Evelyn Somerset

Exclusive: Portuguese Spy Arrested in Newark, New Jersey
By Miss Amelia Snow, Reporter

Bound for the Iberian Peninsula, this cub reporter traveled three weeks ago on rough seas aboard a Portuguese luxury steamship. What was meant to be an adventure holiday to escape the wintertime blues of The Big Apple, turned into a dangerous revelation leading to an astonishing outcome. One of the passengers was suspected of un-American activities: espionage for Adolf Hitler's Third Reich. Formerly living in Brooklyn, New York and later Philadelphia, Pennsylvania, the purported spy was making his sea passage back home to Lisbon where a member of the German espionage system would reward the fruit of his misdeeds! *Mon Dieu!*

Champagne flowed as the orchestra entertained travelers, among them, the spy and his well-heeled group of merrymakers involved in one form or another of espionage. A member of Mussolini's Fascist Politburo, a wealthy German banker, and a Greek shipping magnate had enthusiastically backed his game of skullduggery for their own interests to help destroy America's valiant Arsenal of Democracy. Little did I know that a turn around the dance floor would put me in direct contact with a member of the Fifth Column! The secret agent's sophisticated manner was well rehearsed and as nearly perfect as his proficiency with the German language, not to mention his skilled partnering to "Moonglow" on the dance floor.

Dear reader, what an adventure it was! High crimes on the high seas among the international set of Best Society! Why it was something out of Alfred Hitchcock's cinematic blockbuster *Saboteur*. Little did I know there were spies spying on the spy—and thinking me a spy! Why, it was all so positively lulu. The intrigue, by far, surpassed the home front mystery of mastering ration points and coins!

My arrival into Lisbon was everything I had been warned about by several aboard the ship. The Estado Novo's capital was rife with intercontinental conspiracy, committed by players from every nation, friend and foe, Axis and Allies, allies who became friends, and sources who became…Why there was even romance afoot aboard the ship and in Lisbon, but my lips are sealed on that account.

Here are the official sordid details of that suspected Nazi-collaborating thug. On a tip from British sources close to the investigation, this reporter has been informed that the Federal Bureau of Investigation has arrested John Da Silva Purvis, 43 in Newark, N. J. on charges that he acted as a spy for Germany. Purvis transmitted information to his principals in Europe, and on two occasions received cash payments for his services. Purvis, a Portuguese citizen, allegedly began his espionage activities early in 1942 when he was contacted by a crew member of a neutral vessel who had been recruited by German Intelligence. Those intimate with the arrest confirm that the Portuguese received a letter by courier from a representative of the German espionage service in Europe, and that he sent a reply through the same person who delivered the message to him. He met at least two couriers, one of whom saw him on two occasions. While Purvis was in the United States, a Nazi representative delivered a personal letter to him containing certain identifying code words. Within the letter were sixteen specific assignments to be executed by Purvis. The assignments included gathering information on: warship construction, damage at Pearl Harbor, losses in sea action, and convoys. Additional information was requested on American bases in Central and South America and on the African coast, as well as mine fields in the Atlantic. A four-month long investigation into un-American activities was assisted by the use of motion picture cameras and a network of agents both in America and abroad. If convicted of high crimes, the penalty for espionage carries a death sentence by the electric chair.

March 17, 1943

Estoril, Portugal

My Dearest Marjorie,

You were right, darling. Portugal has been an exceptional diversion and just what I needed to lift me out of the doldrums. Ship travel was memorable, and I'm learning to overcome my fear of the water. Although I have not swum, the seashore is simply divine, and the view from my suite is exquisite—particularly in the moonlight. As for the food it is well-suited to my finicky palate. Can you believe?—I have built quite an appreciation of sardines! The weather has been spotty, but that has not deterred me from traveling the countryside in a delightful little car. On the Q.T—I have learned to drive and play poker!

I miss you terribly and hope that you had an enjoyable time at Washington's Birthday Ball and the Rockefeller fundraiser. Although I have not danced much, I have enjoyed the music (both on board and the local Fado) immensely and have stumbled upon the most darling book shop in Lisbon.

Of course, I am curious how Queen Louise and Albert took the news of my departure for "Philadelphia," but not curious enough to write them at this time. But don't worry, sister dear, I eventually will set pen to paper explaining my ruse, and I'll do so with a gay smile and my chin held high. I'm beyond their censure now, peculiarly confident in myself and determined to live life on _my_ term, not theirs. This renewal in Lisbon has proved to be quite rewarding for both my spirit and my heart. More importantly, I feel liberated from Mother and Albert. When I do write them, it will set me free from their control as well as that of Best Society. I have no doubt that you are ready to burst with news of this letter to them, but please wait to do so, until I have written them. Mum's the word, darling.

Oh, and yes...you'll be pleased to know that an American man of Portuguese extraction has been quite good for my constitution. However, I am off to England for my next adventure. I promise to write when I get settled, but you'll have to be satisfied with that little bit of gossip for now. No torrid details to follow in the romance department. I'll not admit to a paramour, so both you and Brewster will have to use your imagination! Ha. Ha.

Please be a doll and stop by The Dakota to check on Alice and Victor and assure them of my safe passage and sojourn plans. They do so worry about me now that Richard is gone. Also, inform Victor to expect a package I'm sending ahead of me. It's my travel journal. Instruct him to place it, unopened, in my desk drawer in the library.

Best wishes for a joyous Easter and my warmest regards to my dear brother-in-law.

All my love,

Evie

P.S. I am entirely disinclined for a British lover, so don't get any silly notions about my whirlwind adventure!

Continue with Evie's exciting journey in
Flying with the Swallows, Volume Two: Rendezvous in Berlin.
Turn the page to read a sneak peek of Chapter One.

SONNETS FROM THE PORTUGUESE
by Elizabeth Barrett Browning

XLIII

How do I love thee? Let me count the ways.
I love thee to the depth and breadth and height
My soul can reach, when feeling out of sight
For the ends of Being and ideal Grace.
I love thee to the level of everyday's
Most quiet need, by sun and candlelight.
I love thee freely, as men strive for Right;
I love thee purely, as they turn from Praise.
I love thee with the passion put to use
In my old griefs, and with my childhood's faith.
I love thee with a love I seemed to lose
With my lost saints,—I love thee with the breath,
Smiles, tears, of all my life!—and, if God choose,
I shall but love thee better after death.

RENDEZVOUS IN BERLIN
Sneak Peek

 ONE

London Pride

Foreign Office—London
March 19, 1943

An Intelligence agent. She was about to become a spy. *Her?* New York socialite, debutante, wealthy heiress, and war widow. Yes. *Her!* Oh, what a story it would make.

Seated between two British officials Mrs. Evelyn Somerset faced an empty seat on the opposite side of a desk in Great Britain's Foreign Office. The chilled room and the annoying throat clearing of the man to her right upset her composure. Perhaps that was the purpose—a tactic of psychological warfare as she awaited Foreign Secretary Anthony Eden's arrival and subsequent interrogation. At this ungodly hour in the morning looking bright-eyed was a feat. Despite the two-hour wartime clock advance, her body knew it was six in the morning, not eight, and she needed coffee.

Carl Wilson had prepared her for this highly unusual meeting, explaining it necessary given her brother's position. This would most likely be trying, at best, but neither he nor the two officials knew what it was like to stand strong against Queen Louise or her brother-senator Albert's scrutiny. When speaking with her oftentimes cranky, fastidious brother it required all her poise and good humor and the recollection of the sweet young man he had once been. Politicians were all the same no matter the country and she suspected, evident by what she'd seen of London in the last twenty-four hours, the British had been pushed to its limits by German assault. She had not been prepared to see entire city blocks destroyed by massive bombings or protective sandbags stacked against buildings. Odd-shaped balloons hovered above the city as some sort of deterrent, she supposed. If Britons could endure all they physically and mentally have, then she could withstand the coordinated offensive of three old-boys against one woman; three bureaucrats against one socialite. Even when at her lowest, that terrible afternoon at The Dakota, she'd withstood and rallied during Albert's interrogation, which had sent her on an international adventure to find herself—and unexpectedly—lose the woman she'd become. At this moment, she wasn't sure if she should thank her brother or curse him for being such a hard-nose.

The mantle clock's resonating tick-tock filled the awkward silence until another annoying throat clearing preceded the uniformed man named Stewart Menzies' Scottish grouse. "This is getting tiresome. I have work to attend."

Clearly the official to her left was a different sort of man, wearing an expensive suit and a contrite smile.

"I'm sorry for the delay, Mrs. Somerset. The Secretary shan't be much longer."

"Waiting is no problem. I am at the Crown's service."

"Would you care for some tea? I can call the assistant."

"Jesus Christ, Hambro. What are you?—some nippy at Lyons?" Menzies complained.

Charles Hambro ignored the frustrated outburst and offered her another apologetic expression for the swear. She didn't know who or what role these two men played in her recruitment into British Intelligence, but it was obvious there was no love between them. As for her, she cared little for the supercilious military man. Did he not know who *she* was?

She scanned her surroundings. Ordered chaos of books and maps within paneled walls resembled Richard's library. He was here with her—and so was Carl, his poetic gift tucked in the clutch purse rested on her lap. She missed him fiercely, but he was right: this was her time to fly. Even Mr. Drucker was here, and she imagined his encouragement from that day when she sat on the opposite side of his desk. *"It's a mess over in Europe, but you can handle it. You got moxie, more than you realize."*

Suddenly, a tall, distinguished man burst into the room and both men bolted to attention. She remained seated.

"Thank you for coming, gentlemen," he greeted, but approached her with a warm smile and an outstretched arm to shake her hand. "Mrs. Somerset, I'm truly sorry to keep you waiting."

She liked him instantly. "As I told the other gentlemen, Secretary Eden, I'm at your service."

"Very good. I've just returned from Washington and there are so many pressing matters coming from all directions at once. Well, I trust I left you in good hands during your wait?"

"You tell me."

"Touché," Eden laughed, then took his place at the helm of the meeting. "These men are the tip of Great Britain's spear."

"That is reassuring."

The secretary leaned forward and gave her all his attention. "How was your travel from Lisbon? I hope uneventful?"

"Quite so."

"Capital. As you can imagine, the cable we received from Lisbon has taken us by surprise. It's rather unprecedented and that is why I have called both chiefs from our Intelligence sections to meet you. Lieutenant-Colonel Stewart Menzies is the head of MI6, the Secret Intelligence Service and Sir Charles Hambro is our leader in the Special Operations Executive."

"I didn't realize there were two branches of British Intelligence."

"The only departments you need to know about. Under normal circumstances, I rarely involve myself in the recruitment or the training of agents, but as I understand it, after vetting you, our Iberian Section sought to *enlist* you without authorization and under most irregular, and dare I say, manipulative grounds. Is that correct?"

"It was not as deceptive as you may believe, Secretary Eden. I willingly accepted the offer made in exchange for several exit visas for Jewish refugees having difficulties in Lisbon. I'm here because I am eager to assist the British government as repayment for the aid given in deference to my brother."

"And who is your brother?" Hambro asked.

"United States Senator Albert Rousseau of New York."

Hambro sat back in his chair and dragged his hand across his frown.

"I would like this arrangement between the British government and me to remain...our secret. The senator has no knowledge of my affairs or my travel to Europe." She said bending the truth as she touched the wave of hair above her eye. "We are estranged."

"Unfortunate for you, but beneficial to the work ahead," Eden said. "I met him briefly in conference. Senator Rousseau is a fine man, indeed."

Another throat clearing came loud at her right. "We demand the strictest secrecy at all cost."

"Thank you, Colonel."

"Don't thank me. From the minute you left Lisbon and for the next thirty or so years, you are bound to secrecy through the government's Official Secrets Act. Not even American senators or Lord Somerset are allowed access to British intelligence."

"Sallingham?" asked Hambro.

"Right."

"Hmm...Mrs. Somerset, are you aware of the danger you face in this undertaking?" Hambro asked.

She pulled her shoulders back. "Fully aware. Both Mr. Musgrove and Mr. Wilson explained the hazards perfectly."

Eden furrowed his brow and looked to Menzies. "Wilson?"

"An alias of one of sub-Section Five's agents engaged in Operation Midas. A Yank we recruited out of hospital. Flew with the Eagle Squadron."

"And your relationship with this Wilson fellow is…?" Eden asked her.

"One of great friendship, fealty, and trust."

"Did he also explain that in volunteering for espionage activities on behalf of the war effort, you will not be protected under the Geneva Convention," Eden added.

"He did not think my feelings so delicate. His manner was more direct—if I'm caught behind enemy lines, I could be shot."

"Correct. But it will be the job of *both* these men to see to it that you *don't* get caught."

"Now, wait a minute!" Menzies balked.

"Hold up, Menzies. You are already working with the SOE in Lisbon on Operation Midas. So why should training be any different for the same mission?"

"Sir, the Iberian Section sees no other means, but I must draw the line at training co-ordination," Menzies said.

"Although the SIS recruited Mrs. Somerset it does not mean we should throw her into the wolves' den without some specialized training. There is little time to send her to Preliminary School, but hand-picked instruction within Finishing School will at least provide her skills directly suited to her mission. She's no ordinary recruit and, given her relations, we must take judicious care to return her home safe and sound."

Menzies sat forward. "The SIS is in no position to hold the hand of an American heiress, and I am not agreeable to lending vital agents to the Prime Minister's bogus SOE department of rabble-rousing misfits. We will handle her like every other recruit, with the same expectations for performance. If she fails in training, so be it. Otherwise, her fate is left to the Almighty."

She was a hair's breadth away from letting lose her temper and glanced to Hambro's sly smile.

"Of course, the colonel objects, sir. He still thinks my department is a bunch of ineffective amateurs, unable to teach anyone anything of use," Hambro shot back.

"I merely question what the SOE could possibly teach a New York City socialite that would actually benefit *intelligence* gathering? How to hike the Alps and bomb a rail station won't be of any assistance to my team. Perhaps you plan on teaching her how to pour tea so she can at least poison the enemy! Unlike her brother's efforts toward victory from Washington, I doubt a society chippy has the stamina for your brand of training...well, apart for the latter, of course. To which, she is probably quite proficient."

How dare they speak of me in such a manner—as though I'm not even in the room! How very disagreeable!

Hambro remained calm and courteous in the face of the horrible Scotsman. "I agree that sabotage and subversion are the scope of our organization, but they do not exclude the need to learn ciphering and the unconventional warfare employed by our female agents."

"Intelligence is a gentleman's game and, as such, MI6 does not condone the SOE's brand of clandestine warfare."

"As you repeatedly make clear...except when it conveniently furthers your mission in the Iberian quarter," Hambro defended.

"Enough. We are making a terrible impression on Mrs. Somerset," Eden firmly stated.

Yes, they are. Particularly Menzies who was too much like Albert in his disregard of her abilities and quite ungentlemanly in his personal warfare against Hambro's department. He was a downright insufferable oaf! She glanced down at her purse and thought of Carl's encouragement, *his* belief in her despite her womanhood and position in society. Angered and feeling peevish, she defied all the good manners she'd been taught and looked straight at Eden's sympathetic expression. "If you will permit me, gentlemen…"

Immediately, they silenced.

"Allow me to dispense with propriety for a moment. I'm sure I don't know what is involved but can assure you I am not some feckless, timid girl from Polite Society who cannot think or climb her way out of challenging situations."

"My apologies, Mrs. Somerset, I meant no disrespect," Menzies offered.

"Not consciously perhaps. I am aware that Lisbon's section chief chose me due to Wegener's obvious fascination with me, but neither he nor you are aware that apart from my exceptional academic achievements at Vassar College, I also excelled in athletics, as was the institution's expectation. Mountain trekking is not such an anomaly for *this* New York City socialite. As for stamina, I'm not opposed to challenging any of your agents in a vigorous tennis match. I also learned how to shoot a rifle at an early age, thanks to my late father who was an avid pheasant hunter."

"You must admit, Menzies, Mrs. Somerset appears to be in a better position than most of the women we've begun recruiting for the SOE. In fact, I conclude she is spades over some of the *gentlemanly* chaps with the SIS," Hambro quipped.

"And I do believe her social standing will serve well in Berlin," Eden added.

"I didn't realize you also have reservations about my ability to infiltrate German society. If you'll further indulge me, I speak fluently five languages, three of which are German dialects: Plattdeutsch, Hochdeutsch, and Bairisch, as well as Italian and French. I also possess conversational skills in Portuguese, Spanish, and Latin. Further, having had an Austrian governess from infancy until my formal education began, I understand the culture and regional dishes. I am familiarized with taste nuances, such as between pate, *foie gras,* and Germany's *hühnerleberpastete,* or the French crêpe and Austria's *Palatschinken.*"

"Naturally, a multi-linguist is advantageous in the field, and I will concede I am impressed," Menzies said.

She held her chin high as though knowledgeable in the Intelligence business. "Small details are equally important. For example, having dined with Best Society's international set, I have observed the distinctions. I know the difference between, let's say, an ice cream fork and a pastry fork." She turned her head to Menzies and raised an eyebrow. "Unlike the SIS's agent Irena Olszak. Why, I knew she was a fraud in the first five minutes upon seeing her. She ate with the wrong hand and dripped in tasteless jewels, which any woman of respectable breeding would find vulgar. Her fakes may have been good enough to deceive a fool such as Purvis, but I assure you, she wouldn't pass muster under the scrutiny of German aristocracy. Gentlemen, my diamonds are as genuine as my airs and upbringing. My pearls are as cultured as my manner." If she did say so herself! Of course, Purvis had conned her. She genuinely thought him quite refined.

The colonel furrowed his brow.

"You know of Purvis?"

"I do. I'm a reporter for the *New York Daily Spectator.* Nothing escapes my observation." Well, that was a lie, too. She smoothed the hair at her nape then noted the twist to Menzie's thin lips. She changed the topic. "As you can see, I have attributes that could be of use. Would you care for a treatise on Salzburg's Bavarian identity?"

"That won't be necessary, but I would like to know how you came to learn of Purvis's espionage activities. Did Wilson have anything to do with confirming your observations?" the red-faced SIS Director asked—in Plattdeutsch.

Taken aback, she paused. He was testing her, and she smirked before responding in kind. "None in the least. In fact, he claimed ignorance and, if I recall correctly, he laughed at me. Mr. Wilson merely charmed me with his clarinet, not wild tales of British agents and German spies." She then switched to Bairisch. "Purvis himself expounded on his plans, hoping to enlist my fortune in his schemes. He thought me a sympathizer to the Nazi cause."

"Very well."

In French, she added. "One last thing, Colonel. I'm surprised that you, a Briton, underestimate the value of tea service. While I do have a number of house staff to attend to that for me, as I am sure you do, it is universal of good manners in *every* station. Regardless, I assure you all...I am an eager student and a quick learner."

Oh! —that felt as good as it did when she went head-to-head with Albert that afternoon in the parlor. Perhaps when—if—she returned from this assignment, she would do the same to Queen Louise.

"You do understand there will be no article, no scoop for your newspaper in regard to anything you learn, see, or do, Mrs. Somerset," Eden said.

"Of course."

"Hambro? Menzies? Do you have any doubt that Musgrove has chosen well?"

"I do have quite an unconventional question for Mrs. Somerset," Hambro said. "I mean no offense to such a respectable woman as yourself, but...tell me, how skilled a liar are you?"

Eden sat back into his chair and tented his fingers, awaiting her answer.

She tittered, having done nothing but lie at every turn beginning with her flight from Manhattan. "I suppose, I'm skilled enough to have secured the impossible endeavor of interviewing the elusive Madam Lupescu, inserted myself into the German ambassador to Portugal's social circle, and befriended the Estado Novo's premier banker over roulette."

She paused, secretly reveling in their stunned attention. "Further, as mentioned, I lured Purvis to uncover his espionage activities aboard the *Serpa Pinto*. All the while I charmed not only one of your secret agents but also the *Wehrmacht Sicherung's*, General Otto Wegener. To my credit, I accomplished all this under the presence of British Intelligence at my back and the PVDE at my every turn as I went about my business of searching for and extracting Jewish refugees under the menacing scrutiny of the Gestapo."

"And have you lied to us about anything this afternoon?" Menzies prodded.

"Why don't *you* tell *me*? You have already vetted me according to Mr. Musgrove, and if you *truly* are the 'tip of the spear' in Intelligence as Secretary Eden claims, then surely you can read a woman's body language."

Menzies laughed, which surprised her because she believed him incapable of it. "Very well. You have a distinct habit of touching your hair when you lie, Mrs. Somerset, and have done so on four occasions during this interview. While your professed acumen, cultured manner, and bravado are somewhat convincing—your tell is that tiny nervous habit. Wegener will pick it up immediately, if he has not already. Control the impulse. While I'm not entirely in concert with Musgrove's recommendation for your suitability in field Intelligence, I will concede that if you excel in your tutelage and dispense with your bombastic Americanism I will reconsider. Perhaps you may even survive the mission to serve tea back in the states."

Bombastic Americanism? Oh goodness; she was mortified. Rather than portraying confidence she came off as pompous and pretentious! Further, she'd never noticed the habit of hers before. Had Carl noted it, too? He mentioned how she always touched the bird watch fob, but never mentioned her hair.

Again, the clock's tick-tock filled the electrified room as the men awaited her recovery. She had reduced herself to a braggadocio! She fidgeted, trying her best not to stammer. "Duly noted, Colonel. I will do my absolute best on all accounts. You can depend on it."

"Well! I say she is on her way!" Eden announced. "I must disagree with you, Menzies. Mrs. Somerset has exactly what it takes to graduate from abbreviated training and meet Wegener in Berlin in five weeks' time."

"Five weeks?" she asked, flabbergasted.

"Unfortunately, there is precious little time and much to learn. Wegener is expected back in Berlin on the fifteenth of April."

"Where have we temporarily billeted Mrs. Somerset, sir?" Hambro asked.

"Where she would feel right at home—The Dorchester. But it is imperative we move her at once, so I'd like for you to personally drive her tonight to Station Thirty-one. I have already notified Buckmaster to meet you there in the morning."

"And what of wireless training with my men?"

"That's not the plan for her, Hambro. I'm sorry, Mrs. Somerset, if we are talking around you. I want to make clear to everyone what the Foreign Office's expectations are for your training. No sense in teaching you how to radio operate or parachute when the colonel has other plans on how to get you into Germany. Hambro, I would like your absolute cooperation in allowing SIS trainers access to the facility and to work in conjunction with F Section until Germany X Section is up and running. This is an unprecedented situation and there must be no strife between the departments. Our utmost focus must ensure Mrs. Somerset's success and survival once in occupied territory."

"You have my assurance, sir."

"I don't want you to fret, Mrs. Somerset. These men and the team we are organizing to help you in Berlin are top notch."

"I'm not afraid in the least," she lied for the fifth time in thirty minutes yet clasped her hands so as not to touch her hair. Oh dear, what had she gotten herself into?

"Why are you *really* doing this, Mrs. Somerset, when you could be back in America safe and sound?" Hambro asked.

She thought long and hard before answering. "There is the obvious that Hitler must be stopped but...I do this also because...avenging a loved one is a powerful motivator. So is the love of that person when he believes in you against the violent tide of naysayers."

"I see...you would like to avenge your late husband's unfortunate death in the Pacific. Bereavement is a strong inducement for service."

She meant Carl, but simply smiled leading them to believe Richard was her motivation behind her daring committal.

———◆◇◆———

SONG LIST

Prologue- "I Let a Song Go Out of My Heart," Benny Goodman and His Orchestra/vocals Martha Tilton, 1938

Chapter 1- "Don't Cry, Baby," Erskine Hawkins/vocals Jimmy Mitchell, 1943

Chapter 2- "Your Socks Don't Match," Fats Waller, 1943

Chapter 3- "Boom Shot," Glenn Miller and His Orchestra, 20th Century Fox film *Orchestra Wives*, 1942

Chapter 4- "Always in My Heart," Glenn Miller and His Orchestra, 1942

Chapter 5- "I Walk Alone," Dinah Shore, Universal Studios film *Follow the Boys*, 1944

"Boogie Woogie Bugle Boy," The Andrews Sisters, 1941

Chapter 6- "I Hear a Rhapsody," Dinah Shore, 1941

"Frenesi," Artie Shaw and His Orchestra, 1941

"I Have Eyes," Artie Shaw and His Orchestra/vocals Helen Forrest, 1938

"Moonglow," Artie Shaw and His Orchestra, 1941

Chapter 7- "Strictly Instrumental," Harry James and His Orchestra, 1942

Chapter 8- "And the Band Played On," Guy Lombardo and His Royal Canadians, 1941

"Begin the Beguine," Recorded by Artie Shaw and His Orchestra, 1938

Chapter 9- "Pennsylvania Polka," Andrews Sisters, 1942

Chapter 10- "Oh Look at Me Now," Tommy Dorsey/vocals Frank Sinatra & Pied Pipers, 1941

Chapter 11- "A Room with a View," Artie Shaw, 1938

Chapter 12- "From Twilight Til Dawn," Freddy Martin & His Orchestra/vocals Bob Haymes, 1942

Chapter 13- "Tea for Two," Art Tatum, 1939

Chapter 14- "Stormy Weather," Lena Horne, 1941

"Deep Purple," Artie Shaw and His Orchestra/vocals Helen Forest, 1939

Chapter 15- "Spring is Here Again," Marion Harris, 1942

Chapter 16- "Moonlight Cocktail," Glenn Miller and His Orchestra, 1942

"Minnie the Moocher," Cab Calloway, 1930

Chapter 17- "You Made Me Care," Vera Lynn, 1940

"The Things I Love," Jimmy Dorsey/vocals Bob Eberley, 1941

Chapter 18- "Over the Hill," Vera Lynn, 1941

"When the Swallows Come Back to Capistrano," The Ink Spots, 1940

"Hi-Ho-Hi-Ho," Walt Disney film *Snow White and the Seven Dwarfs*, 1937

"That's a Plenty," Benny Goodman, 1927

"Sing, Sing, Sing," Benny Goodman, 1937

"Boy Meets Goy (Grand Slam)," Benny Goodman Sextet, 1940
"Swingtime in the Rockies," Benny Goodman and His Orchestra, 1936
Chapter 19- "Amen," Woody Herman, 1941
Chapter 20- "All for You," Nat King Cole, 1943
"Blue Champagne," Benny Goodman, 1942
"The Wang Wang Blues," Benny Goodman, 1942
Chapter 21- "We'll Meet Again," Vera Lynn, 1939
"Perfidia," Glenn Miller Orchestra, 1942
Chapter 22- "All or Nothing at All," Harry James and His Orchestra/vocals Frank Sinatra, 1943
"I Had a Dream," Harry James and His Orchestra/vocals Helen Forrest, 1943
Chapter 23- "Solo Flight," Benny Goodman, 1941
"Chattanooga Choo Choo," Glenn Miller, 1941
Chapter 24- "Bluebirds in the Moonlight," Glenn Miller, 1939
Chapter 25- "My Shining Hour," Glen Gray and Casa Loma Orchestra/vocals Eugenie Baird, 1943

Poetry Attributions:

Credit: Edna St. Vincent Millay, "On Thought in Harness" from Collected Poems. Copyright 1934, © 1962 by Edna St. Vincent Millay and Norma Millay Ellis. Reprinted with the permission of The Permissions Company, LLC on behalf of Holly Peppe, Literary Executor, The Millay Society, www.millay.org.

"The Spring and the Fall," Edna St. Vincent Millay, Published in her collection of work *The Harp-Weaver and Other Poems* (Harper & Brothers, 1920)
"Amar" and "III," Forbela de Alma Conceição Espanca, published in her collection of work *Charneca em Flor*, 1930
"XLIII," Elizabeth Barrett Browning, *Sonnets from the Portuguese*, 1849

GLOSSARY

Abwher- German military Intelligence
Alpen-und Donau-Reichsgau- German: Alpine and Danubian Gaue, Austria renamed 1942
Amar- Portuguese: Love
Anschluss- Annexation of Austria into the Third Reich
Arroz doce- Portuguese: Sweet rice pudding
Arsenal of Democracy- Refers to the collective efforts of American industry in supporting the Allies
Bairisch- Austrian-German language
Bello- German: Barker
Big Cheese- head boss
*Bissel-*Yiddish: money
Boa fortuna- Portuguese: Good fortune
BOAC- British Overseas Airway Corporation
Brenda Starr- 1940 comic strip character, adventurous Chicago newspaper reporter
BSC- British Service Coordination
Campo da Morte Lenta- Portuguese: Camp of Slow Death, Tarrafal
Corajoso- Portuguese: Fearless, gutsy
Cri de Coeur- French: impassioned cry
Cub Reporter- Inexperienced newspaper reporter
Deutches Heer- German Army
Dies ist von ihrem Cousin- German: This is from your cousin.
Die Meinigen- German: My family
El- Elevated train
Engelchen- German: Angel
Frau- German: Married woman, Mrs.
Fräulein- German: Unmarried woman, Miss.
Hatikvah- Hebrew poem (1878) turned song, meaning "The Hope"
Hen House- Female columnists at newspaper
Heim ins Reich- German: Back home to the Reich
Herr- German: Sir
Herzchen- German: little heart

Herzlichen Dank- German: Many thanks

Hochdeutsch- High German

Intrepid- Sir William Stephensen, head of the BSC

John Thomas- Erection

Mein Name ist Evelyn Somerset aus New York- German: My name is Evelyn Somerset from NYC

Muito Obrigada- Portuguese: Thank you

Münchner- A male resident of Munich

Nazi Parteiadler- Eagle above swastika symbol

Nob- One from old money wealth

Oma- German: Grandmother

Onde Fica- Portuguese: Where is?

Opa- German: Grandfather

Pochen- German: to bluff, Poker

Gnädige Frau- German: Madam

Parlez-vous français?- French: Do you speak French?

Polícia de vigilância- Portuguese: Surveillance police

Plattdeutsch- Low German dialect mainly from Northern Germany

Shipway- Structure supporting a ship during construction

Sieg Heil- Nazi salute: Hail Victory

SIS- Secret Intelligence Service

SOE- Special Operations Executive

Sprechen sie Deutsch?- German: Do you speak German?

Stringer- Freelance journalist

Swallow- Female Agent for British intelligence

The Four Hundred- Mrs. William Astor's list of New York's "best families," 1887

Você fala inglês- Portuguese: Do you speak English?

Wehrmacht- German military forces

Wir sind Deutsch- German: We are German

Wo bist du?- German: Where are you?

Wolfram- Tungsten ore

Yinzer- Nickname for someone from Pittsburgh

Author Note

Although this is a work of fiction, I simply adore calling upon important characters that have shaped history during the era. Taking artistic license, these personages helped to add color by placing them in fictitious situations, using fictitious dialogue. In the case of Flying with the Swallows: *The Lisbon Affair*, the inspiration for our first colorful character, John Da Silva Purvis, a Portuguese spy for Nazi Germany, comes from two newspaper accounts regarding his factual arrest for espionage. The "official sordid details" outlined in Evie's cable to Hank Drucker were borrowed from a September 17, 1943 article printed in *The Canberra Times* and the November 6, 1943, *The New York Times* article.

I could not resist the delicious temptation to introduce the controversial historical personages ex-King Carol II of Romania and his then-royal mistress turned wife/princess in 1947: Elena (Magda) Lupescu. Sketching Madam Lupescu's character came with its share of challenges as much of what was written about her contradicts either things she, herself, had said and contradicted!— as well as articles and blog posts written about her, which comingle truth (both sympathetic and not) with unflattering, salacious rumors and allegations. The research source I ultimately relied upon was the book: *Lupescu*, written in 1955 by Alice-Leone Moats an acquaintance of Madam Lupescu to help paint the picture of the complex woman hated by her own country but loved by the ex-king. Of course, I couldn't resist peppering the book with some of those rumors, for they do so color a romance novel. The articles Evie quotes in her interview with Lupescu are actual publications.

As for the S.S *Serpa Pinto*, the noble passenger steamship made departures from both Lisbon and Casablanca to Baltimore, Philadelphia, New York, and Rio de Janerio. I have relied upon actual passenger accounts from both book and information on the American Jewish Joint Distribution Committee and Chabad.org websites. Other ship-related sources helped to paint the picture of how it looked, how it traveled, and the dangers it faced as it transported 7,800 Jewish refugees toward freedom.

And lastly, I would like to remember the valiant crew aboard the U.S.S *Jarvis* who perished in what became known as the "Ironbottom Sound" in the Solomon Islands. All hands went down when the destroyer split and sank under heavy Japanese plane bombing forty miles from Guadalcanal as the Marines stormed the beaches. It is said that if not for the *Jarvis's* beleaguered sailing after having suffered torpedo damage the day before, the air assault on the Marines would have been devastating had those thirty-one Japanese planes not pursued the *Jarvis* but rather continued onward to Guadalcanal.

Thank you, dear reader for taking this journey with me and Evelyn Rousseau Somerset. I hope you will join us for a new exciting chapter in her life in Volume Two of the Flying with the Swallows duology: *Rendezvous in Berlin*.

If this was a pleasant reading experience, please consider leaving a review on Amazon. Thank you!

ACKNOWLEDGEMENTS

It's been a long, challenging road both personally and professionally since embarking on Evie's journey in the Flying with the Swallows duology. My unwavering champions remain throughout each new book project, but this one required patience from them all.

Thank you, Lord for giving me the desire and New York stick-to-itiveness to see it through when family health crises, coupled with Covid, sought to waylay my plans to see Evie's growth and happiness at the end of Volume Two, *Rendezvous in Berlin*.

My darling Bill, you never complained and you always—cheerfully and logically—encouraged. I love you more than words.

To my cherished nonagenarian parents. Thank you for patiently waiting —and gently asking—for another completed chapter to be read to you as you recuperated. Your confidence in me and this story has kept us all going!

A special shout out to some wonderfully supportive and talented people in the writing/reading community: Debbie Chandler Hughes, Glynis Whitelegg, Angela DeThomas, Zoe Burton, Ree Hudson, cover designer Hannah Linder, and the amazing ladies in the Tampa Branch of the National League of American Pen Women.

And lastly, to Kristi, dear friend, and the best darned editor in town. Your loyalty to me and the project humbles me. Thank you for staying the course beside me these five years of Flying with the Swallows, and our nine years' collaboration of publishing. You are an amazing individual with a heart of gold and a diplomatic red pen.

ABOUT THE AUTHOR

Cat T. Gardiner is a Long Island girl who has fallen in love with the romance of an era known as the Greatest Generation. She and her husband, now Floridians, love to explore the 1940s home front and military experience as living historians, wishing for a time machine to transport them back eight decades.

Second to her husband, her passion is writing Historical Fiction, WWII-era Romance. Her debut novel, *A Moment Forever*, was a 2017 Next Generation Indie Book Award Romance Finalist.

A member of the Tampa Branch of The National League of American Pen Women, Cat takes her readers on a swell journey at The 1940s Experience™ blog and gallery where she shares her writing, reenacting, and the stories of those who lived through the trials and joys of the era. It is her belief that everyone should have an understanding of the 1940s experience.

Connect with Cat and her WWII-era world
cgardiner1940s.com
cattgardiner.wixsite.com/homefrontpodcast
facebook.com/cat.t.gardiner
facebook.com/CatTGardinerHisFic
payhip.com/CatGardinerBooks

OTHER WWII-ERA BOOKS BY CAT T. GARDINER

A Moment Forever
An Unforgettable WWII Historical Fiction Epic Romance
Romance Finalist, 2017 Next Generation Indie Book Awards

Time & Again Antique Shop Series
Contemporary, WWII-era, Time-travel Novelettes
Vintage Valentine
Vintage Victory
Vintage Halloween
Vintage Beginning
Seasons in Time – E-book & Paperback Boxset Bundle

www.ingramcontent.com/pod-product-compliance
Lightning Source LLC
Chambersburg PA
CBHW030924260626
47169CB00002B/374